STARSTRUCK

How Far Would You Go to Make Your Dreams Come True?

PHIL BARNHILL

Copyright © 2025 Phil Barnhill.

All rights reserved. This book or any portion thereof may not be reproduced or used in any manner whatsoever without the express written permission of the publisher except for the use of brief quotations in a book review.

To my boys,
Ethan and Ben

ACKNOWLEDGEMENTS

Writing a novel is never a solitary journey, and I am deeply grateful to those who supported and encouraged me to begin, and to not give up.

To Annie Greenlees, my English teacher when I was just 15 years old. You were the first person to whom I declared that one day, I would write a book. It only took me 35 years, but I got there in the end! Thank you for lighting that creative flame, all those years ago. It never went out.

To my FITfactory friends, I want to thank you for your constant and unwavering encouragement, and being genuinely interested in this project. Your excitement to read the finished product has meant the world to me.

Arlene and Natalie, you endured countless conversations about plot twists and character arcs - your insights and enthusiasm shaped this story more than you realise, and motivated me to keep going.

A special thanks to Lasairiona, without whom this book would not exist. Thank you for giving me that initial push, for helping demystify the process, and being a sounding board for my doubts and insecurities.

To the readers, thank you for choosing to spend some time in Tommy & Gina's world. I hope you enjoy your time there as much as I have, and look forward to more in the future.

Lastly, to anyone who has ever dared to chase their dreams, this book is for you.

Phil

PART ONE

'Follow the Sun'

Saturday, June 8th 2002

1
TOMMY

The golden hour before sunset still held a special place for me, even though I moved to Los Angeles nearly six months ago. Here, that warm dusky hue adds an extra touch, infusing the air of this mystical place with a sense of enchantment. But then, of course, it would, for a hopeless romantic, I thought, unable to suppress a smile.

I hope I never get used to this...

My gun metal grey Mustang purred at the lights on Lincoln Boulevard, giving me a few more seconds to gaze out towards the sun preparing to set beyond Venice Beach. 7.09pm, my watch shows, as I slip it off my wrist and toss it on the empty passenger seat. My tummy rumbles in recognition, like it too saw the time. I glance at it lying there like a discarded prize and shake my head, smiling at how much my life has changed despite all the Hollywood bullshit which came with the dream. Currently, my dreams are uncomplicated. Sal's Pizza and a rare evening to switch off. Well, everything but my phone. *He* might call at any time with another micro drama.

The phone rings as I slowly edge southbound in traffic. "Fuck sake," I mutter…that didn't last long. My brow relaxes though, when I see who is calling.

"Alright Tommy you big Hollywood dick, ye," booms the speakers, forcing a welcome laugh before I can reply "Alright Ollie, what's happening big stuff!?"

"Shattered mate, sitting up to fucking 2am to call you, but who else is gonna make sure you're still alive out there?"

"You're the last of the true living saints!" I laugh. "How'd the match go today?" I ask even though I already know the score.

"Beaten 2-1 sadly, but I did score a crackin' header!"

"You're a crackin' header!" I bellow back and we both laugh, hiding the homesick pang I feel in my heart every time I hear that unique Northern Ireland accent.

"Well done though! A couple of days off now?" I inquire, keeping an eye out for my turn-off down Venice Boulevard.

"Home leg on Tuesday night mate, so off tomorrow. Then the gaffer has us back on Monday morning. Hopefully, we can turn it around and blag another private jet to some unpronounceable place in Europe."

"Sounds great, I hope you smash it matey!"

"So, what are you up to? Heading to some swanky party to charm the knickers off Angelina Jolie?"

"Nothing quite so exciting," I chuckle. "Just about to pick up some pizza and have a quiet one."

"No way? You're still a boring bastard then?"

I'll never tire of his banter and how it brings me back to reality, even if hearing our accent still stirs up painful memories.

"I'm almost there mate, so can I call you back in a bit? Ah shit no, it's the middle of the night there. You have to come over for a visit so we can talk in the same damn time zone!"

"I will, I will, I promise! If we can get through this next round then a tasty wee bonus will have my butt on a plane in no time….but only if you promise to introduce me to Angelina!" Ollie's dirty laugh is gonna stand out here like a sore thumb.

"Mate, she wouldn't even be able to understand you!"

"Who gives a fuck about talking!?" Ollie snorts.

"Well I suppose you're fed up with all your wee football groupies?"

"I wish mate!" he shouts, and his "Yeoooo!" trails off as I turn right, towards the beach…towards the sunset.

"I'll catch up in a few days Ollie. Good luck win the match! Make sure you win so you can come see this unbelievable sunset!"

"Oh aye, rub it in, ye dick! he shouts. "Talk soon mate. Enjoy the pizza. Be good!!"

Passing the bars a few blocks back from the beach, the atmosphere forces an involuntary grin. I'll never get bored of how laid back and happy this place is. The sun has set closer to the horizon now as I get lucky with a space right outside Sal's Pizza.

This time of the evening the clientele starts to gradually switch from surfers, skaters and tourists, to the party crowd. It's my favourite time of the day here, and Saturday of course has its own extra energy. They say often in life you don't appreciate things until later, but on this day, and in this moment, I feel so much gratitude that it gives me a weird tingly feeling on my scalp.

Some songs I listen to have this same effect, but I've never known how to describe it. I suppose the common denominator is when I feel inspired or moved by something. Emotionally, of course. I sometimes wonder if other people ever experience that feeling, or am I just weird?

Grinning at a guy passing by, carrying his girlfriend in a piggyback like it's completely normal, I slip my phone into my jacket pocket and undo a couple of buttons. My tie gets loosened before I loop it over my head and toss it to the passenger seat.

Shit, better hide the watch if I'm leaving the top down.

A few seconds later I'm in Sal's - maybe not the busiest pizza spot, but definitely one of the best. A half dozen tables take up one side of the small front area, partitioned off slightly from the takeaway waiting area. The open plan kitchen beyond the counter has an enormous pizza oven, from behind which Sal himself appears, his apron covered in flour and chatting in Italian to the woman behind the counter. I suspect she's his daughter by the look she gives him and the tone of voice, prompting only a mischievous smile from Sal. They're even happy when they argue here, I love it!!

"What's yours?" Sal's possible daughter says, forcing a smile my direction.

"Order for Millar - a 12 inch meat feast please, no cheese"

"That'll be a few minutes hon, take a seat" she smiles, already looking over my shoulder towards the doorway.

Stepping off sideways towards the corner, I pick the stool with the best line of sight to the doorway. I've always loved people watching - especially here as it's so full of joy and full of surprises, not like home. I'm only there a minute or so when my outside gaze follows two girls enter Sal's, hand in hand. One is clearly leading the way, a long-haired brunette in baggy cream trousers. They're slung low around her waist, allowing a little glimpse of a tan beneath her t-shirt. She's more confident in her steps than her blonde tipsy friend, who almost stumbles as she whispers something into her ear. I lock eyes with her, trying to read her face to see what she's just heard, but she gives nothing away. Yet.

2
GINA

"Aw come on, just one more. Pleeease!!" begs Amy, dramatically throwing her arms around Gina from behind as comes back to the table.

The girls are seated on the open terrace, raised up a few feet above the boardwalk, carefully positioned to catch the last rays. The Venice Beach Bar is one of the best spots along the ocean front to get the full Venice experience, or 'the circus' as locals would nickname it.

"Babe, I'm starved! I haven't eaten since, like 11am!" Gina mimics back with the same playful whine.

"OK OK! Pizza then can we come back? There's a guy inside who looks like he needs my help." Her exaggerated wink is typical Amy, as she slides back into her seat.

"Oh I'm sure he does, but who's help is he gonna need once *you* get hold of him?" I tease as I knock back the last of my third mango & pineapple mojito. "Let's go!" I'm on my feet before Amy has a chance to argue.

"I'll let you away with that one…" Amy fires back with wide eyes and a sarcastic smile, "…but only because I'm too tipsy to think of a come-back….and not because I'm not funny!

I'm the funny one!" Her straw slurps loudly as her Mojito disappears, making her snort and burst out laughing.

"Come on, you!" I'm giggling as I grab Amy by the hand and lead her down the three steps onto the Venice Beach boardwalk.

We're still holding hands as we weave through the early evening crowds, the music from the street performers makes for the coolest of soundtracks as I leads the way. Being a Venice tour guide has it's perks, including knowing the best spots for pizza…

As we turn left away from the sunset, the simple Sal's Italian Pizza sign comes into view only 30 feet away. "Oh look, someone's slumming it," Gina mutters, eye rolling as we pass a Mustang parked outside, gleaming in the sun, and slip into Sal's.

The deep house beats inside fit the Saturday sunset vibe outside, and are just loud enough to keep Amy's reply between us. "Douchebag. Two o'clock" she announces just behind my ear. I have to stifle my laughter as my eyes meet his, and his hint of a smile. I feel my smile widen, not for Amy, but for him. My eyes flick down for the smallest of moments, struggling to hide my coyness and instant attraction to this dark haired stranger on a high stool facing the doorway.

Don't blush! Don't blush!

"Nice wheels!" Amy manages just the right mix of sincerity and cheekiness. He frowns briefly with fake indignation, playing along, before raising one eyebrow and letting his smile widen. He doesn't reply with anything more than that, and despite myself I glance back over my shoulder to see him still looking at me.

Right at me. The way he's looking at me makes my face warm, and gives my tummy a new feeling. It could just be hunger though, trying to hurry me up.

Amy gets her order in first - demanding nine inches of pepperoni passion with a wink.

"I think you only choose that one because of the name".

"A girl's gotta take whatever passion she can get!" she fires back, raising both hands in fake protest. "...and nine inches sounds like something I could do with right now!" She tries to deliver it straight, but starts to break into laughter straight away.

"Keep your voice down! You're like a horny teenager!" I scold, playfully pushing Amy away. It's only once I push her that I realise I've just used it as and excuse to steal another towards the handsome stranger with the intense eyes.

"What are you having Gina?"

I bring her attention back to the counter, after another few seconds of the kind of eye-contact which almost carries words across the air.

This is not normal.

I'm not usually drawn in so quickly by someone. I could flirt as well as anyone - it definitely makes for more tips on tours - but having dealt with more drama than my twenty five years should have felt fair to inflict, I'm definitely guarded enough to play it safer than most, or so I thought.

I certainly had never, until now, experienced the feeling I have right now. Not with a stranger anyway.

50% excitement, 30% curiosity with the other 20% a mystery. There were butterflies though…lots of little butterflies. I try to chase this rush of thoughts away, passing it off as hunger and alcohol. As if a few seconds of eye-contact meant anything, I tried to rationalise.

This is something that only happens in cheesy rom-coms, right?

I realised I'm blushing slightly as I try to give Gabby my full attention. Thankfully Amy is too drunk and too busy rifling though her handbag to notice, while Gabby raises her eyebrows in anticipation of an order.

"Yes!! Sorry!! I try to sound assertive enough for both of us. "A meat feast please Gabby. No cheese."

"Nine or twelve inch?"

Amy snorts, and I give her a 'Don't embarrass me' sideways look.

"Ummm…twelve please, I'm starved" I reply, giving Amy a playful push on the shoulder, just hard enough to make her lose her balance, prompting more snorts of laughter.

It was pretty obvious that Gabby had heard the nine inch and twelve inch jokes too many times now to even play along. She raised her dark eyebrows to me, with the most subtle of nods towards the oblivious Amy, who's little finger was now applying lip balm with from a tiny round pink tin.

"'Yes I apologise for my friend. She's researching a role where she's 16 years old trapped in an adult's body."

Amy's head slowly, with theatrical drama, lifts towards us.

"I could pass for 16…" she says dryly, before closing her eyes and pouting like she's waiting for her first kiss. Seeing the opportunity, I quickly grab her face and pull her in like I'm going in for a kiss, but instead quickly drop a wet lick on her nose instead. Amy's eyes pop open wide, stunned for a moment, before throwing her arms around me, her hysterical laugh only breaking long enough to wipe her nose on my hair and called me a bitch.

Gabby smiles a jealous smile. "You guys are a little bit crazy tonight," she says, before turning towards the kitchen behind. "Another twelve inch meat feast with no cheese" she calls towards Sal.

"*Another?*" Amy inquires conspiratorially, leaning over the counter towards Gabby.

"Another what?" Gabby asks.

"Another fucking weirdo who has pizza with no cheese?" she almost whispers now, leaning in even closer.

Gabby smiles and glances at me. This must be a wind up, as I've been getting stick about this for years. A pizza isn't pizza without cheese etc. Blah blah blah! But I've never actually met anyone else who shared my odd dislike.

Gabby looks back at Amy then nods towards Tommy off to her left.

Amy turns completely towards me, suddenly standing up straight and formal, like a bridesmaid preparing to ready the bride. With a deadpan look she says "Oh. My. God." All I can do is roll my eyes and give her a sarcastic tip of the head.

"What?"

"Don't what me. You and your cute wee red face and sexy Mustang man are maybe the ONLY two people on earth who eat pizza without cheese. What are the chances!?"

"I'm sure there's plenty" I dismiss, feeling my cheeks getting warmer, almost on Amy's cue. Before the words have even left her mouth, I can already see the mischievous glint in Amy's blue eyes, before she wheels around and moves towards him.

Oh shit!

"So Mister Mustang!" Amy has suddenly adopted the persona of a chat show host. "Is it in fact true that you are a lover of the pizza without cheese?" She has perched herself on the edge of a stool between him and the doorway. Her playful interview style catches him off guard, and after a slight pause he replies slowly, looking justifiably wary, "Yes" and forces a casual laugh in an attempt break the weirdness.

"So what do they call you, handsome?" Amy fires, clearly relishing the awkwardness of the sudden interrogation.

"Tom. Tommy" he replies awkwardly, still a little wrong-footed by Amy's boldness, but his smile shows me he's warming to it.

"Well Tom Tommy, that's a funny name, and a funny accent. Are you…" she pauses for dramatic effect, "..Australian?"

"Nope!" Tommy smiles, wider now, like it's not the first time he's been mistaken for an Aussie.

"Scottish?" Amy guesses, with a hint of dismay in her voice that she might be right?

"Amy, leave him alone" I butt in, but staying cool at the safety of counter.

"He's fine" Amy dismisses, without taking her eyes off Tommy. "Aren't you?" He just smiles in reply, clearly enjoying the attention, but letting me know with a glance that he sees me too.

"So, Scottish?" Amy asks again, this time trying but failing to ask in a Scottish accent"

Tommy laughs now, happy to play along. "Close! Take a wee hop across the Irish Sea."

Amy's eyebrows dart upwards in cute amusement. "Take a wee hop across the Irish Sea?" she mimics, nailing the accent better this time. Her impression comes closer to a leprechaun though, especially they she flares her elbows as she speaks, drawing an instant giggle from us both.

Even Gabby smiles, enjoying the show. He glances towards me again, and let's it linger long enough that I have to scramble to say something before my face bursts into flames. "You're from Ireland?" I ask, trying to be confident, but Amy notices the nervous waver in my voice and gives me a knowing look over her shoulder.

"Yes, well, Northern Ireland"

"Is that *different* from Ireland?" Amy interrupts, drawing Tommy's eyes away from mine again.

He laughs to himself gently as he looks down briefly, bemused by the question.

"Yes. No!" he stumbles, smiling at how unsure he is himself. "If you only knew how often I get asked that," he laughs again. "Northern Ireland is still Ireland, but just the bit where it's colder and everyone fights more". "But it's home" he adds. "I really should give up trying to explain the difference, as here in the US, you're just Irish. Which usually means you're great craic and drink Guinness every day!"

Amy pouts, studying him as she considers this…and possibly some more mischief.

"So not only do you and my *beautiful* friend here share a liking for pizza with no cheese, god knows why, but I have it on good authority that she is quite partial to an `Oirish` Man." She slips back into full Leprechaun again for maximum with effect.

It's not even enough to make her more embarrassed that I am though.

My mouth drops open slightly in shock, suddenly and completely mortified by my possibly soon to be ex-friend. The stunned pause is seized upon quickly by Amy, having the best time now playing with my embarrassment.

She run with it. "Gina do you remember St Paddy's Day last year in San Francisco?".

Tommy looks like he's enjoying this too, especially now that the attention has been diverted to me, standing speechless staring in disbelief at Amy's audacity. He's looking at me now, though. Actually it feels like he's looking *into* me with a sexy, mischievous expression. Somehow it chases away some of the embarrassment. There's no judgement or ridicule coming from him, unlike my friend. His little head tilt and growing smile let's me see a curiosity, and I bite my bottle lip self-consciously, trying to meet him half-way.

I buy some time by pushed my long dark hair behind my ears, hoping it looks nonchalant and not the anxiety that's bubbling away underneath. I keep eye contact with him, and notice his eyes flick down to my tummy. Lifting my arms lifts my t-shirt too, just a little. It's purely unintentional, but I like his reaction. A little eyebrow lift. He probably caught a glimpse of my favourite tattoo, a floral design on my side which teasingly disappears up under my shirt and down below my waistline.

"Please excuse my friend" I declare after a tension breaking exhale, holding Tommy's eyes and grateful for the softness I'm getting in return. "Not only is she a little bit drunk, but she's a little bit of an asshole!". I deliver the last word noticeably louder and directly to Amy, hoping that it'll make her shut up.

But Amy just smiles at us both, knowing she's done enough to make the moment as memorable as possible without going *too* far.

Gabby's timing could not have been better, announcing the readiness of the three pizzas. She stacked the three on the counter, then slid the top one off for Tommy. He gathered his, close enough now to me to make my heart rate quicken. It looked for a second that he was about to say something as he came close, but I could see the conscious decision to swallow it again. I fight the urge to try to engage more before he leaves.

Be cool. I didn't come here to chase men.

Gabby looked at Tommy, then added a smile when bringing her gaze to me. I'm sure she could feel the attraction and the tension in the air. She was looking at us like some sort of fairy godmother who'd just brought two lonely souls together. Over pizza.

I felt something too, but I was less sure it was anything other than total embarrassment.

"Thank you, Gabby" she said cheerily. "I'm taking the morning tour so we'll finish around 12.30 for lunch here, if that's OK?"

Gabby smiled knowingly, recognising me trying to leave a breadcrumb of a clue for Tommy, and her wink made me bristle slightly in case he picked up how obvious it was between us.

Thanks Gabby!

Completely oblivious, mischievous Amy grabbed *her* nine inches of pepperoni passion along with my meat feast, and the only two no cheese pizzas in LA that warm summer's evening went their separate ways…

3
GINA

Tommy was long gone in his shiny Mustang by the time we burst excitedly into our apartment. The short walk back from Sal's consisted mostly of me deflecting Amy's protests at the lack of exchange of numbers.

We had watched him pull away - I was longing to call him back and ask the things I would have asked if I had been as bold as Amy. Who are you? Where are you going? Did you feel what I felt?

We lingered long enough at the corner to notice him turn left several blocks away. "Hmm…Malibu do you think?" Amy wondered out loud, as curious about this stranger as I was.

"Maybe" I shrugged, pretending not to care.

As much as I loved her, I had learned to keep my cards close to her chest around Amy when it came to anything men-related. Not that she ever meant any harm, but her well hidden needy nature had been known to manifest if I ever became *too* interested in someone. "Girls gotta stick together" she would always say with a smile, painting it positive enough for me to let it slide.

Amy is the archetype insecure commitment-phobe, perfectly happy with the sort of brief, intense flings which leave her men bewildered. I've seen the love-bombing infatuation / ghosting cycle so many times in the year they'd shared the apartment on Pacific Avenue. She wore her intimacy & abandonment issues on her sleeve for all to see, but mixed with such a façade of self-assuredness that most men found intriguingly irresistible.

Amy's romances were like distress flares, and I knew Amy was keen to keep mine just as brief.

"If you're so interested, why didn't *you* get his number?" I tease, sounding sincere as I flick my Doc Marten sandals into the shoe cupboard.

"Oh I might have, if his big dark Irish love eyes weren't all over your cute ass!".

Avoiding eye contact and enjoying the return of the butterflies, I let myself drop, with a satisfied sigh, into our comfy sofa. The sliding glass doors to the balcony allow our beach-facing apartment to be filled with an orange glow from the setting sun, although right now I'm more interested in trying to excavate the remote control from the between the cushions.

"Friends?" I call back to the open plan kitchen.

"If you only want to be his friend then I'm not sure I know you any more" Amy throws back with some sass.

I love Amy's quick wit. I don't reply, but just sit with a smile and a deep, warm content buzz. The kind that reminds you that you are exactly where you're supposed to be.

"I'll be there for youuuuu….." fills the apartment as the FRIENDS logo appears on the large flat screen TV.

The pizzas land on the coffee table, still in their boxes, and I give Amy a cheeky tongue as she sits, just to let her know I have some sass too. She just points a 'behave yourself' finger back at me, too busy arranging our food & drinks. "You just sit there sure, princess!" Amy mutters sarcastically as she pulls a bottle of DeLoach Chardonnay from the under counter wine-cooler.

"Which episode is it?" Amy asks as her bum lands besides me on the sofa.

"The one with the prom video." It's just a mumble as I'm mid bite into my first slice.

"Fucking love it!" Amy sings, pouring two glasses before sliding one towards my side of the table. "Oh my god no way!" Amy bursts suddenly, reaching across towards the pizza box.

"What's wrong!?" I ask, dryly - too used to Amy's micro dramas to get excited.

Amy slowly pulls the tab of paper off the side of my box and ceremoniously drops it into my lap with a grin.

"Bingo" she chirps triumphantly, turning her body away from Joey & Chandler's foosball game to face me. I stare at the slip of paper for a moment, back to Amy, then the paper again, deliberately hiding a reaction but very much feeling the onslaught of tummy back-flips.

Millar
310 1905 188

"Shall I fetch your phone, m'lady?" Amy half whispers, conspiratorially. Her mischievous smile from Sal's returning with glee as she leans in for full effect.

A "Ha!" is all I can muster up, unconvincingly, still trying to process.

Ever since my rebellious phase around age 14, I've been drawn to the mystical side of life. It fitted me well, at odds with the hard-knock life realism my mother lived by. I needed some hope to cling to that this world's wasn't as harsh and unromantic as it seemed.

Growing up in 'Naked City', just off the Las Vegas strip ,was as depressing as it comes. Sentiment was sparse and home life was an echo of all the dashed hopes the city was built on. I didn't blame my mum though. Survival mode dictates a lot, but I always wanted *more* than to just survive. Stevie Nicks was my spirit animal growing up - she embraced all the witchy romanticism I thought would guide me to a happy heart, and a happier place. It was mum listening to Fleetwood Mac which got me hooked. The music transformed her. Watching her dancing around the house was mesmerising, like all the heavy chains she carried just floated away. It's hard not to be deeply affected by that.

Now, looking back, they're bittersweet memories. The chains got heavier as the drugs aged her body quickly, and before she died she was just a shadow of the free spirit I was inspired by growing up.

Venice Beach had always been my spiritual home, though. Unlike Vegas, it's a place where free spirits are nurtured, not crushed, and every day feels like a new opportunity. People always say anything can happen here, and the longer I live here, the more I believe it.

For me, the notions of destiny & fate have never just been romantic fairy-tales. I truly believe everything happens for a reason, even through the shitty times.

It's only really since I moved here that I've been able to acknowledge the unusual ability I have to connect with people on a deeper level than most. Amy spotted it quickly, recognising the empath in me.

The belief that we are all connected, moving further or closer together with the flow of life, gives me a spiritual foundation of hopeful optimism which I think draws people to me. Not always the good ones, either. In fact, usually not.

Everyone is drawn to hopeful people, aren't they? Even the bad eggs. Probably those more so, actually. Not enough good energy of their own, so they need to suck the life out of others.

This guy in Sal's seemed different though. A different energy that something inside me recognised, as much as my wounded little heart tried to ignore.

"No no no, I *know* you!" Amy begged. "You believe in all that Serendipity crap, so you can't ignore this. It's a sign!" she finally shouted in a mock-religious way, throwing her arms in the air.

"Dammit!" I thought, suddenly fearful that life was about to throw me another banana skin to slip on. I had followed 'fate' before and fate gave me a black eye in return.

"What have you got to lose?" Amy said casually, before taking a sip of wine, noticing me close my eyes and purse my lips like I was making a wish. "Babe, an attractive Irish man with a nice car orders the same pizza as you, in the same place at the same time, with NO CHEESE. Are you really gonna tell me, little miss destiny, that you think ending up with his pizza box and phone number isn't the universe sending you a pretty fucking loud message!?"

The forcefulness and breathlessness of her speech makes me laugh, but also tightens the knot in my stomach.

Even without thinking this through, I know I have to accept what has landed, literally in my lap.

"OK. Where's my phone?"

4
TOMMY

The palm trees along San Vincente Boulevard stood vivid against the dimming sky as I turned off the wide street and paused to allow the tall, wide oak paneled gates to part.

My short journey back to Santa Monica hadn't been the usual mood slide into a less busy head-space. I just couldn't get this girl out of his head, as much as I tried to distract myself by flicking radio stations.

My encounters with LA girls had so far mostly been fame hungry starlets looking to get close to my boss - film producer, mogul and frequent asshole Liam Fletcher. That suited me well to be honest, happy to be a supporting character in someone else's story for a while.

These girls had opened my eyes to how shallow and ruthless Hollywood really was. They were all chasing a dream. Nothing wrong with that, but High School beauty quickly becomes ordinary in the ruthless corridors of LA casting agencies. When that reality hits, panic usually follows. One of my most troublesome tasks was deflecting these vulnerable girls, ironically often for their own good.

The abuse of power in this town was well known and mostly unspoken about, and my wealthy employer wasn't averse to taking full advantage.

The house was mostly dark inside as I emerged from the lane, just a small light in each bedroom balcony, and the blue glow from the large T-shaped pool. A motion sensor security light awakens as the Mustang glides over the perfect tarmac, towards the garage. The doors open slowly and quietly, revealing the large brightly lit interior, painted bright white and large enough to be a car showroom.

I had never been a car person, but recognise most of the badges on this mix of sports cars and luxury sedans. Any excess space in the garage has been filled with rentals or cars borrowed just for filming. MTV Cribs had just shot an episode for season 3 here two day ago, and I wondered how many of these cars did the rounds and popped up in multiple episodes.

Cribs typifies the fascination with celebrity lifestyle, allowing anyone with a dream to imagine themselves in a mansion like this. A twist of fate away from a life of luxury where problems don't exist. Not the kind of problems normal people have, anyway.

It wasn't too long ago I was outside this world looking in. I'd been on holiday on the French Riviera at the same time as the 1997 Cannes Film Festival, deliberately timed of course. Being so close to the likes of Sly Stallone, Johnny Depp and Sharon Stone gave me goosebumps for sure, but it struck me immediately how subtly myself and my fellow unprivileged were kept at just the right distance, noses pressed longingly against the travelling Hollywood fishbowl.

Only in the last couple of years, with the rise of websites like 'Ain't It Cool News' and tabloid style magazines, that the carefully constructed images of our idols had noticeably began to crumble, and it was clear they were just as fucked up as the rest of us. Not that it did much to kill the fascination. Ironically it probably just fueled it more! There's nothing that will help you relate to someone on a pedestal more than reading about their flaws and watching them take a tumble from their lofty perch once in a while.

What bothered me the most though was the growing trend of talent-less people being made tabloid famous, sharing magazine pages and weblogs with *actual* stars.

I have a resentment towards them for diluting the traditional idea of celebrity, and timing it with my arrival. Some would argue that we're all just chasing our dreams in different ways, but in my book it has less value without some integrity, and talent.

Despite this, my fascination with all things celebrity was still strong - only ten years ago I was the proverbial movie geek who spent his evenings absorbing Hollywood's version of the world. My brain had, for a long time, seemingly been wired to retain movie facts, lines & character names. Remembering things which might have been actually useful in life was never my forte.

This fortunate affliction has helped me fit in easier in Hollywood though, so I now just pass it off as training for my dream job. I was wired that way for a reason, obviously.

I reverse into my usual spot, tonight between a black Lexus and an orange Toyota Supra. Not just any Toyota Supra, but the actual car Brian drove in last year's street racing movie 'The

Fast and the Furious'. I asked if i could take it out and they just laughed at me. I wasn't even allowed to sit in it! It was worth a shot!

Pizza balanced in one hand, phone in the other, I side-step carefully between the cars towards the two exit doors. One leads inside the house and the other up the steps to the helipad on the back roof. Using my bum to push open the left hand exit door, I pivot as the automatic lights reveal the short hallway into the downstairs kitchen.

It's usually hectic at this time on a Saturday, catering for one of Liam's famous parties, which is usually a collection of pretentious 'friends', industry acquaintances, and hungry young talent.

Tonight the stillness is very welcome. It's been a bust week.

Thanks to MTV it was even more immaculate than usual, and as I slip my phone into his trouser pocket it vibrates gently against my leg.

Liam never texted, either too old school or just beneath him, so the message could wait. Given the time difference between here and Seoul I figure my plans for a work-free evening could end any moment. 8pm here means 12 noon Sunday over there, and even though the trip was supposed to be a romantic getaway, the choice of location and South Korea's emerging film industry was no co-incidence.

Liam Fletcher never stops hustling.

The pizza slides from its box onto a wooden slab and into the microwave for a quick reheat as I quickly pour a Budweiser into a branded beer glass, perfecting a head on the beer worthy of an advert.

Sixty seconds after the beep, my backside is making itself comfortable on the luxurious corner sofa in my 'apartment'. Cleverly segregated on the left of the house, I have private use of almost 2500 of the 22,0000 square feet the property extends to, but tonight I don't need much.

Just this couch, food, beer and a movie…and this huge house to myself.

The pizza is gone about 25 minutes into the film. A rom-com isn't my usual choice of genre for a night to myself but I'm a sucker for *anything* with John Cusack. I've always thought that if they made a movie of my life, he would be my ideal alter-ego.

I'm not sure if the average person connects so deeply to films and characters as I do. I've been this way as long as I can remember, especially through my impressionable teenage years before all the romantic ideology which the movies promised turned out to be bullshit.

Growing up in a small town in Northern Ireland offers little hope of a movie worthy story, not that my surroundings ever stopped me trying.

I missed the film 'Serendipity' when it hit cinemas just after Christmas last year. I was too lost in the chaos of moving my broken little life 5000 miles to care about John's fateful love affair with the beautiful Kate Beckinsale. Tonight I'm loving it though, and quite happy to catch this one alone. It's probably not very 'cool' for a 28 year old man to enjoy romantic comedies as much as I do, but I don't care.

John Hughes, you have a lot to answer for.

It's only when I pause the DVD to grab a second bottle of Bud that I remember to check my phone, wondering who it would possibly be. Most people I know are in a 4am time zone and unlikely to be texting. Maybe Ollie is still up.

I stand up and pull the Nokia 3310 out of my trouser pocket, opening the unread text which has sat patiently waiting for a little over thirty minutes.

It's a good job we like the same pizza ;-p

I raise my eyebrows, completely bewildered at first as to what this means. The two girls in Sal's - could it be one of them? Who else could it be? But how?

I feel my brain suddenly become more alert and my heart rate quickens as I stare at the wink at the end of the message. Definitely a little flirty.

Could it be the quiet girl?

The really pretty one with the dark hair.

She did get a pizza with no cheese too, I think.

Fuck! What was her name again?

How did she get my number?

I smile at the screen as I head towards the fridge, wondering how to respond, or *if* I should…

My pledge to myself to not get involved with anyone for at least a year has been going well. It's advice I'm trying to follow after my world fell apart. Ollie's advice had been a little more laddish - something along the lines of "Just go shag as many people as you can until you can't remember that bitch any more".

Not my style.

Work has been so all-consuming that it's been easy to keep my heart closed for business. When I first arrived in LA, I had sometimes wondered if I should take even a little of Ollie's advice, just to see how it felt. Girls wear much less clothes here than back home, and it's hard not to notice. I may be heartbroken, but I'm not blind, and everyone has needs, right?

The opportunities hadn't been forthcoming though, or I hadn't really sought them out. Either way, it's probably been for the best.

I do miss it. Just don't ask me exactly *what* I miss, because I couldn't tell you.

Fuck it!

I've already surprised myself tonight in Sal's. I sure haven't felt that tingle in a long time, and I'm enjoying this little twist in the evening. A little innocent flirting can't hurt anyone!

Thank you, John Cusack & Kate Beckinsale, for reminding me what it feels like to meet a random stranger and have an instant connection.

Leaning back against the counter, my brain freezes at the same time as my fingers, poised over the keypad. Tapping my thumb on the small screen, her words are staring back at me, waiting on the perfect witty come-back. I'm a little out of practice.

My sense of humour is definitely on the surreal side and I remind myself to keep that in check. That and the nervous teenage boy inside me who's just decided to re-emerge.

I start to type, then delete it…three times.

Keep it light. Keep it fun.

Good job indeed! I hope mine is as tasty as yours ;-)

5
GINA

The phone beeps loudly, and suddenly, making me jump. Amy snatches it off the coffee table lightning fast, like going for a buzzer on a quiz show. The Friends episode had run its course along with Amy's vocal impatience in the forty minutes or so since my semi-flirty little text bounced off into the ether.

Why has he not replied?

Is it the wrong number?

Is he married?

Is he gay?

"Well why else would he not be interested in you?" Amy had also said out loud all the things I had been thinking. None of it helping the rising apprehension about my number being in the hands of a total stranger.

"You're *sure* he isn't some guy sent there to spy on me for Brandon?" I had begged nervously after about fifteen minutes of no reply.

"Brandon doesn't even know where you are babe! And how would a spy know you were going to be in Sal's and be there waiting for you? Spy's aren't commonly psychic…or Irish!" Amy smiled, trying to relax my anxiety.

A wry smile accepts her logic but the worst-case scenario dread hasn't been fully quietened. For how long longer would my trauma randomly manifest, tarnishing my experiences and tinting my perceptions?

"Everything is OK, I promise," Amy adds reassuringly, knowingly, before chirping, "Anyway, if anyone wants to hurt you they'll have to get past me first. I'll pull some combat moves on the fuckers and kick them back under the rock in the desert where they belong."

She take her attention to the phone screen once she sees my worry begin to subside.

"Oooh he thinks you're tasty!"

"Oh I'm sure he does," I reply dryly with my signature eye-roll.

Amy passes me the Nokia then turns quickly to sit cross-legged on the sofa, facing me, waiting impatiently on me assessing the message.

Good job indeed! I hope mine is as tasty as yours ;-)

Amy can't keep still. "What are you going to say back?"

"Oh, you're loving this!" I let out a nervous giggle as I stare in admiration at Tommy's text, before looking up at Amy. "He's good! So what do I say to that, queen flirt?"

"Simple. Your address," Amy deadpans, pausing before, "…and then ask him how big his penis is?"

This makes me throw my head back, laughing at the idea, and at the audacity of my friend. Typical Amy.

"Does that work for *you*?"

"Everytime, bitch!" Amy deadpans again, this time pretending to blow dry her fingernails. "Or you could ask him if Irish sausages are as tasty as American ones?"

"Oh yeah, I'll tell him I'm doing a research paper on international sausages."

"Sounds like my kinda party…" Amy mutters into her wine glass before draining it.

I start typing, then quickly hit 'send' as a rush of adrenaline runs through me.

* * *

Tommy

My finger is already hovering over on the pause button on the DVD player remote control, hoping for a reply that is quicker than I had managed. I didn't expect it to feel like this, or maybe I had just forgotten what it felt like. It had been a long time.

I know lots of people in LA already, so it surprises me how much this feels like I'm connecting with someone for the first time in this huge city.

I can't fully define it, but going purely by the warm glow in my chest right now, it feels right.

So if i asked what a guy like you was doing in a place like this, would that be too cheesy? ;-p

I smile wide at this, tossing the remote control aside to give the phone all my attention, and acknowledging the soothing sensation of someone being interested in me again.

I'm also aware of the contradicting emotions. The fear of even thinking about letting someone become close enough to hurt me is there, but it's losing the battle against the other sensation. An intoxicating one. The feeling of being validated again as a person worthy of getting to know in that way. If this is nothing more than some flirty text messages, I'm happy. It's already refilling something in me which I hadn't realised was so empty, until now.

That's the only kind of cheese i like. Or we like? :-D

We already? Do they all move as fast as you back home? :-O

ha ha fair point. I'm not very good at this! Was my number on the pizza box?

Yes Mr Millar! You're better at this than you think - i didn't even see you swap boxes to slip me your number :-P

I wish i was that good! Everything happens for a reason though, right? Too cheesy? Tommy by the way :-)

Maybe it does Tommy! Is it a 'Of all the pizza joints in all the towns in all the world, he walks into mine' kind of thing then? ;-)

She follows it quickly with **Gina x**

* * *

Gina

Amy squeals in delight. "Wow you're good at this! When did you get so good at this?"

"Spending too much time with you obviously!"

"Hold on hold on!" Amy almost shouts, holding one hand up. "Tommy & Gina?"

I look at her blankly, and need to nod to get more information.

"Bon Jovi?" she prompts, before singing, "*Tommy goes to work on the docks.... Gina works the diner all day.*"

"Aaaah Living on a Prayer. I love that song!"

Amy grabs Gina's hand and with her best fake serious look says "Babe, your life is a song now. This is your destiny!"

I give Amy an eye-roll after an involuntary laugh. "Not quite, but how weird though!" My brow furrows as I try to focus on the screen, at the exact moment it lights up again with another reply.

Tommy & Gina? Like the song? Is this a prank?

I know right. Amy just said the same thing. I don't work in a diner though lol and I'm guessing you don't work down the docks?

Maybe i do ;-)

Don't see many dock workers in nice clothes driving around in a new Mustang

Gina, you were paying more attention than I realised

My tummy flutters when simply seeing my name in his message for the first time. Anxiety has a word with my boldness and threatens to come out on top…just for a moment. I'm enjoying this too much. A sip of wine and a smile to the enraptured Amy and I tap out a simple reply.

;-D x

* * *

Tommy

I need a minute to process this message, smiling at my attempt to take a sip from my now empty glass. Two beers have added just enough buzz to make this flirty back and forth feel a little surreal. How refreshing, though, to talk to someone about something other than work.

How do I reply to this though?

It feels like raising the stakes in a poker game.

I head to the bathroom to give me time to think of a witty reply, or if I should just leave it there. I take my time washing my hands. More time to process this and decide which of the two opposing instincts to follow, even though I already know, deep down.

No matter how much my heart has been trampled on, I will always be pulled towards the romantic, especially when it's playing out like a scene in a movie. Pausing to look at myself in the mirror, I shake my head at the ridiculous instinct to make sure I look presentable.

For text messages?

I don't really understand why - but it does make me think that maybe I want to make a good impression on this girl.

Riding high on that thought and swept up in the moment, my next message is the only next move. If he don't raise the pot, so to speak, it might look like I'm not interested.

I'm also unsure if I'm a match for her banter, so matching her boldness instead feels obvious, as I begin to type with a mischievous grin.

* * *

Amy

"Oh fuck, he's not replying now. I've scared him off"

"Babe, relax, he's probably away for a pee or something" Amy called over her shoulder, on the way for a pee herself.

The phone beeps as Amy returns a moment later, like it was waiting on her.

I wonder where Tommy & Gina had their first date?

I reads it slowly, several times, deliberately keeping my expressionless face a polar opposite to my insides, where my tummy and my heart are right now doing some pretty spectacular back-flips.

I nonchalantly pass the phone to Amy who reads as she sits, pouting slightly, impressed.

"He's good. Time to dig out your best underwear chick".

I smile as I give Amy a firm shake of my head, "Nope. Six week rule."

"Oh jeez are you still on that? What guy is gonna wait six weeks?"

"The ones who's worth my time will!"

I deliver this as definitively as I can, and Amy's hand gestures concede that it's non-negotiable. I give her an appreciative smile before returning to the phone, a reply already eagerly waiting in my fingertips.

Can you roller-skate?

Not without falling over!

lol OK maybe play it safe then and meet for a drink?

Sounds good! My boss is back in the country Monday so if it's not too soon does tomorrow work for you?

Working till around 4 but could meet you after, on the boardwalk near Sal's? You could introduce yourself to my group lol

Your group? Is this how they do first dates in LA? lol

lol I'm a tour guide, I'll be finishing up a walking tour there at 4 x

Aah i see! Thats pretty cool! See you all there then x

:-D

I press the button to darken the screen and set the phone triumphantly on the coffee table.

"Guess who's got a date at four tomorrow?"

"Holy shit!" Amy shouts, almost perfectly mimicking Julia Roberts' same line in 'Pretty Woman as she starts to bounce on the sofa. "So what's the plan then, Cinderella?"

"Just a drink and see how it goes. I mean he might be a nut job - I don't even know what he does for a living. Knowing my luck he'll be a gangland accountant or something."

"In Sal's on a Saturday night? You watch too many movies babe," as she gives me one of my own eye-rolls back.

"Criminals eat pizza too you know…..will you come with me?"

"A threesome? On the first date? OK but only if you go first and let me watch."

I scold her with a playful slap on her leg.

"Will you hide somewhere nearby and keep your phone on in case I need rescued?"

"Can I wear a disguise? I could do an accent and be your waitress. Oh that would be so much fun!"

"Can you just be serious for one minute, please? Now that I've arranged this I'm flipping out a little…" I trail off before Amy interrupts.

"Yes, of course, sorry babe I've got your back!"

I'm not sure if her hug is one of congratulations, or to calm the anxiety she can probably see building.

Either way, it's very welcome.

6
TOMMY

It's a busier than usual Sunday afternoon along the Venice shore-front, and I'm lucky to grab the last space in the car park beside the fishing pier. Another random sign from the universe that I'm on the right track, and with my first LA date less than an hour away I'll happily take it as a thumbs up.

Being late is one of few things which stresses me out, but this was early even for me. Then again I had no idea that fate was keeping me a space, and with it gifting me some time to take a walk around my favourite place in the city. Perfect.

I can see it's busier further up Ocean Front Walk, so I walk slowly in that direction, with no particular plan to pass the time.

It's not a place to rush. I want to take in the eclectic mix of people and relish the complete sensory experience of this unique place. The smell alone is unique. The aromas from burger joints and various internationally themed street food outlets are a weird mix when blended with the smells of incense and candles from new age stores. Every so often you'll get a whiff of board wax or marijuana, all cornerstones of the bohemian Venice which is famous around the world.

It's only when I stop to watch some street performers - a troupe of six guys drawing a crowd with their fusion of acrobatics and break-dancing, that I suddenly remember Gina had said she was leading a walking tour before our date.

Shit, what if I bump into them? How awkward will that be?

I briefly considered just going back to the car, but glancing out to sea, seeing the gentle shimmer on the water, quickly change my mind.

Shoes dangling in one hand, I pad barefoot through the soft warm sand away from the crowds and towards the water's edge, passing a volleyball game in full flow. I've been in Venice several times but never on the actual beach. It's amazing how quickly it becomes quiet as you walk towards the water.

This truly is heaven.

I check my watch as I let the gentle tide wash up over my ankles.

I wish it was 4 o'clock already.

Sal's isn't too far from here, so I can take my time, but the peacefulness which descends as I walk creates space for some nerves too. A wave of resentment comes next. I should be feeling nothing but happy. The anxiety is not welcome. Clearly I can travel thousands of miles away from home but *she*, or rather what she did, is going to follow me everywhere.

How long do I have to carry this pain?

Squinting towards the sun, I take a deep breath and remind myself again to focus on gratitude, and how good this day is hopefully going to be. I was only been around Gina for a short time last night, but it was enough to feel her warm energy and feel an instant and powerful attraction. I for sure had never experienced that before, like she had an invisible glow which radiated out into me.

Does everyone feel that from her?

Just thinking about it makes me crave being around her again, especially after the flirty messages. So far, this had all caught me completely unaware, just how much I've been craving a meaningful, safe connection with someone.

Will I be able to be myself around her?

Do I remember how to do this?

What would Ferris do?

This had been my 'thing' in my late teens, obsessed with 'Ferris Bueller's Day Off'. If ever I found myself unsure of how to react or behave, I just put myself in the shoes of the coolest person I'd ever seen.

I have long since realised that Ferris Bueller was just a selfish, entitled asshole and no role model for anyone, but annoyingly it hadn't stopped him still popping his head around the door in my brain to ask the question.

Ironically Ferris' advice would probably be spot on - just relax. Don't over think it.

* * *

Glancing up Venice Boulevard, the sign for Sal's about 30 feet away is as familiar as an old friend waving hello as I pass.

The frontage of the Venice Beach Bar is a huge wooden decked balcony, split in half by a few steps leading up to the main door to the bar & bistro inside. Fate again had held the last table - a small wooden one in the front corner of the balcony, and as I slid smugly into one of the two empty wicker chairs I only relaxed long enough for my watch to bring back the nerves.

3.45pm wasn't too early, right?

The thought of arriving at the corner at the same time as Gina and her tour made me cringe. I consider briefly losing the watch, thinking it's too showy.

Why do I have such a hang-up with this watch?

It came with the job, but it makes me feel like I'm tagged. I wouldn't be surprised if it did have some sort of GPS tracker built in! It's not my style but I'm so scared of losing it that I wear it more than I want to.

Stop over-thinking!

The waitress returns with a beer and a smile, and its coldness lands perfectly as I lean back into the chair and make a concerted effort to relax. I still struggle a bit with the heat here, but as they say back home on an unseasonable warm day 'We shouldn't complain!'

A sudden cluster of chat and laughter catches my attention as it passes a few feet to my right, a group of maybe 20 people. This has to be a tour group, recognising the difference in clothing & nationalities. It must be Gina's too, but I can't see her, or any guide for that matter.

The scared, broken part of me sees its opportunity and starts to gloat.

She was winding you up.

There is no date.

You're not worthy of anyone!

The lies had just reached the pit of my stomach when the group began to part, just like it would in a movie, and suddenly, as bright as the sunshine she's bathed in, there she is.

The universe could not have positioned us more perfectly, because as she was revealed, about twenty feet away, our eyes meet simultaneously. Hers widen slightly in recognition, as her speech pauses for a split second. Just enough to allow a smile.

It's like the whole world pauses in that tiny, most magic of moments, and I honestly feel her smile in my soul. She looks even more beautiful than I had memorised, which is quite a feat, given how much I've idealised her since yesterday . She holds a bold eye-contact for a good five seconds while giving facts about the famous Muscle Beach Gym, and smiles again in response to mine.

Only one of her group notices, glancing round to me and smiling herself at the cuteness of the connection between us.

She asks the group to head towards the corner of Venice Boulevard for the last stop on the tour and allows them to move either side of her, still facing my direction. As they pass, she lifts one hand up in front of her chest, fingers spread wide. "Five minutes" she mouths, eyebrows raised hopefully and a cute little head tip forward, like she's whispering close to me.

She pauses for my nod back, before beaming me a huge smile. One that lands even deeper.

Spinning the opposite direction, she throws her arms in the air with a shout "OK my beautiful people," and strides off towards the tour group.

7
GINA

Here we go!

Tucking the last of my tips into my bag, I can feel the needy gaze of a few lost souls who linger in the aftermath of the tour. No better place to be lost than Venice, and all it's hidden delights to discover. I try to send them off with a flutter of my lashes and a reassuring smile. I've had clingers before. Well meaning of course, but I don't have time for new friends today. My phone chimes, giving me the perfect out, and I can't help but grin at Amy's message;

Secret agent Dickinson in position, ready for extraction.

If I know Amy, right now she's wrapping some bronzed lifeguard around her little finger. She's not the type of person to simply wait. She'll always find some mischief to spice up the moment.

Moving in lol wish me luck I quickly thumb back as I head back towards the bar, taking a deep breath and making a conscious effort to relax. I'm aware of the need to dim the sparkle of my boisterous tour guide persona to something more subtle. Slightly manic is not a good look for a first date.

Amy's quick reply jolts a genuine laugh out loud; **No anal on the 1st date!**

I'm thankful to see Tommy's attention is on his own screen as I get closer to the bar. This is awkward enough without having to nail the approach with grace and style. I can just sneak up and be in the seat before he realises.

No such luck - his eyes flick up as if he can hear my thoughts, and I instinctively slow to a pace I hope looks relaxed enough to hide the nerves. The goofy wave I throw him from no more than ten paces away kills that immediately, especially when combined with an over enthusiastic grin.

Oh my god stop acting like a game show host!

Be cool.

Let the mystery linger a little.

I go for the classic casual hair tuck behind the ear as I bound energetically up the steps before settling in the seat opposite him, with all the calm of a serene lake. Or rather the proverbial swan on the lake.

'You're here!' he exclaims with effortless charm, completely unaware of my racing heart. His appeal is undeniably stronger than my memory serves - the sexy confidence in his eyes, that rogue shadow of stubble, and oh, that accent.

Trying to play the cool card, I drawl, "Well. I had a spare hour, y'know?" flipping an unintended eye roll that I immediately internally chastise.

He volleys back quickly with an ease which throws me off guard even more, "You do dates by the hour? What kind of tour guide are you?" The way his right eyebrow arches as he leans in closer, like we share a secret, whips up a little whirlwind in my chest.

I find myself replying before any thought or composure can temper my words, "Oooh, and you said you weren't good at this. Handsome *and* funny. If all Irish lads are like this, then I've been looking for love in all the wrong places".

He just cocks his head to the side, saying nothing, and I feel exposed. Instant heat creeps onto my cheeks, broadcasting an awkwardness I wish I could swallow back down.

Feigning calm, I deflect, "I blame Amy's influence", only to be met by his grin - wide and indulging, as he silently watches me squirm.

The waitress comes to my rescue, perfectly timed - just like she would if this was a scene in a movie.

"Hey guys, what can I get you?" She giving the table a token wipe with a damp cloth that was hanging on her belt.

"Jen, what's that new cocktail with the three colours, the pineappley one?" I'm grateful for the break in tension, and to see a familiar face.

"Sea Breeze," she replies with a 'I just realised you're on a date' mischievous smile.

"I'll take one of those please," I reply, using my eyes to plead for her discretion, doing my best to deliver my words with the intent of "Please don't embarrass me".

This wasn't how I planned to first use this technique from my acting lessons, the 'subtext method' they called it. A cornerstone of the famous Meisner technique - it's the ability to say the same line different ways, depending on your intention. Basically saying one thing but *meaning* another.

The practice exercise that tickled me most in class was a time we used the question, "Would you like a cup of tea?". Various random intentions were called out with a context, and the one involving a couple which was most hilarious. "You've just invited someone back from a date to your apartment for the first time, and you're only allowed to ask them if they'd like a cup of tea." the coach had instructed. Simple enough, until you have to say it and convey that you'd like them to leave, or the best of one all was conveying that you're actually inviting them to bed. What a laugh we had with that one.

I don't know if I'm very good at it though. Jen's wink and "Sure thing hun" doesn't fill me with confidence.

Maybe I should have asked her if she'd like a cup of tea?

"Another Bud light? Jen blithely asks Tommy, as she waves at someone on the path below us.

"Ah, I'm driving unfortunately, so just a water and lime cordial please?"

Jen nods and disappears back inside as my phone beeps loudly from my bag.

"Are you excited to see the eclipse?" I ask, as brightly as I can muster, ignoring the beeps.

"Oh wow yeah, that's soon isn't it?"

Instinctively, we both look out towards the sun, hovering out over the Pacific Ocean.

"About an hour from now I think, at its peak. Have you ever see one?"

Tommy shrugs. "No…well yes, kind of. There was one when I was really young. I remember it being a thing but don't actually *remember* it, if that makes sense?"

Jen appears back at the table before I can reply with more than a nod, setting the drinks down and leaving me with a look that I read clearly as "Not bad". She's clearly a better actress than I am, and I make a mental note to ask her sometime.

The clink of our glasses, "To first dates" feels like the official start of something, and I happily let my gaze connect with his, sealing the moment in my memory.

Attempting nonchalance, I ask about his reasons for landing in the City of Angels, keen to peel back the layers and let him do the talking.

"So what's brought you to LA?" I inquire with a playful lilt, aware of my instinct to interrogate. "Chasing your dreams like the rest of us starry eyed souls?"

He pauses, slightly tipping his head in consideration, then glancing down at the table.

"Chasing a dream or running away from a nightmare - take your pick," Tommy says flatly, trying to deflect it with a weak laugh as his eyes meet mine again.

There's a flash of something in his eyes, which I recognise as pain, before he continues in a brighter tone. "I'm not quite sure which of those it is, but I'm all for dreams coming true."

His openness, laced with vulnerability throws me - taking me aback in a way I had not anticipated. With just one sentence he has managed to show me a level of emotional maturity I thought was a myth in the male of the species. The men I've encountered until now all wear their masculine bravado like it's a medal and a symbol of pride, completely oblivious to the fact that this makes it profoundly difficult to see the person beneath - to truly understand and connect with them.

Tommy's unexpected openness is disarming, and invites a connection that goes beyond what I expected on a first date. I'm immediately curious.

Before I can think of how to reply, he follows with "What about you? What's your story?" He's leaning towards me again, trying to regain confidence.

I open my mouth to speak but the phone cuts in again, this time ringing. "Sorry!!" I beg, as sorry for the nerve I've touched as I am for the untimely interruption.

Scrambling through my bag, my phone has found its way to the very bottom, and by the time I retrieve it, it has rung off to voicemail. 1 missed call. Amy. Crap! She'll be thinking I've been abducted!

I'm OK babe, I'll call you soon xx I type quickly and hit send.

"Sorry about that, I told Amy to check on me in case you tried to kidnap me or something…..you're not going to kidnap me are you?"

"Ha! No I gave up the 'oul kidnapping when I moved here. Trying to be a better person."

"Well thank goodness for that" I smile, enjoying the banter, and feeling more at ease with this guy than I expected. "You have good energy!" I blurt out. "LA must be working for you."

"Yeah, I love it here," he smiles back, sidestepping the energy comment. "Especially the weather…" He pauses mid-sentence and gives me a look that I can literally feel inside me. "…and the view!"

"Oh, I thought Ireland would be lovely!" just letting his flirty comment hang in the air between us, but unable to hide the slight flush he's given me.

"Oh it is, but not the weather. Northern Ireland is like the complete opposite to here. Always cold, usually wet, and everyone is miserable about it most of the time. The shitty weather is the number one topic of conversation back home, yet we stay and put up with it."

"You didn't…"

"Yeah, true. I suppose not everybody gets to be as lucky as I am." That's the second time he's used the Meisner method on me in less than a minute. His mid-sentence change of tone and sexy smile makes me feel special.

Why is everyone better at this than I am?

"I've always wanted to go - it looks beautiful! So green! Is Northern Ireland different then?" I inquire with playful innocence. I'm hoping if I pretend to ignore the flirting he'll keep it up.

He chuckles, more to himself, like he's been asked this question before. "Yes…..well no not really. It's complicated". An ironic chuckle now, realising it sounds stupid when he spots my frown. "North and South Ireland. Two religions…which are actually just two versions of the same religion, fighting over who owns which bit, although it's mostly only the northerners fighting each other. I'm so glad to be away from it, to be honest."

"Oh shit, it sounds dangerous."

"I'm probably not being totally fair - it's not like it's Beirut, with gun battles in the streets or anything…and it is getting better…I think. No it's a beautiful place on the whole, and some of the most genuine people in the world. Don't let me put you off going - the chances of getting shot are pretty slim." he says brightly, trying to lift the vibe again.

"Hey, don't worry. There's plenty of places not far from here where they'll happily pop a cap in your ass for no reason too."

"Oh great!" he laughs back, "Now I should be worried that *you're* actually the dangerous one!"

"You never know!" I give him wink, deciding the time is right engage my own flirt mode.

Tommy leans back, letting a sexy smile of appreciation change his face. "So, tell me your story. The life and times of Gina…..?"

"Sawyer…and hey a girl has to keep some mystery. Not that my life is that exciting."

"How long have you been a tour guide? I'm sure you meet some characters doing that?"

"Oh wow you have no idea! But I absolutely love it. You get to spend two hours at a time in the company of such interesting people. Some you're very glad it's only two hours, but mostly you get the best of people, relaxed and happy to be on vacation. It still makes me feel like I'm still on vacation here too."

"Oh? You're not from here?"

"No, I'm a blow-in like yourself, although from a little closer - Las Vegas"

"I like Vegas....for three days max!" He laughs, hinting at a story which I might ask about later.

"Yeah, try living there for 26 years."

"So you're chasing some dreams here too then?"

I instinctively bite my lower lip, letting my own vulnerability show. If he only knew what lay behind the door of that little question.

"Well, let's just say that you and I might have more in common already than I thought - but that's a story for another time. I think we should both keep our eyes fixed on the dream eh?". I give him my best 'we're big brave adults now' energy, and a confident smile.

"Sounds good to me" he grins back, happy to keep it light, and to recognise a kindred spirit.

We're been so engrossed in our connection that we've been oblivious to what's unfolding above us, until the daylight slowly begins to dim, casting an otherworldly hue over the world around us.

The foot traffic between us and the beach has slowed to a standstill now, and it feels like the whole world has stopped to watch the sun disappear behind the moon.

What a rare and magic moment, and to be experiencing this on a first date feels very much like a message from the universe. The planets aligning, almost literally.

A rush of awareness comes quickly, and my body responds with warm flush of excitement and anticipation. I make a conscious effort to burn this moment into a deeper layer of memory, The eclipse and it's romantic light. The world stopping around us. The buzz from my second cocktail. The mellow house music and the undeniable spark between Tommy.

It's one of those rare moments in life which I know is special while I'm in it. I lock into the magic, and let all my senses heighten to take it in.

Not since fleeing Las Vegas in fear that cold February night have I allowed myself to feel this relaxed, despite my anxiety whispering some justifiable caution.

I don't know this guy at all, but I know with surprising certainty that I am safe.

Basking in the soft glow of the emerging sun, there's an unspoken excitement of something new and thrilling surrounding us…just us. The rest of the world begins to move again.

The sun will be gone again in a couple of hours, but I know I'm not ready for this date to end. We order more drinks, with Tommy giving in to my protests about his boring water & lime and ordering a fruity mocktail recommended by Jen.

The chat is easy and comfortable between us, and how he takes the ribbing I give him about his new drink only intrigues me more. How refreshing it is to be with a guy who's confident enough in himself to not only sit in public with a huge pink mocktail, but to let me tease him about it without taking it as picking holes in his fragile masculinity.

Choosing to keep private the driving force of my upheaval, I take the comedy route and dramatically frame my LA arrival as the usual cliché - fresh off the Greyhound with dreams of instant fame. A Hollywood megastar discovered in Ben & Jerry's! This amuses Tommy more than I expect, and before I make a mental note to come back to his reaction, I first have to work to quieten the anxious squatter in my brain.

How long will I have to live with this irrational radar, over analysing every innocent joke or reaction which doesn't perfectly fit my expectations?

Over the next hour, the chat is light, flowing so easily but avoiding anything too personal. He seems content to listen to my stories of countless failed auditions and how often my dorkiness lets me down when I meet someone even semi-famous. When Amy phones to double check I'm OK, he takes the opportunity to ask about her. This works well for me - three cocktails in and hyper aware of not giving away too much about myself.

Just in case.

"She seems a bit…ummm…crazy?"

"Oh wow you have no idea. How she functions in normal life I have no idea. Actually now that I think about it it, she doesn't function normally at all. We work well together as room-mates though, and I'm *so* grateful for her. She's my crazy safety blanket, and she does *so* much to not let me quit on my myself."

"That's amazing. Everyone needs someone like that in their corner. You're a lucky girl. Did you know her from Vegas then?"

"No, just here. I got lucky with a Craigslist advertisement, and we hit it off straight away. And when I say lucky, you should see her amazing apartment!"

I pause to down the last mouthful of alcohol in my glass. "I think she wanted a friend more than a room-mate, because she takes very little money. I think she took pity on me…"

"Take pity on you? Why?"

He's on this quickly, and my frustration at letting my guard down enough to slip up like this makes me freeze, only serving to make it even more suspicious.

"Oh! Umm…no nothing, I don't know why I said that," failing miserable to sound convincing.

Tommy's expression tells me that he doesn't buy this for a second, but his smile lets me know he won't pursue it.

Keep it together girl.

That little slip up is a reminder to myself that I need to stop with the cocktails.

I glance at my watch, led a little by anxiety, but mostly by hunger. That sudden realisation you're hungry which only happens when you've had a few drinks, or been lost in conversation. In this case, it's most definitely both. It's also a useful diversion.

I lean across the table, the alcohol bringing out more flirt than I would otherwise normally allow. "I'm hungry!" giving him wide eyes. Too wide, and too flirty, judging by the reply.

"You look like you're ready to take a bite out of me!" he laughs as he leans forward too, rising to the challenge of my unintentional flirt. Our faces are no more than six inches apart.

Oh fuck! Oh fuck he smells so good.

"You should be so lucky," I whisper, too intimately and too inviting. Not the cheeky cute I was aiming for.

Only our closeness allows me to notice his eyes widen in recognition, and the smallest movement towards me, testing the water.

Suddenly I'm hyper aware of just the space between us, and the involuntary hormone rush in recognition of being so close to this beautiful human being. My bum lifts off the seat to bring me closer and our lips meet softly, not moving for what feels like several seconds. He presses deeper into the kiss, just enough to signal more intention that a simple peck, before he lets go.

My head stays still, our faces still so tantalisingly close that I can feel the warmth of his breath for a moment…then his lips are on mine again. I instinctively let him lead and when his hand cups my face, fingers touching so gently on the sensitive soft skin behind my ear, I have to make a conscious effort not to let out a moan of pleasure.

Oh my God. Who is this guy?

Pulling away very slowly, and very reluctantly, I smile with a shyness I would have preferred to keep hidden.

"That was nice. Unexpected, but nice."

Be cool. Don't say any more.

He smiles in sexy agreement and a slow nod, holding on to the moment with an intense gaze. "Now I'm starving!" he half-whispers with a wink, and just enough innuendo to make me cover my embarrassed giggles with the back of my hand.

"Back in a sec" he says, touching my other hand gently, before standing and disappearing inside.

Oh. My. God.

We kissed!! is on my screen and Amy-bound within seconds.

I take a take a deep breath and look around, bringing the rest of the world back into focus. It's disorientating at first.

Did everyone not experience what just happened?

Is anyone watching us?

This is too good to be true. Isn't it?

"Ready to go?" Tommy arrives back breezily, his confidence and relaxed demeanour somehow managing to make my anxiety disappear.

"Definitely!"

"Thank you" I say, touching the back of his arm as we walk slowly away from the bar, through the crowds on the boardwalk.

"What for?" he looks at me with eyebrows raised.

"The drinks, silly."

"Oh I didn't pay, I thought you did. I just went to the toilet."

This stops me in my tracks, and Tommy walks on a few paces before spinning round with his a cheeky, 'gotcha' grin on his face.

"Oh my goodness don't do that. There are people who pull that shit here all the time!" I half-laugh, catching him up and giving him a firm but playful shove with both hands.

We settle on a taco each, after a hilarious and flirty discussion on what we'll do if one of us spills chili on our clothes. We eat as we walk, and I completely embarrass myself with multiple hilarious attempts at an Irish accent. It's one of those walks where you just go with the flow. The best kind, with no particular plan, and we've ended up a block or so back from the boardwalk, around the canals.

"I've never walked around here before. It's so beautiful." Tommy's enthusiasm is genuine, and I enjoy seeing him as a tourist.

"I love it. It's so peaceful…"

The familiarity is also comforting. I've led so many tours over and around these iconic bridges, but it feels more special today to introduce this place to Tommy.

"Will we go for a drive?" he asks suddenly.

My reaction takes *me* aback as I stiffen, but not so much as Tommy would notice. My unwelcome friend, anxiety. Always waiting in the wings for its cue to take centre stage, or crash the party.

"I dunno, I should maybe get back…"

Can he hear my anxiety?

"You have another date eh?" he teases softly, adding a perfectly affectionate nudge to my shoulder.

Dammit, stop being so good at this.

"No, no!" I'm light but quick with my reply, keen to avoid an awkward pause. "One date is enough for one day, thank you very much."

Oh my god, shut up you dork!

"I didn't mean it like that," I add quickly, nudging him back, in the hope that I can get away with how cheeky that sounded.

"That's OK, you probably need a nap after that big taco anyway?" he teases again, as we stop in the middle of the bridge.

We're leaning on the handrail, side by side, looking down towards the seafront, and suddenly it feels even quieter.

What's left of the evening sun is on our faces, and that early evening magical calm is settling over Venice. I'm a sucker for the vibe, and all my positive instincts are inviting me to stay and see where this goes.

"I want to….I just…." I swallow the rest of my unfinished sentence before the words can even fully form in my mind.

Tommy doesn't reply, and his body language gives nothing away. He just gazes in the middle distance, and when I glance at him he gives me an easy smile.

What is he thinking?
How do I know if he's safe?

The devil on one shoulder is telling me that no one can be this perfect without some serious flaw, lurking, just waiting to hurt me.

Bail out before it's too late, and enjoy the 'what if'.

This isn't worth the risk.

You're better off alone now.

It's easier.

The devil on my other shoulder has clearly watched too many rom-coms and wants to see what else Mr Tommy Millar has to offer.

Go for it girl, it's just a drive!

There's no way the universe has put you here with this dreamy Irishman just to run away.

"Drive where? Tell me more…" I ask after several awkward seconds, trying to temper the rejection by moving a few inches closer until our arms are touching. My body's response to the sensation of his skin on mine makes all objections fade into background noise.

It's like my body has just been plugged in, and every square inch of my skin feels the electric tingle.

Oh wow.

What is this?

I can feel the flush again on my cheeks, excited and surprised at my boldness, and the effect this guy is having on me right now, while trying to ignore devil number one's cries of caution.

"Somewhere to enjoy the sunset I think" he replies with sexy confidence, grabbing the rom-com reins with both hands. "I think that would be perfect right now, don't you?"

"Yes!" I nod with no hesitation.

Fuck it!

We look at each other, and I soften for the inevitable second kiss, but no such luck! He smiles at me in a way that makes me feel he can read my mind, forcing more redness into my already sunset cheeks.

Dammit!

"OK handsome, where are you parked?"

8
TOMMY

The walk back to my car is slow, and as soon as we reach the boardwalk it takes me a moment to adjust. Everything that felt so familiar before, now feels like I'm enjoying it for the first time. Just by having her beside me.

Is this what all American girls are like?

She's been hard to read for sure, and despite my own wariness quietly chatting away in the background, I've been happy to just let this unfold today. It's amusing to hear just her side of the call to her friend Amy, trying to reassure her that she hasn't been abducted, and she'll back before midnight. "Yes…just like Cinderella," she said sweetly before hanging up.

"She's very protective, is Amy?"

"Ah….yes….it's OK isn't it?"

"That she's protective of you?"

"No, that I'm getting in a strange man's car." Gina frowns, giving away more anxiety than she probably intends.

"Well *I* think it's OK, but it's my car so I'm biased. And I'm really not that strange. I hope!" I give her another playful shoulder nudge.

"I do BODYCOMBAT you know" she says flatly.

"What on earth is BODYCOMBAT? And should *I* be worried now?"

"An exercise class," she laughs. "I'm just letting you know I can hurt you if I have to."

I wince a little at this, but don't let her see. Instead I'm silenced by the surprise at how quickly, and how easily my internal alarms went off, sensing danger. False alarm.

She doesn't mean that kind of hurt.

"Hey, I'm just kidding. Amy teaches it in Santa Monica. You should come sometime," she adds, sensing the awkward pause.

Fuck, she's gonna think I'm some kind of wimp!

"Just so you know, I bruise easily," breaking the tension. She fires me the most beautiful smile. The kind where someone smiles with their entire being and it shines out through their face. That's what I see anyway, but I'm quickly starting to realise that I might be biased.

I can't believe how beautiful you are!

Weaving through the rental bikes beside the car park, I press the key in my pocket and the Mustang flashes in response.

* * *

Gina

"This is beautiful, you have to let me drive it," I can't help but purr as I slip into the passenger seat. "I feel like I'm on a date with a movie star! Oh god I'm in your car and I haven't even asked what you do!"

"Movie star," he fires back quickly, deadpan, and has me fooled for a split second. "Well you are handsome enough. Just about…"

Again I'm surprised at my confidence, but I feel completely at ease with Tommy. He lets it sit for too long with a smug smile, letting me feel my boldness. "Come on then hotshot" I demand, as he pulls out of the space, the engine growling with it's own bold confidence.

"Nothing *quite* so exciting, I'm afraid. But I do get to meet plenty of movie stars."

"Oooh, go on!" I pivot and pull my now bare feet up onto the seat.

Where did all this sass come from?

"I'm a PA for a movie producer," he says, throwing a smile in my direction. "Cute feet, Cinderella…"

"Kindly stop flirting with my feet please, and tell me more. Do you know anyone famous?"

"I wouldn't say *know*, but I've met plenty…"

"Oh wow that's so cool!" I grin, anything but cool myself.

"Trust me, the idea of it is better than the reality. The excitement soon wears off when you realise they're not the gods and goddesses you assume they'll be." He pauses, aware of my disappointment. "*Some* nice people though…and to be fair when I meet them it's usually in situations where they're not as in charge as they'd like to be. That's never gonna bring out the best in people like that."

"Still amazing though! Who's the most famous person you've met?"

"Angelina maybe?"

"Angeline Jolie? No fucking way? Really? When? I *love* her!"

Tommy laughs loudly at my over enthusiasm. "Alright calm down there fan-girl, you're as bad as my mate Ollie."

"Seriously though how sexy was she in 'Gone In 60 Seconds'? I'm not into girls but I would make an exception for her!"

Tommy raises his eyebrows in surprise. "That's a movie I'd pay to see!" This prompts a slap on his shoulder…his very firm and muscular shoulder.

"So where do you park this bad boy every night? If you say it's at Angelina's I'm jumping out into traffic," I ask, while turning down the radio. "I *hate* this song! Don't you hate this song?" not giving him a chance to answer the first question.

"Hey, Nelly is an under-rated song-writing genius I'll have you know." Tommy's sarcasm is laid on thick.

"Oh yeah, sure, he's a proper Elton John. It's getting hot in here, so take off all your clothes? My accompanying eye-roll goes unseen.

"OK but can I pull over first? I'm not sure naked driving is allowed in LA anymore."

This makes me actually snort with laughter…then we both fall into a relaxed quiet and I study him while he drives, turning carefully onto Santa Monica Boulevard and towards Beverly Hills. His warmth and quick humour are making him even more irresistible.

Calm down fan-girl

"Oh yeah, where do you live? You didn't say"

"You didn't give me a chance," Tommy replies, laughing gently. "I'm in Santa Monica."

"Nice…whereabouts?

"San Vincente Boulevard."

"Holy shit, you *do* live at Angelina's. I knew it!"

"Wanna call by her house and see if she's in?" Tommy says in a half whisper, leaning over towards me.

"Now you're definitely fucking with me!" landing another slap, but this time letting my hand linger a second or two longer. A little feel never hurt anyone.

"Yeah I am," he chuckles. "Even if I did know where she lived, I'm pretty sure we'd get arrested, or eaten by guard dogs if we just turned up there."

"Would be one way to get on TV," I shrug, realising immediately how stupid I sound.

Stop being such a dork!

Tommy lets that one slide.

"So where we headed? It's gonna be dark soon…" I ask, trying to mask my vulnerability.

"Well I was thinking we might be in time to catch the sunset from Griffith Park?"

My anxiety reacts quickly, assessing exactly where my phone is. Griffith Park is not somewhere you'd want to be wandering around after dark, from what I've heard.

"Griffith Park? Is it safe?"

I get the impression that Tommy picks up that my "Is it safe?" actually means "Am I safe?" as he tries to reassure.

"Yeah, just the observatory - there'll be lots of people about. I promise you, you're safe… I'll keep you safe."

The last part comes after a slight pause, but those four words, the way he says them so confidently, makes me feel like he's got his arms around me already, warm and strong. And safe….

"OK!" is out of my mouth as soon as that feeling lands. The devil on one shoulder was quicker than the other, and I flash him my best 'I'm OK' smile in reply to his check-in look.

"Are you sure? I don't want you to feel I'm up to anything. Anytime you wanna go just say, OK?" he pauses, before; "I'm just having the best time with you and don't want it to end just yet."

Damn, how is he so good at that? The dramatic pause before a killer line.

He's clearly feeling the awkward pause while I think about how much I agree, and follows with "Was that too much?".

Oh my god, how cute are you?

All I can do is just shake my head and grin…

"So what's your place like?" I ask, dying to know more about him.

"Well, it's not really mine as such. My boss's place has a wing of the property on the ground floor which is kind of separated into an apartment. It's pretty awesome to be fair - the only people ever in it are myself and the cleaner."

"Is her name Angelina?" My cheeky grin gets the laugh and sexy look I was hoping for in return.

"You're not gonna be content until you meet her, are you?"

"Nope!" I turn round a little more in the seat, completely sideways so that I'm facing him, and hug my knees into my chest.

"Are you cold? We'll be back in the sun in a minute I think," he asks, with a courtesy and awareness I'm unaccustomed to, as we wind our way up the shady part of Canyon Road towards the Observatory.

"I'll be OK!" and with a wink, "You'll keep me warm…"

A minute or so later we pull into the car park in front of the Observatory, on the opposite side to the city beyond. I regret not thinking ahead and bringing a jacket as we walk without much purpose up the pathway.

"I can't believe I haven't been up here yet," I think out loud, gazing at the Hollywood sign set into the hillside. We wander towards the right hand side of the building, closer to the sign off to our right. We follow the path along the side of the observatory, and as we come around to the back, the entire city comes into view.

"Wow!" I exclaim, at double volume, such is the impact of this sudden view.

"I know, right. Isn't it stunning?"

Los Angeles, in all it's glory, fans out beneath us like a spectacular tapestry, all the way out to the sea and the shoreline we walked along not so long ago.

"Oh my god Tommy, It is fucking amazing! It looks so vast from up here, I can't believe it."

He sits on a little white waist-height wall and casually throws his legs over. When I join him, nervously, I see that our feet are dangling over another walk way just below, so it feels safe.

It also gives us a completely uninterrupted view, and the thrill of the moment - the view and the company, brings an excited, giddy rush from my tummy to my chest. I shiver just a little at the slight chill in the evening breeze. He notices and edges his bum closer until we're touching, then wraps his arm around me.

I'm grateful for the warmth, but still snuggle in just a little bit more than I need to.

"So lovely…" I trail off in a whisper, absorbing every bit. Not just what I see, but the feel and the smell of his body, and the strangely comfortable calm that washes over me.

How can I feel so safe with someone I barely know?

Any chatter from others around us gradually quietens as the sun edges closer to the horizon beyond Venice Beach, and we watch in silence too, huddled close. The changing light is so dramatic and fast from this vantage point, and I glance to the Hollywood Sign to enjoy the mystical glow it's now gloriously bathed in. The same glow it has enjoyed every day since the golden era of Hollywood.

It has it's last glimmer of magic, before darkening into the hillside as the sun falls.

"It seems like it's setting really fast. Does it always set so quickly?" I half ask and half wonder out loud.

"I guess so," Tommy whispers back into our little huddle.

"It's incredible!"

We watch in awe as our little part of the world spins into night and the sun slips out of view. The entire city, almost suddenly, illuminates. The grid pattern of streets become a satisfying map of light, framed by a purple/pink sky which right now looks so vast.

Beautiful...

"Thank you" I offer quietly, resting my hand on Tommy's leg as I sink into him even more, as if that was even possible. He doesn't reply, but I can feel his smile without even seeing it.

Neither of us move or speak for five minutes or so, both soaking in the moment. We've both been in relationships long enough to know that this is exactly the kind of uncomplicated moment that sinks deeply into that part of the brain which holds the best memories.

This one won't need to be romanticised any further in hindsight - it's just perfect the way it is.

"Should we go get warm?"

"What had you in mind?" I flirt back, our closeness making it feel bolder than the banter of earlier. It's good he can't see my blushes.

"You're funny" he says warmly, giving me a squeeze.

"Yeah, let's go see how fast that Mustang can go?" I suddenly sit up straight, excited and mischievous. "We can find someone to race for pink slips!"

"Oh yeah lets! And I'll end up going home in a taxi to pack my bags," Tommy laughs. "We don't have much street racing in Northern Ireland you know, so I'm a little out of practice."

"I'll drive!" sticking my tongue out before swivelling on the wall and hopping off.

"Oh really? I thought Americans couldn't drive…what is it you call it? A stick shift?"

"How hard can it be?" I parry back, playing along.

"Well, OK but if I get the sack there'll be no second date."

"Maybe there won't be one anyway. Don't you be getting presumptuous Mister Millar!"

He gives me a fake shocked face in reply, not believing me even slightly.

Cheeky boy…I love your confidence.

The warmth of the car with the roof on is welcome, and as follow the same route back in reverse, I'm secretly hoping he takes a longer way. This feels nice, even though I barely know him. It feels like I'm exactly where I belong…but then devil number one reminds me how low my bar is set after my experiences with Brandon over the last few years.

"Straight home, or would you like to go anywhere else?" Tommy inquires, gentlemanly.

"You sound like you're my chauffeur," I giggle.

"I'll take that job! Where to m'lady?" suddenly super formal in a posh English accent.

"Back to the beach, my good man, there's a good chap".

Tommy's head snaps round mid-sentence. "Holy crap, that's a good English accent! Where'd you learn that?"

"Acting class," I say coolly, like it ain't no thing.

"It's good! Much better than your Northern Ireland accent, or any kind of Irish accent. You sound more Jamaican when you try my accent."

"Oooh rude!" I pout with fake indignation. "I suppose I'll have to work on it, if I'm gonna be chilling with the Irish now."

"Lucky them," he says, nodding in pretence, making me smile in appreciation.

Just the right amount of confidence with no cockiness.

We make it back to the beach a little quicker now that the traffic is lighter, and it's just after 9pm when we park up again. Ironically the exact spot we left is still empty, like it's been waiting for us to come back. The chat for the last part of the journey has been mostly me quizzing Tommy about his life back in Northern Ireland.

I've always been fascinated by Ireland. When you grow up in the desert, a place that's so green and lush with all the lakes and mountains feels like a different world. It's easy to romanticise far off places I know, but I would so love to see it. I don't tell him though, in case it feels like I'm fishing for an invite. It's a bit soon for that just yet.

I've found out that he's from a small town.

Aren't all towns in Ireland small?

He has two older sisters, his mum is alive but his Dad passed away five years ago. I didn't push for more because he seems to stiffen a bit when talking about family. It has made me really curious to know but I don't want to open up something painful on a first date - talk about a mood killer!

It's a free and easy return leg back to the bar, much more relaxed in each other's company than earlier, and we take our time.

There are fewer street performers now, making for a more romantic walk along the beach front. The bass beats pulse softly from the beach bars and the side-street clubs, perfectly scoring our journey.

We decide to have one more drink as we arrive, and grab seats inside this time, towards the back corner. Tommy has an early start in the morning, picking up his boss from LAX at 7am. I'm sure Amy will be wondering where I am too, not that it occurred to me until Tommy gallantly reminded me.

"I'm actually surprised she hasn't texted. But knowing Amy she's probably taking advantage of the empty apartment by taking advantage of some guy who's followed her home. If there's a pair of her knickers on the door handle, then expect a text to come rescue me, OK?"

"Yeah you definitely don't want to walk in on that. There's some things you don't wanna see and your best friend naked is one of them."

"Stop imagining my best friend naked!" I shout over the music just as it stops between tracks, broadcasting my words to the tables close by, and to the now sniggering waiter as he delivers our drinks. "Oh my god, I'm sorry" I beg through both hands clasped over my mouth, as if to stuff the words back in while Tommy roars with laughter.

"I remember when I was like 16 or something, my mate Ollie was seeing this girl, and a group of us had a sleepover in her friend's house one Saturday night. The parents were upstairs so there was like eight of us sleeping on this girl's living room floor, and Ollie and his girlfriend were at it for hours under a duvet, keeping everyone else awake."

"Oh my god, no way! They were having sex beside you on the floor!?"

"Yes, and not one bit embarrassed about it. Apologies for my crudeness, but she fucked his brains out that night. At one point in the middle of the night, you could hear him say, 'Oh god, again?' It was so funny! In the morning when they came out from under the duvet poor Ollie looked like a vampire had drained all the blood out. I've never in my life seen anyone so exhausted!"

"Wow, that's unreal. Sounds like she needed that."

"She must have! It seemed so out of character too. The nicest girl!"

"Hey nice girls like sex too y'know!" I blurt out, grateful this time that the music has kept it between just us.

Oh my god why did I say that?

"I'm so sorry, I have no filter." My cheeks are already flushed, and I grab his arm with both hands for forgiveness.

"It's OK, I'm just glad you brought up sex on the first date."

I study his face for some meaning to go with that, and he can only hold serious for a few seconds, before "Oh I had you there! Your face!" as he laughs indulgently.

"You did! I thought oh no, he seemed like such a gentleman too. I hadn't even got around to tell you my rule yet."

Tommy's eyebrows lift "Your rule?"

"Yeah, I kind of have this rule that I don't sleep with anyone until we've been dating for six weeks." Somehow I manage both boldness and sheepishness at the same time as I make this declaration, waiting to see what his reaction will be.

Usually it's a fake agreement at the time, with an obvious disinterest shining through pretty quickly. Guys in their twenties are so fucking shallow.

"Oh," he replies after a beat. "That could be a problem."

My heart drops into my gut. Hopes that he was different ripped out with more of a sting than I expected.

"I'm actually more of a ten week guy myself. I mean how much can you *really* know someone in six weeks? I'll need to do a thorough background check first, maybe get a private investigator to follow you for a while. That shit takes time babe."

His sarcastic reply is as refreshing as a welcome breeze, lifting and swelling my heart as quickly as it fell. But by the time he gets to the last bit about a private investigator, fear has taken over instead, sending my brain into a spin and unable to reply with much clarity. I'm certainly not able to play along and give his quick wit the credit it deserves.

It's been my greatest fear that Brandon would hire someone to find me.

Breathe. Breathe. It's OK, he's just joking.

"Wow OK, that's not…that's good. I mean…ummm…I wasn't expecting that. Sorry!" I sit back and try to cover my rising anxiety, but fail miserably. He frowns slightly as I let go of the eye-contact we've had this entire conversation, glazing over slightly, needing a moment to reset and refocus everything.

Tommy leans forward onto the table, and my eyes widen just enough to signal my discomfort and expectation of a big reaction. He spots this and drops his chin just enough to signal submission to whatever has happened, without even understanding it.

"It's OK Gina, there's nothing to apologise for. I was only kidding." He's calm, even and warm with his tone, despite the confusion.

The panic eases a little with this reassurance that I'm safe. I think. I hope.

Get it together. This isn't Brandon. He's just joking…breathe. Don't fuck this up.

He slowly pushes the candle to the side and offers his hands towards my side of the table, palms open.

I give his hands a token squeeze. Peace-keeping instincts kicking in, but then I withdraw them back to my lap. "No I'm sorry, I know you were only joking about the private investigator stuff. My reaction isn't anything to do with you, I promise. It's just…." I tail off not knowing what to explain.

It's only our first date.

"It just spooked me a bit. You must think I'm some kind of freak. I'm sorry!"

His hands haven't moved, like he's scared to move at all in case it spooks me more. Before my brain can think about it, I quickly take his hands again and our thumbs rub a gentle signal that the moment is passing.

"Hey, it's OK! You don't owe me an explanation or an apology. As long as you're OK. Whatever it is, I can promise you with all my heart that right now, right here, you're safe. I've had the absolute best time today and I don't want anything to ruin it."

"Thank you" letting my eyes meet his again and feel more a little more than reassurance. The change in how we look at each other is small but significant. I can feel his look inside my chest, and that gorgeous smile on that gorgeous face isn't helping. Maybe it's only my vulnerability desperate to be soothed, but I'm feeling like I like I want him to hold me tight, breathe me in and feel what I'm feeling.

You shouldn't be doing this. What are you doing? He doesn't even know your real name for goodness sake! Don't let go…

I take a deep breath in, blow it out slowly and let a smile return, squeezing an affectionate thank you into Tommy's hands.

"I like when you call me by my name. It's very sexy." It feels like the perfect time to tell him this, to break the awkwardness. When he used my name a moment ago, I felt the excitement underneath the anxiety.

Without speaking, he leans forward, not breaking our connection. His head tips ever so slightly and he gently kisses my cheek, lingering instinctively after my soft intake of breath. I squeeze his hands even tighter and close my eyes.

Our mouths find each other and kiss number two comes with something extra, for me at least. An excited tingle in my head and a flutter everywhere else.

Everywhere.

Oh. My. God.

Our lips peel away slowly, seductively. More flutters.

"That was lovely," I gush quietly as we separate. "Oh boy!"

"I wasn't expecting this," he replies, meeting me in recognising the strength of our connection, but hinting at more going on in his head. It's Tommy's turn to take a deep breath and exhale slowly, unafraid to show his own emotional headspin.

I think I actually love this man.

"This wasn't part of the plan," he says softly, hesitantly.

"You have a plan?"

"Yeah, well not like that, not for today I mean". He pauses for several seconds after opening his mouth to say more. "A big part of coming here was to get away from a bad relationship. A marriage actually…I was married back home. The job came at the perfect time, when I needed to get away. It was…ummm… pretty bad, and I made a promise to myself not to get involved with anyone. Until I could get my head straight and figure out what I want, you know?"

I just nod, surprised both at his honesty and how well I'm taking this news. Especially coming after one of the top five kisses of my entire life.

I'm grateful for the fact we're still holding hands, taking my opportunity to reassure him this time. His smile receives it, appreciating me settling some of his understandable nervousness at delivering this information. I'm absorbing how important thing this is to him, and how his face is holding the anticipation of my reply.

What are the chances of this?

"I wasn't expecting this either." I choose my words very carefully in recognition of this moment of exposure between us. Two elephants in the room all along it seems. I keep hold of his hands to make sure this part of our connection holds steady regardless.

"Believe it or not, I'm more on the same page as you than you realise. I think today I've allowed myself to be swept along - it's been sooo lovely. I'm not used to feeling like I matter."

The abruptness of how that comes out makes my heart race, then even more so when his brow furrows with concern.

I don't need pity, don't pity me.

Oh god stop talking like you are then!

"That came out wrong. I know I matter," I add, trying to dilute the moment with some lightness. "I'm not good at expressing myself, I don't think. Sorry!"

Stop apologising...

"Stop apologising for being yourself..." He leans closer again with a keenness to be heard.

"Don't tell me what to do!" I laugh now, pointing at him, more comfortable with some banter, than actually letting my guard down again. "Look I've been shit on too. From a great height. By a fucking eagle. So I get it…"

"Hmm, I'm sorry that happened to you," he offers. His genuine sincerity is impossible to ignore. "People can be absolute cunts can't they? Can you say that word in America?" I grin at this, especially that he chose to lower his voice *after* he said the c word.

Stop being so fucking perfect, please!

"You have no idea!" I reply, before pausing. "Well no actually you probably do…"

"It's hard to know what your heart wants when it's broken."

He says this in such a matter of fact way, unaware of how this simple sentence is possibly the most profound thing I've ever heard. From a man, anyway.

More flutters. Mega flutters. Everywhere.

Wow!

I stare at him for several seconds, genuinely trying to figure out if he is for real - this beautiful, kind, funny stranger sitting here with a broken heart and a golden soul.

"To kindred spirits!" I offer eventually, raising a toast from my cocktail to his lite beer.

"I know it's spectacularly uncool of me to say this, but our date isn't even finished and already I can't wait to see you again."

I purse my lips for a moment, letting it sink in that a man just said that to me, before shaking my head slowly. "It's more cool than you even realise, Mister Millar"

"We should probably call it a night. Pray for my soul tomorrow morning when I'm back on duty."

"I think your soul will be just fine," I fire back, with a wink. "I'm dry now anyway so good timing." I say this while trying to find some more liquid below the crushed ice at the bottom of my glass.

A moment later we're out on the boardwalk, a glowing moon now replacing the sun which shared the start of our date. A pretty fucking awesome date.

I send a quick text to Amy: **Home in 5 x**

I take one of his hands in both of mine, ready for goodbye. "Well mister no cheese Irishman, thank you very much for such a great day."

"Am I not giving you a lift home?" he says, surprised

Slow down, I'm not ready for you to know where I live just yet.

"No need, I'm only a block back from here so it'll be quicker to walk," I deflect, "…and if Amy sees you she'll not let you go. Then you'll sleep in and your boss will kill you. You're no good to me dead Mister T."

"Hmm…OK are you sure?"

"Oh totally! I walk home all the time"

"OK, well thank you for the unexpected treat of spending the day with you. It feels cut short, but maybe next time we can get more time?"

"For sure we will," I beam, before kiss number three touches my lips, unknowing that the next one won't be coming as soon as I think. We part ways still holding hands, arms dropping as we let go and I give him my best cute wave.

After the dorky one earlier, I've definitely finished strong.

At this time of the evening, even twenty metres back from the seafront feels like a different place. It's quiet, free of cars and the chatter of people heading to and from the beach. I pass a couple hand in hand, smiling as we pass as if they know that I might be part of their little club again now.

I'm halfway up the block towards my turn onto Pacific Avenue, eyeing the corner and excited to get home and tell Amy all about my day. I've ignored all her texts asking for details.

I spot a guy on the corner up ahead, but on the opposite side. He's standing alone in the doorway of the now closed internet cafe, in just enough shadow of the street lights that I can't tell what he's doing.

What the fuck are you up to, buddy?

My self-protection instincts kick in quick, assessing the width of the road and the head-start I'd get if I have to run.

Girl, you're so paranoid!

Drawing almost level with him, ten metres from the corner, I glance across. I'm trying not to be too obvious, in case he's a creep just waiting to make eye contact with someone. He doesn't move, or shout some crude asshole line. He's just leaning against the window, watching.

The high-alert part of my brain makes the assumption that he's watching me. What else would he be doing? I glance again just as I turn the corner and my heart almost stops between beats.

Brandon?

It couldn't be.

The fear is already making my body physically shake, with no chance that any sort of rational thought has a hope of getting the upper hand in my panicked brain. His face is in the shadows but every fibre in my being knows with absolute certainty that it's Brandon.

When you spend so long with someone you can recognise their shape, their stance, every tell of body language. I don't need to see his face. My eyes react to the pressure behind them, and begin to well up.

Fuck fuck fuck FUCK! How has he found me? Is he behind me?

Keeping a brisk pace, listening intently for footsteps, I keep moving. Every step is one more closer to home, and the limited safety of a door.

Fuck!

I so want to run, but one of the thoughts racing down the self-preservation highway right now is the hope that he doesn't realise I recognised him.

Thirty seconds later I'm opposite our apartment, but I had to cross the road, and back into his eye-line. I make a move to bolt between the parked cars, then force myself to slow to a casual walk, across the road and up the short pathway to my building's main doorway. I punch the code, discreetly glancing over my shoulder as I move inside.

No line of sight to the corner, thanks to some trees.

Have I made it?

Did he follow me and see my door?

I bound up the stairs two at a time and burst through our apartment door.

I close it quickly, quietly, and firmly before looking out through the peephole to an empty hallway.

Then the tears come full force.

Amy! Amy!....Amy!!!!

9
GINA

Amy rushes out from the bathroom, frantically trying to tighten a bath towel around her body. We meet halfway as I throw myself on her, arms around her shoulders, unable to speak. The tightness of my embrace rattles the usually unflappable Amy as I sob into her neck.

"What the fuck babe? What happened? Did he hurt you? she asks urgently, the panic rising to anger.

I continue to sob, still unable to speak but managing to shake my head.

Amy peels me off with, "It's OK, just breathe. It's OK babe, whatever it is we'll sort it!" She grips my shoulders to keep us face to face, taking in the full picture of my distress, while trying to read the situation.

"Take a deep breath Gina. You're safe, I promise!!" she commands, going for an assertive tone now to try bring and me down.

I'm pretty fucking far from safe!

Shaking my head in disagreement brings a flicker of fear to Amy's face - the first time I've ever seen her spooked. "Talk to me babe. What's going on?" She tightly grasps both my hands in hers in an attempt to dampen my panic. "Let's sit."

"No!" I half-shout, shaking my head. "I have to go. I need to leave. Now!"

"What!? Why!?" Amy panics, real fear in her voice now.

I lift my head to meet her eyes, and the fear I see on Amy's face is the first thing to snap me into some sense of clarity amidst the panic.

"Brandon. I saw Brandon!"

"Brandon from home Brandon?"

I can only nod in reply, tears dripping off my chin now.

"Where?" Amy's face, tone and entire body language switches in an instant, suddenly ready for a fight. This triggers another rush of emotion through me, and more sobbing. We hug for several seconds in the middle of the apartment. Strong, angry Amy with me in her arms, feeling pitiful and helpless.

She peels me off again, desperate to get the full picture. "Is he outside? Did he hurt you?"

"Yes, I mean no. I saw him on the corner….I think…." I'm just about regaining my composure, but still teetering on on the brink.

"You think? Amy snaps. "What does that mean Gina!?" verging on scolding now like I'm an irritating child. She sees my eyes widen in response and switches tone. "Was it actually *him* you saw?" she asks, softer and quieter now.

As I open my mouth to answer, the downstairs intercom suddenly buzzes on the wall behind me. It's just as loud and angry as it always has been, but right now it's tone is nothing but threatening, and I'm back clinging to Amy, so so tight.

"Oh fuck! Oh fuck! Amy he's downstairs. Don't answer it! Don't let him in!"

"I'll knock his balls in." Amy pushes me off now, grabbing the opportunity at last to be decisive and take control.

"No! Please!" I beg, frozen with fear as she takes two determined strides to the intercom, and presses the talk button. "Yes?" she barks. No reply. "Who is it?"

Several more seconds pass. Amy raises a hand and makes a patting motion in the air to reassure me. Silence, then suddenly a voice blares through…

"Pizza delivery". Amy frowns at me, then stabs the button. "I didn't order a pizza". There's an agonising pause for several more seconds. "Sorry, pressed the wrong number."

"What the fuck is going on Amy? What if that's him pretending?"

"One way to find out," she announces, already moving towards the door.

"NO!" I shout, raising both hands up, "Stop!! You don't know what he's like!"

"I don't give a flying fuck what he's like babe! If it is actually him he's going to get my footprint on his face."

I recoil a step as she opens the door, half expecting him to be standing there, ready to charge in.

"I'll be back in minute," Amy says with impressive confidence, pointing at me. As if I need to be told to stay right where I am!

What if he hurts her and gets in here?

What do I need to do?

Glancing at the balcony on the living room window, I'm already visualising my escape. Climb over. Drop to the grass below and away.

It's only one floor so if I land properly I'll be OK? Fuck!!

The fast triple knock at the door makes me jump. "Gina it's me," Amy calls from the other side.

"Are you alone?" I call back as I approach the door, tentatively.

"Yes of course…it *was* a pizza guy. It's all OK. Let me in?"

The release from immediate danger is a welcome relief as I let Amy back in. She hugs me again, then leads me to the sofa by one hand. "Sit. Tell me everything"

I do as she commands, hesitantly, and take a deep breath.

Suddenly everything feels different. Tainted.

"Tell me, it's OK." She rubs my shoulder reassuringly.

"OK". Another sigh. "I walked back and there was a guy on the other side of the street who looked like Brandon."

Amy pauses, and I can tell by her face that she's trying to visualise herself in my position. "Did he say anything, or do anything?"

"No, he was just standing there."

"You're *sure* it was Brandon?"

I pause, immediate panic subsiding now that I'm in familiar surroundings, and safe.

Was it?

"I think so…"

"It either was or it wasn't him babe. Which is it?"

"I *think* so!" My head snaps round, to drive this home to Amy. My irritation feeding off the fear and making itself known. "I don't know for sure. It was dark, but it looked like him."

"Did you see his face?"

"No."

Amy's sigh pricks my impatience again - all emotions running on full power just waiting for their moment to be unleashed. But I stay silent.

She's trying to help. She's on your side.

"So you can't be *absolutely* sure it was him?" Amy says in her best 'I need to know, but need to keep the peace too' voice.

"No," I reply meekly, after a pause. My chin drops now in recognition of the possibility that I could be mistaken, and suddenly I feel a little foolish. "But what if it was?"

"How could he know you're here though? You didn't tell anyone back home where you were going?"

"No, definitely not!" I shake my head, my brain frantically sorting through a jumble of incoherent scenarios that could lead to Brandon finding me. "Could it be anything to with Tommy?"

"How babe? He's not even from here."

"It's a bit of a coincidence don't you think? The first day we go out and then I see Brandon?"

"But you don't know that? It probably wasn't. Most likely it wasn't him - just some random guy the same height or whatever. Did anything happen on the date that might have made you suspicious?"

"Emmm….no, not at all. It was lovely actually." I allow a hint of smile.

"If you're smiling after that babe, it must have been good," Gina laughs, grabbing her opportunity to lighten the mood.

"Hmm, yeah. It was." I say this, though still distracted by all the racing thoughts. "But it's too much of a coincidence. I knew I shouldn't have went out with some guy I don't even know!"

"I think you're being paranoid," Amy says, unconvincingly, pulling me into a cuddle, wrapping her arm around me. We lay like that for five minutes, during which time my heart rate comes back to a point where I can no longer feel it literally thumping inside my chest.

Amy breaks the silence with a whisper. "So what are you going to do?"

"I have absolutely no idea. But I need to sleep!" I pull away and sit upright, formally, and face my friend. My protector. "Tell me it's going to be OK."

"It is completely OK! I'm 99% sure it can't have been Brandon."

I want to accept this but the scare is still too raw. My frown is for the other 1%.

I let myself flop back into the sofa, defeated. "I'm glad I have a few days off. I don't think I can handle being around people for a bit."

"What day is your audition babe?"

"Thursday morning...." I trail off, struggling to imagine being even remotely in the right head-space for that.

"Should we get a gun?" I ask out of the blue, scared to even look at Amy as I ask. I know the answer already. Amy thinks she's already a weapon.

"Absolutely not!" Amy says firmly, pointing a long finger to drive it home.

"I'm scared," I reply, feeling scolded again.

Amy stands up and takes me in a tight embrace again, softly reminding me "Just let this pass. It wasn't him. I've got your back babe!"

10
GINA

Thursday, June 13th 2002

The last three days, sporadically alone in the apartment for hours at a time, have been crippling. The adrenaline hangover that greeted me on Monday morning didn't muster up enough rational thoughts to help me relax, but I was grateful for the relative safety and comfort of home.

Happy to keep the world outside, and pretend it didn't exist for a while.

That includes Tommy. Any dreamy reminiscing of our day and evening together is quickly overcome with fear, and the possibility that he *could* be part of this.

What if he knows Brandon?

Was it all a setup to find out my name and where I'm living?

Filtered through a brain in a normal functioning state would draw little probability, but anxiety sees logic as a foreign language.

Amy has been begging me to reply to Tommy's messages, of which there have been three since Monday. I just can't. Fear wins. It's just not worth the risk. I've lost count though, of the times I have re-read his messages, almost hoping each time that they'll somehow suck me back in time to Sunday.

Monday 1.21pm: Thank you for my favourite day in LA so far. Hope you had a good time too. Meet this week if you're free? x

Tuesday 3.28pm: Uncool of me I know to ask if you got my message yesterday? Don't make me beg, it's not dignified ;-p Tommy

Wednesday 8.44pm: Hope you're OK and hope I didn't do or say something to offend you. Thanks again for Sunday x

It's audition day.

The nerves before an audition are bad enough on a good day, so just getting out the door today will be a challenge. I have a taxicab coming at 10am. I'm ready to go fifteen minutes early. Just me and the butterflies, waiting impatiently.

The casting call is on the Sony Studios lot in Culver City, thankfully only about five miles away, so I'll be there in good time. I love auditions on studio lots as it increases the chance of seeing someone famous, despite the undercurrent reminder of my own failure to join their ranks. This will be my first time to the Sony lot, and it bugs me that I'm not more excited. It's the former site of the legendary MGM Studios, where classic musicals like 'The Wizard of Oz' and 'Singin' in the Rain' were filmed.

It's also the studio behind one of my favourite movies from last year.

Like almost every other girl in America, I fell in love with the charm of Legally Blonde, starring my new hero, Reese Witherspoon. We're the same age, and the fact that neither of us are native to LA has created a feeling of kinship with her, even though our career paths are more than a little misaligned.

A girl has to dream though, right?

The audition today is for the inevitable sequel, Legally Blonde 2, and they're casting the Delta Nu parts - Elle Woods' sorority sisters. The fun Amy and I had last night choosing my outfit has been the highlight of this week, and as I check myself one more time in the full length mirror in my bedroom, I start to feel the part. I definitely look it.

My pink and purple floral halter dress is perfect Legally Blonde chic - retro and colourful. It hugs my figure perfectly, with the Wonderbra doing what it does best underneath.

My god, imagine Reese was there today?

This is good for me. I feel like I'm striking back and fighting for my place in the world. My fresh sense of emboldenment is short-lived though, when a horn beeps from the kerbside. The wave of anxiety I expected washes over me, and I do my best to ignore it, as I check my hair one last time.

Attempting to channel the spirit of Elle Woods herself, I stride through the apartment, grabbing my bag and keys off the counter top on the way.

No hesitation. Out the door.

That a girl. You got this!

Fifteen minutes later I'm standing outside the famous entrance at Sony Studios. The huge white archway spans the two vehicle lanes which lead to the security huts ten metres beyond. It's hive of activity, cars mostly in and out of the lot, and more than a few fellow auditionees. The outfits are a dead giveaway.

This is gonna be a good day!

My new mindset for auditions came after a meltdown following my first one a few months back - a complete disaster where I was so nervous I could only giggle like a child when asked to begin. It was either that or freeze. When you've spent years imagining a moment, and that moment leading to something you've always dreamed about - to be there in reality is quite overwhelming.

Amy's well placed advice after that debacle, was just to the enjoy the experience with no expectation. Just be 100% grateful to even be there, and be yourself, unapologetically. She conceded that we had to drop the last part, when I pointed out that being *myself* in an audition might not be the best tactic, if I actually wanted to be cast.

Directed to an office building close to studio four, I take my time on the short walk, but not seeing anything to excite my inner fan-girl. Tommy had called me that, and the unexpected recollection helps keep a smile on my face as I enter.

Once inside, another security check takes me down a brightly lit corridor with a luxuriously thick carpet underfoot. There's a holding room on the left for me and my fellow prospective Delta Nu sisters.

I settle into one of the cushioned office chairs just before 10.30am, and try to get comfortable. My limited experience has already taught me that I could be here for a while. A call time just means you'll be called anytime after that, so keeping a chunk of the day free is probably a good idea.

I pop an earphone bud into my right ear, keeping the left, the one closest to the door, free to hear my name. The iPod was a very generous birthday gift from Amy last month, and a quick scroll lands me on Fleetwood Mac's 'Rumors'. I need me some Stevie Nicks to relax. Her voice has always had a grounding and calming effect. The familiarity of the iconic intro to 'Dreams', my favourite song, is comforting in this strange place. Like Stevie is singing directly to me: 'Now here you go again…'

Ten minutes pass, zoned out and three songs deep when I'm aware of a slight difference in the light coming from the hallway. I glance to my left, letting my eyes scan up from the shiny black shoes to the dark grey suit. He's got his back to me, talking quietly to an older man in a blue striped shirt with no jacket.

Something familiar sparks me into a higher level of alertness, and I instinctively lean to get a look at the younger guy in the jacket, catching his profile for a split second as he turns slightly to let someone pass.

Oh. Fuck. Tommy.

It never ceases to amaze me how quick my body responds physically to awkward or scary situations.

Is everyone like this?

My heart is immediately thumping in my ears, and an embarrassed flush jumps from tummy to face, for full presentation to the outside world. It's no wonder, because my 'too nosy for my own good' lean catches the outer edge of his peripheral vision, and he glances back my direction. When our eyes meet, his conversation stalls for no more than a beat. It's enough to signal that it threw him, just a little.

My first instinct is to get up and leave. Reese probably isn't even here, and I'm probably going to be too old, too short, not pretty enough, or any combination of the above to have a chance anyway. "Just not what we're looking for today, but thanks for coming," they'll say, with well rehearsed fake sincerity and a smile that's whiter than normal in any other place on Earth.

Instead I'm frozen to my seat, paralysed and mortified. My rational brain is temporarily out of order, so I'm unable to run through possible scenarios as to how this could play out. I've never been good at that! I'm envious of the think fast, think-on-your-feet kind of people. Nope, not me. I'm the freeze up and panic type, who thinks of plenty of clever "You should have done this…" or "You should have just said that…" moments later on when I don't need the inspiration.

I'm one of those people.

Then he's gone. Disappearing in the literal blink of eye while mine were shut, praying for rescue.

Maybe he won't be back. Maybe he's just passing through. Maybe he's off to a meeting. It's gonna be OK. It's OK. Just be calm. You've done nothing wrong.

My internal battle of should I stay, or should I go keeps me frozen in place, and when the younger, prettier, taller blonde opposite me is called, it lets me settle some way into the normalcy I felt before he appeared. Stevie is still in my ear. My guardian angel. "You can go your own way...." she sings, talking up my pride and courage to the point where I'm determined to stay and see this out.

I don't owe him anything.

"Gina Sawyer?"

Deep breath, iPod tucked away as I turn down the corridor, following my calling. The assistant shows me into a larger room, set up on one side with two free-standing studio lights illuminating the audition area. I step in confidently, knowing my mark, and smile brightly. "Thank you for seeing me."

"Thanks for coming, Gina." comes the smooth reply from the other side of the room. I think about fifteen feet away. It's hard to tell as the bright lights make it difficult to see. My eyes eventually focus to see three figures - two men and a woman, seated casually with no table between us. Their relaxed body language is a relief, but I'm also a little gutted Reese isn't among them. Adjusting more to the darker side of the room, I take in four more bodies standing behind them in the shadows. One steps forward, and as he bends forward to whisper into the ear of the man in the middle, his face comes into view.

Seriously?

Tommy glances up as he steps back, his smile just one of the typical rehearsed type. All front, no feeling. At least that's how I interpret it.

The older, seated man studies a clipboard as he speaks. "OK Gina, there's a script page on the table to your right. Whenever you're ready."

OK here goes, focus.

The page is highlighted with my lines, and it's immediately familiar as a scene in the first movie where Elle discusses her date with Warner, with her sorority sisters. I give it my best bubbling enthusiasm, visualising the scene in my head as I read, with the other lines read by the same girl who showed me in. Thirty seconds later, it's over. Just like that.

"Thanks Gina, that was really great. You've got something we might be able to use. We'll be in touch OK?"

"Thank you," I beam, with a smile and a nod, unable to resist a glance towards Tommy's dark hiding place.

I leave quickly, but get no more than six paces back up the corridor when I'm called again.

"Gina! Hang on."

His voice stops me in my tracks, and I pause before turning around slowly. That's what they do in the movies right? Just the right amount of attitude, though I know it will be short-lived.

"Hi," drips out of my mouth weakly, not expecting to be called out quite so soon for ignoring his messages. It seems now that he was telling me the truth about who he is, which just makes this even more embarrassing.

"You were fantastic!" he gushes, trying a little too hard. This throws me - I wasn't expecting him to open with that.

"Oh wow! Really? Thank you!"

"Are you OK?"

"Yeah, yeah, sorry, I just wasn't expecting you to be here, so it wobbled me a bit."

"No, you were great in *there*! I mean are *you* OK? I sent you a couple of messages. I thought we got on well. Did I misread things?"

My heart softens with every single word, when filtered though the fresh hope that he might actually be for real, and it's hard to reply in a way which I feel he deserves.

My hand automatically touches his arm, desperate, without being too obvious about it, to make him understand that he's not the problem. "No! You didn't. I'm so sorry, it's…emmm …it's me. I just got spooked."

"By me?"

"No, no, no!" I'm shaking my head, and realising how badly I'm dealing with this. "It's just me," I sigh. "It's hard to explain, but I did have an incredible time. It was a magical day, honestly. I just…I had a really bad experience in my last relationship and I got scared."

I study his face, waiting for the inevitable bad reaction.

"OK that's cool - that's good!" He closes his eyes briefly. "No. Sorry. That's not good, sorry."

His awkwardness makes me smirk.

How cute are you?

"You're not angry?"

"Angry? God no, why would I be angry?" He looks confused, like we're having two different conversations. "I've been burned pretty bad too," he nods. "I'm not really sure how to move on myself, or how this should work, so I get it. It's all good."

"Well I didn't text you back. That was pretty rude of me, so I wouldn't blame you if you were angry."

"I have no expectations of anything. I'm just glad to have met you, and if that's all it is, that's OK. We might end up kind of working together anyway by the looks of it," he smiles, adding a wink.

I playfully slap his arm. "Stop being so good at this!"

He raises his hands like he doesn't understand. "You keep saying that, but…I'm just me…"

"Yes…yes you are!" I sigh. I can feel the energy again between us again, and make a conscious effort to not let him see my love eyes return.

"Look I need to get back, I'm sorry. It was nice to see you today - a really pleasant surprise. What's the chances we'd end up in the same room eh?"

"What's the chances indeed!"

Tommy smiles and touches my arm. Tummy flips. "See you soon hopefully." I don't know if that was a statement or a question, but he's gone before anything more is said.

Just a last look of longing, which I appreciate.

"Hopefully…" I whisper. Just to myself.

11
GINA

Call me when you get a chance x

My text to Amy is sent before I even leave the studio lot, and her name is already flashing up as in coming call as I climb into the taxi.

"Well superstar, how did it go?" she chimes, sunny as always.

"Really good!"

"Was Reese there?"

I laugh at how stupid that now seems. "No, she wasn't there, but guess who was?"

"Angelina? Brad and Jennifer? Oh fuck stop teasing me, I'm wet here at the thought."

"Behave yourself! I didn't see anyone famous."

"Oh! Who then?"

"Tommy."

"Irish Tommy? Really!? What was he doing there? He doesn't look the Delta Nu type."

"His job of course. He was in the room for the audition."

"No. Way."

"Yes - as if it's not hard enough."

"You made him hard already? Good work babe, that's fast!"

"Stop it you! It was proper embarrassing - he chased after me. I didn't know what to say."

"I know what I would have said…"

"Yes, and I'm sure it would have been very inappropriate." I reply, laughing at Amy's persistence to go down the smutty road every time.

"So what happened? How was it left?"

"I don't really know…"

"For fuck sake Gina, I know you were spooked after Sunday, but it sounds like you need to give this guy a chance. He's handsome, funny, Irish and obviously doing very well for himself. Why have you not grabbed this bull by the horn?"

"Horns you mean?"

"No I mean his horn. You know what I mean!" she giggles.

"I'm away!!" I laugh.

"Text him! Text him NOW!"

"OK OK!! I'll see you later at class." I hang-up and slide deeper into the seat. The butterflies back after Amy's reality check.

I'll text him when I get back to the apartment.

I'm already back inside when I realise that I hadn't even thought of Brandon. Nothing but Tommy on my mind as I got out of the cab, and skipped up to the apartment.

That's progress.

I have a couple of hours to myself before my 2pm tour, and have to fight the urge to immediately text Tommy. I can't stop thinking about him.

How can anyone be so cool, and so understanding?

Created with Sketch.

One luxurious bath later, I'm ready for my first shift since the drama of Sunday evening, and finally allow myself to text Tommy on the way. It's a welcome distraction, even though I take a longer route to avoid the corner where I thought I saw Brandon. I'm aware I'm smiling as I walk, carefully constructing the message, but don't care how it looks to passers by. It's a beautiful day in LA. I'm going to have a great tour today. I'm going to make lots of tips and I'm gonna set up another date with the nicest guy I've ever met.

This is gonna be a good day!

It was nice to see a friendly face this morning. Thank you xx

The afternoon tour is full - 24 of them, easy to spot milling around with no particular purpose. Check-in is one of my favourite parts, getting to know the mix of characters I'm gonna spend the next two hours with, and mentally marking the ones who seem like they're up for a bit of banter. My hand written roster has a tick beside every name by 1.58pm, so we're good to go. Half the group are from the US or Canada, with six other nationalities represented; Mexican, German, Japanese, French,

Australian, and typically, an Irish couple. It's not unusual to have Irish people on the tours, but today the accent hits different for obvious reasons, and the compulsion to ask them more about their part of the world is so strong. Especially as Tommy has not told me much.

I wonder do they know him? Are they from the same town? Imagine....

We head south along the boardwalk with the group in good spirits. It's the most beautiful day, at 75 degrees a little warmer than average, and the rush of gratitude I feel gives me a tingle. How my life has changed compared to six months ago!

The few days break has been good, but I've missed this interaction with people so it's good to be back. I've come to suspect that I'm not built to be alone.

The tour is cleverly crafted to begin with a ten minute walk to the first stop - the perfect length of time to get to know the group as we walk towards the pier, and the Marina Peninsula area.

We always start with the history of Venice. I love how it surprises everyone to know that after early tourism success, the area was dominated by 450 oil wells, for almost thirty years, from the early 1930s. The laminated black and white A4 photograph from my bag is passed around the group, attracting some gasps at how different it looked back then. It's only really since the 1970s that Venice began to build it's cool counter-culture status, with artists, beat-poets and writers attracted to the cheap rent, in what was then a very run down and neglected part of the city.

The next couple of hours take us the full length of the beach front. A hilarious sampling of 3v3 basketball game on one of the open courts, then past the famous Muscle Beach, and along to a great viewpoint of the Santa Monica Pier further up the coast. I suggest they visit Santa Monica if they get the opportunity, and maybe catch one of our tours there, before we head back south.

This time we cut in away from the beach, stopping for photos near the famous Venice sign which hangs across Windward Avenue, then towards the canals. It feels a little indulgent but I switching my usual route to take us over the bridge which Tommy and I stopped on.

It's like I can feel his energy still lingering here, and it only makes me crave him more. It's been a long time since I felt a craving to be close to someone. My phone has vibrated twice since the tour began, and the anticipation that his reply is waiting for me lifts my excited energy on the tour.

I wonder if these guys are gonna be good tippers…

The tour wraps up a little after 4pm, on the corner near Sal's. Last time I was here was Sunday, but so much has happened since then. I almost don't recognise the girl who skipped away from here that day to meet Tommy.

Tommy is everywhere now.

The tips today are incredible, the best yet. At least $200 stuffed into my bag amidst beaming smiles, hugs and in-jokes from the last couple of hours. What an awesome group of people. Zero on the asshole scale today. Life is good.

My phone comes out after the last deposit, clutching it, feeling it radiate *his* energy as the group disperses slowly, like smoke in still air.

Two messages.

Tommy: I was hoping you'd text :-) How are you doing?

Amy: Babe would ya grab some milk on the way home? CU at 5 x

I fire off a quick **Sure xx** to Amy as I take a seat on the low stone wall which separates the paved path from the beach. Swinging my legs over for a better view, I gaze out to the sparkling water looking for an inspired reply.

Why am I so crap at this?

After too much typing and deleting, my reply is away before I can analyse it any more.

Good thnks!. Just finished a tour and wondering why you're not here waiting for me ;-p

Just the right amount of flirt. I smile smugly at my screen. It starts ringing and the suddenness makes me jump, accelerating my heart rate when I see it says Tommy on the screen's caller ID.

What the fuck? I'm not ready for this!

"Hey you!" I sing, cool as can be.

"What's the craic?" he sings back, making me laugh out loud. I've heard this from lots of Irish guests on my tours, but not from Tommy yet, and it's totally unexpected. It's about the one phrase that I can attempt in an Irish accent. Irish people definitely get a kick out of hearing our terrible attempts at their accent.

"Not much pal, what's the craic with you?" It's still poor, but it's my best effort at an Irish lilt. I'm keen to play along, marvelling at how effortlessly fun he's already made our first phone conversation.

"Ah very good! But the accent still needs work. It's a good job Elle Woods' pals aren't Irish or you'd be sunk."

"I can just say my character is Jamaican!"

"Oh yeah, you look Jamaican!" he says, with the perfect serving of sarcasm.

"Irish Jamaican? Is that a thing?"

"Well I've never seem any Rastafarians wandering around Belfast, so probably not!"

"Probably the weather. Dreadlocks and spliffs don't work well in the rain ya know?"

"That's very true! That must be the reason," he laughs…then "Sorry for phoning but I'm in the car so couldn't text."

"There was no panic," I shrug.

"I was scared you wouldn't reply…" he says with a hint of cheeky.

"Ha! Fair enough!"

"…and maybe I just wanted to hear your voice?"

"This morning wasn't enough for you?" I reply, try not to let my excitement show in my voice.

"Well, they say once you get a taste of something good, it makes you want more."

My laughing is clearly not what he expected, and I have to quickly explain it away;

"Sorry, I just heard that with Amy's ears, and imagined how she'd turn that into something really dirty. She's such a bad influence!" I explain, finishing with a flourish of fake annoyance to deflect my embarrassment at putting it out there at all.

"Ah, I see, of course that makes sense. I'm saying nothing…other than your kisses did taste *very* good! Is that too bold?"

"Only if you don't mean it!" I tease, absolutely loving this.

"I might need my memory refreshed." he parries back.

Damn you're good…

"I'm sure that could be arranged." I'm grateful that he can't see my reddening face and goofy smile.

"That's good to hear."

"Can I text you in a bit? I gotta get home and eat before class at six."

"Of course, sorry! Yes…which acting class do you go to?"

"Oh no it's an exercise class. Amy teaches it in Santa Monica. It's awesome! She's a beast!"

"She teaches exercise classes? We should introduce her to my mate Ollie - he's into that. He teaches Spin classes when he's not playing football…or being an asshole!"

"Two asshole fitness instructors then? Sounds like they're made for each other. I'll text you later to arrange?"

"Sure thing! Enjoy your class, Gina Sawyer!

Yes! Say my name! Oh my god, that's so sexy!

* * *

I'm back home with the milk, and already changed for the gym before Amy bursts in, like her usual force of nature, just after 5pm.

"Fuck fuck fuck! I'm gonna be late again! Did you get milk?"

"In the fridge. You go get changed I'll sort it." I'm ready to go, just putting away the last of yesterday's dishes that have now dried.

"You're a legend!" Amy whispers as she passes, grabbing my face and planting a big wet kiss on my forehead. "Oh you smell good!" she calls, as she peels away quickly towards her bedroom. "Did you text him yet?"

"Yes, then he rang me!"

Amy's appears in the doorway. jumping up and down trying to pull up her black Nike leggings. "Fuck off, like actually phoned you instead?"

"Yeah, he was driving. I nearly died. I wasn't ready for that." I reply, pouring the milk over Amy's usual pre-class bowl of cereal.

"Was it awkward?" she asked, as the bright orange Les Mills vest slips over her head, hugging her lean torso.

"No, it was really lovely actually."

"He wasn't mad at you ignoring his messages then?"

"No, far from it. He was just more concerned. I don't know if it's an act or he's *actually* this nice."

"Well babe, I hope he's for real - you deserve it." Amy looks up, smiling brightly, seated on the floor tying the laces on her white Reeboks. "Are you seeing him again?"

"Yeah, I think so. I'd like to. Should I?"

"Why on earth would you not?"

"You know why!"

"Gina, you know I love you to bits, but with all due respect, don't be a dick!"

I give her a non-committal smile while she takes big mouthfuls of honey nut O's, choosing a middle finger as my reply to avoid any more conversation about it. I'm scared that if we say any more, I'll end up talking myself out of texting him back.

Created with Sketch.

The class was just what I needed. The adrenaline rush and feeling of empowerment from a BODYCOMBAT class something that, if you could bottle and sell it, you'd make a fortune. Amy was epic as always, blasting her way through forty five minutes of boxing, Muay Thai, Taekwondo, Capoeira,

Kung Fu & Kick-boxing. There truly is nothing more uplifting than punching to a beat with 20 other people in a dark studio.

Showered and changed, we're back in Amy's white BMW soft top just after 7pm.

"Tommy lives here in Santa Monica you know?"

"Really? Do you know where? Let's do a drive by and pretend to break down!"

"Ha ha ha…NO!"

"OK just a drive by then, spoilsport!"

"He lives in his boss's house on San Vincente, but I don't know which house it is."

"Ah damn, OK, well we need an invite some time, to see where he lives."

"We'll probably see it on TV soon. He was telling me they filmed an episode of MTV Cribs there last week."

"Fuck! Off! Oh my god Gina you need to lock this guy down. *Fuck* the six week rule!"

I just eye-roll a reply, but Amy's enthusiasm gives me goosebumps. I've refused to let myself get too excited.

Brandon was nice at the beginning too, and look how that turned out…

12
GINA

Keep your phone on ;-)

It's been two days since we last chatted, promising to arrange a second date once Tommy had an idea of his weekend schedule. His text landing just before 10am on this Saturday morning throws my anxiety up a level.

I don't much like surprises. Mostly because I've had too many shitty ones.

Before I can send the two question marks back, the phone rings in my hand. Private number. Anxiety responds accordingly. I usually just let these run to voicemail, but I throw caution to wind after Tommy's message and hit the green button.

Created with Sketch.

OH. MY. GOD! is what Tommy gets back after I hang up the short call, quickly followed by **Can you talk? x** as my heart almost bursts with joy.

His call comes through almost instantly.

"Tommy!" is all I can muster, giddy at the news I've just received.

"Hi, is the delta nu sorority house?"

"Oh my god I can't believe it! When did you know that I got the part?"

"Just this morning! I'm *so* proud of you!"

Those words land hard and fast in my chest, and everything inside feels like it swells. The only person who has ever said those words to me is Amy. To hear it from Tommy - to hear it from a man, is like an emotional thunderbolt. It shouldn't mean this much of course, but when you've been abandoned or abused by almost every significant male in your life...

"I can't believe it!" My voice is quivering, as much as I'm trying to stay cool. "I was so nervous that day, I didn't think I had a chance."

"Well, they loved you...how could they not?"

I can visualize Tommy's face as he says that, knowing him well enough already to hear his words come with a smile. I love his smile. He smiles with his whole face. Not everyone is blessed with that, and it's something I probably didn't even recognise consciously - how disarming someone is who expresses their emotions so fully and unguarded.

"Thank you," I whisper, in my mind not hiding very well how much I wish he was here with me right now. Maybe it's best he doesn't see how flushed with joy I am right now though.

"We should celebrate! Are you working today?"

"Not 'til tomorrow," I reply, wondering if he can hear my smile the way I heard his. I had forgotten what this rush of excitement and anticipation felt like, and I'm immediately aware and grateful that my usual anxious first response has been overcome completely, leaving only a warming glow.

Maybe my luck is finally changing?

"Do you trust me?"

My heart sinks a little. I'm not ready to trust anyone.

"Ummm….I think so." I try my best to make that sound optimistic. "Do I need to trust you?" I half-laugh to dilute that as much as possible and keep it light, aware of anxiety trying to be heard from underneath all the joy.

Tommy's laugh is sincere enough to defuse my question. "Sorry, I put you on the spot there and made it weird. I'm not a weirdo I promise! I just thought we could get out of the city?"

I swallow, despite myself. "What have you in mind?"

"Let me take you up to Pismo Beach. I was there last month for work, and it looked like somewhere nice to come back to. Have you ever been?"

"Nope, not yet…" I trail off, frantically processing and filtering all possible logical and illogical outcomes. Amy's advice was to live a little. The actual words were 'Don't be a dick', but that's what she meant.

"I've put you on the spot, I'm sorry. You hardly even know me, so…"

"Let's do it!" I cut him off, before one of us talks ourselves out of it.

"Are you sure?" The sweet consideration in his tone melting any remaining reservations.

"Fuck it! Yes, I'm up for that," I blurt out, surprising myself with this newfound boldness. The idea of being away from the city, and the real or not real presence of Brandon was sinking in, and sounding better with every second. Hell, I was used to escaping. For once it would be nice to escape under nicer circumstances, you know, like normal people do.

"That's awesome! How long do you need to get ready?"

"Ummm….an hour or so? Do I need to bring anything? What am I wearing?"

"Casual is fine. Maybe bring an overnight bag just in case?"

My face reddens at this this little bombshell, and my stunned silence is obvious on the other end of the line.

"I'm not suggesting anything inappropriate, don't worry! If we end up having a few drinks we can stay over in separate rooms."

Silence. My imagination sprints to worst-case scenario, trapped 300 kilometres away, locked in a hotel room with a crazy rapist/murderer.

Breathe.

The power-struggle in my brain dismisses that quickly. I need to stop catastrophizing.

Not everyone is out to hurt you. Trust your gut. Just go.

"Sure! Sounds good!" I chime, with not a hint of the work still needing done to make my words truthful.

"Amazing! I'll see you in a hour of so then? Will you text me your address and I'll pick you up?"

Woah, slow down boy.

It's fine! He's safe.

Are you sure about that?

Yes…no…I don't know!

Ah fuck it, yes, take a chance.

"I will….I can't wait to see you!" I've now unable to control my eagerness and excitement, and no longer caring if I sound dorky and needy. I haven't done a great job of hiding it so far, and he's still interested enough to take me away for the night.

Pismo Beach is a small city on the coast, roughly a third of the way up towards San Francisco, and is well known for it's beautiful beaches and summer resort vibes. I've passed through a couple of times but never stopped for more than a wee.

Ten seconds after hanging up the call I'm bouncing on Amy's bed like a kid at Christmas, shaking her out of her one and only lie in this week.

"Amy. Amy. AMY. Wake up!!"

"This better be good," Amy groans, one eye open, not committing to fully waking up yet.

I slip quickly into the double bed beside her, my head on the other pillow.

"Do you want the good news or the good news?"

Amy smiles wide as she closes the one open eye. Her faces softens with the smile as she relaxes again. "You pick," she says, her eyebrows waking up now too.

"Delta Nu…" I whisper.

Amy's eye flash open, wide and warm.

"You got the part?"

"I sure did!"

"Oh babe that's fucking awesome. I'm so proud of you. How do you feel?"

"Scared," I laugh. "Excited?"

"Oh my god, you're gonna be best buds with Reese," Amy teases. "You're not gonna need me any more," she continues, with a very 'me' eye-roll.

"I should be so lucky," I wink back, prompting a furrowed brow, then a deep laugh.

"What's the other good news? Is Reese taking you for lunch or what?"

"Not yet, but Tommy is. We're going up to Pismo and I've to pack an overnight bag." I try to deliver this flatly, with as much nonchalance as possible, hoping to hide my lingering trepidation.

Amy's eyes widen more this time, almost impossibly so. "Fuck. Off." I just smile my reply. "An overnight bag?"

"Hmm. Yeah," I reply, joining the furrowed brow party, but adding some pursed lips too.

"Holy crap. That's major," Amy whispers, more to herself than to me. "When?"

"He'll be here in an hour," I smile nervously.

Amy sits up quickly on this, slipping out of the bed and to her feet in an instant. "Well Cinderella, don't just fucking lie there. Are you *ready*?" Amy's hands cup her groin area as she says the last part, prompting a snort of surprise and amusement.

"I'm ready for *nothing*. Certainly not that. 6 week rule, remember?"

Amy is on my side of the bed now, grabbing both hands and pulling me up to my feet, and into a hug. "I love you, but you're so fucking boring," she whispers, before planting a kiss on my cheek. "Go get packed. And please, pack a razor and something at least a *little* sexy. No Bridget Jones knickers, OK?"

Amy helps me pack a few things after I take a shower, reassuring me that I have nothing to worry about. I kind of know already, but still wish I could share her complete and unwavering confidence. Amy has somehow managed to avoid being shit upon by life like I have, and I'm slightly envious of her 'Everything is always gonna be OK' outlook.

Maybe I need to be more like Amy.

"This works out well actually." Amy tosses her words out casually while perched on the kitchen counter top. Her legs dangle while she watches me stress over which shoes to wear, and which ones to pack.

"Oh? Why's that?"

"I have a date too. At least now if I bring him back for a test drive, I'll not have to gag myself."

"Oh, don't worry. I'm sure once he gets to know you, he'll happily gag you himself." I'm amused for a moment at my own boldness, and the opportunity to counter Amy with some 'Amy'.

"Hah!" she laughs, throwing her head back theatrically. "Very good! That sounds like something I would say."

"Who's your new victim then?" I smile, repacking my bag for no other purpose than keeping myself busy while I wait for Tommy.

Amy doesn't bite at this one. "The gym!" she chirps, like this is a regular occurrence…which it actually is. "A new guy who has made it very obvious he's only coming to *my* classes, and we got chatting after Spin last night. He's nice! He's probably more your type than mine if I'm honest, but he asked me out, so it felt rude to refuse."

"You make him sound like a charity case."

"Well, what can I say. I'm very accommodating. Though if he sweats as much in bed as he does in class, then he's outta here!"

"Ewww. Don't say anything more, please!" I beg. "Brandon was a sweater, and it *always* turned me."

Before Amy can reply, we both hear the recognisable, confident growl of a Mustang pulling up outside. Amy beats me to the window, like a couple of teenagers waiting to be picked up for High School Prom.

"Make him wait five minutes," Amy says with a nudge. "Don't be too keen."

"Alright mom, any other advice?

"Other than sex advice?"

"Obviously."

"Ummmm….just make sure he treats you like the diamond that you are."

The sudden sincerity catches my breath for a moment. It's not like Amy to *ever* be this sincere, and it throws me off balance for a second.

"Oh, don't say that! Do you think he's up to something?" Anxiety floods back, along with all the other irrational thoughts.

Amy sees the shift in me and takes me in her arms. "No, absolutely not. I just want the best for you, that's all. You'll have an amazing time. Now go, before he changes his mind!"

"You said to wait five minutes!"

"Oh, for goodness sake, don't listen to me!"

Amy lifts my bag from the sofa and shoves it, and me, towards the door.

13
TOMMY

Gina appears quicker than I thought. The smile she greets me with, gives me excited tingles I didn't expect. A sunny and confident "Hi" follows as she reaches the car, tossing her duffle bag into the back seat and slipping in beside me. Her scent follows a few seconds later. More tingles.

"You look amazing," I offer, trying not to sound like an eager little puppy.

She's wearing a colourful summer dress, and strappy sandals with a thick heel. Effortlessly cool. She slips her sunglasses on as she turns towards me with a beaming smile.

"So do you." She rests her hand on my thigh, and leans affectionately towards me for a moment, before slipping her seat-belt on.

"I can't believe I'm doing this" Gina says. "Can *you* believe I'm doing this? I don't usually do this. This is so not me!"

Her stream of consciousness ramble makes me smile. It's nice to know she wears her heart on her sleeve. It's so refreshing! Most people are so guarded now that it makes me suspicious, even when there's no need to be. But I can quite safely blame *her* for that. Not her as in Gina of course. My ex wife.

She's the root of almost all my trust issues.

"What's so funny?" she inquires, in a playful offended tone, smirking herself in full knowing as to why.

"Oh nothing! You just make me smile naturally."

"Hmm…" she eyes me suspiciously. "Good answer. I'll let you off. So how long is the drive?"

"A few hours at most," I reply, reversing around the corner so we can head back north.

"Can you believe I'm gonna be Legally Blonde 2?" Gina does a little jump turn in her seat with this, like she's suddenly remembered. I don't what's more cute - her sunny enthusiasm, or the way she's tucked one leg under the other so she can face me.

"Absolutely I can. You were really good. Did they say when you'd be needed?"

"Not exactly, just to expect a call once my agent agreed the contract. Tommy I don't even have an agent, I just saw the open audition notice in the paper."

"I can help you with that. Someone good too."

"Good sounds expensive," Gina says dryly as we pull out onto Lincoln Boulevard towards Santa Monica.

"Standard 20% fee, so they only get paid when you get paid."

"Oh wow OK. That sounds alright. Thank you *so* much!" Both of her hands landi on my shoulder now. After a long time with someone who was closed off emotionally (not that I really understood that at the time), Gina's tactile nature might take some getting used to.

"No worries. Are you excited to see Pismo Beach?"

"I am…but I'm slightly worried about this overnight thing."

"You don't need to be worried about that. We can get separate rooms - I wouldn't put you in that position."

The silence makes me glance over, seeing Gina smile, looking a little embarrassed.

"What is it?" I ask, confused.

"Sorry…when you talk about putting me into positions, I immediately think of Amy."

My eyebrows lift immediately. "Why, what positions do you and Amy get into?" I'm trying to hold back the laughter at both how Gina has phrased this, but also how shocked she is now that she realises how it came out.

As short a time as I've known her, I can tell already this is classic Gina.

"Oh my god, no! You think we're lesbians?" She roars with laughter at this, and I playfully dismiss her attempts to explain.

"No, no, I get it. It's none of my business what you two get up to." She eventually gives up, settling into a content smile as she snuggles into the seat, watching me as I drive.

This is going good so far…

"I forgot to pack my phone charger. Do you mind if we stop off quickly 'til I grab it?"

We're approaching Santa Monica already so we're close to home. I haven't forgotten the charger on purpose, but truth be told I'm glad of an opportunity to maybe impress Gina with where I'm living. I'm pretty damn proud of where I've ended up, compared to what my life looked like not too long ago. So far no one from home has been out here yet to visit, so this is my first opportunity to show any of *my* people where I live.

"Ummm…yeah sure. I'd love to see where you live."

"If my boss is there, I apologise in advance. He can be a bit…emm…direct."

"Was he at the audition?"

"Yup, that was him."

We turn up San Vincente Boulevard in silence. Gina gazes from side to side at the houses as we cruise quietly up the freshly tarmacked road, before turning in towards the gates at number 1525.

"Holy crap," Gina mutters, reverently.

"Want to do the honours?" I ask, passing her a small square remote control, with a stubby aerial. She presses the green button at the top and watches, with a cheesy grin, as the huge gates slowly open inward.

"That's pretty cool. Do you let all your women do that?"

I laugh at her boldness, and the idea of that. "Nope, you're the first. Although I'm not sure I would describe you as 'my woman'."

"Oh, thanks very much!" Gina gasps, perfecting the fake indignance more every time. "For a moment there i thought I was special."

"You're hard work…." I laugh, as we follow the driveway round, bringing the house into view.

"Thanks! I do…fuck me, that's your house?"

"Maybe someday…for now I'm just a lodger."

"It's incredible. I had no idea it would be so…*big*."

"I bet you say that to all the boys."

Gina blushes just a little. "Is that you Amy?" she replies, playfully pushing my shoulder.

The garage is open already open, so we park up in my usual spot and I hop out quickly.

"Do you wanna wait, or come see inside?" Gina is already out of the car before I finish.

"Are you sure it's OK?" she asks, looking like she's having sudden second thoughts.

"Absolutely fine!" I say, taking her hand. It was meant to be more for reassurance, but the romance of it, purely accidental, isn't lost on me. Maybe the same for Gina too, as she squeezes my hand momentarily to signal her acquiescence.

I'm glad it's quiet again in the house today as I lead Gina through the kitchen, into one of a few lounges, smiling at her various exclamations of surprise at the opulence around her.

"I can't believe you get to get to live here," she says, as we pass through the last part of the house before reaching my living quarters.

"Thomas?" calls out from behind us, in a deep voice, managing in one word to sound like it could only come from someone in full command of their surroundings, and also of those in it. I feel Gina pull closer to me.

"It's OK" I whisper, before turning us both to face Liam Fletcher, my boss, and I instantly regret letting her hand drop from mine.

"I thought you were away for the weekend?" Liam booms, always several decibels louder than required. He strides towards us, dressed in dark blue jeans, with a white linen shirt tucked in, stretched over a belly that says a lot about his luxury lifestyle.

He's talking to me, but his eyes don't leave Gina, until he stops in front of us, waiting for an answer.

"Yes, I am. Sorry Liam. I'm just here to grab my charger and we'll be away. Sorry to land back in unexpectedly."

"Hmm, don't apologise. You live here too." He's smiling, but I can tell this niceness is a front for my guest. I'm pretty sure if I had been alone, my greeting would have been, "What the fuck are you doing back here?" or something equally unwelcoming.

I've always marvelled at how Liam can flick his bastard switch on and off at will.

"Of course, yes, sorry," chastising myself at apologising again so soon. Liam hates it when people apologise. A sign of weakness he says, and his narrowing expression is a direct delivery of exactly that sentiment.

"Liam, this is Gina. We're heading up to Pismo Beach," I say nervously, resenting the feeling that I should physically present her with both hands on her shoulders, like a special prize I've just won.

Don't bring fuck-toys to my house. You never know who sent them. This was one of Liam's house rules, eloquently recited on day one. The paranoia was understandable, but I was to learn pretty quickly that this rule in particular was hypocrisy in the extreme. The only time Liam *didn't* have random starlets (half his age usually) in his bed while his wife was away, was when he had food poisoning.

People were commodities to use or consume in Liam's world. A prime example of the Hollywood asshole. Narcissistic, entitled, chauvinist and many other repulsive traits. Yet, still he thrived here. He had no problem being the bad guy. He relishing his reputation, and enjoyed the power.

In any other world, no one would get away with that behaviour, but when your dreams or livelihood rely on someone's money and influence, it's understandable to see why most look the other way.

This had become a huge internal conflict for me. Moving here, or more so what I moved *away* from, forced me to develop some new core values in life. Liam Fletcher had already tested those to the extreme. Still here I was, taking the money and bending over to be metaphorically fucked at will.

"Have fun guys!" Liam chimed, spinning away towards the wide marble staircase. I'm pretty sure I was going to hear about this later, be forced to defend myself and listen to his crude aspersions about Gina. Telling him she's an actress, who's just been cast in a bit-part in one of his next productions would be a bad move. Right to paranoia city centre.

"I'm so sorry about that," I plead, earnestly. I have my back to Liam now, and searching Gina's eyes to see if she's anywhere near as uncomfortable as I am right now.

"It's fine. He seems nice enough. What are you worried about?" Her sincerity makes me resent Liam even more. I briefly consider explaining his bastard switch, but take Gina's hand instead.

"Just you," I say impulsively, and as soon as the words come out, a chill runs through me. How cheesy is that.

Shut up you dick!

I get away with it. Gina's eyes widen just a little, before a goofy smile appears. "Awwww! That's lovely". The fingers of her free hand touch lightly on my cheek as she leans in and kisses me softly on the lips, then pulls back an inch, close to my face as she squeezes my hand. "Let's get your charger," she whispers, as she moves her mouth towards my ear, lifting onto her tiptoes.

Five minutes later we're back in the car, heading south back down San Vincente towards Highway 1. The famous Pacific Coast Highway. This is definitely a day for the scenic route, and we make small talk about Gina's excitement about Legally Blonde, and how much she adores Reese Witherspoon. If you told me a year ago that I would be cruising through Malibu in a convertible Mustang with a beautiful woman beside me, I would have probably suggested some professional help, or at least a career writing fantasy stories. Yet, here I am.

Here *we* are.

Gina has her shoes off now. My god, even her feet are pretty! I have a good view as she has them crossed over on the dashboard, in the kind of free spirit move that fits perfectly with her Venice Beach lifestyle. It couldn't be further from what I've been used to back home, and I get that feeling again of utter contentment. Right place, right time, with the right person. The universe has served me well this year.

By fuck I deserve it

'Steal My Sunshine' by Len is playing on the radio. I love this song, and Gina's cute feet tell me she loves it too.

In this moment, it's especially perfect. Cheesy as hell, but perfect.

Ain't nobody gonna steal my sunshine.

I glance towards her, taking in how relaxed and happy she seems. Her beaming smile my way seals the moment, lifting her sunglasses as she does.
No words needed….

14
GINA

I'm amazed how relaxed this is, but can't help but wonder if Tommy also thinks it odd that we're heading up the coast like we've been together for months, yet don't really know that much about each other. I have definitely surprised myself with how much I've trusted my gut on Tommy. I've learned the hard way to fine-tune my reading of people's energy, and despite a few wobbles, but I feel safe in his company, and happy to just go with the flow.

"Oh! We should stop up ahead. Have you heard of Neptune's Nest?" Tommy asks excitedly.

"Net," I reply coolly, my eyes still closed behind my sunglasses.

"What?"

I open my eyes and turn in the seat, tucking my leg under, and hoping it doesn't go numb this time. "Neptune's Net I think it's called. The place from Point Break?"

"Did they use in for Point Break too? I know they filmed there for The Fast and the Furious last year. Have you been already?". His tone of voice tells me that he hopes I haven't. It's so sweetly obvious that he wants to make this trip special.

"Not yet. Amy shagged a waiter who works there though. That's as close as I got. He was there in our kitchen one Saturday morning. All abs and long blonde hair. I'm pretty sure he just lived in nothing but board shorts and pumps when he wasn't working. He was like some kind of rent-a-butler, but a surfer dude."

"I'm sure there's a market for that," Tommy laughs, shaking his head in disbelief.

"Oh yeah, the rich housewives of Malibu would be all over that shit."

We're both still laughing at this as Tommy pulls into a space opposite the restaurant, on the beach side of the road. We're definitely in the minority between surfers and non-surfers. There's at least a dozen clones of Amy's one night stand between here and the surf.

Tommy gently takes my hand as we cross the road, and up the steps to one of the outside tables under the veranda.

"A cider, and a Pepsi please?" I order, after insisting this one is on me. The waitress nods and heads inside as Tommy's mobile phone beeps loudly from the pocket of his cargo shorts.

"Sorry!"

"It's cool…go ahead"

"It's Ollie. My mate from back home. I made the mistake of telling him we were going out today," Tommy explains, as he punches a text back. The moment he sets his phone down between us, it starts to buzz, vibrating loudly on the wooden picnic bench. I'm quietly relieved to see Ollie's name on the screen.

I wonder will I always be on high alert for signs of deception?

Tommy looks from the screen, to me, without touching his angry little Nokia. His lips purse in frustration at his friend's persistence.

"Maybe it's important?" I offer.

"It's not. He's just being a dick. It comes naturally. Do you mind if I answer? If I don't, he'll just keep pestering me."

I reach across and lift the phone. "Let me answer it and play him at his own game?" I suggest, with a mischievous grin. Tommy shows me his, with a nod, and I hit the button.

"Hello. Tommy Millar West Coast fan club. Gina speaking". Tommy's hand covers his mouth instantly to stifle a laugh, and instead snorts. My eyebrows spring up in shock at this, only making him snigger even more behind his hand. The first snort in any relationship is a big moment! Isn't it?

There's a pause on the other end of the line, before an unfamiliar voice with a familiar accent says, "Oh wow, I was *not* expecting that!" Ollie laughs. "Fair play, you got me there, and now I don't know what to say."

"Are you calling to check up on your friend? I thought only girls did that on dates?"

"Ha! Very good! You got me again. I can see why Tommy likes you." He pauses, and I let him squirm, enjoying this immensely. "Are they all funny as you over there?" he follows with, after several seconds trying to think up a witty reply.

"Only the good ones," I say with a wink. Tommy looks a little uncomfortable now, only hearing one side of the conversation, but amused nonetheless.

"What are you guys up to then?" Ollie asks, still struggling to make conversation, but refusing to concede.

"Well right now we're sitting in the sun in Malibu, waiting on drinks, in the bar that was in that Fast and Furious movie with the hot cars." I add the last part just to toy with him. Like all men, he almost certainly knows that movie.

"Fuck off! No you're not!"

"You fuck off!" I fire back, mimicking his accent, which gets a roar of amusement from across the Atlantic. "Tommy, where are we?" I ask, holding the phone at arms length towards him as he leans in.

"Neptune's Nest, mate, honestly."

I bring the phone back to my ear. "Neptune's *Net*. You should come visit and we'll bring you here."

"I like the sound of that. You're not behind the door, are you?"

Tommy is watching me intently, trying to piece together both sides of this conversation, and notices the confusion appear on my face.

"Ummm….what door? Your door? I'm pretty sure I'm not behind any door Oliver. Why would anyone be behind a door?"

Tommy's chin lifts as he lets out a hearty laugh, obviously aware now of Ollie's question, and how it's completely lost on me.

"That's a fair question Gina. Ask Tommy if he knows anyone who would be behind a door?"

"Oliver says to ask you who if you know anyone who would be behind a door?" I let the phone come away from my ear, unable to hide my utter confusion.

Tommy's reaction to this question isn't at all what I expect, and as much as he tries to hide it with a cover up laugh, the first emotion that flashes across his remarkably handsome face is pain. I haven't seen this before on Tommy, but it's unmistakable.

I know what pain looks like.

"Tell him that's below the belt," Tommy says, quietly. He furrows his brow, struggling to land on a definite emotion. I get strong vibes this is maybe not something I should pursue, and instinctively divert the conversation.

"He's gone to the bathroom, sorry," I announce down the phone line, getting a wry smile as an embarrassed thank you, from across the table.

"Right, I'll leave you guys to it. Hopefully I'll get over soon and get to meet you in person, if you haven't realised by then that he's a boring bastard, and dump him!"

"He's doing good so far," I purr, teasing Ollie. I wink at Tommy, hoping it goes some way to breaking the awkwardness that has resulted from that all that 'behind the door' stuff. "Have a good day, or night, whatever time it is over there. It was nice to speak to you Ollie. Tommy talks about you a lot," I exaggerate. I'm well versed in stroking male ego.

"Ah that's good to know he hasn't forgotten where he's come from!"

"I'll keep his feet on the ground, don't you worry!. Have a great day!"

"You too! Be good!"

We bat a 'bye' back and forward a few times, and this amuses Tommy when he spots my frustration at not just saying goodbye once and hanging up.

"Well that was interesting. He sounds like a proper character."

"Oh he is! He's not the most politically correct, or tactful, but he has a good heart."

"I could describe Amy the exact same way actually."

We finish our drinks quickly, keen to get back on the road. It feels like whatever can of worms Ollie inadvertently opened needs left behind.

We continue north, hugging the coastline, soaking up the sunshine and enjoying the warm breeze with the roof down. It's just after noon when we pass through Santa Barbara. I've never been here either, and it appears more affluent than I had expected. Almost an hour has passed with very little conversation, which for a second date I would usually find odd, but with Tommy it feels like we've known each other for longer.

Somehow, we have already reached that stage of just enjoying each other's company.

I keep wanting to voice this, but the fear of sounding corny stops me each time. Maybe he's just not much of a talker? No, he was very chatty on our first date, and before we stopped at Neptune's Nest. Anxiety, ever present on my shoulder, whispers a few possible reasons for the quieter Tommy, all of course to do with something I might have said, or maybe how I look? Maybe he's just bored of me already? These thoughts are exhausting, and as usual I can't pinpoint anything specific.

It's only when Tommy next speaks, that I realise I'm tugging on my bottom lip, as I often seem to do when I'm anxious, and lost in thought.

"Are you OK?"

I'm immediately a little embarrassed. I'm not keen on displaying anything other than my best self this early on, and I don't want him thinking that I'm not having a good time.

"Oh yes, sorry, I'm just thinking how lovely this is. The coastline is incredibly beautiful isn't it?" If I ignore the elephant in the back seat long enough, he might jump out. Hopefully into oncoming traffic.

"It really is! We have an awesome coast road back home in Northern Ireland too, but you guys definitely win with the weather."

I don't reply to this, but allow an awkward pause instead.

"Are *you* OK?" I blurt out, against my better judgment.

"Oh yeah! What do you mean?"

"I dunno, I just got the impression Ollie said something that bothered you."

I put my hand on Tommy's thigh to soften my obvious prying, but it does little to relax his change in energy.

15
TOMMY

I've always been able to balance things out when it comes to Ollie's behaviour, but this pushed the limits. He's not known for his tact, and always goes down the comedian route at every opportunity, even if it risks offence.

I shouldn't be too surprised that he ploughed my wife's fairly recent infidelity for a cheap joke. I just didn't expect it to be relayed via a girl I like a lot, and who would probably *not* want to be opening that door with me just yet, if ever.

Asshole!

By the time we left the bar, I had already texted him to remind him that's what he was. I haven't read his reply. No doubt a mix of apology, and making light of it a little more. I'll let him sweat a bit more before even reading, let alone allowing him a reply.

It has made the atmosphere in the car a little awkward. I don't want to bring it up, but I can tell that Gina is wondering what it's about. Should I talk about it, so she doesn't think I'm some sort of secretive weirdo, enjoying a private joke in her company?

That's rude. That's not me.

Fuck sake, thanks Ollie. Asshole!

"Are you OK?" I ask, when I notice Gina playing with her lip, looking a million miles away. She snaps back to us in an instant, passing it off as just being lost in the moment with the view. This settles any concern that she was wondering about Ollie's comment, that is until she asks if I am OK too.

She clearly has been wondering.

I'm immediately grateful to feel her hand on my leg, speaking more with her gentle touch, than the three words which hang unanswered in the air between us.

"Ummm…" I start, unsure about what, or how much to say. I've spent such a long time carrying the pain of what happened. Processing and compartmentalising every part, and untangling all the feelings of deteriorating self-worth. I've internalised it all in so much detail, that I don't know if I can vocalise it without giving it more power again.

"He made a joke about something that happened to me - something which hurt me a lot." I pause, flailing inside, trying to land on a coherent but brief explanation which won't prompt more questions.

"Hmm, yeah I could see it on your face." Gina says quickly, with a squeeze of my thigh. The empathy she oozes as she says this pulls the rug from under the script in my head. A script written by shame. If I didn't know better, I would say I felt a rushing feeling of love. I wasn't expecting the sensation I have right now in the centre of my chest.

It's like she has stepped into my pain with me, and let me know it's OK.

"It's not something you have to talk about. I just want you to be OK." she continues, softly but assertively.

This is one of those moments when it's impossible not to make eye-contact with someone, and when I do turn my head, Gina lifts her shades to let our eyes meet properly. All I feel is warmth, reassurance and, yes, love. Or something close enough to love for now. I hadn't realised just how much I needed this.

Vulnerability is something men aren't supposed to show. So I've always been led to believe. I haven't done a very good job at hiding my vulnerability here, but Gina seems unfazed by it. Quite the opposite.

What's going on?

The irony is, I've never been successful at processing things internally. In the aftermath of finding my wife with another man, Ollie was a good sounding board for me to hear my own thoughts out loud, then take them back in with a little more clarity. Often over a few beers, which usually helped.

The urge to tell Gina everything right now is overwhelming, and as much as I believe she would listen and not judge, I can't let that happen yet. It's too soon. I want to just enjoy her company and to be 'us', without outside interference or influence.

I know she has a story herself, and maybe if this works out, we'll get to know each other's pain.

For now though, we deserve to just have some fun like a normal couple, don't we? Whatever normal is, for two broken hearts trying to find where they belong.

I just smile, take her hand in mine, and say, "Thank you."

It's from the heart.

The recognition of the things which lie in each other go unspoken, with words replaced by a connection and understanding I'm sure we can *both* feel as our fingers intertwine.

16
GINA

Whatever experiences Tommy has locked away, they're clearly painful, and I don't want to push him to open up. It'll come in his own time, maybe - if he wants to share it with me.

I'm a little surprised, and a little confused, at how this has already made me feel though. Why do I feel warmed by the idea of him carrying some emotional wounds of his own?

The rest of the car journey into Pismo Beach is lighter. We debate at length, hilariously, the subtext of Legally Blonde, and what it says about traditional male and female roles in society. We come to the same conclusion in the end, that historically Hollywood has been one of the first mirrors on cultural shifts, and in this case we hope that it signals more doors opening for women. It's so refreshing to hear Tommy's perspective.

I saw Legally Blonde in the cinema with Brandon and he dismissed it as "pink fluffy bullshit," and that Elle would "end up pregnant anyway, so why did it matter?" He also added something about her cute little ass, but i had pretty much zoned out by then.

It's mid-afternoon, when we pull off the highway and down Shell Beach Road towards the seafront, and a moment later turn in at large sign that says 'Dolphin Bay Resort & Spa'. The five embossed silver stars shining under the logo tell me this isn't just any old hotel.

"Is this where we're staying tonight?" I half-whisper, with a mixture of surprise and excitement. I'm looking at Tommy, and waiting for him to say he's just turning the car here because we missed the turning for *our* hotel. Surely he wouldn't be bringing me somewhere like this…suddenly feeling very under-dressed.

"It sure is, m'lady".

That's cute.

I'm almost speechless, mumbling a barely audible "Wow…"

The anxiety I felt at the start of our day over the sleeping arrangements has passed completely. Today, something has shifted deeper again between us , though I'm not sure I could describe *how,* if someone were to ask me. Right now I feel nothing but tingles of excitement that we're finally here. Well, that and feeling pretty fucking special. I need to live in the moment, and not manufacture possible bad outcomes. That's a hard habit to break.

Driving into the grounds of the resort, it's like a fairy-tale. Bad things don't happen in fairy tales, right?

It's just a getaway for a day, but already it's more romantic than anything anyone has *ever* done for me.

Pismo Beach is the epitome of classic California. A beach town of only 7000 or so, roughly halfway between Los Angeles and San Francisco. I looked it up online before we left - honing in on some tour guide-ish facts which I won't, or will try not to, bore Tommy with later.

"So how many women have you brought here?" I ask, only partly joking, as we glide up to the hotel frontage. He just smiles and shakes his head, closing his eyes for a second to dismiss my question. "First time," he allows.

I hear that instead as, 'You're the only woman', and feel a little foolish for it, despite the goofy grin.

Don't get carried away.

A huge fountain of three happy looking dolphins in mid air sits confidently out front. The early afternoon sunshine makes the bubbling water underneath the sculptures sparkle like some of sort of magic illusion.

Breathtaking.

I've seen my share of fancy hotels back home in Las Vegas, but this is different. Those fancy facades hide a million stories of seediness, despair and ruthless people waiting to exploit you.

This is everything home isn't. Calm, quiet and effortlessly romantic. No 'all you can eat' buffet here, and no constant ringing of slot machines.

The Mustang stops, as an exceptionally well-groomed man in a smart waistcoat appears from the shade of the doorway to greet us. His subtle nod of deference is a nice touch, and makes me feel like I'm a celebrity arriving.

How the other half live eh?

He opens my door with a "Welcome to the Dolphin Bay madam." Another slight nod. "I trust you had a pleasant journey?" His accent is deliberately, and perfectly nondescript.

"I did. We did. Thank you!" I'm not quite sure how to behave now, feeling like a fraud.

Is he thinking I don't belong in a place like this?

"Good afternoon Sir," he addresses Tommy, as he steps out onto the smooth white paving, leaving his door open. "May I collect your bags?"

"Just two small ones in the back, and the suit bag."

My head snaps quickly to him. "You brought a suit?" I'm not hiding the panic very well. All I have is a pair of slacks and a couple of vest tops. "You said casual."

"Oh! I had one in the boot already. It's no big deal, don't worry."

I'm a little worried, but I can't help but trust him.

"You had a suit in your boot?" I ask, deadpan, with amused eyebrows.

His laugh is so perfect. In my smitten ears it even sounds Irish, although I know that's not possible. Making Tommy laugh is quickly becoming one of my new favourite things to do. I like how it makes me feel.

Like he has never laughed for anyone before me.

"The trunk sorry. We call it a boot back home." He pauses. "It's just..emm…junk in my trunk," he declares proudly.

"Was that supposed to be a joke?" I ask, knowing it *was,* but I want to see how mister confident squirms under pressure.

"Absolutely not," he replies, so completely emotionless that I can't tell for a moment if he's being serious or not.

"You do know we don't do sarcasm here in the U.S?"

"I don't believe you," he fires back quickly, watching with too much amusement at my growing confusion.

"You're not as funny as you think you are, ya know!" is all I can come up with.

"Yes I am." he says, with more sarcasm, possibly, as he takes my hand and softly kisses my cheek.

The silence here, and the warm stillness of the air, is so welcome after the long drive with the top down. I can't wait to see what it's like inside.

The airy reception, lit by a domed glass roof, has cute little semi-private cubicles, with a desk in each for checking in. Another well groomed person, a tall elegant blonde this time, appears with a silver tray. She presents us with two tall stemmed glasses of something bubbly.

How fancy!

"I'll take care of checking in, if you want to take a look around?" Tommy suggests. We chink glasses before I wander off - the hotel boutique shop across the lobby drawing me in, like I'm caught in a tractor beam.

Tommy joins me a moment later, his hand on my waist stirring arousal that I did *not* expect from such a casual touch. The frequency of how he surprises me with little things is starting to sink in more, along with how off balance my emotions are. The bubbly can't be kicking in just yet. Anxiety overthinks everything, so I'm used to fast processing, but this is different. *So* different.

Is this how people feel when they're happy?

Is this how people feel when they start to fall in love?

I'm so glad he can't read my racing and irrational thoughts right now. I can hide those. I *have* to hide those.

Fucking hell, he smells so good!

I've got a dress in my hand when his body meets mine, and I quickly put it back on the rail. Two figure price tags are my limit, so this shop is certainly not for me.

"Our room won't be ready for an hour or so, if you want to explore?"

"Sure, sounds good. Just let me use the bathroom first." I turn to face him, our bodies still close enough to keep his hand on my waist. With a hand on his firm, muscular shoulder, I lift my heels off the floor to kiss his lips, lingering for a few seconds longer than planned.

"Thank you so much for this," I whisper.

"We haven't done anything yet."

"We have. You have. Just being here with you today is the biggest breath of fresh air. I'm not used to anyone treating me so well."

Tommy frowns at this. "Well that makes me sad! You deserve so much more than I could ever give you Gina."

Hearing him say my name again gives me flutters down below.

I'm in trouble.

I just smile, respond with another kiss, then whisper in my best sexy voice right into his ear, "I gotta pee so bad."

He's still laughing as I stride confidently across the lobby.

That was funny. I'm so funny.

"Gina!" he calls, softly enough to not draw attention.

I spin around, aiming for flirty/cool/confident.

"The bathroom is that way," Tommy announces, now just above the necessarily volume for only my ears. He's grinning like the Cheshire Cat from Alice in Wonderland, playing with my embarrassment, but getting away with it.

"I knew that!" I reply, with indignance and a red face. "I just wanted to get my step count up."

I stride back past him, doing my best to own it, as he giggles to himself.

17
GINA

"What's the plan Batman?" I ask brightly from behind Tommy, as I return from the most opulent bathroom I've ever been in. Tommy drops his phone from his ear as he turns, looking perplexed.

"Everything OK?" I ask, restraining anxious thoughts.

"Yeah, sorry, just telling Ollie what a dick he is."

"Oh," I reply, not quite sure what else to say, other than the obvious line of inquiry. My "Oh" hangs in the air for an awkward moment.

"I'll explain later. Will we get some food and a drink somewhere? See what this Pismo Beach place is made of?"

"Sounds good to me. I'm so hungry I could eat you, Tommy Millar."

"Ha! Normally this is where I would make a joke about prime Irish beef, but that might be ungentlemanly."

I ponder this for a fraction less time than I should, riding the flirt wave with wild abandon. "I could go for some Irish beef." I'm not even embarrassed now to say it. I'll blame the glass of bubbly if I have to.

Tommy just smiles, a hint of mischief and appreciation, but coolly not pushing it any further.

The concierge desk is nearby, manned by a stout man wearing a waistcoat, and years of experience on his face. "Where's good for food and a few drinks? Somewhere laid back," Tommy asks him.

"There are a few places sir, but if you're only here for a short time I would recommend Harry's Bar."

"Is it close by?"

"Ten minutes drive south sir. The resort car is available at the moment. I could call our driver?

"What do you think?" he asks, turning to give me more attention than I'd be used to in a situation like this.

"Sure, why not?"

"Yeah! Why not!" he grins, adding another kiss to my growing collection.

The concierge is already on the phone to the driver. "He'll be out front in less than a minute, sir," he says warmly.

My tummy flutters again at the special treatment. I am *so* not used to this, and it feels like it's all happening too fast to properly take it in. I want to absorb every moment, so I'll be able look back on it later with some clarity.

But maybe this is just what life with Tommy Millar would be like....

Tommy thanks him with a handshake, discretely passing a banknote with it.

A black Mercedes S-class appears outside almost instantaneously, like a magic carriage. The sumptuous interior is perfectly air-conditioned for the journey as we sink into the leather seats in the back. Tommy's hand finds mine, perfectly intertwined.

Just like us.

* * *

Tommy

Harry's Bar has the look of a building that's been around since the days of the Wild West, with it's wooden paneling and overhanging roof. It's easy to imagine it alongside a dusty street, with a few horses tied up outside. Instead, today it's a couple of Harley Davidson motorcycles.

The corner upon which the bar sits is lined with palm trees. I'm not sure if they had those on the street in the Wild West, but who knows. I certainly don't remember Clint Eastwood ever dodging bullets behind a palm tree in the movies.

The retro vibe continues inside, though I'm sure they'd describe it as classic. I'm delighted to see that it's exactly how I imagined all American bars would look like, thanks to all the movies.

The main floor area is open plan with lots of big heavy looking tables, most etched with random carvings of names and suchlike, and almost all of them occupied already. A vintage jukebox sits glowing beside a smallish stage in the corner, facing the door we've just entered. The stage is empty, apart from a guitar on a stand and a round stool patriotically displaying an open bottle of Budweiser.

I feel so much at home in a place like this, and like the energy already. Casual and authentic. I'm pretty confident there'll be no pretentious assholes here. What a relief.

"This is a cool place. Good choice" Gina says, leaning both elbows on the polished redwood bar. "What are you having?"

A bartender appears from around the corner of the L shaped bar, and I notice that this place has another area almost as large, round the other side of the bar. The decor there is more like a sports pub - four pool tables, with lots of stools around the perimeter, and walls covered with neon beer logos and sports pennants. Each wall has an enormous flat screen TV as it's centrepiece, and from my line of sight they all seem to be silently showing different games of football.

I never did understand American football. Too much stopping and starting when you're used to football back home. The stubborn part of me still refuses to call it soccer, except when I'm winding up Ollie on the phone, purely because I know it annoys him even more than me.

"What can I get for you folks?" The way the barkeep phrases this makes me want to order a shot of whiskey, and a bucket of water for my horse. But I resist, glancing at Gina to let her order first.

"Do you do cocktails?"

"Sure!" the barman says brightly, sliding an A4 sized laminated menu across to her.

"You go ahead and order. I'll need a minute with this."

"I'll take a beer please, a Bud. Draft if you have it?" He gives me a quick nod, then crouches to grab a glass from under the bar.

"What do you recommend if I like something sweet?" Gina asks him, leaning over the bar a little.

"The passion fruit Martini is a popular one," he suggests, carefully finishing the head on my pint. The condensation on the glass tells me that this is gonna be a very cold, and very welcome beer. I'm ready for it.

"OK sounds good, I'll give that a try," Gina replies, still sounding cutely indecisive.

"To Legally Blonde 2, starring Gina Sawyer," I declare, as we chink glasses a few minutes later. We're found seats in the opposite corner to the stage, with a great view of the entire bar. Instinctively, we've sit facing each other, across a small round table.

Gina laughs, "Oh yes, me and Reese will be fighting it out for the biggest dressing room, I'm sure!"

"See, you *do* do sarcasm!"

"You're obviously rubbing off on me, Tommy Millar," she says, following it with a careful sip from her full-to-the-brim glass.

"I should be so lucky," I say, pretending to mumble to myself, and Gina almost spits out her first mouthful. I get a playful kick in the shin while she swallows and licks her lips.

"There's something you should know where that's concerned." Gina says this with a little trepidation, like she's expecting a bad reaction coming.

"Where what's concerned?" I ask, kind of knowing, but not wanting to be presumptuous.

"Like sex and stuff," she whispers, after checking how close the nearest people are.

"If this is where you tell me you have a secret penis, I'm going to be very upset."

I say this a little louder than I need to. I'm 50/50 on whether it's accidental or mischief, but both the man and the woman at the table about 6 feet away both look up in surprise. It's a good job they're out of Gina's line of sight.

"Shuuuuush!" she whispers urgently, leaning towards me so quickly she almost knocks her drink over. Once she stops giggling, she tells me to keep my voice down in case someone hears. I give her my best blank face agreement and nod apologetically, hoping she'll continue.

"I have this, ummm, rule," she says awkwardly.

"OK….?" I trail off, trying to prompt information that she's obviously unsure how to vocalise

"When I meet someone, I have a no sex for six weeks rule." Her voice wavers slightly in her confident delivery. Her eye-contact is more intense than usual as she tells me this. I can tell straight away that she's studying me closely for a reaction. Her elbows are leaning on the table, and one hand clasps a fist over her mouth.

My first reaction is relief that it's nothing bad, quickly followed by an underlying disappointment from the parts of me I didn't think were capable of much more disappointment.

"Is it some sort of religious thing?" I ask, almost not wanting to know.

"It's a self-preservation thing." Gina pauses, in a way that makes me wonder if this is the first time she's had this conversation. "I had a really bad experience with my ex, so I'm thinking if someone is willing to wait six weeks, then I know they like me for me."

"I can see the logic in that." I reply slowly, nodding and trying to process this.

"Is it a deal-breaker for you? I can understand if it is, but it's important you know where my head is…"

18
GINA

My tummy is in knots of conflict. I have talked so much with Amy about this rule, that it's deeply embedded now as a non-negotiable.

It felt like a great idea before Tommy, but now I'm not so sure. I've committed to it now though, and hearing it out loud for the first time with someone, it sounds more like a test than I had imagined.

It was originally about me. I hadn't considered liking someone enough that it becomes something about 'us' and I feel a little guilty as I only now realise this.

"It's definitely *not* a deal-breaker," Tommy smiles, leaning closer to mirror my elbows on the table. "I'm more than happy to wait," he says, a little too casually.

"Oh wow! Thanks!" I pull my head back an inch or two, in surprise.

Tommy's brow furrows ever so slightly, rightly confused at my apparent indignance at him agreeing with my rule.

"I didn't think you'd be so happy to agree." I'm riding both ends of the see-saw now, and I'm aware of it.

Make up your mind.

He's going to think you're a lunatic.

He leans in more, re-establishing the closeness, his gorgeous face not giving away much in the emotion department.

"Gina, let me make this very clear. I've already imagined what it'll be like to do 'sex stuff' as you call it. It's hard not to, when you're as beautiful as you are, and the spark between us is undeniable. As cheesy as this is gonna sound, just being *with* you, and getting to know you, is so far beyond anything I could ever have expected, so going slow suits me. Taking it further will happen when it feels right for you."

He pauses, considering every word carefully, before continuing in an incredibly sexy semi-whisper.

"You know, I didn't *want* to meet anyone just yet. Things are still so raw from what happened back home. I'm not sure I could cope with any more pain, so my plan was just to focus on work and be happy with that. But then I saw you in the pizza place…and I don't mean I just saw you, but I *saw* you in a way I can't really describe, or understand. I'm not talking just about how beautiful you are - that's obvious, but I've never been in the presence of *anyone* in my entire life who radiates an energy like you do. It was like I already knew you, if that makes any sense…'

Tommy pauses again, leaving me hanging, speechless, before he adds;

"So yes, I have no problem waiting, because I think just being around you is refilling parts of me that I didn't realise were so empty. I'm not sure that makes sense out loud, but it does in my brain". His nervous laugh now is his only hint of being aware of the magnitude of what he has just shared.

I'm smiling so widely now, I'm sure it looks ridiculous, especially combined with my reddening face. I've never heard a man speak with such candid honesty. I am completely and utterly captivated by his vulnerability, and how he's happy to wear it on his sleeve. Every single word has been spoken, and heard, with a depth of sincerity that has removed not just every layer of my second-date nerves, but has touched a part of me I didn't know a man could reach.

I take his hands away from his chin and hold them firmly in mine, bringing them to his chest.

I'm utterly at a loss for how to respond verbally, so instead I lean in and put my lips on his, soft and lingering. This kiss feels different. I swear I can feel the energy he was talking about. Not just mine, but ours, like something invisible but also physical connects us. Whatever it is, it's an intoxicating rush of emotion. All walls are down for now. I feel like I could do or say anything in this moment and it would be OK, and the wetness I can feel between my legs agrees.

I let our lips part just enough to whisper, with an insuppressible smile, "Say that all again. Just like that."

I feel his smile mirror mine before he reconnects with my lips, and we kiss with an eagerness now that's borderline inappropriate for where we are. It jolts me back to reality about our public surroundings, but I don't care, letting the kiss continue for several more seconds. Partly because I have no idea how to reply with words.

How can I match that?

"Maybe we'll make it one week instead of six," I smile as we let the kiss go, only half joking.

"Whatever you're comfortable with works for me," he says carefully, taking a sip of beer. The hint of red in *his* cheeks now makes me want to drag him to bed immediately.

The singer has returned during our kiss, and strums his guitar for a sound check. One. One-two. One-two, he says, before fiddling with the volume controls on his amp. He starts to sing 'Fast Car' by Tracy Chapman, in a country style.

"He's good!" I gush, so grateful for the opportunity to change the subject.

"Yeah! I love this song. I've never heard it sung by a man before," Tommy says, having to shout a little. "Do you wanna get another one here or move on?"

"I'm easy!"

Tommy smirks cheekily, enjoying my timing for a double entendre. I just take it, with a tip of my head and a lift of my shoulder as I smile back.

He can have that one.

He can have me.

We enjoy the rest of the song in silence, and I wonder if Tommy feels the words like I do.

It feels like he's singing to us. For us.

19
TOMMY

I feel a little more relaxed now, as we leave the bar. The beer helped for sure, but hearing about Gina's six week rule has lifted the pressure. The idea of racing into a full blown relationship scares the crap out of me. I made that mistake before with Cheryl, and look how that turned out.

Gina, thankfully, could not be more different to her, and as much as she has pulled the proverbial rug out from under my plan to stay single, I need to be careful. Tread carefully.

Another kick in the heart right now would finish me off.

Holding hands, we cross the road and slowly dander the block and a half towards the beach. It's a wide avenue lined with palm trees, and a perfect mix of independent stores and restaurants.

"It feels so laid back here, doesn't it?" I ask as we walk, swinging our connected arms like carefree kids.

"I absolutely love it. It's like Venice, but with money. Thank you so much for bringing me here."

"That's OK, I'm so glad you're here."

I can see a long wooden pier ahead, cutting out into the ocean at an angle. As we approach, the avenue opens out into a large paved plaza, with purple free-standing letters - each about eight foot tall, spelling Pismo Beach. They stand proudly with their back to the beach, and beside the pier entrance, just begging for the perfect tourist photo.

It's not too busy, thankfully. Not crowded like Venice Beach. It's unexpectedly and perfectly romantic. I'm sure we both feel it. We naturally stop at the mouth of the pier, seeing the length of it, and not wanting to commit to it this late in the afternoon.

"I can't believe it's almost four already," Gina says with a hint of disappointment, as we lean on the railings overlooking the beach below. She slides closer to me and I instinctively wrap my arm around her. It feels good to have someone so physically close again, even with the mixed emotions it stirs.

Gina makes a purring sound, and snuggles in closer.

"Are you warm enough?" The goosebumps on my arm have noticed the light coastal breeze.

"For now, yes," she says, burrowing into me a little bit more. "I feel so safe here with you."

"Safe?"

"Yeah…" is all she gives me, but her choice of word has piqued my interest.

"Don't you normally feel safe?"

There's a pause of at least twenty seconds before Gina speaks, from deep in my embrace.

"No. I don't know if I'll ever feel completely safe, as long as my ex still walks the earth."

I'm not sure how to reply, so offer silence in the hope for some more information.

"I kind of did a runner from him, and came here for a fresh start."

"Oh. OK. I didn't know that." I pause, deciding how to ask the obvious question, choosing the simplest way. "Did he hurt you?"

Gina's shaky "Yes" sends a chill through my veins at first, then an overwhelming feeling of protection and care follow it. Holding her tight to my body makes this easier. Feeling her warmth. Hearing her vulnerability, and realising for the first time that this beautiful girl in my arms is maybe just as broken as I am.

As soon as I say "Well I won't ever let anything happen to you," it sounds like a typical cliché, like a badly written scene in a movie. I curse my inner movie-geek for feeding me that line, even though I meant every word.

"You can't promise that," she whispers, devoid of any emotion.

Before I can think of how else to make her feel safe, she loosens herself from me, lifting her head and kisses me firmly. I take it as a signal that I should say no more.

"Thank you, though. I don't want you to feel like you're responsible for my safety."

I suspect that my expression, and my nod doesn't do much to convince her that I don't feel that it is my responsibility.

"Let's take a walk on the beach before it gets too cold." Gina's voice is suddenly and pointedly bright.

My smile of agreement comes at the right time to cover up the anxiety-driven questions I hear in my head, all at once;

What am I getting into here?

Is this going to be too complicated?

Do I need drama back in my life again so soon?

Is this girl worth it?

Regardless of the answers to any others, the "Is this girl worth it?" question is one that doesn't need any consideration at all. Not being around Gina, and seeing where this goes is definitely *not* an option. I know that for certain.

We only walk for about ten minutes away from the pier, along the soft sand, before turning back, not letting go of each other once. It's only on the way back, with the southerly breeze behind us, that she offers me more.

"Last week I thought I saw him. When I walked home, after you dropped me off."

"Who? Your ex?" I try my best to hide the alarm at this revelation.

"Yeah…but I think I'm just paranoid, you know? Amy told me it couldn't possibly be him. He doesn't even know where I live now."

"Would he be the type to follow you?"

Her delayed reply says yes before the words do.

"Probably. He treated me like I was his property after we got engaged."

My first instinct is jealousy, that she clearly loved someone enough to get engaged, but then remind myself that I'm still technically married.

I should probably tell Gina that soon.

My busy brain just sends an "Oh" to my vocal chords as I process this.

"I should have listened to everyone who warned me. What a fucking cliché. I knew better, and paid for that in more ways than one."

"What do you mean?" I'm confused at how I can, at the same time, want to know everything, but also want to know nothing more about her past relationship.

"Well, me buying my own engagement ring for a start?"

"No way! Why?"

"I was working in Walmart, and his idea was to buy it there so I could use my employee discount. This meant I had to buy it, and then he'd write me a cheque, which of course bounced."

"Wow! What a shitty thing to do. Did he give you the money?"

Gina laughs like this is the best joke she's heard in years.

"Have you ever hit a woman?"

This comes from out of nowhere, and the unspoken truth behind it hits me right in the chest. Her question is an easier way for her to tell me what I didn't want to ask.

"No, and I never would. What a fucking coward."

"You don't know the half of it Tommy, and I don't think I even want you to. I'm free of him now, and that's all that matters. Thanks to Amy, I have a life now that I didn't think I would ever have."

"She's been a good friend to you?"

"Like an angel sent to take care of me, honestly. She's like a mom and a sister at the same time. I don't know what I would do without her."

"I'm surprised she hasn't been checking up to see if you're OK."

"I left my phone in my bag at the hotel. There's probably about fifty missed calls by now," she laughs, a little nervously.

"Let's grab a taxi back then. Get warmed up and ready for dinner?"

"Oooh yes, that sounds good."

The steps back up from the beach have us back at the Pismo Beach sign, and a few taxi cabs sit waiting on the closest corner. I open the door for Gina to get in the back, and her expression of surprise and gratitude feels like perfect closure on the heavy conversation we've just had.

"Thank you," she says, taking my hand when I join her in the back seat.

"What for?"

"Everything. Listening. Not running away. Just being you…"

* * *

Gina

What the fuck?

"Tommy, I thought we were in separate rooms?" I demand, as we walk across the lobby towards the elevators.

"We are."

"But there's only one room card."

"You'll see. Trust me." I let him take my hand, knowing he'll feel how clammy it is all of a sudden.

We're on the top floor, and as each building in the Dolphin Bay complex is only 4 stories high, it doesn't take long before the doors ping open.

This suddenly feels like it's happening very fast.

The luxuriously thick carpeted hallway leads us softly all the way to the end of the corridor. 'Ocean Front Penthouse Suite' boasts the plaque on the wall beside the door.

What the fuck?

The lock beeps, and Tommy pushes the heavy dark wood door wide, stepping in before holding it open for me to enter. I give him a suspicious look as I step inside slowly.

A longish corridor opens out to an enormous open plan room and, possibly for the first time in my life, my breath is *actually* taken away. Well, as long as I don't count the time Brandon kicked me in the stomach, when he thought I was pregnant.

An eclectic mix of chairs and sofas surround a giant glass coffee table on one side, facing a grand looking fireplace. The other two thirds of the space is a kitchen. An *actual* kitchen in a hotel room. A curved marble breakfast bar with four high stools separate the appliances from a glass topped round dining table, which rests on a very expensive looking rug.

A spectacular view of the Pacific ocean draws my eyes to a three part window which covers most of the entire opposite wall.

For now, I have completely forgotten the sleeping arrangements.

"Tommy, what is this?" I ask weakly, still stunned.

"Do you not like it?" he teases, walking past me and opening wide the two glass patio doors. "It's a bit stuffy in here."

I follow him out onto a patio which is larger than my bedroom, even with the square hot tub which sits in one corner. We lean side by side on the thick wooden railing, overlooking the water.

"You don't do things by half. I'll give you that," I say in an amused tone, gazing out to sea. The tranquillity and luxury surroundings combine to already relax me more than I have in years.

Never in my wildest dreams did I expect to be in a place like this…with a guy like this.

"I promised myself when I moved out here that I would make the absolute most of everything. Life is too hard, as well as too short not to. Don't you think?"

"Can't argue with that…but…?"

"But…?" Tommy asks, still fixated on the view.

"I'm wishing you'd waited six weeks before bringing me here."

Tommy turns his head as he grins. I open my mouth to say more, but instead get drawn into a kiss. It's a soft, tentative one at first but quickly escalates. The deep longing to take this further is difficult to resist.

Damn my six week rule.

If this were a movie, this would absolutely be when we would slowly undress each other between hungry kisses, and we would make love on the balcony with the late afternoon sun on our skin.

We get dangerously close too, when hands begin to explore during the kiss.

Tommy's hands slide down my back and one hand cups my ass. The noise I make invites him to stay, but he moves it around to my hip, gripping my waist. I don't need *my* hands to know he's as aroused as I am, feeling him hard against me as he pulls me against his body.

He holds me here firmly, while as the little gap in my dress allows the fingers on his other hand to slide sexily under my bra strap. When he brings his mouth to my ear, and then to my neck, an uncontrollable moan leaves my mouth. My head falls back, and I feel limp in his arms. The throbbing between my legs is winning the battle of whether or not I should allow my hands to undo his shorts. I pull my hips away to make space, and lay my palms on Tommy's chest before undoing the top button on his shirt.

I get to the third button and pull his mouth onto mine again, our tongues dancing passionately, then he pulls away, breathing heavily. I'm dizzy and disorientated for a moment, and equally breathless.

"What's wrong?" I pant, confused.

"Nothing. My god, nothing, that's the problem!" Tommy clasps his hands behind his head, as if to keep them under control. He's breathing hard, and his partially unbuttoned shirt gives me a teasing glimpse of his toned, and very kissable chest.

"I don't understand."

"Your rule. We can't do this yet."

Wow. Are you for real?

I'm stunned into silence by that. But I can't argue.

What would that say about me if I say 'fuck the rules', and let him take me?

He's right. Dammit!!

I take the deepest of breaths, and let it out slowly through pursed lips.

"You're right. I'm so sorry!"

"Gina, you have nothing to be sorry about! I'm the one who should apologise."

"I think we both got carried away," I laugh, moving to button up his shirt again, punctuating it with a soft kiss, with one hand on his cheek.

"This is gonna be hard," Tommy whispers as I withdraw, answering him with my best sexy smile and a glance downwards.

"If it's gonna be harder than that, then I'm in trouble," I say, raising a mischievous eyebrow.

"Oooh, you're getting *very* bold," Tommy laughs. "I love it!"

"Right, let's see the rest of this ridiculously expensive hotel room then." I'm enjoying the compliment, but need to rescue us both before it gets hot and heavy again. "I still don't see how we have separate rooms."

"Come see," Tommy says, grabbing my hand to pull me with him as steps back inside. He leads me back to the corridor, and I spot three doors Two on one side, and one on the other. He opens the first and pushes it wide, then does the same with the other beside it. Two large adjoining bedrooms, each with a huge, plush looking bed under a massive ceiling fan.

"Take your pick," he says, smiling like he a real-estate agent proud of his show house.

"I think *that's* mine," I say, noticing my bag on the cushioned table at the foot of the bed. "Thank you for being a gentleman". I give him another kiss before we divert to our own rooms.

"Oh, where's the bathroom?" I spin around quickly when I don't see another door in my bedroom.

"It must be there somewhere," Tommy replies as he opens the single door opposite the bedrooms, revealing an enormous bathroom. "I thought they said both bedrooms were en-suite."

"Ho-ly crap! Look at this!"

The centre of the bathroom wall has a rectangular mirror at least 10 feet wide, above a marble his & hers sink area. Both sinks are wide and deep, their curved corners making each an elongated egg shape.

Pure luxury.

To the right of the vanity area, a deep free-standing bathtub sits, mirroring the odd shape of the sinks.

Is it too dorky just to climb in now with my clothes on?

An open doorway at to the left has a toilet, and a corner shower which looks big enough for at least four people. Or two people with room to move. It's on the tip of my tongue to suggest this, but resist, though now I'm imagining us in there under the rainfall shower.

That sounds like some *very* hot foreplay.

Tommy calls from off behind me, "There's an en-suite in my room, so yours should have one too. If not, you can have this room."

I run my fingers across the marble at the sinks with an excited grin, before I go to check.

"Found it!" I call. The door to my en-suite opens to reveal an adjacent dressing room area with a full length mirror, ornamental free-standing clothes rail and various shelves and cubby holes. I flick a light switch and it's suddenly brightly lit by halogen bulbs from above and the side.

Perfect.

There's a long zipped up clothes bag hanging on the clothes rail, and three shoe boxes on the floor to the side.

"Tommy, I think someone left some stuff behind," I call, but he doesn't reply.

"Tommy?" I push his partially closed door open to reveal him stripped to the waist, in nothing but boxers.

Shit

"Oh shit, I'm so sorry." I turn away quickly, but every part of his toned body is already burned hard into my vision.

He laughs lightly at my reaction. "It's OK, come back in. I'm not naked."

"You're pretty close," I say, opening the door slowly, trying to look at him without staring. The ceiling fan whirls softly above him, so I try to look at that instead.

"I suppose so, but you'll need to wait to see the good bits."

The way he says this with a wink, as he unpacks his carefully folded clothes, makes me feel exposed. That's quite a feat when I'm fully dressed and he's almost naked. I have no reply but another blush.

"There's stuff in my room that someone must have left behind. Should I call down to reception?"

"No, that's yours," he says both plainly and cryptically at the same time.

I tilt my head in confusion. "What do you mean?"

He smiles at me with a hint of mischief, standing there full of confidence.

Stop being so sexy, and put some clothes on.

"Go and have a look. I'm gonna take a shower. There's cider in the fridge, and some premixed cocktails if you're thirsty. I'll get a beer once I'm done, and join you."

He's so matter of fact, it's actually a little frustrating. He see the confusion on my face, my mouth slightly open.

"The concierge gave me his card earlier, so when you went to the bathroom in Harry's, I called him and asked him to chill some drinks for us arriving."

My mouth drops open just a little more. "You can actually do that?"

"Sure, why not?"

"Hmm…I guess I'm just not used to this kind of place, and this kind of treatment, or deserve it…"

My eyes widen a little when Tommy starts towards me. Perfect abs, and a sexy curved line of muscle on each side of his waist disappearing below the band of his trunk style tight black boxers.

What's happening?

The tingle between my legs is not helpful right now.
His hand lifts to my cheek when he reaches me.

Fuck, he smells good with no clothes on.

The kiss is firm and brief, dropping his hand to take mine at my side.

"The fact that you're not used to this kind of place, and being treated better is a fucking crime."

Nice touch adding the swear word. That could have sounded corny otherwise.

"This might sound a bit corny, but…"

Uh oh, here we go.

"…I've met a lot of people, and almost every single one carries themselves through life with a sense of entitlement or self importance that they wear like they're proud of it, not realising how unattractive it is. One of the first things I noticed about you, even before we spoke, was how you radiated the exact opposite to that. My god that was attractive. It still is! I'm glad that you told me about your experiences with your ex, because it explains perfectly what I see."

I'm frozen on the spot, the only visible movement being the lump in my throat as I swallow, trying to take this in.

"What do you see?" I ask, hesitantly, thrown completely off balance by his earnestness. It feels like he can see right through me, and for the second time, I'm the one who feels naked.

He tips his head ever so slightly, with an expression that he suspects what he's about to say isn't going to be news to me.

"Someone who's wounded, but survived, and hasn't been hardened by it. Shy but somehow confident at the same time. Someone who's more deserving of the absolute *best* things in life than anyone I've ever met, and I mean *anyone!* But instead you've been shit upon by life. Actually not life, just by other people. There are fuckers out there who are drawn to good people with good hearts, because they see them as easy targets to manipulate. They don't do that shit to people who are like them, because it wouldn't work. Shitty people see shitty behaviour a mile off, because they understand it. Whereas for the rest of us, we're drowning in it by the time we realise."

Tommy pauses, and I see the same expression flash across his face, as I saw when Ollie was on the phone.

"All I'm trying to say is that you deserve this, and so much more. The fact that you don't feel you deserve it is more attractive than you could ever know."

"Wow". My face must be a shade of beetroot now, and I'm aware I'm shaking a little.

"I'm sorry," Tommy says quickly. "That was a lot all at once."

I just nod, head spinning, not knowing whether to cry or run away. Or both.

"Look, I'm not gonna pretend that I'm not trying to impress you, because I definitely am…but it's only because I like you so much. I love how you make me feel when I'm with you, like I'm not alone any more, and I just want to make the most of it. If it's too much, I understand." His shrug of nonchalance is a tell for how exposed he feels right now, given that I'm not saying much.

I shake my head slowly as a tear makes it's way down my face, and I gather myself to speak.

"I'm just not used to feeling wanted. I'm not used to being with someone who values me, and cares about how I feel." I quickly wipe the tear away, like I need to pretend it wasn't mine. "This feels like a dream, or a movie, or something that isn't real."

"It's real, Gina." Tommy hugs me warmly.

Don't ever let me go…

"I'm sorry for making you cry"

"Don't apologise. I cry a lot, you'll see." I try to laugh it off to break the tension.

"Hang on one sec," he says, turning towards his bed and lifting a t-shirt. He slips it over his head, then turns towards me.

"The Goonies? Seriously" I have one hand over my mouth to stifle the ridicule his choice of shirt deserves.

"It's my pyjama top!" he replies with grin, as if that makes it OK.

I nod my head my head as Tommy passes me and heads down the corridor. "And still you manage to make it look sexy."

"Stop flirting and come get a drink. I think we need one after that."

Fuckin' A we do!

Tommy pours while I take one of the bar stools at the breakfast bar. He passes me a tall class of something mysterious and sits beside me.

"To open hearts, good times, and no more bastards" he declares, chinking my glass and taking a sip of beer.

"Eloquently put!" I smile, wondering how he always knows the right thing to say.

Is he real?

"Did you check your phone?"

"Oh shit no, I haven't." I'm already off the seat mid-sentence, reaching to plant my glass back on the counter as I dash off.

Two missed calls and one text from about an hour ago;

Hey honey, just checking you're OK while I've still got my knickers on ;-)

I snort at this. Classic Amy.

Having the BEST time, can't wait to tell you all about it. Love you xx

I come back out a moment later and lean on the door frame. "So what's with the stuff in the bedroom?"

He looks a bit sheepish. "Go and have a look," he implores gently.

I unzip the clothes bag, and know what it is before even taking it out fully. It's the green dress I was admiring in the shop downstairs. The one that was almost $2000. My bum lands on the stool behind me, saving me from the dizzy rush of shock that just hit me.

What is going on?

I feel like crying. Especially after our conversation, I'm not sure how I feel about this, and definitely can't accept it.

Maybe it's a rental.

No, a shop like that doesn't do rentals.

I take it to the bed and lay it out. It's stunning. Beyond stunning. I'm shaking. Do I go back out and demand that he takes it away again?

Why? Why?

I don't deserve this.

What do I do with this?

Regardless of whether I'm keeping it or not, I *have* to try it on. My light summer dress slips easily over my head and gets tossed on the floor, before I step into the new one. I zip it up the side, and turn to the mirror in the bedroom, tossing my hair as i take it in.

I have never worn an item of clothing so utterly beautiful, or felt anything so rich against my skin.

I walk out barefoot to the kitchen, slowly and quietly. Tommy looks up as I stand still before him, and his expression speaks all the words.

"Tommy, it's stunning," I whisper, feeling almost ashamed to be wearing it.

"You're stunning! It's absolutely perfect."

"For what, though? Why am I wearing this…and how did you know?"

"I saw you looking at it, so I bought it when you went to the bathroom. I thought it might be a nice surprise for going out for dinner."

"A nice surprise? Are you kidding me? I feel like I'm Julia fucking Roberts!"

"And just as beautiful too."

I tip my head and purse my lips at this, as if to say, "Don't bullshit me"

"I'm serious. I can't even think of words to describe how incredible you look."

"Tommy, I can't keep this."

"Why on earth not?"

"Because it's $2000 and it's our second date. For fuck sake!" I can't help but laugh, because hearing that out loud, it sounds even more ridiculous than it does inside my head.

"Shoes…" he replies slowly, enunciating every syllable slowly with relish, and clearly enjoying this.

"What shoes?"

"I asked the woman in the shop to pick out some shoes she thought might go with the dress, and send them up. If you like any of them, we can get them sent up in your size."

"Fuck off!"

"No, you fuck off!"

I just scowl at this, but inside I'm doing cartwheels. Sitting beside the shoe boxes on the bed, I'm almost scared to open them. Three boxes of treasure. Jimmy Choo. Dior, and Manolo

Blahnik. I immediately think of Carrie Bradshaw's obsession with Manolo's in Sex and the City, and another wave of dizziness washes over me.

I go for the Dior ones first, carefully lifting the lid while holding my breath. Fuck, the box alone is probably worth more than any shoes I have ever owned. I peel back the folds of the branded paper to reveal a pair of slingbacks, and lift one out carefully.

Stunning.

The heel and back half is shiny black leather, with the front half a black tightly woven fabric. What sets them apart though is the fabric strap - white, with J'Adior printed black in contrast, and finished with a beautiful bow on one side. I've already noticed each box is size 7, my size.

Just like a fairy tale.

Onto box number 2, with the bold Jimmy Choo 'LOVE' logo on the top of the box. These are simpler, but so classy. Black glossy patent leather stilettos with thick gold embossed J C letters intertwined on the each heel. Simple and sexy, with a white leather sole reminding you who made these little beauties. But I'm already thinking of box three.

This is like Christmas morning.

The simple white box has Manolo Blahnik printed in black on the lid, and on the side. Inside are the most stunning dark green stiletto pumps. A lush satin finish, with the classic square crystal buckle proudly adorning the toe piece.

I hold one in my hands like they're a gift from God, before slipping it onto my left foot. The other follows, and I stand slowly. A perfect fit. I haven't worn heels since December last year - in my previous life, so to speak.

That feels so long ago, and that girl feels like a different person to the one I'm now staring at in the full length mirror in the dressing room.

Who are you?

The shoes change my posture like magic, making me look tall and elegant as the dress hugs my body, before the side split allows the perfect amount of classy, but sexy flair. The Manolo buckles catches the light, drawing the eye to their magical sparkle.

"How's it going in there, Cinderella?" Tommy calls from the other room.

I take a deep breath, even though composure feels like a tall order, and make my way out…after checking my hair of course. I feel like a beauty queen making an entrance on stage. Nervous, but excited.

I hope he's not disappointed…

He's still perched on a stool, one elbow leaning back on the counter, but sits upright instinctively when I enter the room and stop several feet away.

"What do you think?" I ask, already sure enough of myself to strike a catwalk pose, complete with a pout.

"Breath-taking Gina. My goodness. You were born to wear that dress."

"And the shoes, don't you dare forget these shoes!" I demand, pointing to my feet.

"Carrie Bradshaw ain't got shit on you," he says, shaking his head, making me double over laughing.

"This is like a dream. I can't believe I'm standing here in this room wearing this dress and these shoes."

"It all fits you well." he says, with that sexy smile, before bringing me my drink. We chink glasses.

"To good times and sexy shoes?"

"The sexy goes way beyond the shoes!" he enthuses, and kisses my wet lips. "I'm gonna get a shower now. We could leave in an hour so for dinner? Does that give you enough time to get ready?"

"Perfect" I whisper, *still* playing catch-up.

20
GINA

It's a little after 7.30pm, when the Mercedes drops us off at the same plaza we left this afternoon.

The entrance to The Oyster Loft is unassuming, and for a second I question if we're over dressed.

Who cares!?

Tommy, impeccably dressed in pinstripe grey suit trousers, waistcoat and white open neck shirt, leads me the hand up the stairs to the restaurant, and we're quickly attended to.

"Table for two, in the name Millar."

"Of course sir, please follow me," the waiter replies, lifting some menus from under the podium.

Our table is perfect, of course. The balcony is wide enough for one table at a time, and spaced out enough to grant a feeling of intimacy. I hate when restaurants seat you so close to others that it feels like they're in your party.

I'm so glad we'll be able to chat freely here without being overheard. We're right on the beach front, perched one story up, with an incredible view of the sunset over the ocean.

Just perfect.

Ironically, neither of us order any of the seafood dishes they are obviously famous for, instead going for steak. I choose the Wagyu New York steak, salivating at the prospect, and Tommy opts for the Prime Fillet.

The same but different, just like us.

I *love* that we eat in almost silence, savouring the food, the view and each other's company…and a tequila based dessert cocktail called Aztec Gold. Checking my phone while Tommy is at the bathroom, I see two missed calls from Amy. It's a little odd that she hasn't just texted, when she knows I'm out, but she's a law unto herself.

After sending a brief **R U OK?** I decide to call her back as well, driven by a ping of anxiety. Straight to voicemail. Probably in bed already.

I feel a little childlike when Tommy returns, having just watched him pay the bill at the bar.

"Thank you so much. That was amazing!"

"No worries at all." He kisses me before sitting back down opposite me.

Cute

"I don't want to go home yet. The hotel I mean," I say with a deliberate hint of mischief, leaning towards him.

"It's still early," he says, carefully folding his cloth napkin again. "The bar we were at earlier is close by. We could see what it's like at night time? Might be fun?"

"Yes! Perfect!" As stunning the view here, it's a too quiet to hang around after dinner. I want somewhere a bit more lively. Getting to know each other in different environments is so important.

The air outside is crisper now after dark, and if it was any further a walk to the bar, I'd be wanting more layers on. My re-acclimatisation with walking in heels isn't being helped by the addition of alcohol, but it just gives me a good excuse to take Tommy's arm.

"So, how did you end up here?" I ask casually, like it's on the same significance level as "What did you have for lunch?" or something.

A laugh wasn't the reply I expected, though.

"What's so funny?" I nudge him, growing more aware of his hesitancy to open up.

"Sorry…that's just, ummm…if only you knew how big a question that was."

"So tell me." I'm keeping my tone light, so as not to scare him back into his hiding place.

There's a pause. He clearly wasn't ready for this question. Most times, this length of pause from anyone would have me telling them to just forget it, but the hesitation makes me more curious.

"It's hard to know where to start."

For someone so confident and self-assured, this vague hesitancy is intriguing to the point where if he doesn't start talking soon, I'm gonna sit him down and shine a bright light in his face.

"OK. Where in Ireland are you from?"

"A small town in *Northern* Ireland called Larne."

"Never heard of it," I reply quickly, aiming for humour but not reading the room very well.

"I would be surprised if you had. It's not far from Belfast. You've heard of Belfast?"

"Yeah, I think so. Wasn't there bombs and stuff there?"

"Hmm…yeah, there used to be. It's better now. Hopefully."

"So how did someone from a small town all the way over there, end up with a job like yours over here?"

"I started a business a few years back, once things started to calm down with terrorism and stuff. I noticed more film and TV productions wanting to use Northern Ireland, and I got in pretty early with location management."

"Location management? Like locations for where they film stuff you mean?"

"Yeah! It was just an idea at first, but when I saw that the government were offering great tax breaks and incentives for overseas productions, I grabbed the opportunity. When no one else was really doing it, it was as simple as sending letters out to production companies in the UK, US and Canada with links to a website I had made showcasing the range of locations we had. It's incredible how many different parts of the world you can mimic with the diversity of landscapes we have back home."

His enthusiasm already is infectious, and how excited and proud he seems telling me this makes me want to hear more.

"I would *love* to see it."

"So my company would be hired to manage all the things that a local person could do easier or better than someone unfamiliar with the place. Liaise and negotiate with site or land owners for fees, access, stuff like that, or get permits. I could also advise on locations which would suit certain scenes - that was the part I loved the most. Travelling with the production's own location team to identify sites for filming."

"Wow, that sounds incredible."

"Yeah, it was hectic though, especially when I expanded to include arrangements with other operators, like catering suppliers, logistics and transport. The money was great, but being away from home so much wasn't good when I was only married a couple of years.

Hang on!

"You were married?" I stop dead and face Tommy.

"Emmm…yeah. I still am I suppose." He looks at me with a frown, like he's surprised I didn't already know this.

How could I?

"OK….*that* I didn't know."

"I'm sorry. There never seemed a right time to just drop that into conversation. How's your steak? By the way, I'm still married." His follow up laugh is wary of the reaction he knows is likely.

"That's not funny," I fire back. "I would like to have known."

"I'm sorry. It's just that it's *so* over, that I honestly didn't think it was a major issue for us."

"How do you know it's not over? People get back together". We start to walk again, because stopping this long feels like we're having a row, and I don't want that. It's a lot to process though.

"Because I moved here to get as far away from her, and what she did to me, as physically possible."

"What did she do?"

"Cheated on me."

That was the answer I predicted, and it pulls me back to a place of empathy.

"I'm so sorry. I fucking hate when people do that."

"It happened to you too?"

"I think so…."

"I don't understand."

"I never caught him, my ex, but I'm pretty sure he was…on the regular."

Tommy doesn't reply, maybe keen to let me continue. He does however, take my hand again.

This has got heavy all of a sudden.

"A couple of years back, his friends even joked about it on a night out. How when they all went to Woodstock '99 and no-one's dick was dry the whole weekend."

"Fuckin' hell."

"At least you got away. I stuck around like an idiot, with my head buried in the sand"

"Well, you're away now, and I'm sure you're glad?"

"You have no idea! If I had stayed there, honestly one of us would be dead by now."

Tommy's silence is uncomfortable, but I'm not sure how I would respond to that either.

It's maybe better he doesn't know.

"So…you started this company and it's all going great. How did you end up working for Liam Fletcher?"

"Well, he was working on a film in Dublin, and I had a bit of a cross-border arrangement with a location company in the south. The cast and crew were having a wrap party, and I was invited. I had worked with Liam lots during the shoot. He was very hands on…in more ways that one, but we'll not get into that. Anyway, at the party I was telling him about…emmm… what happened to me, and he offered to let me stay at his place in LA to get some head space.

I told him if I came to LA, I probably wouldn't come back, so he jokingly told me he's hire me to replace the PA he just fired."

"And you landed the job from that?" I ask, not sure if it was believable, or not.

Tommy ignores the incredulity in my tone, though. "Yeah, pretty much. We'd both had plenty to drink but the joking turned into a serious offer. A week a later I was on a plane, and never looked back."

"Wow. Talk about landing on your feet."

"Well, it's not as easy a job as I thought it might be, but it's served me well enough so far." He gives me a playful nudge with that, just in case I missed the compliment.

"When did all this happen?"

"January/February just…"

"Fuck me. It must be pretty raw. The shit with your wife."

He laughs at the size of the understatement. "Yes, it has been, but being over here is so much like a fairy-tale, it's easy to forget my old life even had me in it. Does that make sense?"

"Tommy, that makes more sense to me than you know. Especially today."

We stop for a kiss on the corner of Cypress Street, opposite Harry's Bar, marking the new closeness our conversation has allowed. I instigated the kiss, using it as a way to convey my empathy, and appreciation of his honesty.

The music is pumping in the late evening air. Some Latin sounding house music. The bar looks so different after sunset, with it's neon rope lighting following the shape of the roof, making the building glow against the dark blue sky.

We cross the street, and once inside, find two stools at a small round tall table in the sports bar part we saw earlier. The bar is packed, and everyone seems a little more intoxicated than I expected for 9pm. I guess when you're semi-sober yourself, and just came from the complete opposite environment, it is a little jarring.

When Tommy comes back with our drinks, we chink but make no toast this time. Maybe it's too loud to be heard. Maybe toasting anything after our recent conversation would sound flippant. Ah well, we're in the right place now to loosen up.

"Check that out." Tommy points to large blackboard on the wall behind me.

'Karaoke tonight 9.30pm' is hand-written in coloured chalk, and it looks fresh.

"Fuck no!" I say as firmly as I can with a self-conscious laugh, spinning the stool back around. "I'm way too sober for that shit."

"That's easy fixed."

I raise one eyebrow and pull my head back just a little. "Are you trying to get me drunk, Mister Millar?"

"If it gets you to sing with me, then yeah…maybe," he replies cheekily. Sexy grin included this time.

"With you? Like a duet?"

"Oh yeah, I'm much too shy to go myself."

"Are you fuck," I say, suddenly aware that I swear more when I'm tipsy or drunk.

"Seriously! I can't sing a note."

"I'm no Celine Dion myself babe."

"You couldn't be worse than me. C'mon it'll be fun. I've never done karaoke."

"We're already a bit overdressed for this place, never mind standing up trying to sing to a bunch of strangers."

"In that dress and those shoes, they'll think you're a celebrity."

"Until they hear my voice!"

He just smiles at me, sensing I might crack, but not realising that inside I already think I would do *anything* this man wanted. I can't let that show, though.

"You're not going to charm me into it, stop it!" I can't prevent the smile inside me from reaching my face.

* * *

"First up we have a duet. Can we have Tommy & Gina…I'm going to assume that's fake names…to sing 'Living On A Prayer' by Bon Jovi.

There's a weak smattering of applause, and a few 'woo's'.

"You're a fucker!" I whisper to Tommy, after I slug back the remains of my cocktail and grab his hand.

"I know, but I'm *your* fucker," he grins back.

"Maybe not for long," I joke, poking him in the ribs, and finding out he's very ticklish. His contortion makes me snort. Maybe this will be fun after all.

We step up onto a tiny stage and turn to face the screen, as Tommy whispers in the compere's ear.

"Apparently they *are* actually called Tommy & Gina. Take it away guys!".

He hands the mic to me and I fire a 'what have you got me into' look Tommy's way before pulling him in closer to me.

I take the first line, timid at first, as I don't know how loud the mic is gonna be. I haven't sung on a mic since my high school drama production of Calamity Jane. A fucking calamity it was too!

By the end of the first line I'm fully into it, really milking the 'so tough' as best I can, hoping it'll inspire a similar effort from Tommy as I move the mic towards his mouth.

Now *this* I wasn't expecting. Not his singing talent. Truly awful, but at least he's belting it out. The emotional resonance of the lyrics hits me like a punch in the chest. Working for her man, and bringing home the pay.

Well, maybe not a punch as such. I've had one of those for real. But I feel it in the same place, hard. Thank goodness we duet the next part, to hide the momentary shake in my voice.

We're in full stride now, smiling and cheesily looking at each other like it's actually *our* song we're singing. Tonight we *are* Tommy & Gina!

In the pause before the chorus kicks in, Tommy shouts "Everybody!" and the sensation of half the people in the bar singing the chorus with us is the most euphoric rush I think I have ever felt.

We finish the song with more voices joining the chorus each time, and leave the stage to thunderous applause and whistles. Calamity Jane didn't get that reception, but then no one was drunk. This is an easy audience to please with a song like that.

"Holy crap, that was amazing!" Tommy gushes, his enthusiasm so cute despite his terrible singing.

"It really was! Good choice with the song."

"Well it *had* to be didn't it? What else would Tommy & Gina sing?"

"True!"

Thirty minutes pass with another drink each, listening to songs being hilariously murdered - everything from Dolly Parton to Alice Cooper, and I've laughed so much my abs hurt. We've planned to leave after this drink and are just about to go then when the compere comes back on the mic, asking for more singers.

"Come on folks, who's next?"

He's ignored for several seconds as the bar chatter gets louder again, then a girl off in the corner shouts, "Get Tommy & *Gina* up again". I spin around in surprise that anyone would want a repeat of our song, as fun as it was, but also the hint of an emphasis on my name. The corner is just lit enough to see a group of six in a booth, but I can't see faces.

Someone else from another part of the bar agrees with a drunken "Yeah!"

Tommy looks at me with 'shall we' eyes, and I just roll mine back. I'm not drunk, but firmly in that tipsy 'up for anything for a laugh' stage. He takes it as a yes, and bounds up to the stage like an excited puppy, followed by his only slightly more sensible owner.

"Same again, or something different?" the compere asks, looking relieved to have his best received act back on stage.

"What's the other Bon Jovi song with us in it? Tommy asks him, earnestly, and I can't help but laugh.

"You do realise it's not actually *us* in the song?"

"Tonight it is!" he replies, dramatically grabbing my shoulders like I've just got my big break.

Oh my god you're hilarious!

Our conversation is half-picked up by the compere's mic, and someone in the back shouts "It's My Life."

"Yes!" Tommy calls towards the voice, before turning back to me, seeing me unsure. He takes the mic, and turns towards the people in the bar.

"Guys, I don't think Gina is keen, even though in the song it says that Tommy & Gina never backed down." He looks at me as he finishes his sentence, slowing the last three words like a challenge, and I give him the same glare as earlier.

He smiles smugly, knowing he's got me.

Bastard!

"Go on *Gina*!" the female voice from the corner booth shouts again, with that weird emphasis on my name again. I peer over but the lighting from here is even worse.

Who the fuck is that?

I can feeling my anxiety rising.

The song starts. The bar sings along, and cheers on the 'Tommy & Gina never backed down' line when I belt it out in a duet with Tommy, before grabbing the back of his head and kissing him hard. It feels like the perfect time for a complete exit as we leave the stage to applause, weaving through the tables, pulling Tommy behind me.

We pick up an, "Awesome guys", two high fives and a, "Yes! I fucking *love* Bon Jovi!" by the time we're outside.

"That was such good fun! You're fucking mad though do you know that?" I wrap my arms around Tommy for warmth. There's not a taxi in sight.

"Aye, sure we're all a bit mad."

I'm not quite sure what that means, and let it go.

"I'll phone the hotel to pick us up. Will we go back inside to wait?"

I glance back inside, thinking of that girl in the corner who I couldn't see.

Who the fuck was that? I don't know anyone here.

"No, let's walk back down to the beach and they can meet us there."

"OK cool," Tommy smiles, and makes the call as we cross the street. We walk quietly, hand in hand, just like earlier, and I find myself wishing there was a way to slow down time and keep this day going a little longer.

"I can't believe I've to work tomorrow," I complain.

"I thought you loved doing the tours?"

"I do…but…"

"What's wrong?"

"Nothing. I just don't want this to end. I'm not ready to go back to reality just yet."

"We'll do this again though."

"Yeah?"

"Definitely! There's dozens more Bon Jovi songs to be sung."

He just gets a tight 'behave yourself' hand squeeze.

"Have you had a good time?" I ask, a little apprehensive, giving my anxiety a turn to speak.

"Are you kidding? I have had the best day!"

"Me too! I just wish Amy would reply. I had a few missed calls, which isn't like her, and she's not answering now."

"I'm sure she's fine. Didn't you say she was on a date?"

"Yeah she is. God knows where she is, and what she's doing. No doubt I'll get a drunken message in the middle of night."

After the over-dressed karaoke experience, being back in the resort Mercedes feels more befitting this outfit. I'm assuming I get to keep the dress and the shoes, but I'm scared to ask. To be honest, I wouldn't care if I had to give them back. It's been fun to feel like a princess for one night at least, and I need to keep my expectations low.

The car is toasty warm, and Tommy's shoulder makes a comfy pillow for the short ride back. I always get sleepy after a few drinks. Definitely a cheap date. I'm a dinner, drinks and bed for ten kinda girl.

I'm pretty sure that's how I did so well in college, aceing my degree in education. Meeting Brandon changed everything though. We moving in together too quickly, and I had to take a job at Walmart to pay the bills, instead of enrolling in the state required teacher education programme.

The things you do for love.

My dream was shelved for a man who didn't deserve it, and until I fully qualify, I think it will always eat at me. I'm not even sure what the post graduate requirements are in California.

Back in the hotel, the lobby bar is busy, but looks relaxed. No karaoke in a place like this. We bypass the bar with neither of us suggesting a nightcap, and head straight to the elevators. Our fingers are interwoven, as they have been at every opportunity.

It strikes me that I've never felt so loved by a man. Which is stupid I know, as it's only our second date.

Maybe not stupid, rather just a little sad…

Tommy beeps the door, then pushes it open with an outstretched arm for me to enter first.

"Why thank you sir."

"M'lady," he replies with a deferential nod.

"Stop being so sexy!" I flirt as I pass, letting my hand drift across his chest. Entering the room now feels completely different to earlier. The alcohol, and growing connection between us has changed the atmosphere.

The door clicks behind me as I enter the main part of the suite and freeze with surprise. Almost every surface has candles flickering in little jars. There must be at least fifty of them, perfectly illuminating the room in the most romantic way possible. Music plays softly. I recognise it immediately from the movie 'Serendipity'. Moonlight Kiss.

I love this song.

I'm aware I'm holding my breath, trying to take it all in, when I feel Tommy's hands around my waist from behind.

"What is this for?" I barely whisper, feeling a swell of emotion that's almost overwhelming.

"It's for you," he whispers back.

I lay my hands on his arms at my waist, take and hold a deep breath as my eyes well up to spilling point. I'm still taking it all in, struggling with all the questions in my brain, pushing for attention.

Is this really for me?

How did he do this?

Why me?

"This is…I'm honestly speechless"

He lets go of my waist as he asks, "Would you like a drink for the hot tub?"

My eyes immediately dart to the balcony, decorated with what looks like a canopy above the tub, glowing with hundreds of little fairy lights. The steam is rising from the water, and it creates a mystical glow around the balcony.

Oh my goodness.

What IS this?

"Did you bring a bikini? I forgot to say, I'm sorry."
"Ummm…no, I didn't think."

Fuck!

"Shit, sorry…OK. We don't have to use the tub."
"No no it's OK. Can you give me two minutes?"

"Sure!" he smiles, pouring what looks like Prosecco into two tall, narrow glasses.

"Tommy, this is incredible. I'm a bit stunned here. I didn't expect this."

"I hope not, because I wanted it to be a surprise."

"Well you nailed that for sure….but you don't need to do this for me." I walk towards him, suddenly aware that I've been frozen to the spot for a couple of minutes.

"I know that, but I just wanted to make it nice. You deserve to feel special. Because..umm…you are!"

His shift from romantic hero to awkward teenager in one sentence almost makes my heart burst with admiration…and relief that he is, in actual fact, maybe normal. I grab his face with both hands and kiss him slowly with the tenderness this amazing man deserves.

"Thank you. Thank you so much!"

"That's OK," he replies softly, for the first time looking a little embarrassed himself.

"You're the cutest. Will you wait for me in the hot tub?"

"Absa-fuckin-lutely!"

I'm still laughing at this when I reach my bedroom, and go straight to my phone on the night stand.

Fuck sake Amy.

No calls. No texts.

I call her, but it goes straight to voicemail again. It's so frustrating not being able to share this with her, after everything she's done to build my confidence back up.

I take a last look in the mirror, before delicately slipping out of the Manolo's, and unzip the most beautiful dress I've ever worn. My heart is racing.

If I'm going into the hot-tub it's either naked or in my underwear, so it's a no-brainer. The dressing room lighting is great for trying on clothes, but it's very unforgiving when I'm standing here in my bra and panties.

Thank goodness it's dark out there

I reassure my anxiety as I adjust my boobs for the best mix of, 'well hello there, but don't touch me.'

A deep breath, a quick check of my phone again.

Here we go.

Tommy is in the tub, as expected, with his back to the partially open sliding door. His arms and shoulders look so good from behind, and I pause inside to take it in. It gives me more time to gather up some confidence.

I squeeze through the gap as quietly as I can, even though it's inevitable he'll see me in my underwear.

Just own it girl.

It's hard to climb into a hot tub and look sexy. I realise this after I throw one leg over, misjudging the depth, and now straddling the thick rim with much less class than I was going for.

"Fuck sake!" I mutter out loud, unintentionally.

"There's steps round the other side," Tommy points out, smirking.

"Oh yeah, tell me that *now* why don't you?" trying to suck in, while semi-stuck.

"Do you need some help?"

"Either that or you watch me dry hump the edge for a bit?"

Tommy is laughing as he stands up from the bubbles, confident as usual, wearing the same boxers as before. When wet they cling tight to his body, and I can't stop my eyes from pausing on them.

"Hey girlfriend. My eyes are up here," he laughs, still holding my hand.

"Didn't you bring swim shorts?" I ask, trying to justify the look.

"Yup!"

"Why are you in your boxers then?"

"Didn't think it would be fair if you were in your underwear and I wasn't"

"Aw that's sweet! It's a good job I didn't come out naked, eh?"

Tommy's eyebrows lift, and his eyes drop to my cleavage as I finally get my other leg over.

"Hey girlfriend. The eyes are up here."

He grins, then lifts his eyes, giving me a firm look that makes me tingle from the feet up.

How does he do that?

"Sorry, I couldn't resist. You look incredible."

Right now we're both standing up, very close to each other, in our underwear. He's still holding my hand. The twinkly lights are above us. The hot water bubbles around our thighs and the pacific ocean is crashing against the cliffs below our balcony.

It's the perfect moment for a kiss, but we just stand there, too scared to make the first move. We're not moving, but it still feels like the space between us is becoming smaller.

"This feels dangerous," I whisper, not intending it to sound as seductive as it did.

Tommy's expression flickers confusion, looking down briefly.

"The water is only a few feet deep," he whispers back, mimicking my sexy delivery.

A split second of confusion follows before I land on his wavelength, narrowing my eyes. Mostly because I know he just got me good.

"I mean us standing here in our underwear, you asshole," I laugh, letting go of his hand and giving him a playful nudge. It immediately puts him off balance and he lands on his ass with a big splash.

"Oh fuck!" I shout, surprised, but he's already laughing.

He allows me no more than two seconds standing there with my hands on my hips, before reaching to grab me my hand to pull me in too. I pull my hand away quickly with a, "Uh Uh. Behave yourself!"

I feel emboldened now, standing over him in my underwear. Like some sort of dominatrix.

This is very sexy.

I let him take me in with his eyes for several seconds more before slowly stepping my feet either side of his and squatting down slowly into his lap, letting my hands loosely take the back of his neck.

Now this really *is* dangerous…

21
TOMMY

The music merges with my dream for a moment, before I stir and realise it's real, stretching and focusing on where I am. I'd forgotten to close the curtains last night, so my room is lit orange from the morning sun. It's a lovely way to wake up, but it takes my eyes a few tries to open fully.

When they do, the digital clock beside me tells me it's 7.07am.

What is that noise?

Is Gina up already, and playing music?

Reserving the right to be a little annoyed, I slip out of bed and head out to the living area.

I can hear Gina singing along before I see her, and when I do, any feelings of being rudely awakened disappear with the sight of a very cute butt in pyjama shorts, doing little side-to-side movements in time with the beat. She's at the range cooker, so engrossed in the music and the cooking that she hasn't heard me coming.

It's impossible not to lean on the door frame and just watch.

"I feel like bustin' loose" she sings, just she turns to see me.

"Hey sleepy head," she calls, a little louder than needed, beaming.

"Hey yourself," I reply, pushing off the woodwork and walking towards her.

She closes the gap with an excited, and so adorable bounce in her step, throwing her arms around me and landing with a kiss, a "Good morning," and a cheeky squeeze of my left butt cheek.

"Oooh, cute butt!" she winks, before spinning back towards the kitchenette.

"You took the words right out of my mouth."

Gina glances over her shoulder to show me a smile, as she lifts and shakes a large frying pan. It's hard not to stare at how damn sexy those shorts are, especially when she sticks her ass out to tease me.

The memory of holding it last night when she sat in my lap comes back to me, triggering a little movement in my own shorts.

That was so fucking sexy, but torture too!

We kissed in that position in the hot-tub for a good ten minutes, before forcing ourselves apart. We were both as bad as each other. Gina was grinding into me, her pelvic bone rubbing against me so hard that it actually hurt. I had naughtily slipped my hands under her panties to grip her bare ass to encourage it too, despite the throbbing pain.

There's no doubt that if not for my boxers, I would have ended up deep inside her, rule or no rule.

It's a very strange thing as an adult to want something so bad, and know the other does too, yet still not do it. Gina had pulled away first, a few seconds after she started grinding a little harder, moaning a little louder, and gripping me a little tighter. I wouldn't be surprised if there were still imprints of her nails on my skin.

"Oh my *god!*" she shouted, as she pulled away. Anger, frustration and pure and simple horniness all combining. "I could *fuck* you so hard right now!" she said, eyeing me like I was prey.

"That almost sounds like a threat," I replied, throbbing at the thought of just going for it. I couldn't be so hard and stay in those tight shorts for much longer. I'm pretty sure Gina knew it too.

She had pulled back to the opposite side of the tub, like a boxer going back to his corner to recover, letting her head fall back and exhaling slowly towards the clear night sky above us.

"If we had kept going there, you would have me me cum," she said quietly, a hint of shame creeping into her voice.

"*I* would have made you cum? I think you were fully in charge, babe."

All she said was "Hmm," staring at me again, but not giving away anything more, Just a concerned frown.

We managed to keep our distance long enough for libidos to dim, finish our drinks, and enjoy the stars. The night had finished with a long luxurious hug in the hallway, halfway between our bedroom doors. and me setting my alarm for 7.30am to make her breakfast.

"Can I help?" I ask, predicting the answer, as I jump up onto one of the breakfast bar stools.

"No, I got this. I assume it's OK to be using what was in the fridge?" she inquires, turning the music down slightly.

"Umm…yeah, of course," I laugh. Her naivety is so adorable.

"How do you like your eggs?"

"Scrambled, but if you're making yours another way, I'll go with whatever"

"Scrambled it is"! She's already cracking the first one into a glass measuring jug, cursing as half the shell falls in too.

"What time do you need to be back?" I ask, remembering that she has a tour today.

"I wish I didn't have to go back, but my first tour is at 1pm. Does that give us enough time?"

"Oh yeah, as long as we're away before ten. Could no one cover for you today? We could head up towards Big Sur and make a day of it?"

"I would *so* love that, but I skipped out on a couple of tours the other week, so I've used up all my favours," Gina replies, turning the bacon in the grill.

"Aw OK. We could do this again though, and get longer next time? Some weekend you're off?"

"Are you fucking kidding me? Yes! I've had such a good time, it's gonna be real hard to go back to reality."

"Have you heard from Amy?"

"No," she replies flatly, unimpressed. "She better have a damn good reason for not calling me back. She must be at his place, because she didn't even pick up on the house phone this morning. She can be so reckless and unaware when she's partying or, with a guy."

"I'm sure she's grand. Maybe she's making him breakfast too?"

"Oh I doubt that *very* much. Amy's culinary skills usually involve opening a box that someone has just delivered to the door."

* * *

We enjoy breakfast out on the patio. The sunrise is behind us, so it's cool enough in the shade for us both to need a hoodie. The sunlight glistening off the water out to sea is too pretty a view to not take advantage of, and we eat quietly enjoying the early morning calm.

The morning you leave a hotel is always more bittersweet when you've had a special time, so we're both a little subdued as we wash and dry the breakfast dishes. What hasn't helped is me reminding Gina that I've to go away with Liam on Wednesday. He's producing a movie that's shooting in Europe.

"Oh yes," she says quietly. "I couldn't remember when it was though. Do you know where you're going yet?"

"Ireland first"

She's quiet for a few seconds. "Where your wife lives?"

"Not quite. I'll be no closer than a couple of hundred miles, you can be sure of that."

"Do you know how long you'll be away?" She's trying unsuccessfully to sound chipper.

"Honestly, no idea. It just depends how things go, and how quickly everyone can make Liam happy."

"Are you talking days…or weeks?"

"Definitely weeks. We've to sort things in Ireland, Hungary *and* Switzerland. We might fly back home though between locations. I'm so sorry, I'm not sure."

"Don't apologise. I was OK before…but now I think that I'm gonna miss you more. Does that sound dumb?"

"Hell no, I feel the same. The timing feels really bad. I'll make it up to you when I get back."

"You don't owe me a thing," she says, shaking her head before hugging me tight, like it's goodbye already.

It takes only half an hour or so for us both to shower and pack. Joking about saving time by just showering together has helped lighten the mood.

Gina has no idea how much I'm looking forward to *that* experience.

The journey back down to Venice passes quickly between the music, the chat about our favourite movies, and the hour nap Gina fits in. It feels like a privilege to let her sleep, like she trusts me and is content enough in my company. That's what I tell myself anyway. The late night, and the alcohol has nothing to do with it of course.

The softness in her perfect face while she sleeps is incredibly beautiful.

The quote, 'If you love someone, let them sleep' comes to mind, and I have a momentary tussle in my mind about keeping the L word in there. She sure is somebody I *could* love.

Very easily, if I were to allow myself.

It's almost 12.40pm, when I reverse into an empty spot in the car park, about 200 yards from where Gina's tour begins. It's visible from here, near the bar where our first date began. The memories of that night make me smile, though it strikes me as weird how, in such a short space of time, I know her so well. To that point already where you feel low level chest pain just parting. She hasn't even left the car yet, and I can already feel it.

This was not part of the plan…

How am I going to feel on Wednesday getting on a plane?

I kill the engine, and the sudden quietness stirs Gina from her snooze, smiling blissfully as she stretches her arms upwards. She leans across towards me, resting her head on my shoulder, and a hand on my leg.

"Thank you for letting me sleep," she mutters sleepily. "I'm sorry. I hope I didn't drool on your seat."

"Well you know what they say?" This is out of my mouth before the rational part of my brain can intervene.

"What do they say?" she asks, in the sexiest sleepy voice I've ever heard.

I hide the panic in my brain with an, "Ummm…" before she playfully pokes me in the ribs to prompt a reply.

"Nothing at all…"

"What are you talking about?" she laughs softly, obviously completely unaware of what I'm talking about. If she knew she wouldn't be asking.

"Ah it's just a saying," I reply, hoping she'll let it go. No such luck.

"What is it then?"

"If you love someone, let them sleep," I offer, sheepishly.

You actually said that out loud, you dick.

I know it's not possible to hear someone's eyes open quickly, but I'd swear I heard hers. She takes a few seconds before replying. "Yes, I agree"

I think I can hear her smiling now too, as she sinks into me a little more.

What does that mean?

"I knew you'd fall in love with me, just not so fast." She says this so sincerely. It's not fair that I can't see her face.

Now I'm silent, bewildered as to how to reply.

"Have you bought me a ring yet?" she asks, changing tone just enough for me to hear her struggle to say it in full without cracking up.

"You're fucking with me! I knew it!" I laugh, returning the poke in the ribs. She squirms as she lets out a squeal, startling a passer by walking their dog along the beach path.

"You're good for it," she winks, recovering and reaching into the foot-well to grab one converse shoe at a time. "Just don't be going and giving your love to anyone else, 'cos I think I'm gonna keep you."

The shoes are on and she twists to face me.

"Is that OK?" she asks firmly.

"Don't fall in love with anyone else. Got it."

"Good boy," she smiles, and gives me a triumphant nod.

Cheeky. I love it.

"Now kiss me like you're mine, and then let me go work."

The kiss lasts a good ten seconds, upping the ante on the passion for us both. Our goodbye kisses are already different. I'd never in my life felt words and feelings come in a kiss, until that one.

She pulls back with a happy sigh, then grabs her bag from the back, unzipping it on her lap.

"It's good thing I brought this just in case," she says, pulling her little tour backpack out.

"What about your other bag?"

"Ah, I was just gonna see if they'd keep it for me in the bar."

"Why not just leave it here?"

"Cos I'll need it later when I finish, and I have to show Amy the shoes."

"OK, sure I can drop it down to you? I think I'll probably have missed you enough by then, so you could actually be doing *me* a favour."

"Ooh, you're such a charmer. Stop being so good at. It makes me nervous…"

"What time do you…oh here hang on, have you got food?"

"I'll grab something at home between tours. I'll have about an hour, so I can nip home…I can kick the crap out of Amy while I'm there."

"You *still* haven't heard from her?"

"Not yet," Gina frowns, looking more worried upon hearing my concern.

"OK if I leave the bag, you promise you won't be trying on my underwear, or anything weird like that?"

"I'd rather be taking your knickers off than be putting them on," I reply, feeling a little rush of blood at how bold I am.

Gina leans in, kisses me on the lips, and whispers, "I can't wait…but we will," and follows it with an ironic giggle. "OK, I'll call you when I'm done then? What are you doing now?"

"Yup, no worries. I dunno, I might take a walk, and grab something to eat."

"Lucky you! Right, I'd better go. See you soon Tommy Millar." A playful wink and she's off, cutting diagonally across the beach towards the bar. I watch her the whole way, in admiration, replaying the last 24 hours with a warm glow.

When she reaches the group gathered on the boardwalk, I throw our bags in the boot, and start the walk up the pathway. I don't want to be there when she's trying to start the tour, so scan the frontage for a food place, spotting a burrito bar just far enough away.

22
SUNDAY, JUNE 16TH 2002
GINA

One last check of my phone, before I hide it away for the tour.

Still nothing.

This is niggling me now, brewing resentment, because I should be feeling but giddy and excited after the most incredible time away.

Talk about sweeping a girl off her feet!

I cannot wait to tell Amy all about it, but she's getting a telling off first.

There looks to be at least 25 on the group today. I have no roster to check off the names, thanks to falling asleep and not letting Tommy know we should have called by the office to collect it. It'll be OK. It's not unusual for one or two to follow the tour when they haven't booked. Those are usually the ones who tip the most.

It's another beautiful day. I love my tours, but it hurt to leave Tommy. I could have happily spent the rest of the day with him. Hopefully the tips will be good today - I'm certainly in good spirits so it should be a fun one.

I hop up onto the low wall which separates us from the beach, just to help make me a focal point for the gathering. 5 foot 2 isn't very commanding in a large group, when it's as loud as it is here.

"OK lovely people who are here for the 1pm tour, good afternoon!" My acting classes come in useful for projecting my voice. The ones who haven't already noticed me turn on my voice, and they edge closer slowly, like zombies.

"My name is Gina, and I'll be your guide for the next two hours."

"Bullshit!" a voice shouts, from the back of the group. "What's your name again?" he calls.

Fuck! No!

The solid parts of my knees suddenly feel like liquid, unable to hold me up. I know that voice. The feeling comes too quickly, like an anxiety attack that fast forwarded to level 10, and my lungs cease functioning out of sheer panic. Neither fight or flight would be possible right now, despite the surge of adrenaline that follows - like someone has just filled a syringe and injected it right into my heart.

The people between me and the voice part instinctively, as you would, and he takes a step forward. Any thin shred of hope I was mistaken is gone.

Brandon Davis is standing right there, in my world again, no more than 12 feet away.

"Hello Beth," he says with a casual smirk. "Where the fuck have you been then?" This time there's a menace that I'm all too familiar with. All I can do is stare. I can't process this.

This can't be real.

"Answer me, you fucking cunt," he demands, louder now and taking another step forward. Everything falls silent, except for his voice and the ringing in my ears. It feels like I'm trapped in a tunnel with Brandon blocking the only way out.

The silence is broken before his next step. A woman's voice to my right, angry. "Don't speak to her like that!"

"How about you shut the fuck up, and mind your own business?" Brandon says, his voice getting louder to become a full shout. He hasn't taken his eyes off mine for a second. The empty, angry space between us becomes blocked by an older man with his back to me, a few feet from Brandon.

"Hey buddy, I don't know what's going on here, but you've no right to speak to people like that," he says, in a New York accent.

I don't even see the punch. I assume the man in the white t-shirt didn't either. The sound though. I heard that. New York itself probably heard Brandon's fist connect with the man's nose. The noise of the crack pushes another panic button inside me.

I've been on the receiving end of that fist more than once.

The man falls backwards and crumbles to the ground, the back of his head hitting the wall between my feet, with a sickening thud. There's a few screams from my periphery. Brandon drops his eyes to his victim, letting a smug grin appear, before returning his gaze to my terrified face.

I want to look to see if the man is alright, but if I disengage Brandon he'll be on me in a flash.

The movement to my right catches the corner of my eye a split second before it happens. Someone tackles Brandon at full speed from the side, sending them both sliding six feet across the ground, with Brandon underneath. The crowd parts as they fall, and my world narrows to something I never imagined I would see.

Tommy! No!

Tommy is on top, straddling him, with one of Brandon's arms trapped under his body. His other arm is flailing as he wriggles to try to get free. He's on his side, and glaring at me.

Zero fear. Just pure rage.

"Gina are you OK?" Tommy calls, struggling to keep Brandon on the ground, but I'm incapable of any words.

"Gina!? he shouts. The frustration in his voice rising.

"Her name isn't Gina, you prick!"

Oh fuck.

Tommy doesn't reply to this.

"If I let you up, are you gonna calm the fuck down?"

"*When* I get up, I'm gonna take your fucking head off."

"I'll take that as a no then."

Brandon manages to get one knee bent enough to grip the ground with his boot. He pushes, straining, red faced, but only manages to turn onto his back. Tommy takes the opportunity to pin both his arms down, and the two are now face to face for the first time.

I'm still frozen to the spot, on the wall, with limited ability to take in anything else other than Tommy and Brandon.

The poor man on the ground below me has regained consciousness. I think there's a lot of blood. There's crying, and I hear someone mention the police, but it's all an out of focus blur right now.

Brandon spits into Tommy face, and the shock of it brings a sharp involuntary breath, and a rage from deep within that I didn't expect. I'm off the wall before rational thought kicks in. Three strides forward, zero plan, just years of bottled up fury at someone who's finally in a vulnerable position.

Today the tables are turning.

Two arms grab me from behind and pull me backwards. I'm on one foot - the other raised, ready to either kick or stomp. Whatever comes bio-mechanically easiest will do. My loose leg kicks out anyway as I'm pulled away, like the rage needs an outlet now, regardless.

The air between Brandon and I will have to do for now.

My brave but stupid manoeuvre shocks Tommy too, distracting him enough for Brandon to grab his opportunity. He bucks his hips up, lifting Tommy just enough to release his arms, and deliver a sharp right hook. He's on the ground so can't get much power, but it knocks Tommy off balance enough that he's able to push him off completely.

The two men scramble to their feet at the same time, facing each other, several feet apart. I feel vulnerable again, not knowing if he will go for me or for Tommy.

Brandon charges forward suddenly, looking for the element of surprise, but Tommy is ready. He times his own right hook perfectly, landing it flush on Brandon's jaw, sending him stumbling off balance, almost falling.

"Hit him again," I hear.

It's my own voice, seething, and I'm shocked those words came out of my mouth, like I'm no longer in control.

Brandon hears me. His head turns, and in an instant looks from me to Tommy, and back to me, joining the dots.

There are sirens now, very close, and someone nearby shouts, "Over here!"

He pretends to go for me, jerking his body forwards aggressively, faced twisted with fury, and a little smug satisfaction that he's just dropped a bomb into my new life.

"This isn't over! Say hi to your friend!" he smirks, before he takes off, running the opposite direction to the police. I watch him weaving through the crowd, until he disappears.

I wriggle free of the woman holding me and rush to Tommy, throwing myself into him with such force that he almost loses balance. I'm gripping him so tight when the tears start, and my whole body begins to shake uncontrollably.

"It's OK, he's gone," he reassures me, rubbing my back with one hand, and the other protectively cradling my head.

The ambulance crew arrive behind the police, tending to the man on the ground. I take one look at the state of his face, and almost vomit with shock. The last time face I saw after a punch from Brandon was my own, in my own mirror.

That was only six months ago, and up until now, it felt like it was someone else's life.

Someone that I used to know.

* * *

Tommy

The police want a statement, but I tell them they need to give Gina some time, or let her come to the station later.

"She's too upset! Can't you see that?"

The police are so used to seeing scenes like this, or worse, that it must be difficult to not become hardened by it, and forget that normal people need more time to process it.

"Ma'am, do you know the man who committed the assault?"

"I think it's her ex-boyfriend. He's from Las Vegas. Can you ask her these questions later please?"

"If you can come to the station as soon as possible then. What's your name and address?"

Gina manages to take a breath and compose herself enough to answer.

"Gina Sawyer. 1720 Pacific Avenue."

The officer looks up quickly from his notebook before writing anything.

"1720 Pacific?"

Gina nods, closing her eyes again as she rests her head against my chest.

The officer calls to his partner, who is standing with the ambulance crew as they assess the injured man.

"Hey Miguel, what was the address of the domestic last night on Pacific?"

Miguel pulls his notebook out, flicking a few pages. "1720."

"Wait! That's my address! What domestic?" Gina asks urgently, panic in her eyes, as she lifts her head.

"Ma'am do you have anyone else who lives with you?"

"Yes! My friend Amy. Is she OK?" the panic now making her voice waver.

Oh fuck, that's why she hasn't heard from Amy.

"I'm not sure, but she was the victim of an assault at that address last night. I believe she's still in hospital."

Gina is already crumbling mid-way through the delivery of this bombshell. It's like someone pulled the life out of her body in one swift motion. I've never seen that reaction of shock in my life.

I'm holding her up, but she's shaking, and muttering, "Oh my god, Oh my god, it was him, I knew it," before the tears take over. Everything else she tries to say is incomprehensible now.

I manage to get her seated on the same wall she stood on a short time ago, just as her panic attack escalates into hyperventilation. A female medic around our age brings a paper bag for Gina to breath into, and does a great job talking her down. I feel so helpless, and more than a little shaken myself. The flip side of the sudden adrenaline dump is disorientating.

What the fuck is going on?

The police are extra interested now, and the chances of letting this pass until later have been dismissed. They allow the medic to do her job before questioning Gina again.

"Ma'am, I know this is a difficult time, but we don't have anyone in custody for the assault on your friend. Do you think the man today could be responsible?"

"I don't know. Maybe, but he doesn't know where I live."

"Is there anyone else who would have reason to harm your friend?"

"No!" She shakes her head.

"Ma'am, where were you last night between the hours of 6pm and 8pm?"

"Are you fucking kidding me?" I protest, not hiding my anger. "You think she attacked her own friend?"

"Sir, I'm just establishing the facts. It's a standard question as part of any investigation."

"Well, she was with me in Pismo Beach, and her friend wasn't answering her phone."

"And you name sir?"

"Thomas Millar."

"Address?"

"For fuck sake, shouldn't you be going after that psycho, instead of asking us all these questions?"

"Your address please. We've got units looking for him now."

"1525 San Vincente Boulevard, Santa Monica"

He makes a face that lets me know he's impressed, and it signals a nonchalance that makes my blood boil.

"Ma'am do you have identification?"

Gina nods. Her backpack is within reach, resting against the wall this entire time. She unzips a small internal pocket, then pauses.

"Ma'am?"

"Look, I'm very upset by all this. Can I go and see if my friend is OK, and just come to the station later?"

"That's fine ma'am, but if you could just show me your identification please?" His change in tone now, makes it clear that it's no longer negotiable.

Gina sighs, not moving.

"Gina, what's up? Just let him see it, then I can take you to the hospital."

She doesn't reply. She just looks up at me with a look that feels out of place, before handing her driver's licence to the officer, and then drops her chin to her chest.

"Ma'am, this is your photograph, but a different name and address."

Hang on, what?

"I moved here from Las Vegas." she replies sharply.

"You gave your name as Gina Sawyer, but this licence says your name is Elisabeth Sawyer. Could you explain that please?"

The lump in my throat comes from nowhere, all of a sudden, making it hard to even ask.

"Gina….?"

23
TOMMY

The clock in my car says 1.40pm when I help Gina into the passenger seat, reaching across her as she sobs, and clicking her seat-belt into place.

How can so much have happened in such a short time?

An hour ago we were just here, high on life and shining with joy.

I've been here before. A different place and a different person, but the same sensation of having the rug pulled from under my feet.

It should have hurt more last time, but now comparing it, this feels more unsettling. Back then I knew deep down, but with Gina it feels like I've landed on my ass from a greater height.

How can her name not be Gina?

Who is this person I just took a punch for?

I knew it was too soon to let myself get close to someone!

All these questions flood my mind, but still I'm compelled to protect her in the meantime. Regardless of her name, what we shared this last 24 hours was real. My heart knows this, and I'm happy to let it rule my head for the time being.

I put the top up on the car, hoping it will give her a greater sense of protection, and start the engine.

"It's gonna be OK." I pause, before adding, "Gina."

Right now she looks like she wants the seat to suck her in. Her hands cover her face when I say her name, and the sobs become quiet. Only her rhythmic chest movements give it away.

Ten minutes ago I was so angry at the police officer persisting with questions, when she was clearly not coping. Now I want to question her myself.

"I'm so sorry," she manages, aware enough of the situation. "Can you take me to the hospital please?" Her hands still cover any expression. It feels almost child-like. If I can't see you, you can't see me. There's a swell of pain in my chest as this thought passes through my head, tangled up with all my own selfish emotions.

She's not Cheryl. Just wait and see what this is about.

"Yes, of course, it's not far."

I don't know what else to say. I don't know if Amy is OK, which makes me scared to offer any reassurance. So we drive in silence, with Gina gradually becoming visibly more anxious and twitchy as we get closer to Cedars Sinai Hospital in Marina Del Rey.

The journey is only ten minutes thanks to light weekend traffic.

The emergency department entrance on Mindanao Way has valet parking outside, which confuses me greatly. Not only is this unheard of back home, but hospital parking in Belfast usually involves long queues for too few spaces, and at a cost.

Only in America

Gina takes my hand as we enter the building, and I let her, choosing to ignore the newborn voice in my head calling me a mug. She's never initiated that before.

Then again, I probably haven't given her the chance to before now. I feel my face redden with shame for not taking her hand, probably when she needs it most.

But I'm struggling.

Back home, we'd have been given directions and sent on our way, but in the land where customer service is king, we're escorted to the private room they've moved Amy into. A nurse emerges from the station in the wider part of the corridor to meet us, like she knew we were coming already.

Gina is first through the door, and rushes to Amy's bedside, already crying. The girls embrace, hard, until Amy's wincing forces a release. I linger close to the door, feeling even more like an outsider now, after the name revelation.

Is Amy's name even Amy?

She's still calling Elisabeth Gina, so either she doesn't know, or she's just playing along for my benefit.

Should I leave them alone?

The bruises on Amy's face tell only part of the story. A broken nose and severe bruising around the ribs. From her top lip to her forehead is a kaleidoscope of colours, and she doesn't even look like the same girl I saw in Sal's last weekend. A faint red ring circles her neck, with what must be finger marks.

I can't believe that animal did that to her. Actually, I can.

"I'm so sorry for not being there," Gina begs, holding Amy's hand between both of hers as she perches on the bedside.

"Don't be stupid, Gina. If you had been there, he might have hurt you more."

She doesn't have to say out loud, that it was Gina he was looking for. The thought of her trapped indoors with him makes me shudder. I feel some guilt at being grateful Amy took a beating for her. This will for sure, be a test of their friendship.

"How did he find me?" Gina asks, the tears betraying the calm front she's trying to maintain for Amy.

"I have no idea, but he knows where you work as well."

"I know. He turned up today."

"What?" Amy demands, sitting up a little more in panic.

"It's OK. Well it's not OK, but I'm OK."

"What happened?"

"He just appeared out of nowhere when I was starting the tour."

"Oh fuck."

"Someone challenged them, and he hit them, then Tommy tackled him."

Amy's eyes flick to me, scanning for any visible injuries.

"They got him then?"

"No, he got away before the police arrived."

"The fucker!"

"Tommy got him a good crack on the jaw first, though."

They both look at me now. Amy with disbelief, and Gina with admiration.

"They got a good description of him, so hopefully he'll get picked up soon," I offer, taking the opportunity to approach.

"Sit down," Amy says, nodding at the armchair on the other side of the bed. "I'm so, so glad you were there." She reaches out and takes my hand as I reach the bedside.

"I've been worried sick that he was going to be waiting inside the house when you guys got back. He took my phone, and it has all my numbers in it, so I couldn't even contact anyone."

"I did wonder why I couldn't get you, but I never thought this would happen. I'm *so* sorry Amy!"

"Listen, I'll be fine. You just keep yourself safe." Amy turns to me. "Promise me you'll help keep her safe." It's not even a question. It's an order.

"I promise."

I make eye contact with Gina across the bed. I can see the appreciation in her eyes, but the rest of her face is letting me know she owes me an explanation.

Damn right you do.

"How long are you going to be here?" Gina asks, softly, stroking Amy's arm.

"Hopefully out today. There's not a lot they can do. I may as well be at home."

Gina looks towards me with alarm, then back to Amy.

"Amy, you can't go back to that house. *We* can't go back to that house while he's still out there!"

There's silence for several seconds while they consider this, before Amy sighs.

"We can get a hotel or something in the meantime. I doubt we reach the threshold for the witness protection programme."

Gina and I both frown at her ill-timed attempt at humour.

"I'd rather you guys weren't on your own. Not in Venice anyway."

"I don't have the money for a hotel," Gina whispers.

"Don't worry about money, for fuck sake!" Amy replies sharply.

"Listen, I need to make a call, but I'll be right outside in the corridor, OK?

* * *

Gina

"Did he really hit him?" Amy asks, once the door closes.

"Almost knocked him down," I reply, not sure if I should be proud of that fact. Any sort of violence repulses me, but this was different.

"Brilliant! The fucker deserves a few more."

I just nod, silently, my brain already occupied on what we do next.

For a few moments, we argue about the money aspect of getting a hotel, especially not knowing how long it's going to be.

When Tommy re-enters the room, he's slipping his phone into his pocket, and has a hardened look of defiance on his face.

"What's wrong?" I ask, my heart rate accelerating quickly, still on high alert.

"No, nothing, I just have a plan."

"What plan?"

"Stay with *me*. You can both stay with me. At Liam's. I just called him and explained what happened."

"Hold up. You want us to come stay with you?" Amy laughs, not believing her ears. "Why?"

"Because it'll be safer than a hotel. It's secure, and I can keep an eye on you both."

"Wow," Amy mutters. "You've only know this guy a week, Gina."

I look to Tommy, scanning his face for clues to sooth my own guilt. I know well enough already that I would trust him with my life.

"Are you sure?"

"Gina! Fuck sake wise up! Tommy, that's a lovely offer and you've done a great job today tackling that fucker, but we can't stay in a stranger's house."

"Amy. He's not a stranger." I say it as softly, but as firmly as possible, just the way the police officer did.

"Well, fuck me, whatever happened between you guys since yesterday must've been something special for you to even *consider* this. Have you lost your mind?"

"I trust him," I reply simply, but I'm afraid to meet his eyes when that word leaves my mouth.

Hold on a minute.

All the comfort that Tommy's offer has brought vanishes when I remember his travel plans, and he sees it in my face before the words come out.

"Tommy, you're going to Ireland on Wednesday."

"Yes, that's a problem I know, but…"

"But nothing! We may as well stay in a hotel if you're not even gonna be there."

"I know that, so why don't you come with me?" He visibly swallows hard.

"To Ireland?" Amy jumps in, my shocked silence giving her an opening to shut this down.

I look at Amy, silently, and she can see I find the idea appealing.

Why wouldn't I?

"You're not *actually* considering this as well?" Amy pleads, exasperated.

Why does she not understand?

"Is there any way Amy could come too?" I ask Tommy, standing up to face him.

His eyes jump to Amy, just as she says "What? You want me to come to Ireland as well? What planet are you two living on?"

I ignore her for now. "Is there a way?" I ask Tommy, with an urgency in my voice now.

He shrugs at first, and I can almost see the cogs turning in his brain. His silence isn't helping my rising anxiety. I'm not leaving my best friend behind.

I take a few steps towards him, taking both of his hands in mine, ignoring his obvious hesitancy.

"Look, I know this is putting you on the spot, and I know I already owe you so much today…"

Tommy nods in agreement, fixed hard on my puffy eyes. His grip tightens on my hands, just enough to bring me a sigh of relief inside. I know him well enough already.

"…but I can't go and leave Amy here alone. I can't risk him finding her and doing this again."

"I'll be fine. I'll get a gun and blow the bastard's balls off. With great pleasure too."

"I love you to bits Amy, I say sharply, turning my head her direction. "…but would you ever stop talking crap, and let me help fix this?"

I've never spoken to Amy like this. Not even close. It has worked though, because she doesn't reply with anything other than a glare.

I turn back to Tommy. "What do you think?"

"Ummm…yeah. If it means keeping you safe, then we can make it work."

"Oh my god, really?" I cry, throwing my arms around his torso and hugging him. His arms return the gesture, carefully at first, then he holds me properly, like before.

Amy's protests fade quickly when it's two against one, and she finally relents after a brief discussion. She'll go on the condition that she can buy her own ticket, and pay her own way. We'll get open-ended tickets, and come back as soon as we're sure we're out of danger.

Works for me…

Thirty minutes or so later, the doctor who was treating Amy's injuries arrives, and gives her the all clear to go home today. It'll take an hour or so for some paperwork, and get her some painkillers and anti-inflammatory meds.

"We could go to the police station to give our statements, and then come back?" Tommy suggests.

"OK" I sigh. "Let's get it over with." I leave Amy with the biggest hug, and orders to not go anywhere until we get back.

24
GINA

"Thank you so much!" I tell Tommy as soon as we leave the room. "You've no idea how much this means to us both. Even if Amy doesn't realise it yet"

"That's OK," is all I get back.

"I don't want you to think you *need* to do this though. I…umm…I know I owe you an explanation about my ID."

"Yeah," he replies, with a thoughtful nod.

"Do you still like me?"

Tommy laughs, breaking a little of the tension.

"What sort of question is that?"

"Well I would understand if you didn't. I don't know if I like myself right now."

"Don't say stuff like that." He takes my hand again. The reassurance, and the undeserved kindness, hits me hard. "I like you a *lot*, and if hiding from that psycho is the reason for the different name, then I understand."

Wow…

Stopping dead, I tug Tommy's arm to pull him back to face me. "Are you sure you're real, and not some figment of my imagination?"

"Don't get carried away," he fires back, clearly reluctant to be put on a pedestal. "It still hurts that all this time I've not even known your real name. Does Amy know?"

"No. Nobody here does."

"Hmm," he says, allowing his face to soften, leaving only a slight frown of concern.

We just stare at each other for several seconds, and I wish with all my heart that he could see I'm still the same person.

He breaks the silence first, with a deep sigh that I find hard to read as anything other than negative, then, "I'm sure that hasn't been easy for you."

My knees actually go weak. I didn't think that was *actually* a thing.

"Please stop being so nice about this," I beg, dropping my gaze to the floor to hide my shame. "I don't know what to do with it. Why aren't you getting mad, and calling me names?"

He pauses again. "Not my style, Elisabeth." I can hear his smile without needing to look up.

My own smile appears, as I feel his finger softly lift my chin back up.

"We got this, OK?"

"OK," I reply weakly.

Every bit of me wants to drag him home, tear his clothes off, and claim him as mine forever.

"Good! Now what do I call you?"

"Can we stick with Gina? I like Gina."

"I like Gina too," he winks. His smile is like settling into a warm bath.

* * *

Gina

The Venice Beach police sub-station is too close for comfort to where my world caved in, and the anxiety rises to the point that I'm physically shaking, as we exit the car.

Our destination is between Muscle Beach and the skate-park. So it's busy. An easy place for an evil bastard to hide. I cling to Tommy like a scared puppy, as we make our way through the crowds to the safety inside.

It's a weird sensation to need a safe haven like this.

The officers who were at the scene earlier aren't here, so someone else will take our statements. It's a female officer this time, which I'm grateful for. She has such kind eyes, but I get vibes that she has weathered plenty of storms of her own.

She allows us to stay together.

Is it that obvious that I'm not going to let go of this man without a fight?

The statements are brief as we sit side by side, fingers intertwined under the heavy metal table. She has to hand-write each one, so there's no embellishment as she skilfully asks simple, direct questions. The facts and nothing more.

No more than twenty minutes have passed, before we both slide the freshly signed A4 statements back across the desk. I notice Tommy glance at mine and it feels like my printed name, Elisabeth Sawyer, is flashing like a huge neon sign.

Elisabeth is dead now.

The officer puts her pen down and leans back, the shift in energy from formal to friendly not too subtle. "Can I ask how all this came about?"

I explain how I met Brandon when we were in High School, and just slid from being friends in a group, to being a couple. It was an unspoken agreement. He just had a way of making me feel like I belonged to him, without needing to say it.

"Things were OK for a while, maybe even good. It was only when we moved in together that the control became obvious. It had obviously been there all along though."

"That's how they do it. So slowly that you don't even realise, until it's almost too late." Her wry smile hides her own story.

Tommy squeezes my hand tighter when it all begins to spill out. I had thought, while I was on the bus to LA, that the first time I said these things out loud would be amid floods of tears. Instead it all comes out so matter of fact, like it was a different person to I am now. Strangely, that makes perfect sense.

They both listen quietly, while I tell them about how my wages went into a joint bank account, and how I needed permission to spend *any* of it. Of course permission was never a word *he* used.

The punishments were almost as varied as the things I was punished for.

Unauthorised spending of course, but also talking to anyone about him or our relationship - especially my mom. If I got close to making a new friend in work, or even worse, if a man talked to me or even looked at me, I would be questioned for hours about who and why, and what I was doing behind his back.

"How ironic. Alanis Morissette should have put that in her song, as he was the one fucking anyone, and everyone he could. He eventually normalised it so much, he would boast about it when he forced me to have sex with him. I never minded him fucking around towards the end. The way I figured it was, if he was getting it enough elsewhere, he might leave me alone."

Tommy whispers, "Fuckin' hell…"

"He once tried to make me put it in my mouth after he'd just been with someone else, and when I refused he punched me so hard in the face that I had to take a week off work. He made sure from then on, that he hit me somewhere the bruises wouldn't be visible."

"I can't listen to this Gina, I'm sorry," Tommy says, his voice breaking as he moves to stand up.

"No, please Tommy! Stay!" I beg, gripping his hand tighter and tugging him back to his seat with my other arm. "I don't want to *ever* say these things out loud again, so I *need* you to hear it. So you understand why."

He stays, thankfully. He's heard the worst now anyway. I think it's the worst. It's the stuff that's floated to the top at least.

I tell them about how he made me believe that I was to blame when my mom died of an accidental overdose.

"If you had been there for her more, she wouldn't have done that, " he'd said, even though he was the one who created that distance. He would never let me visit or talk to her, unless he was there. I learned the hard way not to go behind his back. He always found out, so it wasn't worth the risk."

"What about your father?" the officer asks.

I shrug, swallow, and struggle to contain the emotions which start to bubble up uncontrollably.

"I don't even know who he is." I manage, eventually.

As I say these words, I'm confused by the swelling feeling of pride which follows.

"Do you have anyone else in your support network?"

"Just…Amy?" I say, pausing before looking at Tommy. My independent streak tries to stop me turning my head.

You don't need anyone but yourself.

It's unsuccessful. Maybe I don't need him, but I *want* him.

As my eyes meet his, I instantly want to rewind. His eyes are glassy, and he looks frightened.

Oh fuck. Don't put this on him as well.

"You've got me," he says, turning to pull me into his arms tightly. His short sharp breaths against my chest are a giveaway that he's more emotional right now than I am.

"If I'd know any of this, I would have *killed* that bastard when I had the chance," Tommy says, the venom delivered with a wobbly emotion undertone.

"I'll pretend I didn't hear that," the officer interjects, but with enough compassion in her tone to let us know she understands completely.

"I'll be getting that satisfaction, thanks," I whisper in Tommy's ear, quiet enough for only him to hear, and softly kiss his cheek.

I could say I love you right now, and it wouldn't feel wrong.

"Will you be returning home?" the officer asks.

"Only to pack a bag. Amy and I are going to stay with Tommy until you catch him."

"I'm glad to hear that. He doesn't know where you'll be staying, I assume?"

"No, there's no way he could. I've only been there once myself."

"What address would that be?"

"1525 San Vicente Boulevard in Santa Monica," Tommy replies. "Your colleague got my address and mobile phone number earlier."

"Very good," she says, jotting the address down again anyway. "Is that your permanent home?"

"Ummm…yes, I guess so. It's owned by my boss, and I live in the property."

"And your employer's name please?" she asks, not looking up from the paper, with her pen poised.

"Liam Fletcher."

The pen doesn't move, but her head lifts quickly to me.

"What?" I ask, surprised by her quick reaction. She pauses before replying, studying me.

"Nothing at all. That's fine. It's a secure property so I'm sure you'll all be safe there."

* * *

Tommy

"That was a bit weird. Her reaction to your bosses name," Gina mentions, as the double doors close behind us on the way out.

"Yeah, I know. Maybe she just wasn't expecting the name of somebody so well known."

"I guess so."

"Are you OK?"

"Yeah, I think so, all things considered. Are you?"

"It was a shock to hear those things to be honest. I don't know how you lived through that…"

"I'm a survivor," she says, in a 'let's change the subject' tone of voice.

Understood

"Back to the hospital, or your house first while we're close?" I ask.

"Let's get Amy first...but can we drive past home on the way, just to check?"

"Sure thing."

It all looks normal, as we cruise past slowly. Like nothing ever happened. There's no sign of Brandon, but I think he'd be too savvy to be hanging around in plain view.

"Do you think he's hiding here somewhere?" Gina asks, as we head away from her apartment, back towards Marina Del Rey.

"I hope not!" I reply too quickly and too honestly, instantly regretting not taking more time to come up with a more positive response.

Gina is quiet, and slides down into her seat. When she did this yesterday, she was relaxed, happy and excited. How things have changed. I can feel my anger rising, as I realise how much he has taken from her already. From us. Now I'm in this too, whether I like it or not.

"I'm so sorry about all this," Gina offers, tenderly, like she can read my thoughts.

"It's OK."

"It's really *not* Tommy. We've only just begun, and I've dragged you into all my shit. You don't deserve it. Yesterday was one of the best days of my life, and today is one of the worst."

"Do you wanna know why it *is* gonna be OK? I ask, putting my hand on her leg.

She looks up at me, like a scared, lost child, and slips my hand between both of hers. "Why?"

"Because we're going to have so many more days like yesterday, but we're never going to have a day like today." I keep my eyes on the road, trying to keep it casual.

She rubs the back of my hand upon hearing this. "Yeah…I hope you're right".

We drive on in silence for a moment, letting the evening sky and the radio lull us into a false sense of normality.

"You're pretty amazing, you know that?"

I can tell from the way she says this that she's getting emotional. Maybe a delayed shock reaction. "I don't know what today would look like without you."

"Anyone would have done the same," I say, passing it off, but knowing I *did* step up today. I'm proud that I did. I wouldn't hesitate to do it again, despite part of me wondering if I would even have got involved with this girl, if I'd known what she was bringing along.

"No. Anyone wouldn't, Tommy. But you did, and I'm so grateful. Amy will be too, I promise."

"It's gonna be OK," I reply, as we pull up to the valet parking bay outside the hospital, for the second time today. "As long as you guys are safe."

25
TOMMY

The golden hour light before sunset doesn't hold the same magic tonight, as we park up in the closest kerbside spot outside 1720 Pacific Avenue.

I think it's the first time anyone has sat in the backseat of my car. Never would I have thought it would be a feisty blonde, with a mind for bloody vengeance.

"I hope the sucker-punching coward *is* here. I'm gonna cut his dick off and stick it up his ass," Amy hisses from behind us, seat-belt already unbuckled.

"Alright calm down there, Lorena Bobbitt." Gina is dry and unemotional, her eyes narrowing as she scans the area for signs of Brandon.

"I'll go check, if you guys wanna wait here?" I suggest.

"No way! We stick together." Gina's reply is quick. She's in no mood to compromise on this.

We're inside with the swiftness of a SWAT team, moving as a unit up the pathway with eyes in all directions at once. There's a relief once we're inside, closing the door quietly, but any such feeling of safety is short lived.

"What if he's in here?" Gina asks in a whisper, looking from me to Amy.

No one speaks, as Amy slides a large knife out of the wooden block on the counter.

Just like the one in 'Scream'.

This isn't the movies, you dick!

I put my hand on her shoulder before she takes a step, and slowly, silently, try to take the knife from her hand. She grips tighter, shakes her head and scowls, so I let go.

We're still for a moment. Just listening.

Nothing. Just the occasional car passing outside. The rest of the world going about it's business, blissfully unaware.

This is my first time in the girls' apartment, and I'm fairly certain this isn't how it normally looks. Three of the sofa cushions are on the floor, and the coffee table is on its side. There's a congealed dark red stain on the wooden floor which I'm assuming is just red wine, judging by the broken glass nearby. The large TV on the wall is smashed, with a fist sized hole in the centre.

It's like an episode of Crime Scene Investigation. I know the police have been here already, sometime since last night, but there's no evidence of that.

The girls stay close to the door, which now has it's security chain on, while I move through the rooms, checking every wardrobe and under every bed.

There's no one here, but Brandon's menace somehow still lingers.

The large mirror above the sink in the girls' bathroom has, 'I WILL ALWAYS FIND YOU" scrawled across it, in what I assume is red lipstick.

What a fucking psycho!

I take a minute to wipe it off with a hand towel, before calling "All clear!"
That's the last thing Gina needs to see right now.

* * *

It takes them no more than fifteen minutes to pack a suitcase each. Brandon has urinated on Gina's bed, but it makes her more angry than upset. She stuffs the duvet into a black bag, ties it up, and deposits it outside before we leave, SWAT-like again.

"We can always come back, if you've forgetting anything," I say, once we're back in the relative safety of the Mustang.

"Thank you for this," Amy nods, still clutching the Scream knife. "It's a shame that bastard wasn't in there though."

Gina rolls her eyes, and neither of us reply.

"Good to go?"

"Yes! Let's go," Gina says confidently, with a grateful smile. "Thank you again."

We pull away from the kerb, turning the corner northbound.

I glance in the rear-view mirror and just catch a glimpse of Brandon, as he steps out from behind a tree opposite the apartment. He just stands still, Michael Myers-like, watching us leave.

A cold wave of fear washes over me, quickly followed by anger at the audacity of this guy. He was outside the whole time. Probably watching us come and go.

"Are you OK?" Gina asks, noticing the flush in my cheeks.

"I'm fine," I lie, faking a smile. "Just keen to get home and get you guys settled."

"I'm excited to see this place," Amy chirps from the back, still clutching the knife.

"Will you please put that knife down?" Gina orders. "You're more likely to hurt yourself, than anyone else right now".

"Are you sure your boss is cool with us staying?" Amy asks as she carefully sets the weapon in the foot-well. It's good to she's off high alert.

"Oh yeah, all good. Just keep your distance as much as you can. He can be a bit handsy, if you know what I mean?"

"Oooh, I've never been felt up by a billionaire before," Amy giggles.

My look says behave yourself, and Gina delivers the words.

* * *

The house is empty and silent when we arrive, and I'm grateful for that. As agreeable as Liam was on the phone, when I explained the situation, he also didn't say much. That makes me nervous. Getting the girls settled in while he's not here is for the best. In an ideal world, he'll not even notice they're here, before we head off on Wednesday.

Amy is as impressed as I was, as *anyone* would be. The house is pretty amazing.

There are four empty bedrooms on the ground floor, all adjacent to the part of the house I use. I give them the option of sharing but they choose to have one each, which is a nice indicator of how safe they feel.

We agree on Indian food, so I order it to be delivered, giving us all time to shower and wash the day off. It's been a day.

The three of us meet in my living room half an hour later, all in our PJs. It's muted, now that the magnitude of the situation has sunk in. I felt it as I dried off after my shower, how something so routine feels considered and important in the wake of trauma. They both have experienced considerably more than I have, so I can only imagine how they feel.

As I portion out the food onto warm plates, I can't help but feel a twisted gratitude that they've trusted me enough to give them a safe haven. Ten days ago, none of us had ever set eyes on each other. Now it feels like we're bonded by something which will never fade.

We eat together quietly, with the normality of two episodes of Friends for company. Gina's choice.

* * *

Amy is the first to call it a night. She's curled up in an armchair, and tells us she didn't get much sleep last night, despite the sedatives and pain relief. Gina and I are on the sofa, with her head on my chest, and her feet tucked under. They both get up and hold a hug for a long time.

Gina goes with Amy to her room, and returns a minute or two later as I flick channels, without even registering what's actually on the screen.

"How is she?" I whisper.

"More delicate than she would admit, but I think a good sleep will do her the world of good."

"And how are you?"

"The same," she laughs quietly, reflectively, as she slips back in around me on the sofa.

"Hopefully you get a good lie in. It should be pretty quiet in the morning."

"Do you have to go to work?"

"Yes, but I'll be here in the morning at least."

"OK. That's good," she whispers, contently, then after a pause, "He won't be able to find us here, will he?"

My brief delay in replying makes Gina stiffen. "No, absolutely not!"

Did he get my licence plate?

What if he can find us with that?

"OK good, thank you," Gina says, softening again as she lays her head in my lap, looking up at me with those beautiful eyes.

We lay like that for a few minutes, in silence, and she closes her eyes as I stroke her hair. Every now and again she opens them, smiling contently.

"I could just stay right here forever," she says sleepily, stretching her legs out more.

"You're so beautiful," I say, without even thinking.

Gina's eyes open wide, shining with the biggest smile. "Aw, thank you. You're pretty fucking beautiful yourself!"

My eyebrows lift. "Can men be beautiful?"

"Absolutely!" she enthuses, then lifts to meet me halfway for a kiss. A perfect kiss for the moment. I wonder did she feel it in her tummy too?

"This is gonna sound so cheesy, but it feels like I've known you for a long time already. Does that make any sense?" Gina asks, with an intensity I haven't seen before.

I instinctively nod while I think about this. "I know what you mean. It is weird. The idea of meeting someone scared the life out of me, but that changed as soon I met you. It feels like I was supposed to meet you."

"Like Serendipity?"

"Yeah, I guess so!"

"I love that movie," she says wistfully. "Kate Beckinsale is *so* beautiful."

I just nod again, not wanting to vocalise my agreement, but my smile gives it away.

"Hey!" she says playfully.

"Are you going to tell Amy about the name thing?" I ask, keen to change the subject.

"I don't know." Her face immediately shows how much this has been worrying her already. "Should I?"

"I don't honestly know. Probably. How will she feel if she finds out another way?"

"Hmm…"

"Is there a need to keep it a secret now that *he* knows where you are?"

"I'm scared she'll bail on me though. I wanted to tell her so many times, but the more time passed, the more it felt bigger. I was starting to believe that the old me was dead now, and that she only needed to know the new me."

"That makes sense I suppose. I don't know how she'd react to knowing that, so I can't really advise if you should tell her or not."

"Hmm…there's no hurry I guess." She pauses now, biting her bottom lip, and looking off to the side in a middle distance stare.

"What's up?" I ask, stroking her hair again.

"Can I ask you something?"

"Of course!"

"Why would you be scared to meet someone?"

"I…emm…just didn't want to risk…"

"Getting hurt again?"

"Yeah" I reply, the shame evident.

"Hey!" she says, gently gripping my chin with her thumb and forefinger. "It's not a sign of weakness you know?"

"It feels like it."

"I get that. But here you are. Here *we* are. Survivors."

Gina lays there with a wry smile, waiting for me to respond. When I do it's with a smile of my own. A smile of agreement, and contentment.

"Can I ask you something else?" she adds eventually.

"Uh oh," I reply, half guessing what's coming. "Go on…"

"What happened with your wife?"

It's a jolt to my system to hear the word wife, and again my face can't hide it.

Gina furrows her brow at the disapproving look I've given her.

"What's that face mean?" she asks, gently.

"Sorry…It's just hard to hear her referred to like that." The bitterness in my voice catches me by surprise, and Gina falls silent for a moment, studying me intently.

"She must have really done a number on you," she says quietly, reverently.

Without knowing the details, I can tell she already understands more than anyone else could.

"You could say that."

"If it's too hard to talk about, it's OK. I totally get it." She lifts up to kiss me again, before adding, "I just don't want you bottling it up. That shit changes you, you know?"

"It's hard, because it's something I want to leave behind. Like it wasn't my life, if you know what I mean?"

Gina gives me an 'Are you kidding me' look.

We're both so comfortable here together. It feels right, but the awkward turn in the conversation doesn't. For the first time, I realise that this isn't going to be as easy as I thought. The trip to Pismo was real of course, but we were as much in a little fantasy bubble as two people could possibly be.

"Has it changed *you*?" I ask, grateful for the opportunity to divert.

"I'd like to think not," she replies, after a few seconds of contemplation. "But yeah. Maybe for the better actually. I've probably learned to actually value myself for the first time these last six months, and be in charge of my own destiny."

"It's only once you're out of a bad relationship, do you realise how fucked up it was."

Gina gives me a wry smile. "For sure." More contemplation. "I think I always wanted to see the good in people, and hope that the bad doesn't run too deep. Do you know what I mean?"

"Completely. The shittiest people are too good at hiding it for long enough to make you question it, you know, when the mask eventually slips…"

"…or make you believe *you're* the problem?" Gina finishes.

I can only nod a reply at first. "You know, if I were to tell anyone about us, and what happened today, they'd probably advise me to run away as fast as possible."

Her eyes close upon hearing these words, and I'm immediately regretting my timing.

"I'm so sorry," she whispers.

People have told me they're sorry before, but never have I believed it so completely as now.

"I don't think you've anything to apologise for, that's what's so fucked up."

"What do you mean?" Gina asks, opening her eyes again. The cutest little frown appears.

"It sounds like you did what you needed to do, to keep yourself safe. You've been so brave and so strong, so you should be proud, not sorry. I just need to work hard to see *you* through it all, and not make it a trust thing. You know?"

"Can you?" Gina asks, hesitantly.

"Can I what?"

"See *me* through it all?"

My first reaction is a smile, and it softens her worried expression quickly. "One hundred percent. If I didn't, you wouldn't be here".

There's that wry smile again.

"Sorry, that sounded more blunt than I meant it to."

"It's OK. You've every right to be unsure. I just wish we had more time for you to get to know me better, before something like this happened."

"Everything happens for a reason."

She's silent again, gazing at me again from below, with that beautiful smile. That perfect face.

"You're amazing," Gina says eventually.

"I'm really not," I laugh.

"Well I think you are, and hopefully I can repay your kindness."

"Just being here is enough."

"See!" She kisses me again. "Amazing!"

"How do you feel about everything today?"

"Emmm…I knew he might find me someday, just not so soon…and I thought if he ever did, he would actually kill me this time. I think I feel more guilt than anything else, for mixing you and Amy up in it."

"I wonder how he found you, and what happened in your apartment last night?"

"I don't know. I'm too scared to ask Amy. I'm not even sure I want to know. As long as she's OK." A tear grows, and falls from the corner of one eye, and she turns her head away, taking a deep breath to control her emotions.

I make a conscious choice to stay even, in the face of her emotion. Just to be present and pragmatic.

"Well you're both safe now, and hopefully you'll enjoy getting away."

"Thank you," Gina smiles, as I very carefully wipe the tears from her face.

We cuddle for a bit, quietly holding each other close. Tight enough to connect, but gentle enough to relax into it at the same time. It's amazing how comforting a simple hug can be.

Who you're hugging makes the difference, I suppose.

"We should probably get some sleep"

"We should" Gina answers, squeezing me a little bit tighter. "What a day…"

"It's going to be OK you know?"

"I hope so…"

I let the hug linger a little longer, before relaxing my grip. "Bedtime," I whsiper, kissing her on the cheek. A cheek wet with tears again.

"Will you stay with me?"

"What do you mean?"

"Can we sleep in the same bed?"

"Emmm…yes, if you're alright with that."

"I don't really want to be alone. I know that sounds pathetic. I'm sorry."

"Stop apologising," I implore, as gently as I can, getting a very cute, but very sheepish smile in return. This smile has dimples too. Be still my beating heart!

I lead Gina to my room, thankful that I'm a bit of a tidy freak.

"The bathroom is there. I'll wait in the lounge while you get ready sure, and you can let me know."

"Thank you so much," she says, hugging the same holdall from last night's overnight-er.

"No worries. Take your time."

"Can I take a shower?"

I laugh at this, and Gina looks like she's wants to sink into the floor.

"I'm sorry. I'm sorry!" I walk back to her and take her face in my hands. "I know it's a cliche to say, make yourself at home, but..stop being a dick, and just make yourself at home, OK?"

Gina's laughter is sudden and hearty, and I'm glad to see everything about her relax.

"OK, understood. I'm being annoying, I know."

"All good! Now go and enjoy your shower."

"Thank you!" She leaves me with a quick peck, then a surprisingly sexy look over her shoulder as she walks away.

* * *

I catch up on some emails confirming the arrangements for County Wicklow, while Gina gets ready. Twenty minutes later she appears in the dimly lit doorway to the lounge.

Affection, excitement, and badly timed but unavoidable arousal all hit at once.

The non-sexiness of her simple white with red hearts pyjamas makes her all the *more* alluring. The mere act of not trying to be attractive right now could not be *more* attractive.

Her hair is tied up in a ponytail. She's barefoot on the thick carpet, and back-lit like a scene in a movie. Only when you're completely entranced by someone, can they make a simple thing like standing in a doorway seem like art.

She's a far cry from the girl of 24 hours ago. The sassy confidence replaced by a vulnerability and fragility that makes me want to just hold her, and never let her go.

* * *

Everything feels foreign in my own bathroom, as I shower and get ready for bed, knowing she's waiting there for me.

In *my* bed.

How on earth am I going to sleep?

All the mundane, regular bedtime routines take on more meaning tonight. Brushing my teeth a little more thoroughly. A little spray of the new Abercrombie 'Fierce'. Wearing a t-shirt instead of just my usual boxers.

Little differences. For her.

Flicking off the bathroom light, it takes a moment for my eyes to adjust to the semi-darkness. I know my way well enough in the dark, but it's only when I slip into bed that I see, and feel, Gina.

All the feelings of weirdness soon pass when she slides over to my side, resting her head on my chest after a simple goodnight kiss. The last time someone fell asleep on me like this was the early days of my marriage. Things were good then too.

Sleep doesn't elude me as long as I had feared.

Instead, the warmth of her body moulded around mine, and the gentle rhythm of her breathing brings a deep calm that has me drifting off to dreamland in no time.

Safe and sound together.

26
GINA

If you were a fly on the wall at breakfast, you'd be forgiven for thinking that we were three people without a single care in the world. Amy's bruises being the only hint of something beyond the free flowing banter, while we cook and eat together

Tommy looks sharp, in contrast to us. Designer jeans, black open neck shirt, and smelling good. He always smells good. Groomed and ready to take his handsomeness out into the world.

Amy and I however - still in our PJs, with little desire to face anything outside these walls just yet.

"I can't believe we're going to Ireland in two days," Amy purrs, curling up in the corner of one of the sofas, a large mug of coffee cradled at her chest. "Do you think they'll let me in looking like this?" she laughs, only half-joking.

"Fighting is a national pastime back home, so they'll probably not even notice," Tommy calls from the kitchen area, while drying the morning dishes.

Amy smiles, but flicks me an unsteady look as I join her on the sofa, with my usual morning green tea.

"I'm sure it'll not even be noticeable by then babe."

"Bullshit. There's not enough make up in the world to make this go away."

I feel those words like a knife. Amy can be sharp with her tongue.

"I'm sorry," I manage, barely able to form any syllables.

"Don't!" Amy retorts, releasing one hand to point at me, eyebrows raised.

"Don't what?"

"Don't *ever* apologise for that asshole. This is not your fault."

"It kind of is. He wouldn't have been near you, if not for me"

"Maybe not, but you can't be responsible for his actions, and shouldn't have to make apologies for them either."

"Are you sore?"

"It's not too bad. Mostly just the ribs now when I'm laying down."

Oh fuck. I didn't know this. Classic Brandon move.

I open my mouth to apologise again, but my face gives it away first.

"Ah ah. No!" Amy points again, wagging the same finger to silence me.

I let this sit for a moment, my brain yelling at me to take the opportunity now to spill the beans.

I take a mouthful of tea, then set the mug on the coffee table, before sinking back to the opposite corner of the sofa.

"I think I need to tell you something," I say meekly, pulling my knees to my chest and wrapping my arms around my legs.

"Oh boy. This sounds serious. Don't tell me you're pregnant already?"

I meet Tommy's eyes across the room for a split second. Long enough for him to signal his approval. Amy looks round to him, then back to me.

"You're not are you? You can't be already."

"No, of course not!"

"Thank fuck for that," echoes into her coffee mug.

Chad Kroeger is crooning "…and this is how, you remind me…' from the radio near Tommy, as he turns it down.

"It's about something I had to do when I moved here. Ironically to stop him finding me."

No words from Amy, just a single raised eyebrow.

Not the reaction I was expecting.

I glance at Tommy again. He's leaning back against the kitchen counter, arms folded. He smiles and gives me an encouraging nod.

Amy rolls her eyes. "You guys keep looking at each other, like I don't know what's going on."

"What do you mean?"

"I mean I know your real name is Elisabeth." She delivers this news completely unladen of any emotion, judgment or surprise.

My mouth falls open. Amy takes a sip from her mug, barely able to hide her smirk.

"What the fuck Amy?"

"What the fuck Elisabeth!" comes back, lightning fast.

"How? Umm…how did you know?"

"I found your passport, about a week after you moved in."

"You've known all this time, and didn't say anything?"

"I understood, and it was your business. It doesn't matter what your name is. You're still you, aren't you?"

"Ummm…yeah. Wow! I can't believe you've known all this time."

"I'm glad I already knew, when Scott, as he called himself, started asking about Elisabeth."

I pause to digest this.

He was using a fake name too?

How long had he been tracking me?

"Did he say how he found me?"

"Nope! But when he realised you weren't coming back, he went berserk. He threatened to kill me, if I didn't tell him where you were. Asshole!"

"I'm not sure I even want to know, but what happened? How did you get away?"

"Stabbed him."

"What?"

"I stabbed him. With a fork. After he attacked me, he went into your room, and when he came back, I stabbed him with a fork that I used for dinner."

"Where?"

"I aimed for his balls and got his leg, then punched him in the balls."

"Fuck me, Amy!"

I so wanted to be the one to do these things. To be brave enough to make him feel a fraction of the pain he caused me over the years.

"If he hadn't have bolted, he was getting more."

"You're so brave."

"I'm not at all brave. I'm just not willing to let anyone away with that shit, and fuck knows what he would have done next if I hadn't."

I'm visualising this happening in our apartment. My safe place. The tears fill my eyes, and by the time the first one reaches my chin, it has become uncontrollable sobbing.

Amy beats Tommy to me, taking me in her arms.

"Let it all out," she whispers in my ear, and holds me tight until I start to relax again.

"I'm sorry," I wimper, using my sleeve to dry my face. "It feels like I've dropped a bomb in both your lives, and I don't know how to fix it."

"Hey! There's nothing to fix. They'll catch him while we're away, if not before, so try not to worry."

Tommy is perched on the edge of the chair closest to the sofa, as he says this.

"I wish it was that easy," I reply, appreciating the sentiment, but a bit frustrated by his 'happily ever after' outlook. Real life doesn't always play that way.

* * *

Tommy has been in and out twice to check on us, and has finally finished up for the day around 4pm. There's an unspoken understanding that, until we leave, it'll be a bit of a groundhog day. Laying low in the house all day, then ordering food in, and watching a movie before bedtime.

Simple, predictable and safe.

Monday night's food is Thai, and the movie is Titanic…well half of it anyway, as I fall asleep just after the iceberg hits.

Tuesday is a hotter day, so Amy and I venture outside for the first time since Sunday evening. Just out to the pool at first, constantly scanning the perimeter of the grounds, and being startled by the movements of the gardeners and visitors to the house.

The alert level decreases after a shared bottle of wine though, and it makes the afternoon pass mercifully faster.

Liam is hosting a dinner tonight. Tommy says he does this every time he's going away for more than a couple of days.

"I think it's to assert his status, so that even when he's not in town, everyone has him in mind. Either that or just to show off. Probably both actually."

"We're OK though, we don't need to do anything?"

"Yeah, I was thinking you could serve some drinks." he deadpans, then laughs at his own humour. "No, it's all good. It's just that it's for the people involved in Legally Blonde 2, and Reese Witherspoon is invited."

"No. Fucking. Way." Amy beat me to it.

"Reese Witherspoon is going to be in *this* house, tonight?"

"I think so, yeah."

"Oh my god. How amazing. Will you get to meet her?"
"Yeah, she's pretty cool. I think you'll like her."
"I fucking *love* her, and I haven't even met her yet."

* * *

Amy and I eat alone, a little earlier than usual tonight. The wine has made us hungry, and Tommy orders food before he has to go and greet the guests. Pizza arrives from Sal's in Venice Beach, and it's not only very tasty, but comfortingly familiar. Oh, how things have changed since the last time we ate from Sal's.

It's just after 8pm, and we're back in our new Amy & Gina shaped imprints on the sofa, with another movie on. Cruel Intentions. Reese, Ryan & Sarah Michelle Gellar, in an awesome modern adaptation of Dangerous Liaisons.

"How weird is it that we're watching her on screen, at the same time she's somewhere in this house?"

"Mental babe. Do you think Ryan is here with her? It's so cute that they met on this movie, and ended up married. Imagine how fucking perfect *their* babies are gonna be?"

Before I can answer, there's a double knock at the door which leads towards the rest of the house. It opens slowly in my eye-line, with Amy sitting up to look round. We always have it dark for a movie, but the light from beyond makes a familiar silhouette in the doorway as Tommy comes in quietly.

"Why are you being so fucking weird?" I ask, before noticing a smaller silhouetted figure beside him."

"I was telling Reese all about you, and she wanted to meet you. I hope that's OK?" Tommy replies, stepping into the light of the TV, with what my mom would call a 'shit-eating' grin.

I'm frozen. *Is that Reese fucking Witherspoon?*

"Hi girls, sorry to interrupt you. I hope you don't mind me coming to say hi?"

It is actually Reese Witherspoon.

"Holy fuck!" Amy blurts out, quickly followed by "I'm so sorry!" and a hand over her mouth.

Reese giggles sweetly, most likely well used to people freaking out a little when they meet her.

"Are you watching Cruel Intentions?" Reese asks, catching sight of the TV from the side.

"Ummm…yeah" I say, managing to get to my feet. I suddenly feel incredibly child-like, even though Reese and I are the same age. "Sorry, let me turn it off."

"No it's OK. I don't want to disturb you guys. I love that movie!"

The weirdness of that statement clearly rebounds back, as Reese follows with, "I mean I had so much fun making it. I hope you're enjoying it."

You would expect a world-famous actress to be insufferably narcissistic, but Reese appears to be the complete opposite. She's polite, almost self-effacing, and seems genuinely embarrassed to be disturbing us.

I press mute on the remote control instead, tossing it onto the sofa before offering my hand to Reese. Amy is now standing too, like we're in the presence of royalty and it would be unimaginable to stay seated. Oh hey Reese. Sorry babe we're in the middle of a movie. Wanna come back later?

She takes my hand with both of hers, then moves closer and before my brain can comprehend it, we're hugging.

What the fuck is happening?

Reese Witherspoon is hugging me.

"It's so nice to meet you Gina. Tommy told me all about you, and since we're going to be working together, I thought I could come say hi?"

Her non-acting voice is more Nashville than I expect, and it only adds to the 'down to earth' regular girl vibe she has going on. If there's an ego there at all, and she'd be well entitled to one, then it's well hidden.

"Oh you didn't…I mean thank you. I can't believe it's you. Sorry!" I fluster, reddening at the incoherent nonsense coming out of my mouth.

Reese smiles the smile I've seen on screen a hundred times or more. "Hey, I should be the sorry one for barging in on you girls."

"Oh, this is Am. My friend Amy. This is Amy" I stumble, getting a giggle from Reese, and a brief touch on my arm that says 'relax'.

"Hi Amy. I'm Reese." Reese says.

"Are you sure?" Amy asks, her cheeky humour almost falling flat, but for Reese's quick wit.

"I mean hi," Reese shakes her head, like she's just had a slip of the tongue. "I'm Annette Hargrove. Nice to meet you."

There's a stunned silence for a moment, at how fast she switched her delivery to sound exactly like Annette, her character in Cruel Intentions.

Wow

If there ever was a moment that would dispel any doubt that great acting requires great skill, that would have been one. So much so that the thought flashes through my mind that I shouldn't even try, because I could *never* switch it on as skilfully as Reese did just now.

Tommy's laugh breaks the spell. He's behind Reese, and starting to look a little uncomfortable, shifting his weight from one foot to the other.

"I'm just going to the bathroom. Will you guys be OK?"

"Us girls will be just fine," Reese says, back in her own voice. "I'd much rather be here anyway. I hate these parties where you feel you have to put on a show the entire time. I would *love* to just put my feet up and have a pizza!"

"You eat pizza?" Amy asks, weirdly.

"Sure I do, doesn't everyone?"

"Are you looking forward to Legally Blonde 2?" I ask, struggling for what else to ask.

"Oh yes, I can't wait. What about you? You're so pretty, I can see you fitting in so well with the Delta Nu. We're gonna have the best time."

Reese Witherspoon just called me pretty.

"I'm *so* excited. Yes. I only got offered the part a few days ago."

I'm suddenly aware that my conversation skills are severely lacking, at the time I need them most. I want to be sparkly, witty and self-assured like Reese, but instead I'm standing here like a star struck twelve year old.

I wonder is she used to people being so goofy around her?

"Do you wanna watch the rest of the movie with us?" Amy interjects, rescuing us all from the cul-de-sac. "Have a glass of wine or something?"

I stare at Amy like she's lost her mind.

You don't just ask Reese Witherspoon to have a glass of wine and watch a movie. Her movie.

"I would *love* that. Maybe for a little while?"

No way!

When Tommy comes back, he stops in his tracks. I glance over and smile nervously. Yes, Reese is sitting between us with a glass of wine. He's as speechless as I am, and I give him my best, 'I don't know what's going on either' expression.

He lowers himself slowly onto the arm of the chair, afraid to relax, like he's a security guard or something. I suppose he is responsible for her, since he brought her through. He looks uneasy, but doesn't say anything.

"You know, I don't think I've ever sat and watched this all the way through," Reese announces.

No one else speaks.

On the screen, Sarah Michelle Gellar's character, Kathryn, is flirting with Ryan's character Sebastian, who plays her stepbrother.

"She's so *bad* in this," Reese enthuses. "Don't you think?"

"Umm…I think she's frickin' awesome," Amy disputes.

Reese giggles. "I don't mean bad acting, I mean her character is so naughty."

"Is it weird watching her flirt with your husband?" I ask, trying to get involved in an actual conversation.

"Well he wasn't my husband yet, but no it's just for the movie. Sarah is a treasure. She's such a good person. The hardest part of making this, was when Ryan and I did the scene when Annette and Sebastian have a fight. He didn't expect me to slap him in the face, and he threw up afterwards."

Amy and I both say, "Oh my goodness" in unison, prompting another laugh from Reese.

How is she so relaxed?

How is she so damn awesome?

"He was OK though. I took it as a compliment!" she says with a wink to me.

Reese's sense of an appropriate time to leave is impeccable, and her glass is empty in about ten minutes. She was clearly aware of Tommy's growing unease, and he's quick to his feet when she signals her exit.

"Sorry I can't stay to the end. If I don't go back soon, they'll think I've been kidnapped again."

"Again?" Tommy blurts out.

"Relax, I'm kidding," she laughs, rolling her eyes for our benefit. "Next time save me some pizza, OK?" she says, hands on her hips in sassy Elle Woods mode.

Amy and I both stand, cordially, like before, and get a hug each.

"Thank you for letting me sit with you guys. And have a great time in Ireland. I'm so envious!"

There's nothing that can really prepare your brain for Reese Witherspoon saying she's envious of you.

As quickly and miraculously as she appeared, she's gone. Tommy's kiss, and her cuteness both leaving an impression.

"Well fuck me! What was that?" Amy bursts, seconds after the door closes, leaving us alone again. De-Reesed.

"That was like some sort of weird dream."

"If we put X-Men on, do you think Hugh Jackman will come through the door next?" Amy says, pushing her boobs up in readiness.

"Ha! You should be so lucky! How amazing is she though? Oh my goodness, can you believe we're going to be on set together, and now she knows me!"

"Yeah, as long as you remember me, when you're the one heading back to the fancy parties."

"This has been the weirdest week of my entire life…"

PART TWO

'Follow Your Fire'

Wednesday, June 19th 2002

It's been exactly 234 hours since our first date began, and now here I am, boarding the 10.40am Aer Lingus flight from LAX to Dublin.

It's been a little more awkward than I anticipated. I hadn't thought much beyond Tommy, Amy and myself, so when Liam and two others appeared this morning, it felt like *they* were the intruders.

They introduced themselves in brief, business like fashion, no doubt wondering who on earth *we* were. Especially the one who looked like she'd just been in the ring with Mike Tyson.

Jason is Liam's marketing and publicity assistant. Mid thirties, clean cut, and working hard to cover up his hair loss. Alexis is his legal assistant, and amusingly reminds me of Elle Woods when she dressed smart, and wore glasses. No pink fluffy pens though, and definitely little danger of a 'bend and snap'.

Two Lexus cars collected us, one black, one silver, and we split into our two threesomes for the short drive to the airport. I've flown a few times, but never had an airport experience like this one. No long queues for check in or baggage drop, just straight to an executive lounge, with our bags trollied off by a handsome man in a smart uniform.

Boarding is fast and hassle free, with the handsome man appearing at 10am, to personally escort us to the plane before regular boarding commences.

This must be what every day is like for celebrities.

"I'm normally over there with that lot," Amy whispers in my ear, as we bypass the impatient crowd waiting to board our plane, held back by two pissed off looking ground crew.

We're led onto the Airbus A330, and turn the opposite direction that 'normal' people usually would, into the curtained off first class area. I've ever only seen this in movies, and it doesn't do it justice. We're shown to our seats. When I say seats I mean semi-private cubicles, with huge comfortable seats, lots of buttons and a private TV screen.

I squeeze Tommy's arm with excitement, and he smiles warmly. Not his first time.

"Are you OK?" he asks in his library voice.

"Are you kidding?" I grin. "I can't believe this."

"Once you fly *this* way, you'll never want to do it any other way."

"I can imagine. Are you OK? You're very quiet."

"Yeah, sorry, it's all very weird with everyone here. It's my first time going back home too. Feels a bit like going backwards."

"Hmm…how close will we be to where you lived?"

"Oh not close at all, the other side of the border. A good few hours away, thankfully."

"Then it'll be OK?"

"Oh yeah, don't mind me, I'm just being dramatic."

"That's my job!"

Tommy laughs at my over enthusiastic reply.

"I called Ollie to let him know we're coming over, and he's gonna try to meet up with us."

"The mad one who called you at the weekend?"

"Yup. It'll be interesting to see how he gets on with Amy. She's like a wilder version of his usual type. Actually, she's probably more like the female version of him!"

"Oh shit, that sounds dangerous!"

We both laugh at this, while unpacking bits from our carry on bags.

"What are you fuckers laughing at?" Amy demands, picking up the glances in her direction.

"I think Tommy is trying to set you up with his mate."

"What mate?"

"His soccer player friend in Ireland."

"Fuck. No. I'm off men for life" Amy rolls her eyes at my 'sure you are' face, as she takes her seat and fumbles in the bag on her lap.

For most of the first class cabin, it's two seats/cubicles each side of the centre aisle, with a couple of single seats offering more privacy and space to spread out.

Amy and I have two together on one side, with Tommy and Liam across the aisle. Amy & Liam take the window seats, on purpose no doubt.

The luxury is incredible. There's even a 'bed mode' button, and another two which activate heat or a massage function in the seat. I can't even imagine how much this costs. Drinks are free of course. Well not free, but included.

None of this shit is free!

The only downside is not being close enough to your seat neighbour to chat properly. It's a bit of an effort, so Amy and I eventually give up and relax. It's a ten hour flight, so I'm very grateful to not be among the regular economy passengers boarding behind us. I don't envy them at all. I've been there. Cramped on all sides, and always either a seat kicker or a screaming baby nearby, or both if the universe decides to sentence you to extra misery.

* * *

The jet lag is definitely going to be a problem. I'm only realising this as we make our approach into Dublin Airport.

I didn't give it any consideration in advance. My body thinks it's 8.30pm, but the cabin crew have just announced it's 4.30am.

"When are we going to sleep, if it's tomorrow already?" Amy whispers, waiting for the seat-belt light to go out.

"You read my mind," I reply with a frown.

We disembark quietly. No escort this time.

Dublin Airport looks like any other airport. I don't know what I was expecting, landing in Ireland. To be greeted by a fiddle-de-dee band like the Irish pubs back home? Maybe some people dressed as leprechauns, and talking in a foreign language?

Nope, just a regular airport. No music, no green hats, and everyone appears to speak English.

Tommy takes my hand, but lets it go again quickly when I also take Amy's. That's understandable. People don't walk holding hands in a threesome, unless it's some sort of progressive free love polygamy commune. You might get away with that back home, but here it's just weird.

To be fair, even in an airport in the US it would be weird.

"What about our luggage?" I ask Tommy, when I realise we're heading away from the baggage claim hall.

"It'll be taken care of, don't worry."

"I could get used to this," Amy mutters to herself.

Liam, Jason and Alexis reach the exit first, and Liam nods to a man in a suit holding up a 'FLETCHER' sign, handwritten in black on a large white card.

Five minutes later we're seated again, this time in shiny black BMWs.

"It's not what I expected," I say with a confused smile, gazing out the window.

"Ah, this part is pretty ordinary, but wait until you see where we're going. It's all motorway for a bit first, so not much to see."

Despite the concrete greyness, it's still hard to not take it all in. According to the signs we're on the M50 southbound, and Tommy tells us it's a ring road which circumvents Dublin City centre.

"Will we get to go into Dublin while we're here? I would love to see it," Amy asks, excitedly.

"Maybe yeah, some evening if we're finished at a decent time. It's not too far from where we're staying."

"What's it like?" I ask?

"Where we're staying?"

"No, Dublin."

"Umm…yeah it's OK. It's not as traditional Irish as you might think. It's a busy city. Galway is *my* favourite. It's a proper Irish town. Great craic!"

"Great craic," Amy imitates, badly, laughing at her own poor attempt at the accent.

"Can we go there?"

"Oh, it's a couple of hundred miles away on the opposite coast. I don't think we'll get time."

"That's cool, maybe another time," I say, nothing but grateful to even be here.

* * *

The roads are quiet, but it is only 5.50am as we turn off into a place signposted as Enniskerry. Other large brown signs heralded our entry into County Wicklow a short time ago. There are way more signs here than back home.

How does anyone concentrate on the road?

"Oh my god, it's so pretty!" Amy gushes, window down now enjoying the morning sun, and the slow drive through Enniskerry town centre.

"It's so quaint. It's like a movie set. Do people actually live here?" I ask, actually sincere.

Tommy laughs. Even the driver smiles.

"Of course! It is beautiful though. That's why we're here. They'll be filming be in the village here, and the surrounding area."

"Wow! Will we get to see any of the filming?"

"No sorry. Unfortunately this is the boring bit when we just plan the shooting schedule, and agree locations. Stuff like that."

The centre of Enniskerry has three roads meeting to form a triangle, with a little 'island' in the middle. It's like a picture postcard - perfectly painted shops and cafes, and expertly manicured greenery surrounding an old clock tower type structure in the island.

We drive up the hill past the town 'square', turning right at multiple brown and white signs saying, 'Powerscourt', 'Powerscourt Hotel', 'Powerscourt House',' Powerscourt Gardens' and 'Powerscourt Waterfall'.

Why can't they just use one sign?

"Whoever makes the road signs in Ireland must be worth a fortune," I say, impressed but confused at the same time.

Tommy laughs like he's never considered this before. Amy is silent, just taking it all in. I see it all for a moment through her eyes.

How did two west coast girls end up here?

At least Brandon can't find me now…

We're not far down this narrower tree-lined road when the cars slow, turning towards Powerscourt Hotel Resort & Spa. I give Tommy's hand an excited squeeze as I crane my neck to get a view as we approach.

Holy. Fuck

Amy says it out loud a split second after I think it, and it's an understatement. We leave the tree-lined avenue behind, as the landscape opens so majestically that it deserves a musical accompaniment.

"This can't be a hotel?" Amy asks.

"It is," Tommy replies. "It's some place, isn't it?"

"It looks like a palace, for goodness sake. It's bigger than the White House"

The White House comparison makes sense. It's not dissimilar in design; bright white and oozing grandeur. The building is so wide that it curves, like it's aware it's too ostentatious and is trying to hide it's size.

The three story entrance in the middle is swollen and bold in the middle, commanding the two wings which arc outwards either side, cradling a gigantic round fountain, spewing jets of crystal clear water about thirty feet into the summer morning air.

Two pathways lead to the fountain from the hotel, one from either side of the entrance hallway, criss-crossing in front of the water, before looping around the back to meet, in what resembles an infinity symbol.

We're all speechless as we exit our car, taking in not just the view, but the stillness.

"How is so quiet?" I whisper. The only sound is the gentle hiss and sprinkle of the fountain beside us.

The lawns extend out into the distance, lush and evenly green, before meeting the trees which border the gardens. A giant chessboard, complete with person sized pieces, sits off to the left, set and ready for a game, or a very cool photograph.

Inside is just as grand, if not more so. Thick, dark wood, white marbled pillars and regency blue upholstered furniture draw the eye first, before noticing the size of the atrium above. Sunlight fills every corner of the lobby, via the two storey curved glass frontage.

I hook arms with Amy, while we wait on Tommy and the others arranging check in. This is the second luxury hotel I've been to in less than a week, in two different countries.

"I can't believe we're here," I whisper. Amy just nods. It must be the tenth time we've both said something similar, but it's still not sinking in. It's a little disorientating to suddenly find yourself 5000 miles from home, in a very different time zone.

Is this what it feels like for rich people to travel the world all the time?

Tommy comes back and kisses me for the first time in Ireland. Just a peck, but perfect.

"Are you OK?'" he asks cutely, but intently.

"I think so. It's just a bit overwhelming."

"I'm sorry, I've had you everywhere the last while."

Amy's eyebrows jump as fast as mine do.

"Have you now?" Amy says slowly, eyeing me with fake suspicion, knowing full well.

"Oh no, I don't mean it like that," he protests.

"Oh she knows! She's just being an ass. Aren't you Amy?" I add, side-eyeing her back.

She makes a 'maybe' face, but says nothing.

"You've nothing to be sorry about." I give Tommy my sunniest smile. "I wanna be with you everywhere."

Tommy frowns, a smirk growing. "Did you just quote me a Fleetwood Mac song?"

Amy throws her head back with a laugh, drawing a few looks from around the lobby.

"Yes she did. Don't worry, you'll get used to it. I'm surprised she hasn't started singing Stevie Nicks songs to you as well."

I instinctively elbow her in the ribs to shut her up, forgetting her injuries.

"Oh fuck, I'm so sorry babe, I forgot!"

Amy can't speak, holding her breath and clutching her side. She gives me a 'don't' look when I move to hug her an apology. I'm shaking already, embarrassed and angry at myself.

"Are you OK?" Tommy asks her, keeping his distance. Amy just nods, and retreats slowly to an armchair close by.

"She'll get you back for that I'm sure," he says to me, handing me a room card in a little cardboard sleeve.

"The rooms are ready at this time of the morning?"

"Yes, Liam had me reserve last night too. He likes to nap when *he* wants. The jet lag and all that. He's not the sort to wait around for a 3pm check-in."

"That's impressive. I would never have thought of that."

"That's because normal people wouldn't dream of it."

"Must be nice to have so much money."

"You can keep it, if it means ending up like him," Tommy says, after checking Liam isn't in earshot.

What does that mean?

"So I've got you and Amy sharing a twin. Is that OK? I figured you guys would wanna stick together, and we have a few weeks yet before we can risk sharing a room."

I love it when his cheeky side comes out.

We will NEVER last six weeks

"Are you sharing?"

He looks confused. "No, who would I be sharing with?"

"That Jason guy maybe, I dunno?"

"I don't think Lexi would be too happy about that."

"Oh they're *together*?"

"Yes, but Liam doesn't know, so be discreet…and maybe don't tell Amy?" he laughs.

"They have separate rooms then?"

"Yes, adjoining rooms."

"Oooh, how romantic! I love it!"

"Are you hungry?"

"Beyond hungry!"

"Me too. Let's go eat," he says, rubbing his hands together. "Amy…food?" he calls.

"Yes, fuck yes, please feed me," she begs, struggling to her feet, still in some pain.

"I think it'll just be breakfast at this time, but you haven't lived until you have a full Irish breakfast."

* * *

Gina

"Sorry, it's what?" I ask, unable to comprehend what Tommy just said.

I'm seated between Tommy and Jason at a large round mahogany table in the hotel dining room, feeling a little out of my depth already. Amy leans in slightly from the other side of the table, keen to either hear more, or make distance from Liam, who's seated beside her. Maybe both.

"Blood sausage. Black pudding they call it. Fried pig's blood and fat." It's obvious he's enjoying our reactions, and I can't tell if he's serious or not.

He can't be serious.

Amy's face mirrors my thoughts. Probably my face too.

"Very funny," I say, trying to play along with the joke, and not feel like the dumb American.

"No, I'm serious. That's what it is," he replies.

"It's actually very tasty, especially with some of this stuff," Liam chips in, lifting a tall square shaped glass bottle that identifies itself as 'HP sauce'.

I glance at Amy. She's as confused as I am.

"Tommy stop messing around. Be nice," Alexis pleads, poking her black pudding suspiciously with her fork.

This sends both Liam and Tommy into a laughing fit. Not cool.

Yeah, laugh at the dumb girls why don't you!

It's obvious Bradley wants to laugh too, but resists. I know why too. Alexis looks like she wouldn't take crap from anybody, so no doubt if Jason is wanting to make use of that adjoining door, he'd best stifle that laughter.

The waitress appears, asking if we'd like some toast with our breakfast.

"Can you tell us what the black pudding is made from please?"

She repeats Tommy's description in a slightly more appetising way, but she can tell from the three female faces that we will not be eating that. She smiles an understanding smile that tells us this is a quite normal reaction from overseas visitors.

"I can bring you more bacon instead, if you prefer?" she suggests, bringing nods of approval and gratitude.

"You won't even try it?" Tommy asks, still too amused by it all.

"No chance, sorry. Even if it does taste good, it's just the thought of it that turns my stomach." I watch as Tommy times a mouthful of *his* black pudding, for maximum effect.

I just close my eyes and turn my head, opening then when I know I'm facing Amy. She's equally horrified.

"Please tell me the rest of breakfast is normal food," she announces to the table in a hopeful, almost desperate tone.

"If we go to Scotland you're in trouble," Liam mumbles through a mouthful of pork sausage.

Ewww, gross

Amy glances at him, but looks away to answer. The sound of his chewing is enough.

Alexis takes the bait. "Why is that?" Jason smiles, waiting for it, while Liam mercifully swallows before answering, taking his time to let the anticipation build.

"Sheep's heart and liver, and maybe it's lungs too."

Amy physically reacts to this. The smallest of retching movements from her chest, lips pursed closed and eyes wide. The other side of the table smiles at this, all except Alexis.

"Actually?" she asks, putting her knife and fork down completely, like she might need to leave.

"Yeah, but there's none here…" Liam nods at her plate, "…so you're OK."

The rest of breakfast is mercifully free of fried animal parts. Well, apart from the sausages and bacon. HP sauce I discover though, is a revelation.

"Do you have your own room Amy?" Liam confidently asks Amy, completely at ease with being heard, as he wipes sauce from his mouth onto a white linen napkin.

Everyone else's eye drop, except mine, which meet Amy's as they widen in realisation. The rest of her face is frozen.

"Emmm...no, Gina and I are are sharing a room."

"Dear dear, Tommy boy. Could you not have arranged private rooms for the ladies?"

"It's OK. Gina and I are used to living together, so it works well," Amy says, regaining some confidence.

"Wouldn't you and Gina prefer a room together now, that you're an item?" Liam asks Tommy directly, expertly making it sound like a question and an order, at the same time.

Tommy looks stuck for words for a moment, hiding it with a slow folding of his napkin.

"We haven't known each other that long, so I thought separate rooms would be more comfortable for Gina, and be safer for Amy?"

"Safer?" Liam asks, with a flash of irritation.

"Oh just *feeling* safe I mean. You know, being in a strange country." Tommy pauses, working hard to talk himself out of this without pissing Liam off. "They've both had a tough time lately, and they only agreed to come on the condition that they share a room."

I'm already nodding beside Tommy, encouraging him to keep going.

"Emotional support for each other. Comfortable is probably a better word than safe to be honest, do you know what I mean?" he smiles.

Well played. Well played.

If I could get away with applause right now, I'd be whooping too. So would Amy, judging by the relief on her face.

Alexis's female solidarity kicks in, and not before time. "The three of us should get a night out while we're here. I'm usually the only girl on these trips, so it's really nice to have you guys here. It's important you feel comfortable, and if I can help with that I will."

I spot Bradley tap her leg under the table, mid-speech, but she ignores it. His next is a double tap when she continues.

Hmm…what's that all about?

"Fine! Next time maybe," Liam says, like he's already claimed Amy.

Thank goodness breakfast is over, and Tommy is first to his feet.

"Liam, what time are we meeting?"

He looks at his heavy gold watch. "3pm. That'll give me time to adjust, hopefully."

"Sounds good," Bradley interjects, probably too excitedly.

He needs to work on that if he's going to keep that relationship a secret.

* * *

Our suite is two doors away from Tommy's, on the first floor.

Amy and I have a queen bed each, and a luxurious bathroom with a separate dressing room too. We're way too tired though to get excited about the room, or the stunning view of the Wicklow Mountains, looking mystical and misty in the distance.

As beautiful as the morning view is, our body clock says bedtime.

The thick heavy curtains glide closed, turning day into night.

The last words spoken before our 8am good-nights are "What a creep!", my vigorous agreement, and brief declarations of hope that this trip doesn't create *more* problems.

27
GINA

Waking up from a daytime nap is disorientating enough at the best of times, but add in an eight hour time difference, *and* waking up in a different country?

My phone vibrates impatiently on the night stand, until my brain does a hard reboot and sends an arm out from under the thick, heavy duvet.

One zombie stumble and two curtains later, it's daytime again. Amy moans a protest, pulling her duvet up over her scrunched up face. "What day is it?" her voice mumbles from beneath.

"No clue. It's today."

"That's not helpful," she says, still muffled.

I give the bottom of her duvet a tug as I pass on my way to the bathroom, but she's got a good grip at the top.

There's a slow knock at the door as I dry my hands, and it brings a smile.

I let Tommy in, and he greets me with a brief hug and a sunny good morning.

"You're way too perky for this room," Amy calls out, from her cosy hiding place.

"What's the plan?" I ask, groggy but still aware of my three in the afternoon 'morning breath'.

"We're meeting downstairs now to plan out the next few days, and make some calls. I booked Liam a massage for 5pm, so I know we'll be done by then."

"Clever!" I smile.

Amy reveals her face. "Eugh, you couldn't pay me enough to massage that slimy bastard."

"Ollie is already on his way down," Tommy winks.

"That'll be nice for you. To see your friend again."

"Yeah, as long as he behaves himself."

"He's not a creep as well is he?" Amy butts in.

"You never know what you're gonna get with Ollie. I think you'll like him though," Tommy says to Amy. "He'll give you a run for your money."

"I don't know what that means," she replies dryly, as she stretches. "But I'm too fucking tired to run anywhere."

"Why don't you guys go back to sleep for a bit, and I'll come back for you later?"

"No way! I want to explore."

Amy exaggerates a groan, before disappearing back out of sight.

"Right well, I'll let you sort it out," he smiles, nodding towards the shape under the covers, and leaning in for a kiss.

Eek. Morning breath!

I jump knees first onto Amy's bed once Tommy leaves, bouncing up and down to get a reaction.

"Will you please fuck off!!"

"No! Get up and play with me!" I laugh, throwing myself on top of her now.

"Ow!" Amy cries, laughing at the same time. "Get off me you big child."

"I'm a human blanket!" I shout, going all the way in with annoying now.

It works. Amy pushes me off, jumps up quickly, and whacks me in the face with her heavy feather pillow.

"Oooh, good shot," I giggle, hair now stuck to my face.

* * *

Thirty five minutes later, we're showered and dressed, and spot the others in a quiet corner of the lobby as we pass through. Tommy waves discretely with just his fingers, mid-conversation.

Cute

We have no idea where we're going, so stop to quiz the doorman who's standing sentry inside, with a red tunic and black top hat.

"Have you visited the gardens yet, madam?"

"No, we just arrived. Is it just out front?"

"A short distance away, in the adjacent part of the estate. Can I arrange to have you taken over?"

"Ummm…yes, that would be good thanks," I reply, after Amy and I look clueless at each other for a moment.

"Of course," he says, formally, nodding. "If you'd like to follow me."

He leads us back the way we came, towards the back of the hotel. Tommy frowns confusion as we pass. Amy of course only adds to it, making a face like we've been naughty, and are about to be thrown out.

I give Tommy a little thumbs up, in exchange for a smile.

I'm sure he'll find out where we are if he needs to.

"It's the third best garden in the world, you know?" he tells us, before commandeering a younger staff member at the back doors. A young lad no more than 18, who looks like his mum dressed him this morning.

"Colm here will take you to the gardens. Have a lovely afternoon ladies."

"Thank you so much," we both chime, before he turns and heads back to his post.

"Shit, are we supposed to be tipping?" Amy whispers. I just shrug. We really have just ended up here with no forethought or planning.

* * *

"This is fucking brilliant!" I'm fairly sure Amy is being sarcastic.

Our mode of transport for the short trip is, of all things, a golf buggy.

"Aw come on, this is fun," I reply, a moment before our bums bounce up off the seat.

Amy giggles, then winces in pain as she lands.

"Ah, sorry there girls," Colm calls over his shoulder. "Feckin' speed bumps everywhere!"

His accent is so thick, it takes a second to decipher it as actual English, and by the time we do it feels too late to reply. Smiles and nods will have to do for now.

Two minutes, and four more speed bumps later, we hop off at the entrance to what looks like another stately home. Colm takes us in, mumbles to a lady behind a desk, and then pushes a glass barrier open, allowing us to pass through.

It takes us a full hour to follow the route on the map we're given. The gardens are beyond stunning - an unexpected tranquil treat for a sunny afternoon, and the perfect antidote to the chaos of the last week.

"Funny how we had to come so far just to slow down?"

"I think I want to live here when I grow up," Amy replies, nodding.

"That'll be never then."

We wander slowly, both loving the Japanese Garden the most, and tickled that they have an actual pet cemetery tucked away. The map booklet tells us that the 47 acre gardens date back to 1731, and are only beaten by those at the palace of Versailles in France, and Kew Botanical Gardens in England.

"Gosh, someone must travel the world judging the nicest gardens," Amy chuckles.

"Sounds like a great job!"

"So what about this Tommy boy then?" she asks, the sudden change of subject a little jarring.

"What about him?"

"Is he for real?"

"Of course he is! Why would you ask that, after everything he's done?"

"Only because you're acting like you're in love already."

"I maybe wouldn't go that far just yet, but it has been amazing. I'm not used to someone being so nice to me."

"Oh thanks!"

"No, you know what I mean!"

"Babe, just be careful. No one can be that perfect. Even if they do know Reese Witherspoon."

"Could you ask for a better character reference though?"

"I just don't want you getting hurt. A week ago you were so spooked, you stopped contacting him. What the fuck happened when you went away?"

"I dunno. I can't really describe it. I just have a feeling about him."

"Look, I get it. He seems like he's a nice guy, and he's obviously got his shit together, but…"

"Not as much as you'd think!" I interrupt.

Amy stops and faces me, squinting like she can't see me any more.

"What do you mean?"

"I mean he's been through some shit too. His wife cheated on him!"

"Whoa, hold up Cinderella, your prince is already married!?"

"Technically. Obviously they're not together since she cheated on him."

"No. Not technically. Actually!"

"Well, I don't imagine they'll be married for much longer by the sound of it."

"How do you know that? What happened?"

I pause, already knowing honesty here is not going to be well received. "He doesn't really talk about it, so I don't know much other than she cheated."

Amy uses no reply to express her disapproval.

"Why do you think I *shouldn't* trust him?" I ask.

"Umm...maybe because he has a penis?"

"Being a man doesn't mean he's untrustworthy."

"It increases the chances drastically!"

I purposefully let another silence fall as we walk on. I can tell she doesn't trust my judgment, but doesn't want to say it. I guess her encounter with my last boyfriend gives her a soap box to preach from. Fair enough.

"Have you see it yet?" she asks, in a gentler tone.

"Seen what?"

"His penis."

"No, I have not!"

"You had a night away and didn't see his penis?" she asks, incredulously.

"Amy! Stop!" I laugh. "I hate it!"

"You hate his penis? What did it do you to?"

"Will you please stop talking about Tommy's penis!"

She makes a fake offended face. "Just wondering!"

An elderly couple pass us, scowling their disapproval.

"Well please stop wondering," I laugh again. "His friend is coming to meet us while we're here, so please be on your best behaviour."

"Oh, OK, that'll be interesting."

"Why?" I ask, suspiciously.

"You can tell a lot about someone by the company they keep. His boss we can forgive, obviously, but it'll be interesting to meet his friend."

Shit!

* * *

We arrive back in the hotel a few minutes before 5pm. Amy cradles a box of six luxuriously thick caramel squares. We found them in a very cute little shop called Avoca in the reception building at the gardens. It's amazing they survived the speed-bumps, and Colm's 'my shift finishes at five' time trial back to base.

Tommy and Liam are alone now, in the same place, but looking much more relaxed. Whatever the meeting was about, it looks like it went well.

Jason and Alexis have conveniently both gone upstairs for a 'shower'.

"We brought you something back," I beam, nodding at the white cake box as I take the armchair beside Tommy. Amy frowns. Clearly sharing our treats with the group wasn't in her plans.

"Aw thanks, that's really thoughtful. Avoca buns are the *best!*" Tommy says, sliding the box across the coffee table.

"Amy! Let's get a drink. Leave these two to it. What will you have?" Liam is already standing up mid-sentence, driving home the negotiation in his favour.

Amy hesitantly rises to her feet, without a word, looking unsure what to do. Liam passes her, striding towards the bar, fully expecting her to follow. She does, after mouthing, "What the fuck?" with a 'help me' face.

"Just stay down here. You'll be fine." Tommy whispers just loud enough for Amy.

It's only for the bar being close by, and in full view, that I let Amy go.

28
TOMMY

"Have you heard anything from the police?" I ask, just as Gina bites the corner of a caramel square.

"Not yet," she mumbles, brushing the crumbs off her jeans. "Should I call them?"

"It would be good to know what's happening?"

"I'm hoping he just gets hit by a truck or something."

"I don't know if we're gonna be that lucky."

"Couldn't your boss just put a hit out on him or something?"

This makes me laugh. A lot!

"He's not a mobster."

"I'm sure he knows a few though."

"Jeez, I thought I was the one who watched too many movies."

"What time is it back home?" she asks. It strikes me that I'm not even sure where 'back home' is for me right now. That's a weird feeling, like you don't belong anywhere in particular.

"Just after nine in the morning, I think. Good time to call."

Gina just tilts her head in vague agreement, but doesn't reply. The tray-bake is getting all her consideration at the moment. That's fair - they are pretty special.

"The card is in my room." she says, pointing up, but relaxing back into the chair.

"Your room card?"

"No, the card with the phone number for the police station."

"Will we go get it?"

"I'm not letting Amy out of my sight," she says assertively, shaking her head. "I'll do it later."

I consider for a moment encouraging her to do it now, but let it go. Phoning isn't going to change whether they've picked Brandon up or not, so I decide to just let her relax, and forget about it all for now.

"OK," I smile. "I can't wait for Ollie to meet you. He should be here soon."

"No pressure!"

"No, of course not. How could anyone not love you?"

Shit, did I just say that out loud?

Gina pauses just long enough to give me hope that she missed it, then let's a shy grin appear.

"Drinks!" I say quickly after clearing my throat. "What would you like?" I ask, standing up, and self-consciously tugging the bottom my waistcoat.

Amy looks up at me, the shy grin turning mischievous.

"I'll maybe take some of that love, if it's on offer?"

The tummy butterflies are back as quick as Gina's boldness, and I open my mouth for a witty comeback. Nothing. I stand there, two seconds feeling like ten!

"It's not often you're speechless," she giggles. "I got you a good one there."

I nod back. "You sure did. I love an awkward silence, but it's usually me who creates them."

"Oh? Maybe you've finally met your match?"

I let those words hang there for a few seconds, until she realises her unintentional faux pas is as good as mine. Gina's cheeks begin to blush.

"What's up?" she asks, the nervous laugh betraying her certainty. "Speechless again?"

"No!" I sing. "Just letting you think I've met my match."

Her cheeks redden a little more, and she instinctively lowers her chin a little, but still looking up at me. Her sudden switch from bolshy and cheeky, to shy and vulnerable is incredibly sexy.

Is she doing this on purpose?

I take a couple of steps towards her, and slowly go down on one knee, not breaking eye contact, and take her left hand in both of mine. Gina's eyes widen. Fear, confusion, bewilderment…anticipation.

"Gina Elisabeth Sawyer. Would you please do me the great honour of having a drink with me?"

The explosion of laughter catches Amy's attention at the bar, her mouth dropping open in shock, at the sight of me in proposal position.

"Well played…" Gina says seductively, once she stops laughing, looking at me with such affection and admiration. It's a look that soothes something deep inside, and my own cheeks warm at the realisation of this feeling…this connection between us.

That, and the fact that I can totally see myself doing this for real at some point.

29
TOMMY

"Does this mean I have to be best man, *again*!?"

The unmistakable voice behind me is my oldest friend, Oliver Randall. Call him Oliver though and you risk at least a prolonged headlock.

"Actually, should you not wait until you're divorced before proposing again?" Ollie adds, bouncing up the two steps from the lobby floor, to the carpeted bar area.

"Subtle as a brick as always, Oliver," I say over my shoulder, increasing volume on his name.

Next thing, I'm on the floor with Ollie on top of me. Twice in a week now I've wrestled a man on the floor. Thankfully this time he isn't a psychopath. Just an asshole.

"Get off me you dick! My boss is over there!" I laugh, trying to gain some leverage to push him off, but he's too strong.

I glance up at Gina, feeling foolish, like my big brother is bullying me in front of my girlfriend for kicks. She's trying not to laugh, covering her mouth, clearly enjoying the shock on my face too much.

"What the fuck is happening?" Amy demands, rushing over, taking the opportunity to escape Liam. He's close behind, but a slow unconcerned walk, whiskey in one hand. "Are they fighting?" Amy giggles.

A sharp poke in Ollie's ribs gets him off me. By the time I climb to my feet, he has already landed in my chair - legs and arms thrown wide, and wearing a triumphant grin that I know well. "Woo! That was fun!" he says. "You've gone soft mate."

I just give him a 'behave yourself' look." Gina and Amy frown at each other.

"It's good to see you too," I reply, taking a seat opposite him, after I tuck my shirt back in. "Everyone, this is my 'friend' Ollie."

"What's the craic guys?" Ollie booms, still grinning. "So which one of you two stunners is responsible for getting my boy here back on the horse?"

The frowns deepen.

"I guess I'm the horse. Whatever that means…" Gina says, apprehensively raising a hand.

"The lovely Gina! Nice to finally meet you!" Ollie says, standing up to face her. Gina stays seated, looking up at him with justifiable trepidation.

"Come on then!" Ollie says, extending both hands towards Gina. She eventually stands up, slowly, after a glance to me, and when he pulls her in for a tight hug she almost disappears.

"You must be the friend?"

"The 'friend'?" Amy times an eyebrow lift with a head tilt, *and* an eye roll. "Great! I've been reduced to the friend, like the sidekick in some shitty eighties movie."

"Alright calm down…?" he tails off, making a 'tell me your name' face, one hand out waiting for it.

"Amy. My name is Amy." she replies, so dryly that I'm a bit scared for Ollie, who has never been good at picking up on such things. I get the feeling that she's only let him away with telling her to calm down, for everyone else's sake.

"Ah, nice to meet you, Amy!" He's already closing the gap between them, raising his arms.

"No! I don't want a h…"

She's already in his arms, hers trapped by her side, and an expression of disgust just about visible in the bear hug.

"Ooh, I hope the other person got as good as they gave you?" he says, letting her go, and being close enough now to see her bruises.

He puts his fists up quickly in a mock fight stance. Amy just deadpans him. If looks could kill.

"Ollie, sit down and behave yourself. I'll get you a beer." He recognises my tone of voice and obliges, but not without a cocky smile to Amy first.

When I return a minute or two later with Ollie's pint, he's arguing that football doesn't involve your hands, unless you're a goalkeeper. That's going to be a losing battle against three Americans, though to be fair, two of them look like they couldn't care less.

"Thanks matey," Ollie smiles, before downing a third of the pint in one go. "Fuck, I needed that!"

"How long are you here for?" Gina asks, trying to bring it back to normal conversation.

"Just while you guys are here. I've got three weeks off, so I'm gonna make the most of it."

"That'll be nice!" Amy exaggerates, but it goes over Ollie's head as usual.

Liam's phone begins to ring, and he heads back towards the bar to take the call.

"What's the plan then, fuckers?" Ollie asks, draining another three inches from his glass.

"Other than work stuff, not very much," I reply. I've been reluctant to plan anything, not knowing how settled the girls would be here.

"Have you girls been to Wicklow before?" Ollie asks, looking to Amy then Gina, lingering just long enough on Amy to make her uncomfortable.

"No, never! It's lovely so far. We went to the gardens today!" Gina says excitedly.

"Apart from the feckin' speed bumps!" Amy butts in, switching accents with average success.

Ollie's booming laugh draws eyes from a thirty foot radius. "Oh we love a feckin' speed bump over here alright! It didn't take you long to find them."

"We're at Glendalough in the morning," I mention. "You guys should come, and Ollie will look after you while I'm working?"

"Look after us?" Amy's eyebrow inquires.

"Is it dangerous?" Gina asks, with genuine concern.

Ollie's laugh is probably enough to answer that.

"What even is it?" she continues.

"It's one of the most beautiful lakes you'll see in the entire world. You'll *love* it!"

"Wow! It sounds amazing! Is it far from here?"

"Thirty or forty minutes drive, up through the Wicklow Mountains. The whole trip is beautiful actually."

"It is fucking gorgeous to be fair," Ollie agrees, looking directly at Amy the entire time.

Gina can only see the back of Ollie's head, but can see Amy's face clearly, and the hint of red appearing in her cheeks.

Gina looks at me with surprise, and I just shake my head to absolve myself of Ollie's behaviour. Not for the first time, and most likely not the last.

There's a resounding agreement to the suggestion of food when Amy suggests it after another round of drinks, small talk, and some persistent flirting by Ollie.

"How about Summerhill House?" Ollie suggests.

"I think we need a proper Irish pub," I suggest.

"Yes! I would *love* that!" Gina says quickly.

"Johnnie Fox's? Is it too far?" Ollie asks.

"I've never been, but I know it's on this side of Dublin, and up in the mountains, so it can't be that far."

"I'll go check. I need a pee anyway."

"Ewww, too much information dude."

"I could always show you, instead of telling you," he says in mock seriousness as he stands, pretending to unbutton his jeans.

"No thanks! I need to go as well, so you can show me where they are," Amy replies bluntly.

"Oh, the toilets are unisex in Ireland, so we're going to the same one." Ollie deadpans perfectly.

"Sorry, what?" Amy says, cocking her head slightly.

"Come on, and I'll show you," he says, as he breezes past, grabbing her hand on the way.

They head off towards the bathrooms, Amy punching his arm to make him drop her hand.

"They're not are they?" Gina asks, amused at the sight of her friend battling off the heavy handed approach to pick her up…literally.

"They might. I think he's wearing her down," I reply with a smirk.

"What? I mean the unisex bathrooms!"

"Oh!" I laugh. "No he's just winding her up. This country is way too repressed to have unisex toilets."

"What were *you* talking about?"

"I thought you meant those two. Getting together."

Gina looks shocked at the thought. "Noooo!" she exhales. "He's so not her type."

"I don't think Ollie is anyone's type, but that's never stopped him."

Gina pauses to think about this, frowning, like she can't read her friend any more. "No, I can't see that happening."

"Yeah, you're probably right. But if it did, it might keep Liam at bay," I say with a wry smile.

"The two of them together would be interesting. They're so similar."

"Totally! It would be a constant battle to have the upper hand."

"Oh, I'm not sure I have the energy for that!" Gina laughs.

A moment later they're back, and we make it too obvious that we're studying them as they approach.

"What??" Amy demands a little too emphatically.

"Nothing!" Gina and I both reply quickly, as Ollie gives us a cheeky wink from behind Amy.

"Why are you both smiling like that then?" she demands.

We look at each other for an answer before Gina replies. "We like smiling. We were just talking about how amazing smiling is."

"You're fucking weird in Ireland," Amy replies suspiciously.

"Well, how far to Johnnie Fox's Ollie?" I ask as he squats to sit.

"Oh fuck, I forgot to ask!" He stands back up, and we both see the look he gives Amy.

"What are you two up to?" Gina asks in a loud whisper, leaning towards Amy, as Ollie marches back towards the bar.

"Nothing. He's an asshole!". The reply is terse and final.

"Hmm…" Gina leans back, and gives me a conspiratorial look. Amy notices but doesn't react.

"Fifteen minutes drive. There's a taxi on the way. It'll be here in five minutes, out back. No messin!" Ollie announces, staying on his feet to down the rest of his beer.

"I'm fucking starving now," He wipes his mouth with the back of his hand, and plonks his glass back down. Another glance to Amy, who just glares at him.

Gina frowns at her friend, but she doesn't allow eye contact. Instead, she takes a purposefully slow sip of her cider.

Two minutes later, we're outside, and Gina points out the golf buggy with the poor suspension, just as the taxi pulls up.

It's a traditional 'black cab' instead of a normal car, and gives us the opportunity to all pile into the back. There are two bench style seats facing each other, with enough room for three people on each side, and two more on little fold down seats, on the inside of the heavy doors.

The suspension is only marginally better than the golf buggy, as we mount one 'feckin speed bump' on the way out of the car park.

All four of our bums bounce simultaneously, setting off a chain of giggles that could only come from slightly tipsy people. Speed bumps are not usually this funny.

The sun is thinking about setting over the Wicklow Mountains as the taxi makes its way up the winding roads

Golden hour here has its own magic, I decide, as my ears pop…

30
GINA

The sky looks bigger here, somehow.

The deep orange is beautifully unique. Sunsets are beautiful at home, but never taking over so much of the sky, so dramatically. The windows along the front of Johnnie Fox's reflect the low evening sun, like it's glowing from the inside.

Just like me.

The highest pub in Ireland, so the sign says, is a rough hewn, old looking building. It's whitewashed walls are almost entirely covered in purple and white flowers.

"It's really pretty! I wasn't expecting all the flowers."

The taxi trundles off again, after the driver hands us a business card for a return journey.

We only have to wait a few minutes at the bar inside, before we're shown to a table for four, near a hearth almost big enough for a person to stand in. The fire isn't lit, being summer, but I bet it's so cosy in here on a winter's night.

"Do you feel bad that we didn't invite the others?" I ask as we take our seats.

"No!" Amy and I answer in unison, making me laugh.

We have a cute little booth with upholstered bench seating, high wood paneled backs, and red scatter cushions. Each table has a candle burning, and is laid out with cutlery already.

A casually dressed waiter passes, leaving us a small wicker basket, and telling us it's home-made wheaten bread. We all get stuck in immediately, spreading the butter thick on the slightly warm bread, before tasting heaven.

The approval is unanimous. The perfect starter, after a couple of drinks.

"How lucky are we to get the last table?" Tommy says, after a contented sigh.

The bar is busy, but not rowdy. Almost everyone is seated for food, except for some old men at the bar, who look like they've been there for a long time. There's an excited hum of voices and music in the air. Van Morrison's 'Brown Eyed Girl'.

"It's meant to be!" I say, putting my hand on Tommy's leg, and giving it an affectionate squeeze.

Tommy and I are on one side of the booth, of course, meaning Ollie and Amy have to sit together opposite us. The booth isn't very big, unlike Ollie, so they're a little too close for comfort. Well, maybe just Amy's comfort.

"Are Irish people really tiny?" Amy asks, irritated, as she tries to push Ollie up the bench a little, and sighs when he doesn't budge.

"It's cosy!" I offer, aiming for optimistic, but knowing it'll just provoke Amy. She just gives me a look to confirm.

"This is going to require alcohol!" Amy says, with a less content sigh of her own.

* * *

We're all on our second drinks by the time dinner arrives. Amy and I are enjoying Pornstar Martinis, with the boys sticking to beer. The food is practically inhaled, before a brief debate about dessert results in two Apple Pies and two Whiskey Cakes being ordered.

"It's like a proper double date…" I tease, as both sides of the table share one of each of the two desserts. "…except one couple are married!"

"Who's married?" Tommy asks, confused.

"Well, you obviously, but less said about that the better. These two though, are like a married couple," I say, pointing my spoon across the table.

"How's that?" Ollie asks.

"Because you don't like each other. You know, like when people are married?" I laugh, over-explaining but still proud of how funny I am.

"Oh yeah, I get it," Amy says, dry as ever, crossing arms with Ollie, as they both take a spoonful from the bowl in front of the other.

"Aw! Look how cute they are!" I poke.

Ollie grins. Amy glares.

* * *

An hour passes, along with two more drinks each. The chat is about movies and music for a while, extolling the virtues of our favourites, and in some cases having to defend their honour.

I share that the movies that mean most to me are Legally Blonde, of course, but also the 1967 classic, 'Guess Who's Coming To Dinner?' To be fair, I needed something a bit more highbrow, to get away with my first choice. My musical taste starts again with an obvious one, well, obvious to three of us. Stevie Nicks, or anything she does with Fleetwood Mac. Playing the contrast card again, I go for Eminem.

"I would love to have such a good outlet for anger and resentment." The blank faces tell me how weird that must have sounded, and thankfully no one pushes me to elaborate. I would just blame the alcohol anyway.

Amy goes next. The Fast and The Furious, seemingly just for a fantasy threesome with Vin Diesel and Paul Walker. She takes the crown for weirdest statement with, "We'd make a beautiful three-way baby together, don't you think?" Again, no request to elaborate. The mental image is already disturbing enough, though Ollie seems impressed. By what, I'm not quite sure. I'm scared to ask.

Her second movie choice is just as out of left field as mine. 'Nine to Five', the early 80's movie with Dolly Parton, Jane Fonda and Lily Tomlin. "It's been more than twenty fucking years, and that shit still goes on!"

Ollie goes for music first, and keeps it mainstream. Rapper Eminem, and rock legends AC/DC, who he and Tommy saw in Dublin in 1996. For movies, he also goes for 'Fast and the Furious', possibly as a ploy. "In years to come people will look back on that movie as a masterpiece!"

A brief but hilarious debate ensues, when Tommy suggests that it's also just a rip off of 'Point Break'.

"Maybe so, but cars are so much fucking cooler than surfboards!" Ollie argues, getting a high five from Amy.

He also insists on an honourable mention for the Rocky, and American Pie films, at which point Amy looks like she wants to withdraw her half of the high five. "Movies about fighting, and movies about fucking? How original. You couldn't be more of a 'guy' unless you pulled your dick out, and slapped it on the table."

There's a stunned pause, and a scary moment where at least one of thinks he actually might, before we all burst out laughing.

Tommy can barely contain himself by the time it's his turn. Talking Heads, The Rolling Stones, Alanis Morissette and some band called Deacon Blue all get mentioned, with Counting Crows added in as an afterthought.

His movie number one is 'Dead Poets Society'. "No film changed my outlook on life like that one did!". He also mentions one called 'Peter's Friends' which none of us have heard of. "There's a funny story with that one, and an ex girlfriend. I must tell you some time."

"And music?" I ask.

"I'm not done with movies yet!" he protests.

"We'll be here all night now. Let's hope they do lock-ins," Ollie laughs.

"Well, you see, you have to understand the magnificent genius of John Cusack. If I had to pick someone to play me in the movie of my life it would be him," he gushes. "The triple of 'Say Anything', 'Grosse Pointe Blank' and 'Serendipity' are masterpieces of comedy and romance."

"I do love that one!" Amy interrupts. "How fucking beautiful is Kate Beckinsale?"

"And then, to crown it all off, the best one of all is 'High Fidelity'. Pure genius!"

"What fucking Ian guy?" Ollie shouts, pointing at Tommy, who's face instantly has all the enthusiasm sucked out.

He recovers it fast, before I can ask if he's OK.

What the hell was that?

"Sorry matey. That was below the belt." Ollie says, but he's still laughing. "Good movie though. Jack Black was fucking hilarious…and who knew he could sing!?"

"Ummm…everybody you moron. He's a singer too." Amy says, elbowing him.

I can't decide if these two are more like brother and sister, or husband and wife. A bit of both maybe.

"Is he aye?" Ollie smirks.

"Tenacious D," Tommy adds, nodding.

Ollie just frowns his reply.

"The band he's in. It's called Tenacious D," Amy says, enjoying Ollie's bewilderment. "It's OK, we'll keep you right," she continues. I can't see, but it looks like she put her hand on his leg as she said that. Ollie's eyes flick downwards, then to Amy, who looks for a second like she's been caught shoplifting.

I can't help but giggle. "You two should be on stage."

"Ah fuck, I hate this song!" Tommy mutters beside me. It's only in that moment that I realise how little he swears, so it catches my attention more than it otherwise would.

'Dancing In The Moonlight,' by Toploader is playing on the jukebox.

"How can you *hate* this song?" I ask. "It's great!"

"Hmm…" he just replies.

"What's *that* all about?" I inquire, a little more pointedly.

"What's what?" he says, dodging.

"This song, and your reaction!"

"Sorry, no, I used to like it, but it just reminds me of something." He's quieter now.

"What are you two whispering about?" Amy asks, leaning over her cocktail glass, and sucking the drizzle from the bottom through a straw.

"What does it remind you of?" I ask, ignoring Amy. I think if not for the cocktails and all the banter tonight, I wouldn't have asked.

"It's the song that was playing on the radio, when I drove away from…." He starts confidently, but tails off.

"Oooh! Away from what?" Amy asks excitedly, leaning in again, like a gossip seeking missile.

"My wife. When I caught her with another man." Tommy's reply is bluntly, with no emotion.

"Fuckin' hell! I'd be furious!" Amy mutters. "Ruining a good song for you like that?"

Tommy bursts out laughing, closely followed by Ollie, but I already feel bad for opening this can of worms.

"So what happened? Was she banging your best friend or something?" Amy asks, too excitedly.

"Amy!" I almost shout. "Don't be rude!"

"It's OK," Tommy says calmly, touching my hand. "No, not my best friend, otherwise he wouldn't be sitting beside *you* right now."

"Who then?"

"Well, as Ollie, and John Cusack so eloquently put it, some fucking Ian guy."

Ollie purses his lips, looking properly awkward now for the first time. Not before time either.

"Did you know him?" Amy presses.

"You don't have to talk about this, Tommy," I implore, taking his hand. I know how difficult it is to talk about things which have hurt you, and this probably isn't the time, or the place. As much as I still want to know as well.

"I know," he replies softly, squeezing my hand like I'm the one needing reassurance. "No I didn't know him."

There's a silence, while Amy expects more.

"Do you want the highlights, or the full story? Ollie knows it all anyway."

"Are you kidding? The whole story. Highlights included."

"Amy! This isn't a fucking soap opera!" I wince.

"No, actually it probably could be," Tommy concedes, adding an ironic chuckle. "Though if you saw this on TV, you probably wouldn't believe it…"

Amy just nods, not wanting to interrupt any more.

"Well, we'd been having some problems already, and had actually separated. I rented a house not too far away, and was totally happy. It felt like a clean break, you know?"

"OK…"

"I'm telling you this for context I suppose. Things were OK for a week or so, then she decided she wanted me back. I wasn't keen at first but she laid it on thick. Said all the right things, and gave me hope that it could work out between us again."

"How long were you with her?"

"Emmm…five years or so."

"How long were you married?" Amy is settling into this, like she's interviewing someone on TV.

"Not even three years."

"OK, carry on," she says impassively. I roll my eyes.

"Well, I didn't want to move back to our marital home, because her mum lived door. She would let herself in at any hour of the day, so it almost felt like I was living with her too."

"Awful!" Amy commentates, agreeing with a shake of her head.

"I agreed to get back together if she would move out, and live in the house that I was now renting."

"And she didn't want to?"

"No, she did! Sort of, but didn't seem in a hurry to move everything from the old house. It was good though, despite that. Hopeful, you know, like we were starting over."

"Right…?"

"So, she'd got this part time job, working in a sandwich bar in the town, and had made a couple of friends there who were single and didn't have kids. Most weekends before we split up, she'd be out at least one night at the weekend, and I looked after her wee girl."

"Hang on, you guys had a child?" I interrupt, shocked.

"No, she was a baby when I met her, so not my child."

"Where was the baby daddy?" Amy asks.

"Around for a bit, then disappeared. He gave her a real hard time too. I never got the full story, but I think it was a bit volatile. I don't think I really wanted to know…"

"So you were willing to take on someone else's kid?" I ask, still surprised.

"Ummm yeah, I honestly never gave it much thought. I liked her, and it didn't seem like a deal breaker."

"OK, so she's sort of moved in with you to the new house?" Amy asks.

"Yeah, then a week or so later she went out to a local bar with her work friends, and didn't come home." He takes a sip of beer, as if for courage.

"Oh!?"

"Yeah, I'm at home, in the new house with her wee girl asleep. I'm phoning and phoning until about 3am. There's no reply, so I go to bed, thinking she must have just be drunk and went back to the house we'd been living in. She still had the keys and most of her stuff there, and it was close to the bar."

"Uh oh," Amy mutters. We can all see where this is going. Ollie's face is solemn, just listening.

"Yeah, so 7am and I'm awake already. It's a Sunday morning, I remember that. I put Hayley in the car, and drive over."

"No calls back by this point, I assume?"

"Nope. So we lived on a one way street, and the house was right in the middle. There was space to park right at the door. Like really close. There was a big curtain on the inside of the front door, and I could see through the glass that it was pulled across. You can only do that from the inside, obviously. I was so cross that she just went there, and didn't think to let me know. I was relieved that nothing had happened, but that just made me more angry. Like just casually don't come home, and don't tell me!?"

"What did you do?"

"I knocked the door, after trying my key."

"She changed the locks!?"

"No, she just put the snib on the door on the inside, so you couldn't even open it with a key. I could see our bedroom window above had the blinds closed... and the window was all steamed up. That's how I knew for sure she was in there."

"I'm so sorry!" Amy interrupts. "I know this is probably hard to relive, but it's so fucking good! And I need to pee. Can you hold on?"

"Sure! Go pee," I laugh, despite myself.

"Thank you!" she almost cries, even giving me half a hug on the way past.

"Are you OK?" I ask.

"I think so. It doesn't feel like it's my life I'm describing now. Does that make sense?"

"It totally does," I reply, giving him a quick kiss. "As long as you're OK."

"You guys are too fucking cute." Ollie chips in.

Amy lands back in her seat, after what must be the fastest pee ever. "OK go on."

"So, I'm stood there knocking on the door for a good five minutes, then the curtain finally opens inside. You know, they say the face is capable of more than 10,000 expressions, and even through the glass of the door, her face gave it away immediately."

"She let you in then?"

"Yeah, she did. She had no option."

"What did you say?"

"I asked her who was here with her, not wanting to believe that there was anyone. It felt like the obvious first question, just in case. She said there was nobody there, but you know, it was *so* weak that I knew for sure, in that exact moment that there 100% was."

"Fuck me. It's so shit this happened to you, but you should think about a career in storytelling."

"Amy!" I interject, but she ignores me.

"It's funny. Nothing can ever prepare you for how situations like this make you feel. It was like suddenly being in a tunnel. Everything in front of me in sharp focus, like it was being burnt forever into my brain. Everything else on the periphery was just hazy. I know that sounds weird."

"No actually, I get it."

I nod agreement as well, my hand squeezing Tommy's.

"There was no hesitation in charging up the stairs. Not a single moment of consideration, just autopilot. She followed up behind me, and I went straight to what had been our bedroom until a few weeks ago. Apologies if this is a bit gross, but the duvet was on the floor in a heap, and the bed was covered in blood."

They all say a version of, "What the fuck!"

"I didn't know that bit." Ollie says, frowning. "Fucking hell, that's mental!"

"Yeah, the blood stains were *all* over the bed, every corner, so she'd been about it. At first I thought she'd cut her leg or something. At least that's what you'd want to believe isn't it?"

We nod, transfixed.

"It was the air in the room that gave it away. Normally, when you smell sex in your bedroom, it's when you've just been to the bathroom and come back. Not when you've just arrived by car."

Tommy's sneer now is something I haven't seen before.

"The smell was unmistakable, and worse because it was so hot in the room. I swear I'll never forget that, like I could almost taste it."

"Where was the dude?" Amy asks, slowly, still processing it all.

"I'm coming to that, don't worry. So I turned around and there *she* is on the landing, leaning on the banister like she suddenly didn't give a single *fuck*." I asked her where he was and she stupidly denied there was anyone there. Like I was just gonna say OK, and go away."

"Of course not!" Amy agrees, enthralled.

"There were two other bedrooms, and a bathroom, and they *almost* got away with it because I checked the bedrooms and there was no one there. I was about to head downstairs for a look, when I thought I should actually go *into* the rooms to check. It's not like he'd just be lounging on a spare bed, so I went on into the second bedroom and turned around.

And there he was, standing behind the door, trying to make himself look small."

"Oh fuck!"

"Yeah, that was my reaction too. It's not until you actually see it, that you believe it. It was surreal, like I was spectating someone else's reality."

"What did you do?"

"I just said hello there."

Amy leans back on this. "You said hello?"

"Yeah, I couldn't really think of anything else to say," I laugh. "It was so surreal."

"You didn't punch him, or go crazy?"

"Nope. I know that's what happens in the movies and stuff, but at that moment I just felt very calm. I was angry at her, I suppose, but the guy was probably just taking an opportunity to get some sex with a girl he met in a bar….although now I know they probably had been seeing each other for a while, as they're still together. I think."

Ollie nods.

"I can't believe you went through that…" I say, unsure what else to give.

"Yeah, it's a very strange thing to experience. It hit me hard, you know. That level of betrayal, when your guard is down. It's hard to take."

"Phew…I can imagine." Amy says, appearing more exhausted by the story than Tommy does.

"So she was fucking another guy in your bed, while you were looking after her kid?" I ask, more just to hear it out loud for how fucked up it actually was.

"Yup."

"Wow! You didn't deserve to be treated like that. I'm so sorry!" I offer, rubbing his arm with my other hand, and suddenly feeling very inadequate. "I can see why you don't like that song now."

"Don't be sorry. It's OK. It all happened for a reason I'm sure. To teach me some hard lesson, and I wouldn't be here with you guys otherwise."

"Are you getting a divorce then?" Amy asks.

"It's already in the works."

"Good!" she smiles. "I'll raise a glass to that."

"You're well rid of her mate. No one needs all that drama in their life," Ollie declares.

I look at Tommy, sheepishly. It's only when Ollie mentions drama, that I realise how much it must have taken for Tommy to *not* run as fast as he could in the opposite direction, when Brandon gate-crashed on Sunday.

"Right, we need to lighten the mood, before we all drown our sorrows." Ollie continues.

"I can't believe that yesterday we had a drink with Reese Witherspoon, and today we're in Ireland. Life is so weird!" It's all I can think of to change the subject, but once the words leave my mouth, I'm embarrassed at how trivial it sounds.

"I need to come over there, and meet some of these famous people," Ollie groans. "You guys are so lucky!"

"You could try out for LA Galaxy mate. They're really trying to push football over there," Tommy suggests. "It's a long way from Larne Football Club. You'll not be playing in the rain every week for a start."

"Hmm. Isn't that where footballers go when they're about to retire though?"

"No idea. I'm sure the standard is pretty similar to the Irish League, and the money is probably better."

"Never even considered it to be honest. Happy enough where I am for now though!" Ollie smiles, barely hiding another flirty glance at Amy.

31
TOMMY

"Is it weird that it felt wrong, going to separate rooms last night?" I ask as I take a seat beside Gina in the restaurant. We share a kiss as she nods.

"How did you sleep?"

"OK." she replies.

"Are you sure? You seem quiet this morning."

"Yeah, maybe just jet-lag." Gina manages a smile. It's unconvincing, but I decide not to press for more.

I wonder did she have a fall out with Amy?

Everything seemed fine last night…

"Amy not with you?"

"I woke her before I came down. She went back to the bar for a drink with Ollie last night, and I don't know what time she came back."

"Oh wow, really?"

"Yeah, she makes all the right noises about not liking him, then goes off with him."

"Do you think they did more than drink?"

"Goodness knows, but she wasn't back when I woke at 2am, so she's gonna be hanging today. She doesn't do late nights usually."

"You were awake at 2am?" I ask, surprised.

"Umm…yeah, but I got back over. So what's the plan this morning?" she asks, suddenly brighter.

"Are you *sure* you're OK?" I ask. "Have I done something, or said something?"

"No."

"Was it all that stuff last night? I probably went into too much detail…"

"No!" she interrupts. "I'm really proud of you!" She lays a hand gently on my arm, and gives it a gentle squeeze. "It was really brave of you to share all that. I'm not sure I could do that."

"Thank you," I reply, still unsure. "I'm so glad you're here, you know?"

"Yeah?"

I nod, trying to read her face. Beautiful as always, but there's definitely something different this morning. I try to brush it off, as the others begin to arrive. Everyone has bad days, and I need to not get paranoid. I wouldn't tell her of course, but I feel responsible for Gina's safety and happiness, now that I've brought her here.

Liam arrives first, checking on the timings for the day ahead, before Jason and Lexi arrive, seconds apart. No doubt they just had a, "You go in first so it's not suspicious," discussion. Ollie is close behind, and I introduce him properly to the others. He's a little bleary eyed, but no less loud, and his banter lifts the early morning vibes at the table.

Amy is last to join us, weaving her way through the tables slowly, like she's hoping someone else invites her to join them.

She sits with a quiet "Good morning," clutching a bottle of water. Definitely avoiding eye contact with everyone, despite Ollie's attempts. The only seat is beside him, and I spot the hesitation when she realises. The pursed lips too. Gina must notice as well, judging by the tap on my thigh under the table.

"Sleep well, Amy?" I ask brightly, with a little mischief.

She glances up at me, then to Gina, looking startled to have been picked out.

The girls are both quiet during breakfast, but seem interested to listen to the discussion. Prior to working in the industry, I had no idea just how much preparation goes into making a movie. Managing and coordinating all the moving parts is daunting. Our morning will be spent around Glendalough with the production's DOP. Only Amy had to ask what that stood for. Director of Photography. Just one of the many acronyms that Gina especially, will soon be used to.

* * *

The forty minute car journey has us split like before, with Ollie hanging back to get some more sleep. I think Liam might have let him tag along, if he wasn't as suspicious as the rest of us about him and Amy.

We pull into the car park at almost exactly ten am. I know Liam notices little things like that. It's a fairly easy way to keep him happy. "Nail the basics, and don't fuck up the big stuff," he said when he hired me, and I always remembered it.

"Where's the lake?" Gina asks. It's the first she's spoken in about twenty minutes, and I pass it off as just enjoying the scenery as we crossed the mountains. She hasn't let go of my hand the entire journey though. This soothes the paranoia loitering in the back of my brain, like an uninvited guest.

"Just behind those trees," I reply, pointing through the back window.

The weather is perfect, and I'm so glad. I remember my first time here, and the impact it had. I want Gina to feel that too. The bright morning sunshine makes us squint, as we climb out of the tinted window car.

"Wait for me. I want to be with you when you see it," I smile, dying to kiss her, but aware that I'm on duty now. Be professional.

"That's so sweet!" she says, allowing a smile to appear, before lifting to her tiptoes to kiss me.

"You guys are sickening…" Amy mutters, nearby. "This better be *some* lake!"

"I'll be back in a minute, OK?" I say, ignoring Amy. The words "I love you," seem perfect for the moment, but they get stuck on the way up. It catches me by surprise though. That instinct to tell her how I feel.

Do I really feel that way yet?

Is it because I sense something not quite right, and feel compelled to fix it? Does that make it less meaningful if I do say it?

It's too soon anyway…

Gina squints one eye, just slightly, even though I'm shading her from the sun. I panic, just on the inside, and feel my heart thump louder.

Does she know what I almost said?

She smiles like she does, giving me a nod and a content, "OK."

The DOP and his assistants are standing by their van, across the car park from us, and Liam is already greeting them with handshakes.

I should be there doing the same. Be professional.

32
GINA

"I need to talk to you!" I say urgently, taking Amy's hand once Tommy's back is turned.

"Oh, please don't!" Amy whines.

"Please don't what?"

"Don't ask me about Ollie. He's *still* a prick."

"What!?" I say, thrown off my train of thought. "Ollie? What did you do?"

"I said don't ask me!"

"Well I can't help it now, can I? Did you go back to his room last night?"

"Maybe…" Amy squirms. "Alcohol is the devil!"

"We don't have much time, so you can tell me the gory details later."

"What's going on G?" Amy asks gently, taking my hand.

"Last night when you weren't there, someone came into our room."

"What!?" Her face flashes horror, fear and concern, all at once. "Who?"

Thank goodness no one is within earshot.

"Tommy's boss, Liam…"

"What the actual fuck Gina!" she bursts, grabbing my other hand too. "Did he hurt you?"

"Please keep your voice down!" I plead. "I don't...I mean no, he didn't hurt me, but I was *so* scared."

"How did he get in?"

"I don't know!"

"What happened?"

"The door clicking closed woke me up, and I thought it was you coming in. It was really dark, and you didn't answer, so I thought you were drunk. I got up to check, and he was just standing there."

"Holy fuck! What did you do?"

"I asked him what he wanted, and how he got in. He said he was looking for you, and I told him you weren't there."

"Oh my god!"

"That probably wasn't the smartest thing to do, because next thing he had me pinned against the wall, trying to kiss me."

Amy's mouth falls open, speechless. She let's go of my hands, and makes a move to turn towards where Liam is standing, with Tommy and the others.

"No!!" I demand, as firmly as I can, grabbing her hand again and wheeling her back around.

"I'm gonna cut his fucking balls off, Gina! Dirty bastard!"

"You're not going to do anything!"

"Why the fuck not!?"

"Because of Tommy..."

"Are you serious!? What has it got to do with him?"

"Please calm down Amy. I *need* you to listen to me. Don't make me regret telling you!"

Amy falls silent, looking wounded, but bubbling under the surface with rage.

"Go on." she says, after taking a big breath.

"If I do anything, or if Tommy finds out, he could lose his job!"

"But you can't just let him get away with that!"

"I know, but…I don't know. I just know that if Tommy finds out, he'll do something."

"Why would that be a bad thing?"

"Because if he doesn't have a job, then he might go home!"

Amy pauses, studying me. I can tell she's blinkered by revenge on my behalf, and I can see her struggling with it.

"Fuck sake, I should have been there. I'm so sorry!" she says eventually.

"Well, I should have been there when Brandon attacked you. I think I got off lightest out of the two of us."

"Why are men so fucking horrible?" Amy seethes. "Are you sure this guy is worth this?"

"I think so," I reply, betraying my heart a little. "Yes, there's something there. He's not like anyone I've ever met."

"That doesn't mean he's good for you babe!"

"I know…but I have a good feeling."

"You need to have sex with him." Amy's bluntness is jarring.

"What? Why?"

"To make extra sure he's right for you."

The confusion on my face must be obvious, but Amy just raises her eyebrows as if she expects the penny to drop any moment.

"I don't see how that changes who he is Amy," I reply, when it's clear she's not going to elaborate on this strange advice.

"No, but if you're both still as interested after sex, then you'll know."

My frown this time, is a reluctant acknowledgment of her twisted logic.

"That's the whole point of the six week rule. The rule *you* made fun of."

I'm on high alert for movement in Tommy's direction, and my eyes flick over Amy's shoulder to see them coming our direction.

"Well, I think you need to readjust your time scale girl."

"How romantic!" I eye-roll. "They're coming now, so we'll talk about it later. Please promise me you won't say anything?"

Amy sighs again. "Fine. For now anyway."

"Thank you…"

33
GINA

"Oh my goodness!"

Amy and I fell in behind the others as they crossed the car park, heading towards a grassy slope. Tommy dropped back and took my hand as the ground levelled out, beyond some trees.

It took several seconds to process the scale and majesty of what was before us, stopping him dead in our tracks as I spoke. Everyone else, except Amy, went on towards the edge of the lake, chattering away.

Do they not see this?

A lake I expected, but not in such a dramatic setting.

Long and narrow, it stretched off into the distance, flanked on both sides by overlapping lush green hillsides, each one cutting down sharply, and disappearing into the water to create an illusion of a deep valley.

The expanse of water is still, like a huge sparkling mirror in the morning sunshine.

"I told you it was pretty special," Tommy whispers, almost reverently, as he pulls me close.

We stand for a few moments. Even Amy is silent.

"I think this must be the most peaceful place in the world," I manage, eventually. "Isn't it amazing Amy?"

"It really is…" She tails off, transfixed. A good time for reflection.

"Why don't you guys take a walk around the shoreline? I might be a little while here."

"Oh. OK sure. We'll be fine!" I say, trying to sound positive.

"Are you sure you're OK?" he asks.

Men aren't supposed to be this intuitive.

"Yes, I'm good. We're good!" I look to Amy for some solidarity, but she's lost in the view.

"OK good. Well, listen, there's a van in the car park if you want tea or coffee, or anything. Just tell them you're with the crew, and they won't charge you."

"You're too good to us!" I smile, sending him off with a quick kiss.

Amy takes my hand as Tommy walks away, and she leads me towards the water's edge. "You're too good a liar, girl."

"Hmm. He still suspects something obviously…"

* * *

It's almost two hours before Tommy finishes up, blowing out an exasperated sigh, as he sits on a rock beside us.

"I'm so sorry! That took longer than I thought. I think they want to come back too, when the light is different."

"That's OK…I could spend the entire day here. It's like, soothing my soul."

"Ah that's nice! I was worried you'd be fed up already. So what have you guys been up to?"

"We got some tea…thank you for that!" I reply, holding up my empty foam cup. "…and we took a walk. How cute are the little duck families?"

We're sitting on a cluster of large rocks close to a shallow part of the shoreline. A thick tree branch arcs perfectly over the water, like it's been planted there for maximum photogenic effect. A dozen or so ducks are swimming silently in circles nearby. Three adults, with lots of little ones following.

"I wish I had brought a camera, to get photos of us all here. It's perfect."

"Of course! It didn't even occur to me…sorry!" Tommy replies.

"Not your fault!". My smile is back. Some time here puts things in perspective for sure.

He gives a relieved looking smile in return.

"OK so, we're going a little further. You're welcome to come along or I can arrange to get you back to the hotel?"

I look to Amy to see what she wants to do, but she's leaning back on the rock, her eyes closed in the sun.

"Amy, what do you wanna do?"

"I'm easy, hun."

"Well everyone's getting to know that, *hun*!" I tease, and she opens one eye.

"Fuck off!" she whispers, and closes her eye again.

Tommy tips his head, and gives me an inquisitive frown.

I mouth silently, "Ollie" three times, but he's not getting it.

"She's saying Ollie," Amy adds, twenty percent louder than her normal volume. "She thinks I had sex with your friend."

"I assumed you had!" I reply, amused at her boldness.

"Ha! He should be so lucky."

"Oh wow, I'm clearly missing something." Tommy says.

"No. You're not," Amy replies, getting off the rock, and brushing her backside with her hand. "Where else are we going today then?"

"We've to head back towards Enniskerry. And to the waterfall…"

"There's a waterfall? No way!" I interrupt.

"The biggest one in Ireland, apparently. I don't think we'll be there as long though, then we've to take a walk around the village itself."

"Sounds like a good time!" I chirp.

"I wish I got as excited about everything, as much as you do," Amy mutters. "Let's go do this!"

* * *

Tommy

"Is something wrong with Gina?"

We're back in the hotel for lunch, as it's on the way to the waterfall, and I've taken the opportunity to talk to Amy while Gina is in the bathroom.

"What do you mean?"

"I'm not really sure. Just a gut feeling. Have you guys heard from the police or anything?"

"Not yet."

"So there's nothing wrong?"

"I don't think so…" Amy's smile is reassuring, and genuine.

"OK good. I'm probably just being paranoid. It's been a bit crazy, and I'm sure she'd tell me if something was up."

"Yeah, for sure!" she affirms.

Gina arrives back, and I give Ollie a call to join us for lunch while we're here, enjoying Amy's discomfort at the invite.

I'm glad when Gina asks if we can we eat somewhere, so it's just the four of us. It has reigned in any thoughts that she was starting to avoid me, and during lunch the chat is light and easy again.

The atmosphere between Ollie and Amy however, is not as it was, and it takes all my will power not to make a comment. My pal is more subdued than normal, so I need to get a chat with him first, before potentially putting my foot in it. One of us has to be tactful and sensible.

The rest of the afternoon drags in.

It's reassuring to have the girls close, to know they're safe, but it's such a distraction. I feel so drawn to be with Gina every minute, so trying to focus on work, and listen between the lines of everything Liam says has never been more challenging. We have built up a bit of a shorthand over the last six months, in that I'll be able to pick out details to take note of, without him needing to explicitly tell me.

It's only when we're in Enniskerry village, and can't spread out as much, that I notice it for the first time. Liam takes a backwards step onto the road to let the girls pass, and the look he and Gina share is unmistakably loaded.

Any idea of more paranoia is chased away immediately, when I see the knowing look Gina and Amy share immediately after. In the space of a few seconds my heart and tummy feel like they've swapped places, and my brain begins a panic cycle of emotions I can't control.

I stop and watch for a second, but everyone goes back to normal.

What's going on? Did I imagine that?

34
GINA

The sunsets are coming around too fast.

"Sorry guys, what a nightmare. I'm absolutely starving." Tommy drops, exasperated, into what has become 'his' chair in the hotel bar. It's almost 8pm, and Amy, Ollie and I have just finished our dinner.

"Go and order something now. I had the steak sandwich. It was yummy!"

"Oh that does sound good…pepper sauce…and I need a beer after that."

Tommy signals to a passing waiter and orders, before anxiously moving to the edge of his seat. "We might have to go back to LA tomorrow, guys."

"Fuck off! Really?" Ollie and Amy make quick eye contact. Not so subtle any more.

"Yes mate. Well I think so…"

"Why? What's going on?" Amy asks, looking rattled.

"I'm not really sure, to be honest. Liam said there's something personal he has to deal with, but he was on the phone with his *lawyer* for almost an hour, while I waited outside the room."

"Sounds serious. Either he's suing someone or they're suing him," Ollie laughs.

Tommy gives him a disapproving look.

I don't like the feeling growing in my gut.

"Well, we better make the most of tonight then!" Ollie flicks his eyes in the direction of Amy again, but she's just looking at me.

Amy reaches over, and puts her hand on my knee. "Are you OK babe?"

I barely summon up a nod, looking to Tommy, and I know by *his* expression that he can see the fear in my face.

* * *

Tommy

Brandon. Of course! Shit!

"Listen, I'll see if we can stay on a few days, if he does have to go back. He might give me some time off. That'll give the police more time?"

I can hear the words coming out of my mouth, but I know deep down that there'll not even be a negotiation about staying here. If Liam gets on a plane, I'll be with him for sure.

It's not like him to be so secretive, so it's got me a little worried. It's fair to say that the imposter syndrome that has always lingered, is making me anxious now.

Have I done something wrong?

Is that why he's talking to people in secret?

The thought of going back home to Northern Ireland is unbearable. There's nothing there for me now, but pain and bad memories.

Gina gets up from her seat. "I'll maybe make a call to see if they've found him."

"I'll come with you!" A feeling of guilt washes over me, that I might not be as in control of things as I thought. As I wanted Gina to feel. "I'll make sure you're safe," I offer, putting a hand on her waist, as we walk towards the elevators.

"Please stop saying that!" It's the first time Gina has snapped at me, but I can tell by her tone of voice that it's anxiety driven. "You can't be there all the time to guarantee that." There's a bitterness now coming though, as far as I can read.

I grab her hand, and stop dead. "Hey! What have I done?"

"Nothing!" Her patience looks stretched now. "I'm not your responsibility Tommy, so I need to be able to stand on my own two feet."

"I just don't understand the change. If we have to go back to LA sooner than expected, you can stay with me until it's safe."

"Look, I need to go and…" She pauses to take a breath before continuing, softer. "I'm sorry for snapping at you." She loosens my grip on her hand, but instead of pulling away, she spreads her fingers and interlocks mine, before closing her eyes for another calming exhale. "I can't put my life on hold while he's out there, and I can't keep hiding."

"So what are you going to do?"

"I don't know. We need to figure out a way to find him, or this will just continue. I know him well enough to be sure that he won't just go away, and he'll enjoy the chase….why are you smiling?"

"Because you said we."

"What?"

"You said *we* need to figure it out, instead of *I* need to figure it out."

Her eyes make an awkward sideways glance. "Oh. I meant *we* as in Amy and I."

"Oh fuck, sorry, yes obviously. I didn't mean to…"

The kiss silences me, mid sentence.

"Just shut up would you…" Her reassuring smile is welcome, but I'm not sure it's 100% genuine.

"Do you want me to come with you, while you make the call?"

"No, I got this. I'll be back down soon, OK?"

"Right OK. Good luck…"

The elevator bings as she kisses me again.

I know a 'go away and let me get on with it' kiss when I get one.

* * *

"Tommy, a minute please?"

I've only just sat down about thirty seconds when Liam appears, close enough to call for me. He's clutching a phone in one hand, and wears a scowl on his face.

"Oh shit. This doesn't look good," I mutter, with a glance to Ollie and Amy as I stand. "Will you make sure Gina is OK when she comes back?"

I'm by Liam's side in less than ten seconds, but it's not quick enough…if his tapping foot is anything to go by.

"Next flight out. Can you arrange that ASAP please?"

I open my mouth for more details, but he's already got the phone back to his ear as he wheels away. I watch him make his way back to the elevators, before turning slowly to give the others the bad news.

Why the urgency?

"Bad news guys!" I'm not even bothering to sit. If I haven't confirmed the flights inside the next fifteen minutes, Liam will be seriously pissed.

* * *

"Has Gina not come back yet?"

It's been twenty minutes since I left them, to find somewhere quiet to make some calls.

"Yeah, she was, but she went back to the room." Amy swirls her straw round her highball glass, while Ollie leans over the arm of his chair towards her.

"By herself?" My eyes dart back and forth between them, in the hope they'll register my concern. No such luck. It feels like I've interrupted two people that I don't even know.

"Yeah, that's what she wanted."

"What did the police say?"

"They haven't found him yet, but they're following up some leads or some such bullshit." Amy turns slightly towards me now. "Gina is not happy…"

"Neither am I, Amy. Neither am I. We're on the first flight out in the morning. The cars are coming at 4am."

"Do you wanna stay a bit longer?" Ollie taps Amy's forearm with one finger, letting it linger on her skin like it's perfectly natural.

"So there *is* something going on between you guys?" My grin is at odds with my churning insides. I've come around to Amy a lot while we've been here, and I'm glad to see she's given in to her very obvious attraction to Ollie.

Beneath the loudness and passive aggressive humour, there's a softer side to her, which she tries her best to hide. Her guard, for whatever reason she carries it, seems to come down after a few drinks, and she lets a gentler nature peek through the bluster.

Not too dissimilar to my best mate, actually.

Amy ignores my question in favour of Ollie's, tapping him back in the smallest, but also slightly provocative public displays of affection possible. "I would like to," she replies, looking right at him with a confidence I know he'll find equally sexy and uncomfortable.

"But…"

"But if Gina is going home I need to go with her."

"I can't stay, but maybe she could?" I offer, breaking the intense eye-contact between them.

Amy looks to me. "Who?"

"Gina. Stay here with you I mean, until they catch this asshole."

"Are you for real?" Amy's face in that moment illustrates the difference between men and women, in understanding the larger emotional picture. The way she looks at me not only speaks a thousand words, but makes me feel like a clueless teenager.

"Ummm…yes why not?" Even I'm unconvinced now.

"Because she fucking loves you dude. She might not say it but anyone with half a brain can see it, as plain as day." Her massive eye roll makes what she just said, a little less romantic.

Not inside my chest though, where it feels like someone just lit a bonfire.

I take a seat, partly to give me time to process this. It also stops me turning and running to her, like I've suddenly been dropped into a John Hughes movie.

Be cool…

"OK…I'm not sure what to say to that." My nervous laugh allows more processing time.

"Don't say anything. Just go see how she is. She'll be waiting for you."

"Waiting for *me*?"

Another eye roll. "Fuck me, yes! Why do you think she's by herself?"

I'm speechless.

"Well go on then," Amy orders me, with a dismissive wave of her fingers.

* * *

Ollie

"Say it again…"

Tommy has left without another word, clearly doing his best not to literally run to the elevators.

"Say what again?" Amy's voice is slow, assured and mischievous, and the way she's looking at me with those wide eyes is sexy as hell.

"Fuck me…" I'd like to think I'm bolder than most, but saying that to *this* girl right now, has made my lower regions feel like I've just hit the scariest part of a roller-coaster.

She let's it hover in the air for a moment, not adjusting her gaze by even a millimetre. Her confidence is almost intimidating. One eyebrow slowly lifts as a smile begins, revealing her dimples. She adjusts her body to face me, just a little, and leans forward so slowly that it's just on the right side of sexy/corny.

I spot her eyes close as she moves her lips towards my ear, and hear her lips part when they reach their destination…

35
GINA

"Who is it?"

The knock on the door was gentle, but a girl can't be too careful.

"It's only me!" Tommy calls from the other side.

"Shit!" I whisper, as the door chain snaps tight to stop the door opening. "Hang on!"

"Are you OK?"

"Yeah yeah!" I reply, hoping he doesn't notice me dry my sweaty palms on my dress.

"Do you always put the chain on the door?"

"No, I…I just. It makes me feel safer that's all."

He just nods agreement.

"Your room is big! I'm guessing the messy one is Amy's bed?"

"No…that's mine."

"Oh…sorry. So did they tell you?"

"About going home? Yes."

"And how do you feel about that?" Tommy sits carefully on the edge of Amy's still made up bed, it being closest to the door.

My hands are on my head before I can answer. My hair gets lots of attention when I'm anxious.

"Scared. Nervous…and maybe a little murderous?"

"Ha! That's funny…but I'd rather keep you out of jail if that's OK?"

"They haven't found him yet you know, but they spoke to some neighbours and they think he's been hanging around outside our apartment. Someone matching his description anyway."

"Holy shit, really? Amy didn't mention that bit."

"I haven't told her yet. I don't know if it's something she should know. I'm sure it will be him too."

"Hmm…yeah most likely."

"You think it is, really?"

Tommy's face is a picture of bewilderment, like we're having two different conversations.

"Emmm…yeah didn't you just say that you *are* sure it's him?"

"Yeah but I'm not *actually* sure! Do you think it is?"

His pause is disconcerting.

Why is he making me more anxious about this?

"What is it?"

"Sit down." Tommy pats the bed beside him, and I take a seat, warily.

"What's going on?"

"That night we were at your apartment, getting some things. When we were driving away, I think I saw him in the rear-view mirror."

It takes me a moment to close my mouth again, then I nod slowly.

"You didn't tell me."

"No. I'm sorry. I agonised over it, but I didn't think it was worth getting you more upset than you already were."

A tear cuts a path down my right cheek, followed quickly by another, on the left. All I can do is nod some more, as more tears come, silently.

"I called the police as soon as we got home though, but he must've done a runner by then."

I lift my eyes to the ceiling, triggering more tears. "He's a monster…but he's not stupid."

"It's gonna be OK."

My exasperated laugh is amplified by the release of pressure built up inside. I'm instantly aware of how disrespectful it sounds, and put my hand on Tommy's knee to mitigate the damage.

"Sorry," he says sheepishly. "I know it sounds like I'm just painting a rosy picture on things, and we can't possibly know what will happen. What I *do* know is that I'll do everything I can to help, and hopefully we can get through this together?"

The words sound perfect. Part of me hears them, but can't act on them just now. The numbness isn't letting much back out. I just sit, staring at the wall, squeezing his thigh to let him know that we're still connected. Torn between wanting him to stop trying to fix this, and just plain rescue me.

"I'm really sorry…" I say eventually, voice breaking.

"Hey! What have you got to be sorry about?" His hand takes mine now, and we sit holding hands on the bed. Holding tight.

"You don't deserve any of this. It's so fucked up! I had such a perfect time with you in Pismo, and the next day you end up fighting my ex on the ground, just to keep me safe. Then you bring me here to keep me safe." More tears, and a quivering lip. "Now we have to go home, and you're promising to keep me safe, and all I can do is laugh at you. You deserve better than me."

"Gina Elisabeth Sawyer." he says, drawing a smile through the tears. "Not for one single second have I given *any* thought to what I deserve. It's not even a consideration, because it's my *choice* to do all these things. Before he appeared, you might not realise it, but you already had me completely smitten. To the point where I'll do anything, and risk *everything,* to make sure we get back to what we had beforehand, and to give you…"

"Tommy," I interrupt, turning and putting my other hand on his cheek.

"Yes?" He swallows nervously. I can read it in his eyes that he's expecting another push back.

"You can shut up now." I lean in and kiss him, with everything I am.

* * *

"Where did they go?" I'm looking around the bar and lobby, but Amy and Ollie are nowhere to be seen.

"I think I know." My smirk says it all.

"No! Really?"

"Yeah, it looked like they weren't hiding it any more, before I came to find you."

"Where do you think they are?"

"Probably Ollie's room." My face has a look of surprise that Gina even had to ask.

"Let's go see," she giggles, grabbing me by the hand. "What's his room number?"

* * *

Two minutes later, we're whispering down the quiet corridor on the first floor, the opposite wing to my room. It's like Gina has shed her skin and become someone else. It's a little odd, given the turn of events, but I'm glad that the tension that sat around her seems to have lifted.

"Shh." Her finger is on her lips, and her bright but slightly red eyes are mischievous.

She carefully puts her ear to door 129 and listens.

I lean in and whisper, "That's the wrong door," but doubling over in a silent laugh gives it away quickly. She fires a leg out to try and kick me, without taking her ear off the door.

"I can't hear anything."

"Maybe they're not in there. Didn't you say she's very loud when she has sex?"

"Maybe her mouth is busy?" Gina whispers, quickly embarrassed that she said that out loud.

"Oh boke. I'd rather not picture my friend's penis in your friend's mouth."

"Yeah I don't really want to picture that either to be fair. Maybe they aren't here."

"Let's go back down. Maybe they went for a walk or something."

Gina doesn't reply, but instead gives me a wink, then knocks the door three times, sharply. Silence for several seconds, but it feels like thirty seconds, in anticipation.

"Yes?"

It's Amy's voice on the other side. Gina has one hand covering the peephole on the door, and the other had shoots to her mouth to block the inevitable audible surprise.

She nods frantically to me, signalling me to speak.

"Good evening Madam. I have the champagne you ordered." Gina's eyebrows raise when she hears my accent, my best imitation of most of the hotel staff. I'm as surprised as she is, that I managed to sound so convincing.

There's another pause, slightly shorter this time, before the door to room 129 clicks open.

* * *

Gina

Amy's head peeks round the door. The room behind her is in darkness, and the shock on her face is priceless. "Holy fucking shit! What are you doing here, you bitch!?"

"Catching you red handed!" I say triumphantly, pushing the door to come in.

"Whoa! No way. What do you want?"

"Can't we come in?"

"No!"

"Why not?"

"Because I'm fucking naked!" she hisses, like it should be obvious, and glancing briefly at Tommy like *he's* the problem.

"You're such a dirty secret slut!" I laugh. "Are you coming back down?"

"Well not right now I'm not…"

"Right, well hurry up! It's our last night here, and I want us to all get together before bedtime."

"OK! Now go away and…just go away!" Amy giggles, as she's being tugged from the other side.

Ollie's grinning face appears above her shoulder. "Later fuckers!"

The door clicks closed again, and we hear Amy's excited shriek from the other side, before it falls silent again.

36
SATURDAY, JUNE 22ND 2002
TOMMY

The soft early morning light filters through the blinds, casting a warm orange glow over the lounge area, where Gina and I sit quietly, sipping coffee. Amy wanders in, still groggy, nursing her own mug.

Even with the TV on low volume, the air is quiet and comfortable. A rare moment of calm after the stress of the last twelve hours.

Jet lag twice in such a short space of time is disorientating enough without feeling like we've had to do a runner from Ireland. When we were waiting in the boarding lounge in Dublin airport, I had asked Alexis what was going on. She had been engaged with Liam the most over the last number of hours so I knew there was a legal aspect involved. She looked very pessimistic when she pulled me to the side, out of Liam's earshot and gave me a few quick details.

Apparently a story is about to break about Liam - inappropriate conduct at a wrap party. A direct accusation and some witnesses, and US Weekly have been in touch for comment before publishing on Monday.

It was a bit of a relief, and not much of a surprise, but still didn't seem like it was enough to drop everything and fly home. The girls agreed. They weren't ready to be brought back to Brandon's new hunting ground, so the journey home had been very subdued until we landed.

We were greeted at LAX by a small cluster of reporters and photographers, and had to physically push through them to get to the cars.

"I'm sorry about all that at the airport. If I had known they were waiting, I would have hung back to let Liam face them himself."

"Hey! It's not your fault. Has he said anymore about what he's done?" Gina sets her empty coffee cup on the table and sits back with her knees hugged to her chest.

"Not a thing…hang on." I reach for the remote control and press the volume button as a picture of Liam appears on the screen. "Oh fuck!".

Gina

The morning show has cut to the news. Not the entertainment news, the *regular* news. The anchor's voice is brisk but carries a tinge of shock.

"This morning, several women have come forward with allegations against Hollywood producer Liam Fletcher, accusing him of years of harassment and sexual assault. Multiple sources claim his actions were an open secret within the industry, but fear kept many silent until now. The producer has not yet released a statement…"

The words hang ominously in the air around us, and I'm pretty sure even our lungs have frozen in time.

I feel my chest tighten. The room seems to close in, and suddenly the once-soothing warmth of Tommy's place feels stifling and foreign. I squeeze my knees tighter, struggling to keep my expression neutral. But inside, a swirl of emotions take hold—disgust, anger, and a rising feeling of nausea.

It's like I'm back in the hotel room in Ireland, against the wall.

Amy's eyes widen as she looks at me, then back at the screen. "I mean... we knew he was sketchy, right?" she mutters.

Tommy shakes his head, his brow furrowing. "I knew he could be a bit touchy feely, but not to this level? And apparently, everyone knew?"

Amy glances at me again, the sympathy in her gaze too pointed to ignore. "Are you okay?" she asks softly, her voice just above a whisper.

I take a deep breath, forcing myself to focus on Tommy's reaction. Part of me wants him to stand up and condemn Liam right then and there. Part of me wants to ask if he's really as surprised as he seems to be. But he just watches the screen in silence, a look of disappointment and anger hardening his jawline.

"People like him don't just get away with this stuff for years," Tommy says finally. "It's disgusting. Everyone who knew should've been speaking up long ago."

The venom in his remark stings, and I shift uncomfortably, heart racing. "But do you think they really knew?" I ask carefully, trying to read his face.

"Of course, some people must have known," he says, his

voice dropping. "They probably just turned a blind eye to further their own career."

I tense on this, missing the guilt in his tone and just feeling my own. I drop my gaze to the floor in shame.

If only he knew what happened in Ireland...

It's too late to tell him now. I've worked hard to keep it a secret.

If I had told Tommy, he would have been in such a difficult position. It's hard to see how it would have ended well. If he believed me and confronted Liam he'd surely lose his job, or he might not have believed *me*. That would be the end of us and I wasn't willing to take that chance.

If only I had known!

The anchor's voice cuts in again. *"It is still unclear who, if anyone, in Fletcher's circle might have been aware of the allegations, but sources say that this has been an 'open secret' in Hollywood for some time."*

Amy's fingers tighten around her cup, and she leans toward Gina, whispering, "Maybe you should tell him."

The words, barely audible, feel like a challenge I'm not ready for. I glance at Tommy, who's shaking his head, disgusted by the news but completely unaware of the turmoil beside him.

I manage a wry smile and shrug, as though the news *isn't* make my skin crawl. "Yeah," I murmur softly, almost to myself, "maybe I should...."

37
GINA

The past two hours have felt like a siege.

I haven't moved from the sofa, just catching parts of phone conversations, and watching Tommy pace every inch of his quarters.

"Fuck sake!" Tommy tosses his phone onto the chair beside me, sighing deeply. "This is all getting out of hand. I don't know where Liam is, and he's not answering calls. A reporter keeps calling me, and won't tell me who gave her my number."

He slumps, defeated, into the sofa beside me. "Reese called as well, and she says I should talk to Evelyn at the studio."

My eyebrows lift. "Evelyn? As in Evelyn Robbins?"

"Yeah, she green-lit *Legally Blonde 2*, but what could any of this have to do with the movie?" Tommy rubs his temples, as his eyes close.

I sit up straighter, excited to hear Evelyn's name. "I read an article about her. She's one of the few women to make it up the corporate ladder in Hollywood on her own terms. Reese wouldn't send you to her unless she thought Evelyn could help."

Tommy nods, glancing toward the kitchen area, where Ollie is making eggs for Amy. She's perched up on the breakfast bar in Ollie's t-shirt, swinging her bare legs like she hasn't a care in the world.

"Are you OK matey?" Ollie calls to Tommy, who gives him a single, cursory nod, before turning back towards me.

"Alright. I'll reach out and see what she has to say, but if she's getting involved in this, it must be really serious…"

* * *

Tommy

Somehow, it's already almost 4pm when we park up behind a small, tucked-away café in West Hollywood, and make our way inside. After we check for reporters of course.

The bright white afternoon sun floods through the windows, making the café a little too bright for such a secret rendezvous. There's only one table occupied, so we head straight for the back corner, taking a little booth and seating ourselves side by side.

"I still can't believe all this is happening," I mutter, glancing around, barely able to contain my nervous energy. Gina takes my restless hand, and squeezes it tight. "Whatever she has to say, we can handle it. I mean you've done nothing wrong, right?"

Before I can respond, the little bell above the front door jangles loudly. I glance up to see Evelyn Robbins in the doorway. She's elegant and composed as she walks towards us, her silver-streaked dark hair tied back. She's dressed in a sharp black blazer, and carries herself with a quiet authority. Neither the staff, or the family near the front notice her. She's as famous as they come inside the industry, but beyond that, she's almost completely unknown.

I rise as Evelyn approaches, extending a hand. "Ms. Robbins, thank you so much for coming."

"Please, call me Evelyn," she replies, her smile warm as she shakes my hand and then Gina's. She sits across from us in the booth, with her back to the door, and rests her hands formally on the table with fingers interlinked.

"Can I get you a coffee, or tea or something?"

"No thank you, I can't stay long. I just need to speak to you about what's happening with Liam." She pauses, studying my face like she can read minds. "How much do you know?" She leans back as the question comes, and I stifle instinctively with the weight she manages to add to her words.

"Nothing!"

It immediately sounds like a panicked answer. I'm aware of Gina's head turning, but I keep my eyes front. "I mean not much! I've seen him be a bit handsy with girls, and he's not very subtle about it, but nothing like what he's being accused of."

"And the parties?"

"What?"

"His parties. Surely you've seen things?". Evelyn betrays her controlled demeanour with this, snapping her words at me like an accusation.

"What *things*?" Gina interrupts, squeezing my hand again.

"His…" Evelyn pauses to take a breath, regaining composure. "His invite only room at his parties?"

What invite only room?

It's my turn to study her face, but waiting for more information only creates a silence which I can feel incriminating me more with every passing second.

I lean forward, in an attempt to recover the air of innocence I deserve. "Evelyn, honestly, I have no idea about an invite only room. If I'm ever at a party, it's only ever in a professional capacity, and I don't hang around. They're not usually the sort of people I want to spend my spare time with."

Fully in control of her emotions again, Evelyn takes her time to respond. Her position affords her that luxury. When she does, it's after she visibly relaxes.

"Look, I don't know you. The only reason I'm here is because Reese vouched for you, and *we* thought you might be in a good position to help."

"Help with what?"

"To make sure this time we take this bastard down for good!"

I can't believe my ears.

"You make this sound personal…" Gina whispers.

Evelyn leans forward. "Oh it is." Her gaze turns reflective. "When I was in my twenties, he took advantage of *me*. I was just starting out, and he knew *exactly* how to manipulate the situation for his own benefit." Her voice softens, and she deliberately leans back again, this time with a less commanding energy.

"For years everyone has known. The 'casting couch' is a cliché because it's true, but no one ever challenges it. Part of the entry fee, they would joke, usually with pants around their ankles."

Gina and I exchange a glance, both moved by Evelyn's sudden shift to vulnerability.

"I want to make sure people like Liam are held accountable," Evelyn continues, her tone gaining strength. "We have an opportunity here to stop not only him, but everyone else who thinks that every young girl coming through the system owes them something more than their talent."

"You say we, but what can I do? He hasn't done anything to me."

"No, of course not, but I'm going to take this opportunity to coax as many women out of the woodwork as I can. Those who are brave enough to tell their story…and I imagine there will be hundreds."

Gina's grip on my hand tightens.

"The police, and more importantly his lawyers, are going to look for statements of those who are close to Liam. You spend more time with him than anyone, I would expect?"

"Maybe. Probably," I nod, cautiously.

Evelyn reads my hesitancy, and hardens her tone. "Look. He's going down. I'm going to make sure of it this time, and if you're willing to help make that happen, I'll support you with everything I have. And when this all dies down, Tommy…"

She pauses, her expression sincere. "If you're interested, I could use someone I can trust at the studio."

"Me? Are you serious?"

"Yes. As much of a monster Liam Fletcher is, he doesn't suffer fools, so that's in your favour. But most importantly Reese vouched for you, and I trust her judgment."

"Reese vouched for me? Really?"

"She did." Evelyn smiles warmly, silencing the cell phone buzzing beside her on the table.

"Wow, thank you."

"Don't thank me yet. This won't be easy. Do you have a lawyer?."

"No."

Evelyn nods once then rises. "OK good, expect a call from mine. I'll be in touch soon as well. Until then, maybe lie low and don't speak to anyone."

"Thank you so much!" Gina stands, prompting me to follow her formality.

Two firm handshakes and three determined nods later, and Evelyn disappears, already on a call by the time the bell on the door falls quiet again.

38
GINA

"You're very quiet…"

We're back in the car, crawling through rush hour traffic on the way back towards Santa Monica. The 5pm news on the radio has hinted at more victims coming forward, with stories of Liam's behaviour, but Tommy remains stoic.

He sighs, showing more emotion with that, than any words or expressions are giving away.

"What's wrong?" I have to ask, because no words follow the sigh.

Tommy looks at me quickly, his irritation barely concealed. "Well all this, of course. I don't know what to do!"

"Isn't it obvious, after what Evelyn said?" I'm a little shocked that I even have to state the obvious.

"Maybe. I don't know. It just doesn't feel right, without speaking to Liam first to hear this side of the story."

"Do you need to hear it?"

"Well shouldn't I?" The irritation is less hidden now. "What does it say about me, if I just turn tail at the drop of a hat?"

"Tommy, women are coming forward accusing him of sexual assault." I'm glad to see my emphasis on the last two words make him visibly stiffen. It's like he needs hit over the head with this, to see the big picture.

"One of them just sat in front of us, and told us she was one of them. Do you have any idea how brave it is to admit that?" My voice wavers with the flood of emotion that bursts to the surface as I finish, and he flashes me a look of genuine concern, and surprise.

"I know…" he says, after a pause. "Look, I'm sorry. I know it must be easy for you to take sides, after what happened to *you*."

I inhale sharply and my heart almost stops.

How does he know?

"Who told you?" I ask tentatively, struggling to control the mix of guilt and relief which rushes to the surface.

Tommy frowns. "You did!"

"What are you talking about?"

"The things Brandon did to you. What are *you* talking about?"

I glance the other way momentarily, to process how I've misconstrued this, and to cover it with some nonchalance. "Yeah…that's what I was talking about." My tone is about as casual as I can manage - the complete opposite to how I feel inside. "I just wasn't sure how much I told you."

Surely that covers up my slip?

Does he buy it?

His face is too hard to read at a glance, and studying him will be even more suspicious.

"Are you sure you're OK babe?" His tone of voice is like a warm hug.

"Yeah! Sorry, this on top of everything that's happened over the last week has me feeling a bit…all over the place."

Tommy's hand finds mine as we stop at traffic lights, and I make a conscious effort to relax. The day is sliding slowly into golden hour, and the warmth of the sun on my face is comforting, but it's difficult to enjoy it fully today.

"I know you hate it when I say this, but everything *is* gonna be OK."

I do feel a flick of irritation, but with the overall numbness, it barely registers this time.

"Hmm, well I do have Brandon to worry about, as well."

"We."

I can't help but smile. As much it shouldn't be his problem, it's comforting to know I'm not alone. "Thank you…"

We arrive back to Liam's, running the gauntlet of not only *more* photographers, but also now a full news crew with a satellite van. Thank goodness for the gates, and the privacy we have at the house, but we have to get there first. For a panicked moment, it looked like the gates weren't going to open for us, while we sat there trying to ignore the clicking cameras and jumble of questions.

"Is Liam in the house right now?"

"Do you have any comments about the accusations?"

"What's your relationship with Mr Fletcher?"
"Are you a victim of sexual abuse?"

Will these people ask anything?

"Have you witnessed any sexual assaults by Mr Fletcher?"
"Do you know anything about so called 'date rape drugs' being used at parties?"
"Have you seen inside the sex room?"
"Are you part of Mr Fletcher's sex ring?"

This is a nightmare! A sex room? A sex ring?

Tommy's face is steely, determined to not make eye contact. "For fuck sake!" he mutters. "They must have been trying to get in, and punched the code in wrong too many times."

"What does that mean?"

"It means we have to wait until it resets, before the gates will open."

"But if they come through the gates, isn't that trespassing?"

"Yeah, I guess so. They maybe did it knowing it would delay any cars trying to get in."

"It's working." I slide a little deeper into my seat, and close my eyes.

If this is what it feels like to be a celebrity, I'm not surprised that some don't handle it very well.

We sit in silence, while the questions repeat on a loop on the other side of the glass. Two minutes or so pass, feeling like an eternity, then the gates begin to part.

Thank goodness for that…

"No one is following!" I'm twisted round in my seat, peering out the back window, as the pack of reporters swarm into the gap where we had been parked. "Is there another entrance we can use next time?"

"Sadly not, but I'm not going to hide away because of those parasites."

"Hmm…" My lack of agreement gives way quickly when a streak of stubbornness kicks in. "Yeah, actually, fuck them!" I spit. "We've done nothing wrong…what's so funny?"

"You…" Tommy's deep hearty laugh is clearly a welcome release. "Hearing you say fuck like that, it's just funny! But you're right babe, fuck them!"

The warm glow inside manifests on my face as a huge smile. "I like when you call me babe!"

* * *

Amy is alone on the sofa when we come in. "Thank fuck you guys are back. I don't like being here alone, while all this is happening."

"Where's Ollie?" Tommy asks, putting the kettle on.

"Let's hope he hasn't gone looking for the sex room." I'm not sure if it's too soon to make jokes like that, and glance to Tommy for reassurance..

"That's funny!" The sexy look he gives me, as he nods approval, is one I know I'll *never* get tired of.

"Hang on…" Amy eyes appear over the back of the sofa, after a pause that a comedian would be proud of. "There's a sex room?"

In normal circumstances, I imagine Amy would be delighted at the prospect, but her deviant curiosity is layered with some hesitation as she asks.

"Not one that I know of!" Tommy's definite tone hints at his unwillingness to have a conversation about this. "Where is Ollie though, right enough?"

"Shower," Amy replies, sliding back down into the sofa, and out of sight again. "I could do with getting some more things from home," she calls. "Do you think we could go?"

Even after we relay the story of being ambushed at the gates, she's still keen.

Ollie joins us mid-way through the conversation, grinning at some of the questions we had thrown at us. "Sounds like fun! We should go. Maybe run a few of them over?"

"Oh yeah, because that'll put us in a less complicated situation!" Tommy says what I'm thinking.

* * *

"Holy crap, it's like being famous!" Ollie is too excited by the slow push through the growing crowd, as we exit as a foursome, some twenty minutes later.

News of extra bodies in the car ripples through the reporters, throwing up new questions, which fade away behind us as we accelerate down San Vincente Boulevard. Ollie and Amy are both turned in the back seat, taking in the rare first person view of a media scandal siege.

It's a relief when we park up on Pacific Avenue, and find the street around our apartment quiet. I wonder to myself, how many people crave a celebrity lifestyle but then want some normality again, when the attention becomes intrusive. It must be difficult to have it both ways.

Tommy jokes about moving in here for some peace. It doesn't sound like the worst idea in the world. As we head inside, I'm enjoying the thought of the four of us living together, like some cute little half-hour per week sitcom.

The fuzzy feeling doesn't last long, when we enter to the reality check reminder of the elephant in the room, or rather the elephant in LA.

It's Ollie's first time in here, and he's uncharacteristically subdued as he surveys the apartment. Tommy and I exchange a smile when he gives Amy an affectionate rub on the shoulder, while helping her pick up broken glass.

"I'm not sure it feels like home any more."

We're almost done tidying the worst of the mess, and I find Tommy in the bathroom polishing the mirror with a towel. "What are you doing?"

"Just cleaning up a bit."

"I think a dirty mirror is the least of our problems…"

* * *

Tommy holds the car door open, as Amy and I squeeze a few smaller bags into the shelf behind the back seat.

"There's still some room in the boot?" Tommy suggests, amused at our packing efforts.

"You mean the trunk?" Amy asks, with a mischievous eyebrow, as she and I exchange a smirk. "You're not in Ireland now, boy!" I add, coming round to the back to see what space we have left.

Ollie is sitting on the low wall on the other side of the sidewalk, joking about the difference between LA weather and Northern Ireland's constant rain, when my body suddenly stiffens in recognition.

Brandon casually steps out from behind the building next door, no more than twenty feet away. He looks immediately out of place. Like Michael Myers, with a smug grin instead of a mask.

A cold wave of dread washes over me, and my heart rate accelerates so quickly I feel dizzy. The familiar knot of panic tightens in my stomach - a feeling no other person on earth has been able to generate.

Just Brandon.

Tommy is first to notice my body language, and my eyes catch his before flicking back to Brandon, as he takes a slow, deliberate step towards us.

"Well, look who's back in town," Brandon drawls, his voice laced with mockery. "Did you really think you could just disappear on me, Beth?"

I instinctively step closer to Tommy, feeling the blood drain from my face. Tommy takes a step as well, in front of me. I can't see his face, but he's frozen in front of me, braced and ready.

"Is that the fucker who hit you?" Ollie is several seconds late to the party, noticing Amy's shocked and frightened face. His fists clench as he jumps off the wall, and he's quickly side by side with Tommy.

Brandon's smile twists into something darker, with a cocky head tilt. "Relax, boys. I'm just here for a friendly word with 'Gina'." His eyes narrow as he looks back to me. "You and I have some unfinished business."

"We don't have anything to talk about, Brandon." The frightened croak in my voice only makes his evil grin grow.

He chuckles, shaking his head like I'm a child. "Oh, I disagree. I know a lot of things now. About you. About your friends." He looks directly, fearlessly, at Tommy. "About your boss."

"Whatever you think you know, it's over," Tommy says firmly, standing his ground. "There's nothing you can hold over her."

Brandon raises an eyebrow, unfazed. "That's where you're wrong." He reaches into his pocket, pulling out a phone, which he waves tauntingly. "See, I've got proof that you're not quite the golden boy you'd like everyone to think you are. And if I don't get what I want..." He trails off, letting the threat hang in the air.

Ollie steps forward, his voice low. "Listen to me now, you cunt. Nobody here wants to hear anything you've got to say. This is all just a bullshit bluff!"

Brandon sneers. "Maybe. But something tells me Irish boy here doesn't want to risk it." His possessive gaze returns to me. "So, what's it going to be? You come with me, and we'll forget about all your little *holiday*."

I shake my head, finding a stronger voice now. "You're actually delusional. I'm not going *anywhere* with you."

Brandon's grin fades. He looks calm to anyone who doesn't know him, but I can see the shift towards anger. "Then you'll leave me no choice." He moves, as if to walk towards me, but Tommy moves to block his path.

"Try it..." Tommy warns, his voice deadly calm.

They hold each other's gaze for a few seconds, as Tommy uses his two inch height difference to purposefully look down on him.

I study Brandon intently, holding my breath and waiting on him to make the first move. I know him too well. There's no way he backs down.

A police siren begins to echo in the distance - not an unusual sound, but I spot the flicker of recognition on Brandon's face when it begins to get louder.

He glances briefly down the street, then backs away slowly, still grinning at Tommy. "We'll finish this next time."

Tommy folds his arms, and tilts his chin up. "Why don't you stick around, and prove to everyone just how tough you are?"

"Don't worry. You'll find out soon enough, Irish boy!"

Tommy and Ollie both chuckle at this, and for a moment Brandon makes a move back towards them, before looking my way. "This isn't over Beth. I'll be seeing you real soon."

And with that, he turns and walks casually away, cutting between the buildings and jumping over the fence, out of sight - just as the first of three squad cars pull up beside us.

39
GINA

If anxiety had mass, there would be little room in the car for the four of us, as we pull away. We waited with the police after we gave statements, but Brandon of course, was nowhere to be found.

It's almost five minutes before I break the silence. "I can't believe he just showed up like that."

Tommy's knuckles are white against the dark leather as he grips the steering wheel tight. "He's bold, that's for sure. He likes to try and get under your skin too."

"Looking for a reaction he can use. He's always scheming."

"...and what was all that about having something on me?" Tommy glances at me as he asks, almost like he expects me to have an answer.

"How am I supposed to know?" I pause to let the next words sit in my brain for a moment, not wanting to say them out loud, but I'm unable to keep them to myself. "Is there something he *could* have on you that I don't know about yet?"

"I can't believe you'd even ask me that..." Tommy's voice is firm but the underlying hurt is undeniable. "You said yourself he says things to get a reaction!"

"Yes, I know, but…"

Amy interrupts, as Tommy gives me an impatient look. "What if he comes back, or finds out where we're staying?"

Ollie, who had been quiet until now, leans forward. "We need to take this seriously. That guy has a screw loose. He's not going to just disappear, and the cops don't seem able to track him down."

"What if I offer to meet him, and let the police catch him that way?"

Tommy looks at me like I've lost my mind. "I hope that's a joke. This isn't a movie Gina!"

"Well, why not? It's *me* he's here for. Why wouldn't it work?"

"Because he's a fucking lunatic, and you don't know what he would do to you!" Amy's voice is uncharacteristically shaky. The shock of seeing the person who violently attacked her, for the first time since that night, is clearly kicking in now.

"I know he is. But what choice do we have? He won't stop until he gets what he wants, and I can't just hide away fore…."

Tommy snaps at me before I can finish. "Gina! You're not hiding. You're being smart. But putting yourself in danger like that? It's reckless. You're not a piece of bait."

"Reckless?" I shoot back, feeling the anger rising. "You think I want this? I'm tired of running from him. I want to face him on my own terms, and put an end to it. He's controlled me for years, and now that I'm away from him, he's still trying to control me. I'm not having it!" The words spill out of me with an increasing venom, to the point I'm a little embarrassed.

The car falls quiet for a moment, and it's like I can hear my own words echo in the small space.

Amy begins to shake her head. "It's too risky Gina. What if it backfires? What if he hurts you?"

"Because I won't let him. I'll have you guys with me. We'll plan this out, and the police will know what's happening. They'll be ready." I just about manage to keep the fear out of my voice.

Ollie crosses his arms, scepticism written across his face. "And if it doesn't go the way you think? What if he doesn't fall for it?"

Tommy interrupts, his voice now calm and steady. "We have to think this through. We can't just jump into something without a solid plan. If we want to make this work, we need to make absolutely sure you'll be safe."

I take a heavy breath. "I know it's risky, but it's our best shot at finally putting an end to this. We can't keep living in fear. I won't let him control my life any more."

Silence returns, letting my words sink in. Tommy finally sighs, his shoulders dropping slightly. "Okay. We'll come up with a plan, but you have to promise me you'll be careful?"

"Always!" I reply, the determination in my voice letting my anxiety know it's not going to win this time.

"If we go through with this, it's not just about you. We all have to be ready for anything."

"Then we will be!" I insist. "I can arrange to meet him somewhere public. You can all be there, ready to back me up. And if anything feels off, I'll signal you or something."

"Yeah, but what if he doesn't show?" Ollie challenges, arms still crossed. "Or what if he figures it out, and does something before we can intervene? This isn't just a game - it's your life."

"I get that! But think about it," I beg, my heart racing. "If we do nothing, he'll keep tormenting me. I refuse to live like this. I'd rather take the risk, than hide away like a scared little girl."

Tommy's expression softens slightly, but he's clearly still conflicted. "It's just... what if something goes wrong? I can't stand the thought of something happening to you."

"Neither can I!" I shout, frustration spilling over. "But I can't stay paralysed by fear. I need my life back. I *need* to do this!"

It's Amy's turn to sigh. "Babes, you're so brave for wanting to do this, but I'm really fucking scared."

"I know you are. So am I, but I'm not just going to wait on his next move. We'll be prepared, and we'll tell the police when we know where he'll be. If we're smart about this, we can catch him off guard. I know Brandon. He'll never accept that I won't crawl back to him. I can use that against him, and by the time he realises it's a trap, it'll be too late."

Tommy exhales slowly. "Okay. But if we do this, you have to promise me that if you feel even a hint of danger, you signal us, and we get you the hell out of there. No unnecessary risks, OK?"

I nod, the fear trying it's best to take hold, but I've had enough. "I promise. If anything feels off, I'll get out."

"Alrighty, then!" Ollie claps his hands, trying to lighten the mood. "Let's catch ourselves a creep..."

40
GINA

"How did you sleep?"

Tommy's voice is warm and affectionate, grounding me after the restless night I just endured. Morning light filters into the room, softening his face as he lies on the opposite pillow. He looks like he's been awake for a while.

"Good…" I whisper, even though my night was far from restful. We lay quietly, studying each other, exchanging silent smiles. If someone saw us, they'd think we were talking without words.

The stillness, and intense re-connection between us feel magical, like a spell neither of us wants to break. There's a few times I close my eyes, smiling self-consciously when I feel his gaze deepen.

"This is nice," I murmur. "Can we stay here forever? Just you and me?"

Tommy's smile widens, and he slides a hand from under the covers to stroke my face, fingers barely grazing my skin. It's the softest touch I've ever felt, and my body sighs in pleasure, as I close my eyes.

"You're so beautiful," he whispers, almost to himself, brushing a self-conscious frown away from my face.

Does anyone react naturally when told they're beautiful?

I open my eyes, embarrassed but still smiling. "Stop it!"
"Stop what?"
"Stop looking at me like that!"
"Like what?"
"Like...I don't know." I let out a nervous laugh, and cover his eyes with my hand.

"Hey!" he says softly. "Not fair. I want to see you..."

I slide my hand around to the back of his head, moving closer, pressing our hips together as I lift my head from the pillow to kiss him.

His hand drops from my face, finding the small of my back and pulling me in tighter. I lift one leg over his body and slide effortlessly on top of him, letting our tongues meet as I straddle him.

Our thin clothes do little to contain his hardness—or my heat—and as I shift my hips, he grips me tighter, holding me in place.

"I want to feel my skin on yours," I breathe into his ear. My words turn him on as my tongue grazes his earlobe. I can feel the response between my legs. He lets out a quiet moan, hands sliding up my back under my vest, sending a ripple of pleasure through me.

Are we really doing this?

Pulling back, I tug at the hem of his black t-shirt, and he sits up, kissing me hard before raising his arms so I can slip it off. He falls back onto the pillow, his gaze holding mine as I take in his toned torso. Not too muscular, just perfect.

My fingers glide down his chest, lingering on his tummy as I revel in his reaction. He's ticklish, and just as my fingers begin to tease the waistband of his boxers, he breathes out, "Wait…"

I shake my head, and give him my sexiest smile. "I don't want to wait."

Slowly, I peel off my vest, letting my hair tumble free, baring myself to him. His mouth opens, momentarily stunned, before he lifts a hand. He slowly traces his fingers down my chest, grazing my boobs with a gentle, but electrifying touch. He drops eye contact for a moment, confidently studying my body, before pulling me back into a deep kiss.

Skin on skin, the sensation is intoxicating. His hands trail down to my hips, then lower, slipping under my shorts and gripping my ass as we kiss.

Shifting my body to the side a little to create space, I slide one hand under the elastic of his shorts and grip him tight, feeling the pulsing heat in my palm.

Tommy's kiss freezes for a moment as he takes a sharp intake of breath.

I squeeze and release him a few times, and he groans with the teasing.

"Gina…" he whispers in my mouth, squeezing me tighter. "Hold on…"

Ignoring him, I take my tongue back to his ear, breathing into it as I change the movement of my hand.

"Oh fuck..." I hear in my ear. Then, "Hold on...hold on!"

"You don't like it?" I smile, voice barely audible, teasing.

"I think that's pretty obvious..." His words trail off, but then a knock on the door freezes us.

"Are you guys awake? Can I come in?" Amy's voice is muffled, but unmistakable.

"No! Hold on!" I shout back, making Tommy laugh as I quickly slide off, grabbing my top and covering myself.

"Good timing..." he whispers, pulling the covers up.

"You think?" I grin, taking my time to put on my vest, letting him have a last, lingering look.

"Depends who you ask?" he smiles, peeking under the duvet to where my hand was twenty seconds ago.

Please stay there, and let me come back and take you...

I kiss him quick, but as sexy as I can manage. "Be right back..."

I not so subtly flick my eyes to the bulge below his waist. "Oops, sorry was that too obvious?" I tease, putting one hand over my mouth, like I've been caught being naughty.

Tommy laughs, swinging his legs out of the bed to sit up.

"Noooo...don't get up," I whine, trying to push him back. I end up falling on top of him, the two of us giggling like kids.

"Please tell me you're not having sex while I'm listening at the door!"

"One minute!" I shout back, winking at Tommy. "I'm almost there!"

* * *

In the kitchen, Ollie raises an eyebrow as I plop down on a stool. "You guys broke the rule already, eh?"

"I'm sure I don't know what you're talking about." I attempt a casual shrug, but my cheeks burn.

Tommy joins us a moment later, thankfully less 'aroused' than he was when I left him.

"You must have slept an extra four weeks last night?" Amy teases, smirking.

"What are you on about?" Tommy asks, looking confused, as he pours himself a glass of juice.

"Just asking Gina how two is the new six," Amy replies with a grin.

Tommy frowns, looking to me for an explanation. "Six weeks?"

"The six-week rule," Ollie laughs. "Thought it was going to last longer, but fair play."

Tommy just grins, unfazed. "Timer's still running, actually."

"Didn't sound like it through the door!" Amy says, smirking.

Tommy pulls me into a hug, ignoring her. "Just practicing for the main event, weren't we, babe?"

"Please, stop!" I protest, cheeks flaming.

The toaster pops, breaking the tension, and I escape, grabbing some toast as I try to ignore their amused looks.

"I think we should go out today," Amy suggests, her voice forcefully bright. "Maybe shopping? We can talk about Brandon, but somewhere away from here. Just a day out - get away from the heaviness for a while."

No one replies, just nervous looks, mostly towards me.

Amy bats her eyelashes at us. "C'mon, please! I don't want to go by myself."

I smile at Amy's clever trick to get her way.

"Right, okay," Ollie says, nodding. "Could be fun. And we could see a movie, maybe?" He glances at Tommy. "You're not working, are you?"

"Working?" Tommy laughs. "I have no boss any more. So, no."

"Yes!" Amy hisses, practically bouncing with excitement.

It's strange, how everyone seems so ready to leave the house.

Maybe I should trust their confidence.

Shouldn't I?

What are the chances, really, that Brandon could follow us?

41
TOMMY

After a brief debate on where to go, we opt for the new Hollywood & Highland centre. As we pull into the valet parking lane, just off Highland Avenue, the mood in the car has two distinct camps.

Ollie is enjoying Amy's giddy first date energy, while Gina and I have fallen into a rather tense silence. She asked me, after we navigated the increasingly large pack of reports and paparazzi at the gate, why I keep ignoring the journalists who persistently call me for a statement.

"Are you hiding something to protect him?" she asks. pointedly. She's tried to make her question sound casual, but I can see through it.

I can't believe she would even think that?

Since the story broke, I've been backtracking through every memory of every party I've been at. I know I've done nothing wrong, but still I'm uneasy when I try to reconcile that with my knowledge of his liking for young actresses.

Why does it seem worse now in hindsight?

Could I have done more to intervene when he had girls at the house?

Maybe I am guilty of something, even just by passively accepting what I saw happening?

These things are weighing heavy on my mind now, and I also feel guilty that it took Gina's subtle accusation to whip them into focus.

Have I just been burying my head in the sand?

"OK fuckers, what's the plan?" Ollie has that 'just arrived in Hollywood' wide-eyed wonder, especially after spotting the famous sign on the hill.

"I think we should split up, and meet up in a couple of hours. Some food, then a movie? Keep this big lug happy?" Amy nudges Ollie, who's scanning a board listing all the outlets in the centre.

"Sounds good…but it has to be Spider-man, right?" Ollie's eyes drift to follow two girls passing by in tight yoga pants, rolled up mats tucked under their arms.

"At least don't be so fucking obvious about it?" Amy says, sliding into his eye-line, and grabbing his face with both hands.

"Possessive *and* crazy? Nice combination!" he teases, with a cheeky grin.

"Yes, and don't you forget it either!" Amy delivers this with a Godfather-esque cheek slap.

"It's 12.15 now. How about two o'clock? Back here?" I touch Gina's hand, and I'm relieved to feel her take it, intertwining our fingers securely.

"Sounds good! Let's go spend some money!" Amy is already pulling Ollie off in the direction of Victoria's Secret.

Gina and I wander aimlessly for a bit. We haven't had much opportunity to do normal couple things, so this is a nice downshift in drama. We only let go of each other in the Virgin Megastore, flicking through the CD racks, debating the genius of Eminem and disagreeing over the future prospects of Beyoncé's new solo career.

"Have you still not heard from Liam?"

"No, but Lexi messaged back while you were in the shower."

"Oh? Why didn't you say?"

"Not much to tell really. She just said that Liam had gone to his place in Palm Beach, and asked me not to talk to the press."

Gina frowns at me across the music rack. "Not much to tell? That's definitely something Tommy…but I'm glad to hear he's not in town."

"Sorry, I should have mentioned it. I'm still hoping it's all going to go away."

"Seriously? This is *not* going away." She moves round beside me, and lowers her voice. "Why don't you speak to Evelyn, and see what she thinks you should do. About speaking to the press I mean?"

"If I do that, I'm definitely out of a job. Do you really think it's worth it?"

"Do you really want to work for someone, or even be associated with someone, who assaults women?"

"It's easy for you to say that…"

"No!" Her sudden angry interruption makes a few people nearby glance up. She notices, and visibly composes herself before continuing. "It's really *not* easy for me to say that, not when I've…" She trails off, closing her eyes for a second, and when they open again, they're moist.

"What's going on? Why is this so important to *you*?"

"What's important to me is knowing that I'm with someone who will do the right thing. I maybe wouldn't be so persistent, if not for the job offer you have from Evelyn…."

"That's not a sure thing!" I interrupt, and Gina takes another deep breath, while carefully wiping away a tear.

"Yes, Tommy, I know. But maybe you could trust *her* over the man who forced her to have sex with him?"

I take a deep breath of my own.

She has a point.

"The longer you do nothing, the more it looks like you're on his side. Can't you see that?"

I don't have a reply, so Gina continues.

"This town is ruthless. You should know that. If you stay in his corner, you'll be seen as guilty by association…unless there *is* something you know, or been involved in?"

"What are you accusing me of?"

She puts her hand on my chest, just softly enough to defuse the tension. "I'm not accusing you of anything Tommy. If I thought you were anything like him I wouldn't be here with you, but you won't talk to me, or anybody, about what you do or don't know. Can't you see how that just leaves big gaps for people's imagination to run wild? Including mine!"

"Why would…" I begin to argue.

Gina stops me with both hands urgently taking my face, her eyes imploring me to listen.

She speaks slowly and deliberately. "Because I've been on the other end of abuse, and I've seen people look the other way. I need to know you're different."

"I'm not like him Gina." The hurt in my voice comes as a surprise, even to me.

"I know you're not, but it's important to me that he doesn't get away with…" Her voice quivers, and both eyes are all of a sudden heavy with tears.

I quickly cradle the side of her head with one hand. "Gina what's going on? Why is it so important to you?"

She closes her eyes, and keeps them closed while she speaks.

"Because he attacked me as well."

Her eyes open only after the words leave her mouth, releasing two heavy tears which drip off her face as she looks up at me, her eyes desperate for the right reaction.

42
GINA

"Let's go sit somewhere," he says, eventually, slowly relaxing his arms from the tight hug, and placing the softest of kisses on my temple. I wanted to stay in his arms a little longer. Especially when a staff member asked if everything was alright, such was the intensity of my sobbing.

We end up in a nearby Starbucks, and Tommy leads me to a table farthest from any other customers.

"Are you OK?" I ask, hesitantly. My face must be an absolute mess.

"Am *I* OK!? It's *you* I'm worried about. Why didn't you tell me?"

Shame drops my chin to my chest. "I know it sounds stupid now, but I didn't want to put you in a difficult position." When he doesn't reply immediately, I glance up. Tommy's expression is a mix of bewilderment and fascination. "I didn't want you doing anything about it."

He leans forward and takes my shaking hands. "Why on earth would you not want me to do anything?. His head is shaking in disbelief, and I feel foolish now in hindsight. "Will you tell me what happened?"

It's the sudden rush of relief which brings back the tears. Not the thought of what happened. I've replayed that in my mind so many times, that it feels like a movie or something now. If I was telling Brandon this, by now he would be smashing things and accusing me of instigating it.

Maybe Tommy really is different?

"He came into our room in Ireland, when Amy was with Ollie. It was pitch black and I thought it was her coming back in drunk, but when I got up to see what she was doing, he pushed me against the wall."

I can't look Tommy in the eye while I'm recounting this. The Starbucks table can't judge me.

"And then what?" I can tell simply by his tone that he's seething.

"He kept trying to kiss me but I just turned my head. He was so strong!" I'm surprised at myself. I imagined telling Tommy would turn me into an emotional wreck, not the resolute calm I've settled into instead. It's like I'm describing something which happened to someone else.

"Is that all?"

"What do you mean is that all!?"

Tommy's head moves back as mine snaps up, the instant boil of anger taking him by surprise, as I pull my hands out of his grip.

"I'm sorry!" he replies, lightning fast. His eyes are wide with panic. "I didn't mean it like that. I just meant is there more? I'm so sorry!"

It's the first time I've seen a man so vulnerable. His words were a huge trigger, dismissing my trauma, as Brandon would have done so often, delighting in the cruelty. His face though…and his eyes. He looks like he's about to cry, and it flips my emotions like a coin tossed in the air.

Past patterns would have taken me off somewhere to listen to Stevie Nicks and lick my wounds, waiting for the storm to pass, but this is new. My scalp actually tingles as a tremendous wave of emotion cascades up my body, leaving a fullness in my chest that feels like excitement…except it can't be excitement.

I feel suddenly regretful for snapping at him, now that I can see his own pain.

How is he feeling this as well?

I take a breath, and take his hands again. Me holding *his* this time. "We maybe don't need to go into so much detail? It was horrible, but It could have been worse…"

Tommy's eyes are glassy now too, and his tunnel vision gaze burrows into me so deep, it's like he's reading my thoughts. "I'd like to know what he did to you, if you're able to tell me…"

Pursing my lips, and allowing a slow nod, I continue carefully and matter-of-factly. "When I wouldn't stay still, he grabbed my hair and banged my head against the wall. Then he tried to turn me around. His hands were all over me, and I didn't think I was going to be able to fight him off."

I can't describe the look of horror on Tommy's face, and for a second he closes his eyes. Maybe so he doesn't have to look at me. He opens them to the ceiling instead, trying to control his breathing. I can feel his fists tighten under my hands.

"You were able to fight him off though? Please tell me you did?" His voice is quivering now, and I quickly reach to his face to bring him back into focus with me.

"Eventually yes…"

"What does that mean?"

"He banged my head again, and got me facing the wall, holding my hair, and pulled my bottoms down a bit."

"Oh no, please!"

"That was as far as it got, I was…"

"How?" he interrupts.

"Listen…I was able to bang the wall and started shouting for help while he tried to…"

Tommy closes his eyes again. Another controlled breath.

"…and that worked. He stopped, mumbling something I couldn't make out, and just left."

"Holy fuck, Gina. I'm going to kill him. I'm so so sorry!"

"It's not your fault, and you're not going to kill him. I'm pretty sure someone else will eventually do that for us."

He stands up, pulls me to my feet and takes me in a tight hug. I can feel his heart beating hard and fast against me, and I let myself hide inside his embrace.

43
GINA

"Well, I told him."

I'm whispering, because I don't know if anyone is in the toilet cubicles. The ladies bathroom in Mann's Chinese 6 cinema has an echo as well, so we need to be extra careful.

"You told Tommy about Liam?"

"Ssh…don't use his name. You don't know who could overhear…but yes I had to tell him."

"Wow OK, and how did he take it?"

"Not well, as expected. But I think he understood why I didn't tell him until now."

Amy is quiet while washing her hands, studying my face in the mirror.

"And how do you feel now?"

"I'm relieved, obviously. I didn't think it was weighing me down quite as much as it was, so I'm glad it's out in the open now."

"That's good!" Amy smiles sympathetically, as we dry our hands under the noisy driers. "So the obvious question is what is he going to do about it?"

"Hmm...he offered to kill him." My laugh and shrug isn't reciprocated.

"Sounds like a good plan to me," Amy nods.

The confused shake of my head finally brings a smile to Amy's face. "I told him hopefully someone would take care of that for us."

"So I assume his hesitation to speak out is going to stop now?"

"Yes! He called the reporter back. The one from E! Entertainment Television. They wanted to come to the house, but that was a crazy idea. So we're going to their studio on Wilshire tomorrow morning."

"Wait, you're going as well?"

"Yes, I want to tell my story too. Fuck him!"

Amy smiles broadly, before taking me in a tight hug. "I'm so proud of you, you know. You've been *so* strong about this."

"Do you think? It doesn't really feel that way."

"Yeah, especially with all the shit with Brandon thrown in the mix."

I sigh when I hear his name. I had actually forgotten about that. "Oh yeah, him."

* * *

"That was fucking brilliant!" Ollie says, taking one last mouthful of popcorn, before dropping the box in the black rubbish bag, as we exit screen one.

We've just sat through Spider-Man, though I don't think I could tell you much about it. After Peter got bitten by the spider, my brain drifted off to replay everything that's happened since I met Tommy Millar. For a moment I did feel a pang of resentment towards him…well maybe not Tommy per se, but how much I've had to deal with since.

How much of it would still have happened, if I hadn't texted him that night?

I can't blame him for Brandon anyway, and who knows what would have happened if Tommy hadn't taken me away that weekend.

Up until that point, it had been a dream. Cute flirting, tipsy kisses, a beautiful hotel suite…and of course *that* dress and *those* shoes. The Liam thing in Ireland could have been worse, but it was damn sure bad enough.

I can't really blame Tommy for that, can I?

If it hadn't been for Brandon appearing, and Tommy trying to keep me safe, I wouldn't have been in Ireland. Then again, I could have been attacked much worse by Brandon. Despite the confusion, at least the thoughts are freely roaming around my brain, now that I've confessed to Tommy. I've even had an internal argument over whether it can be classed as a confession, when I actually did nothing wrong.

My brain is a fucked up place sometimes.

* * *

"Alright guys, what do we fancy for food?"

Tommy has been noticeably more present since we left the movie. Some people say they do their best thinking while driving, but maybe Tommy is like me. Watching a movie certainly frees my mind. Whatever the reason, I like it. It's never easy to be vulnerable with someone. There's always the risk that they won't recognise it, and not give you the metaphorical hug you need.

I can tell he gets it. I can tell by how tight he holds my hand, how he touches my waist as I pass through a door, and even just how *close* he is.

"Oooh, you know what? I think since we're so close, it would be a crime not to take Ollie to Miceli's? It's only around the corner. It's so refreshing to see Amy's giddy side back again, and it's fascinating to see how she behaves around a guy she's seeing. Since I've known her, she's never had more than casual flings, and there's certainly never been an opportunity for a double date.

Actually, it's not even something *I've* ever done. I smile to myself, and appreciate the buzz it gives me, just to be feeling like a normal person in a normal couple. Then the irony hits. It's pretty messed up, that despite all the drama that surrounds us, I still consider this normal. After living with Brandon though, it most definitely is.

"What's Miceli's?" Ollie perks up, rubbing his tummy with one hand, and Amy's butt with the other.

"Will you stop feeling me up?" Amy's mock offence just makes Ollie up the stakes by pinching her backside. "Ow!! Knock it off you! We're not sixteen."

"It's an Italian restaurant, where the waiters sing to you." Tommy interrupts them, before they either start fighting, or making out. With these two, it could go either way.

"Fuck off! Really? Actually sing to you?"

"Yup, well I've not been, but it's well known for it."

"America is fucking nuts! Back home you just get slabbered at, but here they sing to you!"

"Well they expect tips here, that's the difference," Tommy chuckles.

As we walk, Amy, who's been to Miceli's a few times, turns into a bit of a tour guide herself with some facts. Apparently it's the oldest Italian restaurant in LA, and lots of movies and TV shows have been filmed inside. Frank Sinatra, the Beatles, Jim Carrey and even JFK have eaten there.

"How do you know all this?" I laugh. Amy never ceases to amaze me.

"A guy I knew once worked here." Her look lets me know not to ask any more. I can fill in the blanks, so just give her an eye roll and a smile.

We turn off Hollywood Boulevard, making comment at the volume of homeless people, into Las Palmas Drive. Miceli's is close to the corner, and as Amy said, proudly proclaims 'Hollywood's Oldest Italian Restaurant Since 1949'. A huge mural of Frank Sinatra sits beside the red and green entrance canopy, with the remainder of the frontage made up of random shades of brown brickwork.

Inside, the brown tiled ground floor is tightly packed with four seater wooden tables, each covered with a red and white check gingham tablecloth. Raised mezzanine levels around the other three sides are not as busy, but no less packed with tables on the black and white tiled floors.

"Wow, it's like stepping back in time!" Tommy is turning to take it all in as we wait at the hostess podium.

"Yeah, I think they wanted to keep it as close to the original décor as possible, " Amy adds, confidently.

Even before we're seated, I know the elephant in the room is already here waiting. This is the first time since we agreed to lure Brandon out, that we'll get to sit together around a table.

This won't be just pizza, but pizza and plans…

44
TOMMY

It's pretty obvious that we've been taking our time to finish dinner, delaying as long as possible the unavoidable conversation.

We've already been serenaded twice, going through what I imagine is the standard mortified embarrassment, before starting to enjoy it. We had a solo rendition of 'O Sole Mio' before we even ordered. Our reward for being good little boys and girls, and eating all our dinner, was the Dean Martin classic, 'That's Amore.' By the time it reached its third verse, six other wait staff, *and* most of the diners (including us) were singing along. The cheer across the entire restaurant, when we collectively reached the final crescendo…well it sure will live in my memory for some time.

"I can't decide if it's really cringey, or really fucking awesome!" I think the rest of us know already, since Ollie sang the loudest at our table.

Once the song ends, the usual restaurant noises return. We've ordered desserts and more drinks, so we can keep the table longer. Especially now that it's getting closer to evening time, and becoming busier.

Gina's grip on my hand tightens, and I can feel the tension in her fingers. She's nervous. I can't blame her.

This is not the kind of place you'd expect four people to hatch a plan to catch a bad guy. It's too normal. Or is it? Maybe in the movies, this is *exactly* the sort of place. Either way, it feels like we're acting out some kind of play. But it's real. Every second of it. And potentially very dangerous.

Ollie and Amy are trying to act casual, but even they can't hide the fact that they know what's at stake. We've been through a lot, each of us in different ways. And now, we're about to lure Brandon out of hiding, and hopefully bring the whole damn thing to a head.

I glance over at Gina. She looks nervous, but there's something else in her eyes too. Determination. This is *her* fight. We're just here to make sure she gets out of it alive.

"So, we're really doing this Brandon thing then?" Ollie says, his voice lower than usual. He looks to Gina, then at me, like he's waiting for some kind of reassurance.

I meet his eyes and nod confidently, even though I'm not sure if I'm reassuring myself, or him. "We are."

Amy leans back in her chair, taking a big sigh, and scanning the restaurant like she's ready for anything. "Gina's got this, I think. I mean, he's going to show up. I don't see why he wouldn't, and it should be pretty simple to just keep him talking until the police show up."

I watch Gina carefully, noticing the slight tremble in her hand as she fiddles with the edge of her napkin. She hasn't said much since we sat down. She's been quiet, but I can tell she's ready. This is something she has to do. She needs to see

Brandon face to face, to let him know just how wrong he is to think he can get away with everything he's done...then watch him being led away in handcuffs.

"You sure about this?" I ask, my voice low.

Gina looks at me, and her lips curl into a small, tight smile. "Yeah. I'm ready." Her hands are still trembling as she begins to type the text message.

It's me. What is it you want?

She sets the phone on the table like it's a bomb, and looks at it for several seconds, like it could actually explode.

Dessert arrives. Usually a mood lifter, but the waiter delivers the plates to our place-mats with a wariness. No songs this time. He can read the room.

Gina lifts her spoon, just as the phone suddenly awakens, and she jumps, dropping the spoon on the floor. We both go for it at the same time and almost bump heads. When we come back up, her face is flushed.

"Do you want me to check it?" I ask, trying to calm her shaking hand with mine.

"No, it's OK." Her smile is one of resignation, but also an admirable attempt to summon up strength.

You back where u belong!

She reads it out loud, but not one of us can give much more than a nod, or a shake of the head. Gina looks at us all, one by one, then begins to type again. The messages ping back and forth almost instantly, and she reads each one without emotion.

I'm not sure that's what I want

You cant hide here forever. I won't let u

Why??

Because ur mine thats why

Maybe once, but u ruined it!

I'm not giving u an option Beth

You hurt me too many times

There's a pause this time, before Brandon replies.

Then i wont hurt you any more

I really want to believe that. I miss home

Gina sees my reaction to this message, and my instinct to protest.

"I don't mean it of course, but I have to make him think there's a chance so he'll agree to meet me."

Then give me another chance

Gina delays replying this time, faking consideration of Brandon's suggestion.

If we talk about it first, then maybe

OK

OK we can talk first?

Yes. Tonight

Tomorrow

Stp fucking about Beth

I need time to think first

Fine but if you mess me about ull be sorry

I won't. Can we meet somewhere public?

Where?

How about Hinano café? It's near the beach in Venice

OK 12

OK

The entire exchange took no more than five minutes. Gina relayed it all, and no one even lifted their spoon while we listened.

"My god," Amy whispers, in reverence to Gina, as she reaches across the table to rub her arm. There's no more shaking. "That was amazing! You're so brave."

Gina breathes a sigh of relief, gives a single firm nod and digs her spoon into the corner of her cheesecake. The rest of us just watch in wonder as she takes a mouthful.

"What?" she mumbles, with a full mouth.

"You just did all that, and then casually take a bite of cake. You're fucking ruthless girl." Ollie is shaking his head in amazement, and saying what we're all thinking.

She just shrugs like it's nothing, but I would be surprised if that outward bravery travelled all the way to her core.

45
TOMMY

I'm awake before Gina again.

I don't think I've slept for more than an hour all night, each time waking with all manner of worst case scenarios playing out in an anxiety-laden fantasy-land.

For most people, events of the magnitude we're facing often don't come around even once in a lifetime, let alone two in one day. Weirdly, it feels like one is fortifying my resolve for the other.

I hope Gina feels the same when she wakes. I'm already happy that she should be well rested for what's to come. Her day of reckoning, and mine. There's a twisted romance in that I think, as I lay here, enjoying my girlfriend's beautiful, completely serene face.

It's just passed 6.45am, and we're to be at the E! Entertainment studios for nine. This will be my opportunity to help take down Liam for what he did to Gina - and, God knows, how many others.

I slip out quietly to the bathroom, rinsing away my morning breath with some mouthwash, before I return.

When I come back to the bedroom, Gina is up. I feel a pang of guilt that I must have woken her. She's seated on the edge of the bed, her back to me, shoulders visibly tense already.

I come around the bed and sit beside her, placing my hand on her back. "You OK babe?" It feels like a stupid question, but also feels equally stupid not to at least ask.

Her eyes meet mine, and there's a deep resolve there as she nods. "I am."

Breakfast is muted. Neither of us are sure about which part of the day to talk about first. Ollie and Amy haven't surfaced yet, by the time we leave, which is welcome today. It's a morning for undistracted reflection and focus.

The car ride to the E! studio on Wilshire is quiet, but there's a pulsing energy growing around us. Neither of us needs to say much. After a long journey of dodging truths and running from pain, we're finally taking steps towards them, and facing them down.

We're going to expose what Liam did, and then we'll take Brandon down. Gina's gaze stays steady as she looks out the window, her fingers wrapped tightly around mine, saying nothing.

We arrive early, not taking any chances with the morning traffic.

We're ushered into a quiet conference room, with a camera and bright lights on a stand set up at one end. Three comfortable looking red leather arm chairs sit empty, waiting, and at odds with their sterile surroundings.

The journalist is a veteran reporter with a reputation for being sharp and uncompromising with her questioning, and isn't afraid to ask difficult questions. Some say she thrives on knocking people off balance. Liz Weaver might be an industry heavyweight, but physically she's a slight woman with hawk-like eyes, and an unwavering serious expression.

"Thank you both for coming in. This is incredibly brave," she says, looking from Gina to me as she quickly shakes our hands. "We're here to support you both in any way possible."

Yeah, sure you are.

Gina gives a small nod, but I can feel her fingers trembling. She lets out a small, shaky breath, and I tighten my grip on her hand.

We sit down, side by side, facing the camera. Liz checks her notes, a sombre expression on her face. "OK so, before we start, you don't need to hold anything back," she says gently, her gaze focused on Gina. "We're not live, so if anything goes off topic, we can kill it in the edit, OK?"

Liz nods an affirmative on our behalf before giving us a chance to speak. Straight to business.

"Are you ready to start?" she continues, louder this time, for the benefit of the camera operator and others who have joined him behind the bright lights.

Gina straightens up, her voice steady and confident. "I'm ready."

Liz signals with her hand, clicks her pen and begins.

"I'm joined today by Tom Millar, the personal assistant to Liam Fletcher, who as you know has faced an avalanche of accusations in recent days. Unwanted contact, inappropriate sexual suggestions, trading movie work for sexual favours, and some reports of sexual assault or rape. Mr Millar, given your close working relationship with Liam Fletcher, how much of this did you witness?"

If it was possible for my stomach to physically leave my body, this is the moment it would choose to go. Her last sentence was obviously constructed for full viewer pleasure.

"Well…" I shift uncomfortably in my seat, and quickly chastise myself for doing so.

Why is it when you try not to look guilty, that you're most likely to look the opposite?

"…the short answer is I didn't know."

"But you live in his house? You organise his affairs, including his parties. You're as close to his right hand man on a day to day basis, and you didn't know *anything*? Do you think that might sound implausible?"

"Ummm…yes, I suppose it might, but I don't think it means I'm guilty."

Now I know why celebrities receive media training. I've just referred to myself as not guilty. Exactly what a guilty person would say. My face is starting the show the heat I'm feeling.

"I suppose the obvious question is in that case is, "How could you not see it?"

"Well, It was obvious that he liked girls, especially younger girls, and now in hindsight I should have seen it for what it actually was."

"What did you *think* it was?"

"Well, I suppose that there's always been an unspoken... *element*...of those sort of things in Hollywood. The casting couch kind of thing. I've only been working for Liam for six or seven months, and it just seemed to be the way it worked here, and that everyone was OK with it."

It's Gina's turn to move in her seat, with an uncomfortable clearing of her throat.

"Sexual favours and sexual assault is OK, if you get a job?"

"No, of course not! That's not what I said!" I'm trying to be calm, but it's hard when I feel anything I say can, and will be used against me. This is not an interview, it's an interrogation.

"By your admission, you've been with Liam long enough to see how he works. The kind of parties he throws. The ones that no one talks about."

The way she's looking at us makes my skin crawl. There's a hint of a smile on her lips, but it's the kind of smile that makes me think she's already got everything figured out. And she's right. She knows exactly what she's doing.

I can feel the weight of her words settle over me like a heavy cloud. I've heard the rumours, of course. Everyone has. But hearing them out loud, with her looking at me like she already knows everything, is a different animal. It feels like my throat is closing up, and my heart is racing.

"Yes, I've seen parties," I admit, trying to keep my voice from cracking and making me look even more guilty. I glance at Gina, and she gives me a small nod, like she's telling me to be honest, and be brave. "But that's all they were to *me*. Just parties."

Liz watches me closely, and I can feel her wanting to push for more. "Parties?" she repeats, drawing out the word as if she's savouring it. "Or something else? Something darker?"

I'm stuck. I can't lie about everything. I've always known there was more to those parties than just the glitzy Hollywood surface. I've seen the whispering. The people who came and went. But I was always too busy keeping things running smoothly to ask questions. Too busy keeping my head down. Too terrified to confront what might, or might not be going on, behind closed doors. Liam's closed doors.

I shake my head, trying to gather my thoughts. "I…I don't know. I never saw anything like what you're talking about."

"Tommy," she says, leaning in slightly, "you were close to Liam. You worked closely with him. Many people have come forward with details of a so-called 'sex room' in his house. A room where women were taken after they'd been given drugs, or gotten too drunk to resist, or where they were just tricked into going. What can you tell me about this room?"

The words hit me like a punch, and I grip the edge of my chair. "I didn't know anything about that," I reply firmly. "If there was a place like that, he kept it hidden from me. I wasn't invited to his parties as a guest, at least not the ones that turned into…whatever you're describing." I take a pause, but should have just stopped there. "I didn't ask. I didn't need to know."

Liz looks at me, and I see the judgment in her eyes. "Really? You didn't need to know?" She scoffs, with a little tilt of her head.

Liz doesn't back down, instead pushing harder now I'm on the ropes. "But you *must* have seen or heard things, Tommy.

People say you were with him at some of those parties, saw him escort women into side rooms, or at least looked the other way."

"I was at a few events, sure," I concede, feeling a pit in my stomach. "But I never saw anything like what you're describing. And if I had, I wouldn't be sitting here now. I would have called the police myself. Look, I thought I knew Liam. But I didn't know this side, and I didn't want to."

Her knowing smile doesn't falter. It's the smile of someone who's seen too much, heard too many confessions. She knows exactly what she's doing.

"You didn't see anything." If her eyebrows could speak, they'd call bullshit.

Liz leans forward, her voice dropping lower, more pointed now. "You didn't see how he treated women? How he isolated them? Forced them into his private room? The one that no one ever talked about?" She's practically pushing the words into my face, each one feeling like a slap.

I don't know what else to say. The pressure is growing, and I feel like I'm suffocating under the intensity of her gaze. My stomach twists, my hands begin to tremble and I have to grip the chair tighter to stop it.

I don't want Gina to see how much I'm struggling. How much I want to buckle under Liz's scrutiny, but I know she can already sense it. I can feel her eyes on me.

"I…" I start, trying to find a way to escape this conversation, but the words don't come. Liz is already moving on, relentless and ruthless.

"You've been there through all of it, haven't you?" Liz presses, her pencil moving across her notepad, scratching out something I can't see. "You were the one who watched over the guests when things got out of hand. You were the one who kept things quiet, who kept the lights dimmed just enough for no one to see what was happening behind closed doors. You were the one who stood by, and let him get away with it." She lifts her eyes to meet mine, for full dramatic effect.

I feel like the air's been sucked out of the room. I can barely breathe as she throws these accusations at me, each one heavier than the last. It's not true, not entirely. I never stood by and watched him hurt anyone. I was too busy playing the part of the good assistant. The one who could smooth things over, and keep things moving.

But how could I not see what was going on?

How could I have been so blind?

"I wasn't part of any of that," I reply weakly, my resolve fading now. "I promise I didn't know what was happening behind closed doors, and would never condone it."

Liz leans in even closer, her eyes boring into mine. "And Gina?" she asks, her voice almost a whisper now. "You didn't know what happened to Gina?"

I feel my heart skip a beat. Gina stiffens beside me, and I can feel the extra tension. She's not looking at Liz any more. She's looking at the table, her lips pressed together in a tight line. Her breathing is steady, but I can tell she's fighting to keep her composure. I want to say something to protect her, to make it stop, but the words stick in my throat.

"Gina is your girlfriend, and has recently been cast in the upcoming sequel to Legally Blonde?" Liz switches quickly back to her broadcast voice, luring me into a false sense of security.

"Yes, that's right."

"And you think that was just a coincidence?" Liz continues, her eyes flicking from me to Gina. "She's a very pretty girl. You think she wasn't targeted too? Just like the others?"

Gina finally looks up quickly, her gaze steady but hardened now. She's not going to let Liz reduce her like this, so casually, and she's certainly not going to let anyone talk about her like she isn't in the room.

"I wasn't a coincidence," Gina says slowly. Her voice is calm, but filled with a cold fury I haven't heard before. "You make me sound like some hapless little girl who was just picked out for a cheap lay. I know that's not the case, and it's most definitely not something I would allow."

Liz raises an eyebrow, clearly intrigued by Gina's response. "Oh? Then what was it? What exactly happened between you and Liam?"

The question hangs there, heavy and charged. I saw this coming. I knew this would be the hardest part of all of this. Gina's encounter with Liam, albeit brief, is a mess, and bringing it into the light feels unnecessary to me. But I see her square her shoulders, her jaw tightening in determination. Then I get it.

"He *tried* to hurt me...to force himself on me, yes." Gina says, her voice unwavering, though the pain is still there, lurking beneath the surface. "But I wasn't going to let him."

"And Tommy? What did you know?

"I didn't know about it," I reply, my voice hollow. "Until recently."

"Were you surprised?"

"Of course! I was shocked to hear it, even after all the accusations became public. You're making it sound like I'm complicit in all this, like *I'm* the one on trial here."

"You were one of his assistants, Tommy. You were the one in charge when things went south. You were the one who kept the parties running smoothly, kept the people coming back…looked the other way when it suited you."

I feel the weight of her words. She's right and wrong at the same time. I was there. I was a part of it, even if I didn't fully know what was happening. I didn't want to know. And now, I have to own up to that.

"I was trying to keep my job," I mutter, my voice barely audible. I don't even recognize the person I'm talking about any more. The assistant. The guy who kept the chaos under control, while the world around him crumbled. That's who I was.

Liz nods slowly, but her eyes don't soften, and she doesn't need to say anything in response.

"Tell us more about what happened in Ireland, Gina." Liz's shift in focus and tone is jarring.

Gina glances at me, before looking back to Liz, then to the camera.

"Did Liam threaten you, or suggest anything in exchange for sex?" Liz asks, leaning in, her tone almost too calm. But I can see her eyes - she's searching, pushing for something more salacious to wrap this up.

Gina swallows hard, but then her voice is soft and clear. "He didn't get that far, and he didn't say anything."

"So nothing actually happened?"

"Oh it did. He came into my room in the dark, and pinned me against the wall."

"Was he under the impression this was something you wanted?"

My turn to stifle, but before I can speak, Gina replies with a calmness I can only describe as a superpower. She has more of a measure of Liz than I could ever have, and I just listen in awe.

"Liz, I'm surprised you would even ask that, given the accusations against him. I would have thought that you, as a woman in Hollywood who's no doubt had to work hard to get were *you* are, would understand the opportunity we have now to change the narrative. To stop victim blaming. Isn't that as bad as accusing people who bury their head in the sand? Actually I think it's worse."

"Well..." Liz looks slightly rattled as she begins to speak, but Gina cuts her off sharply, with a raised tone of her own.

"No, I'm not finished! He acted like he was entitled to whatever he wanted, *whoever* he wanted, and I'm sure we both know that he's probably not the only man who uses his power, his reach and his influence in that way. I'm not describing any details of what happened to me. I'm not going to sacrifice my dignity for a good headline, or a juicy story for your viewers. That's part of the problem that feeds all this. Don't you see that?"

Wow!

Liz nods, her pen tapping lightly against her notepad. She doesn't give anything away in her expression. The only acknowledgment is her longest pause yet since the interview began.

I want to give Gina a round of applause, but instead I just quietly enjoy the moment. Her moment.

"And how has this affected you both?"

If Liz was rattled, she's not letting it show. The way she looks at Gina as she asks, lets me know she's enjoying the challenge.

I look at Gina, waiting for her to answer, but she just looks back at me. She's letting me speak.

"Well I don't want to speak for Gina. As you have just seen, she's quite capable of that."

Liz properly smiles for the first time today. I look to Gina again and she nods, reassuringly, basking in her new glow of confidence.

"Well, she didn't tell me at first, because she didn't want to put me in an awkward situation. I think that just makes her more heroic in my eyes. It's possible Liam knew she wouldn't say anything if she cared about me, and he took advantage of that. Or maybe there wasn't that much thought behind it. I'm not sure. Maybe he just didn't care."

Gina's hand reaches out to take mine, a silent but strong connection as we face the camera.

Liz pauses again, considering her next question, her eyes darting back and forth. "What was your reaction when you did find out?"

"Obviously, I was livid. It was a good thing that he disappeared. I haven't seen him since, and to be honest, I no longer want to work for someone who could do these things. It's not something I want to be associated with. I can't even imagine how hard it was for Gina to endure that, then to keep it a secret for the sake of our relationship."

"Why do you think Liam gets away with this?"

Gina's face hardens again, and takes the question. "Because people don't talk," she says, with a sadness in her voice. "People who know, or even just suspect - they're too afraid to stand up to him, or anyone like him. Too scared of losing everything that's being dangled in front of them. But we're here to say no more."

Liz's eyes register something like admiration. "If you had one thing to say to him now, what would it be?"

Gina's breath catches, but then she finds her voice again, firm and steady. "I'd tell him that he's not going to get away with it any more. No one deserves to live in fear because of someone else's power, or have to compromise their self respect as a woman just to get a fair shot. We're here to say, me and the other women speaking out…that it's time things changed."

I give her hand a squeeze, feeling the strength in her resolve, as much as in my own.

Liz looks at both of us, her expression softened. "Thank you for speaking out. You're doing something powerful. Something that could inspire others to come forward."

There's no going back now, that's for damn sure.

"Lastly, what's your message to any woman who might be watching, or listening, who has also been a victim of Liam Fletcher?"

"My message isn't just to them, it's to *any* woman who's a victim of abuse from *any* man, not just Liam Fletcher. It sounds like there's a loud enough voice against him already, so I think that'll take care of itself. It's the others who are suffering in silence. Speak up, but do it safely. Take this opportunity to take your power back. It's time men realised that women are not a piece of property to be passed around, used and abused like we only exist to make men happy."

"Well said Gina." Liz's whole demeanour thaws in the space of three words. It's actually incredible to watch. "Thank you for joining us, and thank you to Gina and Tommy for speaking out today. We'll be back soon with more on this story on E! Entertainment Television, as it unfolds."

A voice behind the camera calls cut, and the lights dim as Liz stands up. We follow her lead, a little taken aback by the suddenness of how it ended.

"You guys were incredible. Well done. That was some really good stuff." She gives us her full attention only while she speaks, before turning away to speak to the person who called cut. A fidgety woman around our age taps Gina on the shoulder.

"I can show you guys out, and have your car brought round, or get you some refreshments first?"

We exchange a glance as much for politeness. I think we both can't wait to get out of here.

"No thanks, we're good."

"Can I just say, I've never heard anyone ever speak up so well about those things. You made me proud, and I don't even know you."

"Aw, thank you. I'm just sick of it." Gina looks embarrassed, like she's a newly crowned celebrity being stopped by her first fan.

"Me too!" The girl leans in closer to whisper. "It's everywhere. Even here…and between you and me, I think Liz Weaver has a nerve asking *anyone* why they didn't speak up."

"If this is what it takes to make sure men like him never do this to anyone else, we'll keep speaking out. No matter what."

Gina looks to me as she says this.

I'm more than happy to let her speak for *me* now…

46
GINA

All I can do is cry. Not ordinary crying, but ugly crying. Convulsing, and barely able to breathe between sobs.

We're back in the car. As soon as the doors clunked shut and it was just us again, the floodgates opened, and I just fell into him.

I've just begun to regain some control, when Tommy kisses my wet cheek with, "I'm so fucking proud of you!" and I'm off again. He holds me tighter this time, like he's trying to squeeze it all out of me quicker. That's how it feels anyway.

The sense of relief is like an exorcism of guilt and shame.

"That was really tough." I'm just staring into space now, having drained all emotion out of my body, for the time being. "It wasn't what I was expecting at all…"

"No, me neither."

"What the fuck was all that? She was making out that you were involved in what he was doing, or helping him. Nasty!"

"Yeah, I feel a bit stupid that I didn't see that coming. Of course they're gonna go down the road of what makes the best TV. Entertainment is more important than facts in their world."

"I guess, but…"

"What got me was how quick she could shift from interrogating us, to being almost completely empathetic."

"Totally!" I finally look at Tommy, pulled back into it being *us,* instead of just me, or just him. "And she was so nice and matter of fact, afterwards."

"She'd make a good prosecutor in court. She's ruthless."

I nod agreement, then shake my head in bemusement at how surreal the experience was.

"How do you feel?" Tommy asks, squeezing my hand.

"Scared!" I look at him for a reaction, maybe a way out of what's coming next, but he's just got a wry smile for me.

"I'm still not sure you should risk meeting him alone, you know…"

My shoulders sag in resignation. There's lots of reasons to not go through with this plan to trap Brandon, but none of them are going to make me sleep easy tonight, or any night… until he's out of the equation.

"I know. But it has to done, and there's no point in delaying it. If we leave it too long, the police might lose interest in him."

Tommy thinks about this for moment, and his face tells me he knows I'm right. "I just think this is something I should be able to sort out for you."

My smile confuses him, especially when I turn in the seat, take his face in my hands and kiss him gently. "That's very sweet of you, and I appreciate it, I really do…but this isn't the 1950s. I don't want to be anyone's responsibility to keep safe. It's me alone he has tortured for years, so I can't pass up the opportunity to be alone in turning the tables. Does that make sense?"

Tommy nods in hesitant agreement, clearly still struggling. Male pride is a powerful thing to overcome.

"We've just sat and got torn to shreds in that interview, ironically by a woman who's probably experienced that shit herself, just to try and pull back some control for women. The things Brandon did are different to the things Liam has been doing, but really it's still the same, if you think about it. It's still men taking advantage of old fashioned ideas. Cherry picking bits of 1950s ideology to either get their jollies, or paper over the cracks in their own shortcomings as human beings. It really annoys me that he has stolen part of *me*."

I pause to let my words sink in. The silence threatens to stir emotions that my brain immediately recognises as weakness.

Don't cry.

You can't make a speech like that and then cry!

"What I mean is, it's like he's taken the best of me, and I hate him most for that. I feel closer to you than I thought was possible, and I resent the fact that *he* has made me *less*. Like you're now left with a broken version of me."

"Gina…listen, I get it. I could tell you the same thing. I know *exactly* what you mean. You just vocalised it better than I ever could."

I look to him, but quickly feel annoyed at myself. I'm looking for signs that this is bullshit. That he's only telling me what I want to hear. Just like Brandon would, when he needed to pull things back from the brink. But this is different.

I decide in that small moment, to give him my best. Starting with my best smile. "I know you've been hurt badly too. I feel a bit guilty for being slightly grateful for that."

Tommy smiles, knowingly.

"It's fucked up, I know, but…"

"I get it!" He interrupts. "If we both have healing to do, what better way to do it than together?" He shrugs like it's no big deal. "We *should* probably *both* be a little grateful. I don't think that's fucked up at all. I think it's being grown up enough to understand that life is shit, and has been shit, but it doesn't define who we are, just what we've learned. We can use that experience to build each other's trust back up, so ummm… things don't need to *stay* shit. Don't you think?"

"Wow!" I'm just staring.

Are you sure you're real?

"I know. That's a lot of shit, isn't it?"

His earnest tone, and his cute little frown, make me burst out laughing.

How is he so good at breaking the tension at the right time?

"Umm…yes!" My grin fades slowly to a more sombre expression. "I agree one hundred percent. I think!"

"What do you mean?"

"Do you know what? I'm not even sure. I guess I'm just watching and waiting for you to show me that you're *not* actually this perfect."

"Babe, I'm most definitely *not* perfect!"

"Compared to what I know, you are."

"That's OK…and you're allowed to be wary, after what you've been conditioned to for years. I'm just going to be normal though. Just me…and hopefully time will help that wariness fade. You might not even feel it, but one day you'll just realise it's gone. The way you've been treated is not normal, and it's not how I operate. I think we have a connection that goes way bey…"

"Tommy."

My tone is curt, and his face reacts to it with a flash of fear. "Yes?"

I sigh and look away, then turn to look at him as intensely as possible, as a cheeky pout gives way to a smile. "Stop talking…"

The kiss we share is a milestone of relief, deep connection, longing, understanding…and for a moment, pure lust. The kiss, with the touches and sounds which layer through it, convey much more than words.

You can say a lot with a kiss.

You can say I love you with a kiss…

47
TOMMY

Amy and Ollie are waiting for us at the beach front, beside The Venice Whaler Bar & Grill. They'd got a cab down to Venice, and picked up Amy's car on the way. They look even more anxious than we are, as they sit stiffly on the wall. Their expressions would probably look to passers-by like they'd just had a fight.

It's only 11.30am, so have some time to get into position, but briefly fill the pair in on the interview this morning. Just the highlights for now, but it's enough to make them even more fidgety.

Hinano café is just out of sight, around the corner, and about a block back on Washington Boulevard.

Ollie is tapping his fingers on his leg, his face tight with worry, while Amy has her arms crossed, eyes shifting between Gina and I. We all know the plan, and how simple it *should* be, but it doesn't seem to ease the tension.

"Okay, let's go over this one more time," I say, addressing the three of them like we're about to rob a bank or something. "Gina will sit at one of the outside tables at Hinano. Ollie...you, Amy and I will be outside The Whaler. It's close enough, but as it's down a bit, on the other side of the street, hopefully he won't see us. We should stay as far back as possible though, to be sure."

Amy shifts her gaze to Gina, her face showing clear concern. "And you're sure you want to go through with this, Gina? Once he shows up, you know we can't predict what he'll do."

Gina offers a shaky smile. The reality is setting in now, and competing with her bravery. "It's the only way. I need to face him, and before he gets taken away, I want him to know that I'm not scared any more." Her voice wavers slightly, but she straightens her posture, eyes hardening. "And with you all watching, I know I'll be safe. Right?"

Ollie nods in agreement, though he's frowning as he turns to me. "But why don't we just all wait inside in the same place they're meeting? If things go wrong..."

"No." I shake my head firmly. "Brandon needs to think he's got her alone. If he senses even a hint of a trap, or sees us inside, he'll bolt. We'll have a good view, and once he's there I'll call the police. It's the middle of the day, and in a public place. What's the worst that could happen, especially if he thinks Gina might come with him?"

Amy stands, and takes Gina in a tight hug. "Just...be careful babe, alright? And remember, if he threatens you or anything, just shout or run, or signal to us, and we'll be there in a flash."

"Thank you. Threats are to be expected, but I'll be careful. Try not to worry," Gina replies, squeezing Amy's hand before turning to me. There's a silent exchange between us. An understanding that this will be one of the hardest things she's ever done.

My turn to hug her. "You've got this. We'll be right there, I promise."

"You've got your phone?"

"Yup, right here."

"OK let's do this then," she sighs.

With a final nod, Gina turns and marches toward Hinano, with a courage that makes my insides glow with admiration.

* * *

Gina

As I settle at one of the square, rustic wooden tables outside Hinano Cafe, I try to *appear* as calm as possible, even though my insides are twisted with dread. The vibe here is the complete opposite to my churning insides.

There's only one other outside table occupied, by a young couple, and I've chosen one furthest from them. The last thing I want is someone intervening, and scaring Brandon off before the police arrive.

A coffee comes in quick time, like they know I need something to stop my hands from shaking.

Every passer-by, every break in the crowd, makes my pulse quicken as I wait for Brandon.

I casually glance across the street at The Whaler, where I spot Amy and Ollie taking their seats, and then look around, knowing Tommy must be close by, though he's out of sight.

The minutes tick by, and the midday sun starts to feel uncomfortably warm on my face.

Maybe he's changed his mind, if he won't come after all.

Maybe he's been here before us, and saw the others.

In an attempt to ground myself, I study the frontage of the building I've walked past so many times, with rarely more than a glance. They've gone for a vintage, rustic beach hut style, like it's been that way since the 1960's. Maybe it has. I know from my tour guide knowledge that it opened in 1969, and has epitomised the shabby chic, laid back Venice vibe ever since.

It's only when I turn my head to check my friends are still there, that I see him.

Brandon steps out of the crowd, walking casually toward me, his usual uncomfortably intense gaze locked onto mine with an ominous combination of smugness and anger.

He gives me a thin smile and takes a seat across from me, without waiting for an invitation.

"Beth." His voice is low, almost a murmur. "Fancy seeing you here."

I do my best to match the confidence of his stare, but he knows me too well, and the corners of his mouth let me know he sees a little crack in my mettle.

I fucking hate that you know me so well…

He leans back, folding his arms as he studies me. "You look…different. You've toughened up. LA has been good for you."

There's a dangerous glint in his eyes. It's one I recognize all too well, and I remind myself not to provoke him. He's right though. His condescending comment would have been taken on the chin a year ago, but now it makes me want to punch his.

"But I see right through it."

I glance down, trying to control the rising panic in my chest. "Things have changed, Brandon. I've changed."

He laughs, cold and dismissively. "Oh, have you now? Running to strangers for help? Hiding behind them to keep me away?" He leans forward, voice dropping to a near whisper. "I could burn down this little fantasy life right now, if I wanted to."

"Brandon, you don't scare me any more." The words are out before I can stop them, and for a split second, he falters, surprised at my courage. But then his face hardens, a look of pure malice taking over.

"Oh, you should be scared, Beth. Unless you come with me now."

* * *

Tommy

I've stayed on my feet, partially obscured from Gina by the thick pole supporting the parasol over our table. I'm too nervous to sit, and I want to be ready to move fast if need be.

Amy sees him first. She signals it with just a sharp intake of breath, and we all freeze.

Watching from a distance, I can't hear their words, but their body language says plenty. Brandon leans closer to Gina across the table, too close. He has his back to us, so I'm trying to read Gina's expressions. She's not giving much away. She looks calm, but I know she won't be feeling calm inside.

Every muscle in my body is on edge, and I'm holding my phone, ready to dial.

"Tommy! What are you waiting for?" Amy pleads.

I glance to her, suddenly snapping out of my trance, and drop my eyes to the phone in my hand. I have the direct line to the station who have been looking for Brandon. The same one where Gina and I went for our interview. That feels like so long ago now.

They answer after three rings.

"Venice Beach LAPD Substation, Officer Martinez speaking. How can I help you?"

"Yes, my name is Tom Millar. I'm involved in a case with a guy called Brandon Davis. You guys are looking for him for assault and criminal damage. I'm looking at him right now."

"Can I have your location please, sir?"

"Yes, I'm outside the Whaler on Washington Boulevard, but he's sitting outside Hinano Cafe across the street."

"Can you give me a description of the suspect?"

"Yeah, he's about six foot, with short dark hair. He's wearing cream shorts, and a baggy black hoodie. He's wearing white trainers too, I think."

"Please stay where you are if it's safe. We'll dispatch units immediately. Do not approach the suspect."

"He's with my girlfriend now. We're trying to keep him there, so he doesn't get away."

There's a short pause on the other end, before, "Officers are on their way sir. Could I have your girlfriend's name?"

"Gina. Gina Sawyer. But she used to be called Elisabeth Sawyer, so might be on your system under that name."

There's another frustrating pause. "Is she with the suspect?"

"Yes."

"Is she in immediate danger?"

"No, I don't think so. They're sitting outside at a table, talking."

Suddenly, as I'm speaking, Brandon stands, gesturing toward the door. Gina stands up too, her face suddenly tight with tension.

My heart leaps into my throat. This wasn't the plan.

"They've just stood up. It looks like they're going inside. I need to go."

"Sir, do not approach the suspect. Officers are en route." Her switch in tone lifts my state of alarm ten levels, in a heartbeat.

"Tommy mate, what do we do?" Ollie's voice is behind me, panicked, but I can't process it fully. I just keep my eyes on Gina as she walks slowly towards the door, and pushes it open. A hard push like she's pissed off.

"Get here fast. I can't see her unless I go inside too!"

Two things happen in the next five seconds which change everything.

Just before stepping into the open doorway, Gina drops one arm by her side and straightens all her fingers to make a flat palm, facing it backwards towards us, moving it slowly in a way I can only read as "Stay back."

Why would she want us to stay back now? Fuck!

Suddenly, Brandon spins around to face the direction of her signal. In our direction. I've already stepped out for a clearer line of sight, and our eyes meet immediately. His cocky smirk is one I've seen before, but this time he lets it linger, as he slides his hand slowly out from the pouch at the front of his hoodie.

A gun?

I catch just a glimpse, not even enough for the sunlight to fully catch it, but something he's gripping that has a handle. He clearly showed me, before turning back towards the doorway, and following Gina inside.

"Oh my god, did you see that?"

"What!?" Amy and Ollie both reply at once, their sudden panic a reaction to mine.

"Does he have a gun? Did you see it?"

"Fuck off! No, he doesn't!" Amy is on her feet quickly. "Did you see it?"

"I think so...I don't know. He has something he was trying to show me. What else could it be!?"

* * *

Gina

After the bright sunshine, it takes my eyes a few seconds to adjust to the light inside the cafe.

Did they see me go in?

Have they called the police already?

I decide quickly that they must have. I can't even consider any other option, but this was not part of the plan, and I'm struggling to control my body from shaking.

Brandon leads me to the back corner, away from the other patrons, and my stomach sinks as I realise he has no intention of letting this stay in public view.

He grips my arm hard enough to bruise, as he pushes me into a seat. His eyes quickly scan the room before he leans close, his voice low and menacing.

"You think you're clever, Beth? You think I didn't see yourr little friends across the street?"

"I'm not 'Beth' any more, Brandon," I hiss back, my voice shaking. "I'm done being who you want me to…"

The slap is fast and hard, making my head jerk back in shock.

My eyes immediately look in desperation for someone to have seen or heard it, but no one did. The shock of the slap, and the realisation that I'm at his mercy again fills my eyes with tears. I gently touch my cheek, and find it burning hot.

What do I do now?

Brandon begins to laugh at me, letting all his evil show again as he relaxes back into his seat. It makes my skin crawl.

All the times I've seen him congratulate himself this way, and delight in the control.

Why did I think this would work?

"They're not coming, you know."
My eyes dart back to him.
"Your pathetic little rescue party." He glances over his shoulder to see if anyone is there, before slowly reaching into his pocket, and carefully laying a small pistol on the table.

He lets go of it, almost challenging me to grab it. I've never shot, or even held a gun, in my life. Right now all I can imagine is Tommy coming charging in, and Brandon shooting him. A fury begins to form in my tummy, like a tornado gathering momentum, and when the rage reaches my eyes, I lift my gaze from the gun to Brandon's face.

There's that smirk again.

I'd love to slap it off his face so hard.

"Go for it?" He lifts his chin slightly, in a taunt straight out of a gunfight scene in a Spaghetti Western. "Ooh, look at you, all fired up and angry!" His laugh, and dismissive shimmy with his body and head only infuriate me more.

The door creaks and my eyes shoot up, half hoping it's a SWAT team or something. Just not Tommy.

"Awww, nobody to come save you."

"What are you gonna do, Brandon, shoot me? You'll never get away with this. You've gone too far this time!"

His eyebrows jump slightly at the venom in my voice. I know he's never heard strength like this from me. The sheer knowledge of that alone, fortifies me even more.

"Oh, you think so, do you? He leans back, taking the gun with him. "You have no idea what I'm capable of."

Nothing would surprise me now.

I glance toward the door again, wondering what's happening outside.

"So what *is* your next move, Brandon, shoot your way out of here?" I add a mocking laugh, in the hope that it'll rile him up enough to make a mistake. No such luck.

"No need, we're not going out the front door."

Footsteps approach behind Brandon, and he glances over his shoulder to see the waitress coming towards us. She's smiling welcomingly, completely oblivious. For a moment, I consider giving her a signal for help, but quickly dismiss it.

"Hi there!" Brandon says brightly, turning on the charm. "Can you give us five minutes please?"

"Sure thing!" she smiles, not even noticing me, before turning back towards the bar.

"Give me your phone." His eyes are back on mine, and his face transformed.

I frown at him. It's an involuntary reaction to an unexpected demand. "Why?"

I see it coming this time, tensing up and closing my eyes 1/10 of a second before it lands. Same cheek. This one doesn't hurt the same. The sting is there, but now it's like throwing hay on a fire. I open my eyes slowly, and almost invite him to hit me again, just to prove how much of a big brave man he is.

Bastard.

Instead I show him nothing. No emotion.

"Hmm…I like this new feisty version of you. The sex is finally gonna be interesting.

Don't give him a reaction.

I want to cry and scream at the same time. The ferocity of hatred I feel right now surpasses anything I've ever felt before. It burns me, now that I've seen a different way to live.

"Well this is fun Beth, but it's time to go. Up you get!"
"Where are we going?"
"Home!"
"You think you can just walk out? You think anyone is going to let you?"
"Yes, I do, because I don't think anyone will wanna take a bullet for a white trash bitch like you."

This time I can't control it, and I lurch over the table towards him, swinging my arm to hit him as hard as I can. Years of resentment boil over. I don't care if he shoots me now, as long as I get to slap that smugness off his face, just once.

He catches my wrist in mid air, stopping it dead with an ease that kills my fight before it's barely begun.

"Now now, play nice Elisabeth." It's remarkable how comfortable he is with violence. My attempt to hit him seems to have only relaxed him more.

"I hate you!" I seethe, through gritted teeth, hoping that if he keeps hitting me here, someone will see it.

He just laughs at me. The kind of dismissive laugh you'd use to put someone in their place.

"Whatever…let's go. Side door." He stands up and nods towards a heavy looking service door close by.

"What's out there?"

"Your ride home. Let's go."

I stand up slowly, trying to stall time for rescue, but he grabs my forearm and pulls me up, and towards the door. It's only the gun which makes me hesitate shouting for help.

The police will surely be here any moment.

* * *

Tommy

Two minutes feel like thirty, as we wait anxiously outside, watching the door and willing Gina to reappear. We're directly across the street now. Brandon has already seen us, so there's no point hiding any more.

"Why are the police not here?" Amy wails, literally hopping from one foot to the other. "I wanna go in. He's not going to shoot *me*."

"No fucking way!" Ollie grabs her from behind as she steps towards the road, holding her in a bear hug. "Just wait. He's not going to shoot Gina either, so don't make him do something stupid."

I can't wait any more. All rational thought has gone now. If it hadn't been for Ollie, both Amy and I would already be inside.

"Tommy! No!" Ollie shouts, as Amy wriggles, and I break into a jog across the road towards Hinano. My heart hammering with blind panic, but the rest of me is on autopilot.

I don't even look back, but typically as I pass the point of no return in the doorway, that's when I hear the sirens.

The door closes quietly behind me, and I stop to survey the interior, taking in zero detail as I scan for the face I love.

They're not here.

"Excuse me!" I jump forward quickly as a waitress passes, startling her with my sudden movement and tone of voice. "Have you seen the guy and girl who came in here about five or ten minutes ago?"

"Oh yeah, cute couple! They're down back," she points behind her, already moving away to a waiting customer.

It gets dimmer towards the back, away from the natural light from the windows at the front. The metaphor of running headlong into the dark is not lost on me, as I stride that direction, before my eyes can properly adjust.

Empty. I spot the two bathroom doors, and without hesitation go for the men's first. Empty.

They must be in the ladies. The propriety of it isn't even considered, as I push the door open with a fake confidence and stride in, ready for anything.

Empty. I check each cubicle twice. As you do when you can't comprehend why what you're looking for isn't actually there.

I can hear the sirens getting closer, as I come back out into the bar, and then I spot it. Another door, along the side wall. It looks like an emergency exit, or a door to a staff area maybe. It's a plain metal door, covered in scuffs and scratches.

It's the only possible place they can be.

The bright sunlight catches me by surprise as the door creaks open, and I step through quickly and close it behind me, quietly.

I'm in a yard between Hinano Cafe and the building next door. There are several empty metal cages on wheels, a haphazard stack of empty cardboard boxes, and three huge dumpsters. Two red ones on my right, and a green one on my left. My line of sight is only to one end of the yard, the Washington Boulevard end. There's a high chain-link metal fence spanning the gap between the two buildings, and I can see a heavy metal chain hanging in the middle, padlocked to keep the two gates in the middle of the fence secure.

As I take it all in, and realise Gina isn't in sight, two police cars appear. One stops just out of sight, probably at the cafe entrance, and the second stops with it's back end just visible through the fence. The loud sirens stop suddenly, but the lights keep going, and I can hear another faint siren in the distance, getting louder.

My ears stop ringing from the sirens as I step forward tentatively, looking down and up the yard, like I'm waiting to cross the road between parked cars.

"Tommy!"

Her voice, strained and frightened, comes from the other end, furthest away from the police.

"Gina!" I rush out into the middle of the yard, and freeze at the sight of them.

"Brandon, let her go!" My demand sounds pointless in my own ears, but I can't think of anything else to say. He tightens his hold on Gina's arm, flashing me a look that manages to be triumphant and deranged at the same time.

"You think you can just take her?" he sneers, pulling Gina closer, his fingers digging into her. She flinches, eyes wide and terrified, and it's all I can do to keep myself from lunging at him then and there. It's the gun waving in his other hand that freezes me in place. One wrong move, and this could end very badly.

"She's not yours," I reply, forcing my voice to stay calm. "She never was. Let her go. Now. Before the police know you're here."

Brandon's laugh mocks me.

Why can't he see there's no way out now?

"Are you OK, Gina?" She looks too scared to speak.

Brandon looks from Gina to me, shaking his head in a way that sends a chill down my spine. "You think you're some kind of hero, don't you? Big Hollywood guy running in to save the girl, like you're her knight in shining armour."

His face screws up with rage and scorn. "But you don't know her. You don't know what we've been through. She needs me."

Gina struggles to break free of his grasp, but Brandon's grip only increases. I can see her anger and frustration, but also fear, as she looks at me helplessly. One of her cheeks is bright red, and when I notice, I have to make a conscious effort to set aside the rush of anger which follows.

My sole focus needs to be getting her out of this.

"She *doesn't* need you," I say, louder now, and revealing my anger more with each word. "She's afraid of you, Brandon. You've done nothing but hurt her. That isn't love."

"Afraid?" He spits the word back at me with a new level of rage. "She's afraid because you put ideas in her head. Lies about who I am, what I am. You think you're better than me?"

He raises the gun, pointing it directly at me. My heart pounds, and as I hold his stare, it feels like everything in my peripheral vision narrows into a tunnel. Having a gun pointed at you isn't something you ever imagine happening, not for someone like me anyway. Even still, my reaction doesn't feel like what it would be if I had thought about it. Panic is the obvious emotion, but there's none. I felt more panic outside when I couldn't see Gina.

Now i just feel a weird deep calm, like this is coming to a head now, either way.

"If you really loved her, you'd put the gun down," I say quietly. "Let her make her own choices."

A flicker of something, doubt maybe, crosses his face, but it's gone as quickly as it appeared, replaced by more fury.

I'm aware of the door opening to my left, but it closes quickly, and I get the feeling no one else has entered the yard. The last thing I need is the police bursting in now, while he has his gun pointed right at me.

"Choices? She doesn't know what she wants! She's mine." He jerks the gun toward Gina's head, and her eyes widen in terror.

In that instant, every instinct screams at me to move, to do something, anything. I know that if I don't act now, I may lose her forever. He's getting more erratic, and if the police steam in now, anything could happen.

With a surge of adrenaline, I charge forward, launching myself at him. He wasn't expecting it, and his grip loosens on Gina just enough for her to pull free, stumbling back as I crash into him. I've been here before, but without the gun.

Brandon's free arm swings quickly as he uses his momentum, and his fist connects with my jaw, sending a flash of pain through my head, but I don't let go. My hand clamps down on his wrist, struggling to twist the gun from his grasp. He fights back viciously, snarling while he lands two or three more more punches on the side of my face.

"I'm not letting go!" I shout, wrestling him to the ground. The gun slips from his grip and skids across the ground, stopping just out of reach. But before I can fully pin him, he twists out from under me, scrambling back to his feet.

Out of the corner of my eye, I see Gina, clutching her arm and watching in horror. "Run, Gina!" I yell, my voice straining. "Get out of here! Go!"

But she doesn't move, frozen in place as Brandon grabs the gun again, and stands with it by his side.

Behind me I hear an engine rev, then a crash of metal as the fencing falls, but I keep my focus locked on Brandon. I see him look beyond me, a flash of panic in his eyes before it hardens into defiance, as he slowly raises the gun in my direction.

"Drop the weapon!" a voice behind me shouts, booming with authority. "Hands in the air!"

Brandon looks to them, then back to me. I can see the wheels turning in his head, the decision hanging in the balance. He could surrender. He could end this all right now.

"Stay back!" he yells, his voice becoming hysterical. All his calm cockiness has gone. "I'll shoot!" The gun is still pointed directly at me.

* * *

Gina

The officers are frozen in place, their weapons fixed on him from their positions behind the car that has just broken through the gates. "Put down the gun, Brandon!" a second voice orders. "It's over. Don't make this worse."

Brandon's hand trembles, the gun wavering, and I see his finger twitch on the trigger. He's trapped, and he knows it. There's no way out, but he's too consumed by his own rage and fear to think rationally.

Brandon has never backed out of a fight.

"Brandon," I say gently, trying to catch his attention. "Think about what you're doing. You're only digging yourself in deeper. Just let go of the gun. It doesn't have to end this way."

For a moment, his eyes meet mine, and I see the slightest flicker of hesitation, maybe even regret. But then his face twists in fury again. "You did this to me," he mutters, his voice low and filled with venom. "After everything I did for you, you bitch!"

Almost in slow motion, his arm swings and the gun is now pointed directly at me. His hand steady now, and I can see a familiar madness in his eyes. My blood turns to ice. I know he's not bluffing any more.

"Brandon, don't!" Tommy says calmly, as he steps quickly between us with his hands raised. "Please just put it down!"

"Stay where you are ma'am!" an officer shouts from closer than I expect, crouched beside the dumpster to my right, but I'm already moving on instinct.

* * *

Tommy

"Please, Brandon," Gina implores softly, her voice trembling. "I know you're hurt. I know you're angry. But this isn't the answer. Please."

As she speaks, Gina moves beside me, takes one more step forward, then finally sidesteps in front of me as she says, "Please."

For a second, it looks like she's gotten through to him. His hand lowers slightly, his gaze softening as he looks at her. But then he shakes his head.

"No," he whispers, voice choked. "It's too late. You made your choice."

In a sudden movement, he raises the gun toward her. I don't have time to think. I rush forward, shoving Gina out of the way just as he fires. The shot rings out, echoing in the narrow alley, and I feel the heat as it grazes my arm, a searing pain burning through my shoulder.

Gina spins around when she hears me cry out in pain, just in time to see me stumble backwards clutching my arm.

"Tommy!" she cries. I look up to see the shock on Brandon's face harden again, as Gina rushes to me.

The police officers react instantly. "Last warning! Put down the gun, or we will shoot!" one of them yells, his voice more forceful than ever. But Brandon doesn't listen. He slowly raises the gun one last time, aiming it towards Gina and I, with a look of pain and resignation that sends a chill right to my core.

And then, in a sudden, deafening volley, the officers open fire.

The gunshots fill the air like claps of thunder, and I watch as Brandon's body jerks and crumples, hitting the concrete with a thud, twitching a few times before becoming still.

It's like we're in a confined space all of a sudden. Every sound is clearer and louder. Footsteps surround us. I feel Gina's hand on my arm, steadying me. Her face is pale, and she's shaking. I hear someone mention an ambulance. The disorientation lies beyond my central focus. Gina. She's breathing heavily, almost hyperventilating, and I try to smile through the pain to comfort her.

I look down to Brandon, lifeless on the ground, with blood pooling around him. His eyes are open, and the look on his face is one I will never forget. Another trauma indelibly burned into my long term memory.

Gina follows my gaze, her lips parting in shock, but there's relief in her eyes after she re-opens them and looks back to me. I know the tears aren't for him.

The officers begin to holster their weapons, one of them crouching to check on us. "Are you two all right?" he asks, his tone softer now, more human. "There's an ambulance on the way."

I nod, although the pain in my shoulder throbs, and pulses down my arm with every heartbeat. Gina wraps her arms around my torso, her quivering body feeling warm against mine.

"I love you!" she whispers, her voice cracking, before she gives in to almost silent, heaving sobs.

"I love you too. It's over now."

48
TOMMY

My favourite late afternoon glow filters through the small windows of Gina and Amy's apartment, making the space feel instantly warmer...or at least just me.

It hasn't felt crowded with the four of us here, just messy, mostly thanks to Ollie. Amy has definitely found her kindred spirit where that's concerned. It's a comfortable mess though, and a welcome contrast to the large, sterile spaces of Liam's mansion.

It may only be a temporary arrangement, but I feel a deep sense of peace here, maybe more at home than I've felt anywhere before. Gina has a lot to do with that, obviously.

She feels like home now.

Two weeks have passed since the showdown with Brandon. My shoulder wound is healing up nicely, threatening to leave a scar that Gina insists will make me look heroic.

The real scars, the ones that run a little deeper, are healing too. Just slower. I know we'll carry what happened for a long time, but there's something even more solid between us now - a bond forged through more than just our survival.

We had come through it together.

Ollie comes in from the direction of the bedroom, typing on his phone before flopping down beside me on the sofa. "Did you hear anything yet about your new place? I'm not sure how much longer Amy will put up with me. She keeps dropping hints about me missing my football, even though I tell her I don't need to be back for another ten days or so. I don't wanna have to book into a hotel."

I laugh. "Maybe if you stop leaving crumbs everywhere, and dirty underwear. But yeah, soon. I just want to make sure Gina's got everything she needs first. After everything we've been through…"

Ollie nods, a rare serious expression on his face. "She's a tough one you know, but I still can't imagine you two living apart now. You're good for each other."

"Yeah, I think so. I'm not going to rush into moving in together though. What about you and Amy? That girl's practically glued to your side."

Ollie shrugs, but there's a relaxed warmth, instead of his usual diversion banter. "Funny, I suggested last night that she could come back home with me for bit. See how it goes, and if we can avoid killing each other, I might end up back here. It's hard to not love this fucking weather!".

"Wow, that's a big move for the king of one night stands. What does she think?"

"Yeah, she seems open to it."

I give him a friendly nudge with my good shoulder, and smile at his goofy loved up face. I'm so happy for him. Amy seems to bring out a side of Ollie that I'd never seen before. More grounded and, dare I say, an actual adult.

Thankfully, before our conversation crosses that uncomfortable line when two guys start talking about emotions, Gina and Amy burst in. Their excitement, energy and perfume fill the room with exactly what we were missing.

"Are you two ready?" Gina asks, eyes bright, as she leans over the sofa to plant an upside down kiss on my lips. "We don't want to be late!"

Tonight we've been invited to dinner, with Evelyn Robbins and Reese Witherspoon. Partly as a thank you for speaking out against Liam, but also to celebrate my new job. At least I assume that's what it is. When you get that phone call, the only question you ask is where and when?

I'm scheduled to start at Evelyn's studio in a few days. We had a long conversation on the phone, a few days after our segment aired on E! and she kept good to her promise. It's a daunting step up, but a starting salary that I just can't turn down, especially when she's allowing me to bed in slowly to the role under the mentorship of a colleague. I'll be working as a Production Manager, directly under her head of production Paul Anson.

Filming on *Legally Blonde 2* is due to begin next week as well, and I'll be shadowing on the the production. Evelyn has told me already that Reese will look after Gina on set, after she was told about everything that had happened.

After such uncertainty, our fortunes were now coming good in ways we hadn't dared to imagine, and it felt especially perfect that they were so intertwined.

Thirty minutes later, we leave the apartment and Gina takes my hand, lacing her fingers through mine. "Are you nervous?" she asks, as we climb into the long black limousine that's been sent to collect us.

"Not when I've got you by my side. Nothing can ever be as good as that."

"Ah you're lying. Dinner with Reese Witherspoon will beat everything, surely?"

"Nope. It'll be nice, sure, but you're the one I'm looking forward to being with tonight."

"Are you flirting with me?" Gina laughs, leaning into me as she whispers into my ear.

"Definitely! Is it six weeks yet?"

Gina throws her head back into a relaxed laugh, enjoying my cheekiness, then looks me dead in the eye. "Six weeks or not, I'm not waiting one more night."

"Sounds like a threat babe!"

"Oh you're in trouble alright!" she giggles, gripping my hand tightly on the leather seat between us, and both of us just grin like teenagers as the car pulls away from the kerbside.

* * *

The restaurant Evelyn has chosen is an understated gem in Beverly Hills. The kind of place where the waiters glide by with trays of tiny, intricate dishes on large plates. Reese and Evelyn are already seated when we arrive, and they wave us over, welcoming smiles on their faces.

Now this feels surreal.

Evelyn, elegant as ever, rises to greet us. "Tommy, Gina! And you must be Ollie and Amy. It's so lovely to see you all."

Reese greets us with her usual effortless warmth, hugging Gina like an old friend. "There she is! Hollywood's bravest new star!"

Gina blushes, but I see the look of pride in her eyes, and it fills me with pride on her behalf. Hopefully now, she'll finally realise how much she deserves to be here, to be seen and appreciated.

Our food order is taken quickly and efficiently. This isn't the kind of place with a six page menu, so it doesn't take long to choose. Evelyn leans in, looking directly at Gina and me once the waiter leaves. "I want you both to know how much I admire what you did, speaking out so honestly. That kind of bravery isn't easy, especially in an industry that so often protects its own, as you well know."

Reese nods. "You've definitely helped set off something important. Even now he's been charged, there are more women coming forward. Your courage has paved the way."

Gina squeezes my hand under the table. "We just did what we had to. No one should have to go through what I did with Liam…or Brandon, or the even worse things that others have suffered. It's time for things to change."

Reese's eyes light up. "You know, Gina, with your experiences and your voice, you could help lead something really incredible. A campaign maybe, to raise awareness about domestic abuse. It's a cause that needs strong, real voices like yours and Amy's."

Amy looks taken aback to hear Reese say her name, when she's just been listening, passively, until now. "Me?"

"Absolutely!" Reese's smile is encouraging, and irresistible. "People will listen when they see women who've lived through it, coming together to make a difference. And you've got all of our support."

Gina begins to nod, her voice steady, and after a glance to Amy. "I'd like that. If it can help others find the strength to get out of bad situations, to take a stand...then it would be worth it. We would love to be involved in that, wouldn't we Amy?"

"Wonderful. This sounds like a plan!" Evelyn raises her glass, signalling a toast.

* * *

The chat over dinner is mostly about Legally Blonde, with Reese delighting Gina and Amy with stories of the filming on the first movie, and how much of a pleasant surprise it was to find Elle Woods become such a strong role model for girls.

As we say our goodbyes inside, then walk back toward the car, Gina is quiet, lost in thought. I watch her, noticing how differently she carries herself now. There's a new confidence - an obvious pride and purpose, and it fills me with so much admiration.

She looks up at me. "Tommy, do you think I can actually do this? Be someone who makes a difference?"

"Babe, you already have. I hope this doesn't sound too cheesy, but as far as I see, you make a difference to everyone you meet already."

Her face softens as she stand on tiptoes to kiss me, the warmth of her lips lingering. "Thank you. For everything."

* * *

Gina

"Can you believe it, G? Just a month ago, we were hiding from Brandon and now…now we're talking about starting a campaign with Reese fucking Witherspoon."

"Amy, please promise me you won't call her that to her face," I laugh, cuddling behind her on her bed, while the boys are chatting in the living room. The talk of football was maybe deliberate to get rid of us. Either way, I'm grateful for some one-to-one time with my best friend.

"I'll do my best." I can hear her smirk, without needing to see it.

"I love you, you know," I say solemnly, after a pause.

"I love you too, babes…are you OK?"

"Yeah…" I whisper. "So much has happened so fast, I don't know how much of it has sunk in."

"I know. It's been worth it though, right?"

"Ummm…yeah, for sure. Just hard."

"You're the bravest person I know…"

"Ah, I don't know. I don't feel brave." I shift a little closer to Amy, and hug her tightly.

"I think the bravest thing you did was get on that bus out of Vegas, and you've protected that decision ever since."

"Hmm…feels like she was a different person."

"Well she kinda was, Elisabeth."

"Oh Amy, what am I gonna do about that?"

"Who do you want to be? If that's not too weird a question?"

"Gina. Elisabeth is just an old version of me now. Gina has always felt like a fresh start."

"So change your name legally. I'm sure it can't be that difficult."

"Yeah…maybe. Do you remember when Reese and I went to the bathroom together, at the restaurant?"

"Yes! How fucking weird was that? And you didn't even invite me. You and your new bestie. How can I compete with her?"

"Oh shut up you." I give her a tighter squeeze that makes her groan, then giggle.

"So, when we were in the bathroom, she said she'd like to know more about my story. She said that it might make a good pitch, for a fictional version of my life."

I think Amy stops breathing for several seconds, before she finally breaks the silence with a whisper. "Fuck. Right. Off." She wriggles free of my arms, and rolls to face me, greeting me with a beaming smile. "That's incredible! Oh my goodness! What do you think about that?"

My enthusiasm is much more muted. Modesty won't allow more. "It's wild, isn't it? It gives me some comfort, I suppose. I've always believed that everything happens for a reason, but the stuff with Brandon was hard to reconcile with that. Maybe this is why. Let's just see, eh? I'm just so glad I have you. You've been like my guardian angel."

Amy's eyes close briefly, an unusual bit of vulnerability showing through. Her face is different when her eyes open.

"What's wrong?" My whisper helps hide the emotion in my voice.

"I'm thinking of going with Ollie, to Ireland. Just for a while, to see what it's like, and see how things go with him?"

My heart jumps in my chest. A happy jump, and I realise suddenly how much I've been focusing just on myself. She's been through so much, and Ollie has brought out a softer side of her I hadn't ever seen.

"Amy! That sounds amazing. You guys are so good together!"

She smiles shyly, her cheeks pinking. "I think so too."

* * *

It's just after 11pm. Ollie and Amy have gone to bed, leaving Tommy and I alone, finally.

We're leaning against the kitchen worktop, waiting on the kettle to boil. The only light in the room is from the muted TV, flickering colours against the walls. We're both already showered and dressed for bed, and I wonder does he feel the same nervous anticipation I do.

Tonight feels like the right time. Marking the transition into exciting new adventures for us both.

He's wearing the same Goonies t-shirt as he did that night in Pismo Beach. It'll only be a turn off while he's wearing it, which won't be for long.

"Are you up for something a little different?" I ask with a hint of mischief, as I pour from the kettle into the large round mugs. The hot chocolate powder bubbles up through the water, and I begin to stir the first one.

"Ummm...shouldn't we just do it the normal way first?"

I turn my head quickly, grinning in goofy appreciation of his wit.

That answers that question at least.

"That's not what I mean..." I reply, but my nervous girly giggle doesn't back up my words.

"Oh? Now I am intrigued."

"Well..." I let that linger as I slowly stir the second mug. "Amy and I would sometimes go up onto the roof on a nice night. Would you like to do that with me?"

"I don't think I've ever been up on the roof of a building. Back home if you did that, people would think you're either a sniper, or you were gonna jump."

"Hah! Well both of those things happen here too."

"It sounds nice though. Very romantic."

"Yeah!" I give him another grin, loving how open he is, and how perfectly relaxed this is. "I've only ever been up with Amy of course, so there wasn't much romance."

"You want me to be your first then?" he winks, aiming for cheeky, but landing on cute.

"I want you to be my last, Tommy Millar."

My voice wobbles on the last sound, and my already warm cheeks lead the way with the embarrassment. I think I have some sort of emotional Tourette's syndrome, but maybe not. It's only with Tommy, that all semblance of a filter between my brain and my mouth fail completely. Not the normal, sensible part of my brain either, but a part of my brain that's apparently been programmed by hundreds of cheesy romance movies and novels.

It's a part of me which I've only recently discovered.

Thanks for that Tommy Millar. You've turned me into Molly Ringwald.

"That's cute!"

That's it?

Then I look at him, and I see it.

He sees me. The softness in his face is completely without judgment, and his reply wasn't sarcasm. It was appreciation, maybe even admiration.

Wow…

We're quietly climbing the fire escape, with just socks on our feet, and I'm still processing the magnitude of that moment in the kitchen.

Just two words and a smile.

With those two words and smile, he let me be me, without need for a filter. I'm sure some people spend a lifetime together without that level of transparency between them. To be completely self *un*conscious in the eyes of another, and feel safe to do so.

That's something beyond love.

"Are we allowed to be up here?" Tommy whispers from below me on the narrow steps. I'm moving slowly, holding on to the wobbly railing with one hand, and trying to not let the mug in my other hand burn me.

"Probably not, but sure. Rules are made to be broken. Wait until you see the view…"

"I'm liking the view I've got already. I don't expect the roof will beat this."

I pause immediately, appreciating the compliment. Maybe someday It'll just make me roll my eyes, but right now it's stirring up some seriously erotic urges. I let him see my gratitude over my shoulder, before I continue up the last few steps onto the flat rooftop.

"This is exciting!" Tommy says giddily, taking my hand once he's beside me.

"This way…" I whisper, like it's a special secret, and lead him across to the part of the building facing the sea.

Tommy watches carefully as I set my mug on the low, thick wall which runs around the perimeter of the rooftop, then sit and swing my legs over to face the sea.

"Oh fuck, Gina, that's dangerous!"

"It's not," I smile up to him, reassuringly. "Look…"

He peeks over to where my feet are, dangling only five or six feet above a lower roof. "Oh, OK good, that's a relief. I'm not so good with heights," he adds, joining me on the ledge, then sliding closer to me.

"What does this remind you of?" I ask, nudging him gently.

He pauses to think, as we both gaze out towards the boardwalk, and the dark ocean beyond.

"Ah, our first date. Of course."

"Up at the conservatory at sunset. Sitting on the wall there." My words come more wistfully than I expected, but it's how I want them to be. "

"It was perfect wasn't it? So much has happened since then, it's really weird."

"You mean it's not perfect any more?" I look at him and he smiles before meeting my gaze.

"Not at all, it's more perfect than ever."

"Why?"

"Because I didn't love you then…"

"Gee thanks!" I say, making a goofy face to try and hide the embarrassment. You never know how you'll react, when someone says something so beautiful, so sincere, that every cell in your body listens up.

Tommy's laugh, as expected, defuses my discomfort instantly, and we let our attention get drawn back to the gentle hum of Venice Beach on a warm summer's night.

"Tommy…" I whisper softly, breaking the comfortable silence.

"Yeah?"

"We've come so far together already, don't you think?" I lean my head on his shoulder. "For the first time ever, I think, I'm excited for life. I can't wait to see where we go next."

He kisses my temple with a lingering softness that makes me close my eyes. "Wherever it is, I'll be right here with you."

If only hearts could glow when they're happy. They'd see mine from miles away.

I lift my head to look up at him, smile and nod my head back towards the fire escape.

"C'mon handsome, bed time. We've got some rules to break…"

THE END

AUTHOR'S NOTE

I want to take a moment to thank you for coming on this journey with me. Writing this book was more than just putting words on paper - it was a way to explore themes of trust, connection, and how love grows in the messy, grey areas of life.

I've always been fascinated by the idea of new starts, and all the romantic idealism which goes with it. As a self-confessed movie nerd, growing up in a small town, I'll readily admit that Tommy was a little bit of fantasy wish-fulfilment for the twenty-something me of the past. I do hope you forgive the self-indulgence.

At it's heart though, 'Starstruck' is, of course, a love story.

Love can be incredibly beautiful, but also stunningly painful. It was important for me to show those contrasts, and how life experiences may affect your openness to love. It's never simple in real life, and I tried to allow Tommy & Gina's story to reflect that.

Going through a painful breakup of my own, while writing this book, was a challenge, but actually allowed me to tap into deeper layers of emotional complexity for the characters. I truly believe that everything happens for a reason, and that even through the toughest times we can learn, grow and evolve with an open heart.

I hope Tommy & Gina's story resonated with you in some way, and if it did, I'd love to hear your thoughts.

Thank you for your support, for believing in these characters, and for spending your time in their world.

Until next time...
Phil

Printed in Great Britain
by Amazon